PRAISE FOR THE AWARD-WINNING *BOAHIM TRILOGY*

"With a ferocious-yet-fragile heroine, resonant themes, and a sweepingly gorgeous backdrop, *Amaskan's Blood* delivers food for thought and frank enjoyment."

— MAIA CHANCE, AUTHOR OF THE *FAIRY TALE FATAL* SERIES

"Holy crap, this is good!"

— SEATTLE GEEKLY

"[Oak] will surprise you, frighten you, charm you, and, ultimately, move you profoundly."

— CHANTICLEER REVIEWS

"The prose itself is...a cut above the rest as Raven Oak playfully dances with the reader...Oak is loquaciously talented and the writing in the book shines."

— OPEN BOOK SOCIETY

"Adelei undertakes to save the kingdom, protect Margaret, and discover what truth, loyalty, duty, and family really mean—a tall order for any heroine...."

— PUBLISHER'S WEEKLY

"A suspense-filled YA fantasy adventure set in a complex fantasy world. A FINALIST and highly recommended."

— UK WISHING SHELF AWARDS

"The dialogue is authentic, the world is exquisitely depicted, and Margaret herself blossoms into a power-house before our very eyes. If there is such a thing as a 'sloggy middle' when it comes to a series, it appears nobody told Raven Oak that."

— JAMIE MICHELE OF THE READERS' FAVORITE AWARDS

"An exciting epic fantasy filled with intrigue and layers upon layers of well crafted secrets and lies."

— STEPHANIE HILDRETH OF 100 PAGES A DAY

"This is a novel for readers who enjoy plots filled with twists and intrigue and characters that are emotionally on edge, multidimensional, and solidly developed...It is cinematic and outright entertaining."

— RUFFINA OSERIO OF THE READERS' FAVORITE AWARDS

AMASKAN'S HONOR

The Boahim Trilogy Book Three

Raven Oak

GREY SUN
PRESS

Seattle, WA

AMASKAN'S HONOR
Book Three of the Boahim Trilogy

Raven Oak

Grey Sun Press
PO Box 1635
Bothell, WA 98041

ISBN: 978-1-947712-18-8

Library of Congress Control Number: 2025942684

I dedicate this book to myself. No, really.

Due to complications from COVID, this book was five long years in the making. What I overcame physically and mentally to write it is enough that I deserve this dedication. I certainly earned it.

I also dedicate this book to all the readers who waited patiently with grace and compassion. You've earned this a million times over.

THE Little Dozen Kingdoms OF Boahim
Harren Sea
Aruna
SADAI
Baudwin Bay
NARIBOR
Legend
Boahim Senate
Order of the Amaskans
Capital City
Major Town
Tribor Clan
Holy Temple of Adlain

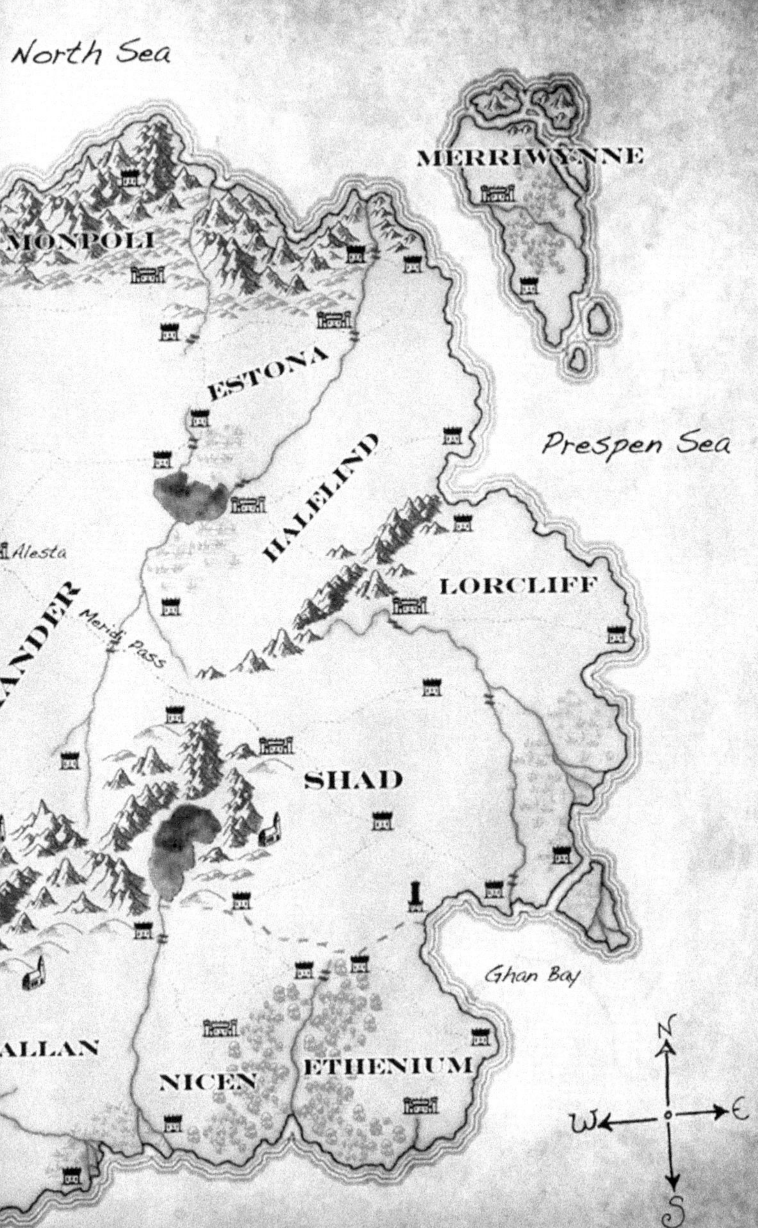

North Sea
MERRIWYNNE
MONPOLI
ESTONA
Prespen Sea
HALELIND
Alesta
LORCLIFF
ANDER
Meric Pass
SHAD
Ghan Bay
ALLAN
NICEN
ETHENIUM
N
W E
S

AUTHOR'S NOTE

As with any epic fantasy saga, there are many characters and places that take place across this trilogy. Readers are heavily encouraged to read *Amaskan's Blood* (Book I) and *Amaskan's War* (Book II) prior to reading this book. The author has written book three with the assumption that the reader has done so.

To help keep track of characters and places, some additional information follows this author's note.

It may help to remember that in *Amaskan's War*, Queen Margaret of Alexander killed Senator Whitlen *(aka Itovah)* of the Boahim Senate by smashing the orb inside of Alesta Castle. Senator Montero *(aka Asti)* died in Alesta Castle after delivering a message to Queen Margaret after the Boahim Senate arrived at the Meridi Pass. Senator Ammons *(aka Diomus)* died at the Meridi Pass. As of the beginning of this book, ten Senators or gods remain.

<u>**Rulers of the Little Dozen Kingdoms**</u>

ALEXANDER: Queen Margaret Poncett
ESTONA: Queen Catia Racci II
ETHENIUM: Queen Delia Benavent
HALELIND: King Marco Paolo
LIALLAN: Queen Helena Lorellyn
MERRIWYNNE: King Bernd Lizana
LORECLIFF: King Darach Killian
MONPOLI: King Damiano Carrasco
NARIBOR: King Ermen Clavine
NICEN: Queen Tera Beleviar
SADAI: King Adir Monsine
SHAD: King Havin Bajit

<u>**The Boahim Senators aka The Thirteen (gods)**</u>

1. Anur, God of War, Warriors, & Justice aka Senator Oranall Lattimore of Sadai
2. Luthia, Goddess of Silence, aka Senator Lissa Melani of Naribor
3. Farimun, God of Journeys & Luck, aka Senator Milan Keene of Monpoli
4. Itovah, Goddess of Death, aka Senator Adela Whitlen of Estona*
5. Echana, Goddess of Chaos, aka Senator Farah Loreen of Ethenium
6. Diomus, God of Logic & Reason, aka Senator Weldon Ammons of Nicen*
7. Delorcini, Goddess of Family & Love, aka Senator Rhiana Forst of Lorcliff
8. Asti, God of Peace, aka Senator Adan Montero of Alexander*
9. Atlina, Goddess of the Sea, aka Senator Shava Trayan of Halelind

10. Adlain, All-Father, aka Senator Liam Trenton of Liallan

11. Sharmus, God of Healing & Protection, aka Senator Anas Raj of Shad

12. Cerci, Goddess of Joy & Love, aka Senator Annet Leda of Merriwynne

13. Agaia, Goddess of Life & Air, Senator Mara Sveva. Serves all the Little Dozen Kingdoms

** Deceased as of the end of Book II, Amaskan's War*

<u>Months within Boahim / Little Dozen Kingdoms</u>

Itovan (Beginning of the Year/Winter)
Luthian
Adlian
Again (Beginning of Spring)
Delorcin
Cercian
Echain (Beginning of Summer)
Diomusin
Farimun
Astin
Atlinas (Beginning of Fall)
Anurus
Sharimus

PROLOGUE

The Boahim Senate

Ten gods remained, their eyes steeped in loss and fury.

As watchers of Boahim, they had served as peace-keepers since time had been a mere fleck of creation, and the loss of three amongst their rank was a reminder that they were drowning in years. For over a century, standing amidst the Boahim Senate meant being surrounded by greatness, by twelve individuals representing each of the Little Dozen Kingdoms. The thirteenth member, an elderly woman with glints of gold flickering in her eyes, held them together.

Adelei had complicated events.

Before her, the Order of *Amaska* had been little more than a nuisance, much like the *Tribor*. Nothing more than assassins who thought themselves important, though their actions changed little. But Adelei's return to Alexander had brought real change, and the Senators had murmured amongst themselves of the prophecy.

Was she the one who would bring about their downfall?

Rather than risk it, Senator Whitlen had taken matters into her own hands, though the damage had been done. Margaret walked a new path, one that would lead to a place of power rather than ineptitude.

No longer would she be content being led by others. Armed with a newfound knowledge and strength, Queen Margaret was leading her people towards a future not even the Thirteen had foreseen. Worse still, her training with the Grand Master of *Amaska* himself had resulted in proving the prophecy still at play.

The Senators might be gods, but the death of Senator Whitlen had proven them expendable.

Many citizens of the Little Dozen Kingdoms had laid down their lives at the Meridi Pass, but even then, the people of Boahim had prevailed while the Thirteen fell. In order to survive, the Senate required a shift in power.

Ten senators stood in a circle on their island, some angry, some chagrined, but all of them afraid.

"If we strike at the queen of Alexander, the rest of the rulers will fall into line," whispered Anur.

Heads nodded, though four remained still as they watched a hooded figure pace through a field of corpses. The figure gathered the remains to her as if every life had meaning, even in death.

Sharmus pointed at the orb's image, and Anur ceased his litany. "There is great telling in how one treats their dead. The care in the way she walks this field—a field of our own making I might add—gives me pause. How long have we remained on this island, scheming and spying on those who once worshipped us? To what purpose? When was the last time we helped them? Why is this queen only a threat now? Has she not been inching her way towards the prophecy since her sister's death?"

"She has, but now she brings the Little Dozen Kingdoms into her conquest!" shouted Anur.

Farimun broke out into a full grin. "Let her. We are gods, are we not?"

"Gods she's figured out how to kill, or have you forgotten?"

Sharmus shook his head at Anur and remained silent.

"Itovah couldn't control her temper any more than you can, and look where it got her. The orb's shattering was purely accidental. I doubt the child understood what it meant. I'd like to remind you that Asti's death was our doing. And Diomus? He exhausted himself, something we can't afford these days, so remember that before you decide to battle with this war queen."

So lengthy a speech from Atlina made Sharmus's bushy brows shoot up. Demure and soft-spoken, the Goddess of the Sea rarely raised her voice, yet this time, she had spoken with purpose.

Anur raised his hands in defeat. "We hear you, sister."

For now, they would watch this queen and plan accordingly.

Though one in particular had his own plans when it came to the young woman who carried out the death rituals as if every soldier had been one of her own. She beared watching, but not for the reasons his brothers and sisters held. Perhaps she could be persuaded to ignore the prophecy, or help use it for the betterment of all...

ACT I

1

The smell of rotten, cooked flesh reached her long before the Pass came into view, and Margaret ground her teeth to keep the bile in check. Six guards had accompanied her, though three had fallen in the fight to escape the City of Alesta. The three who remained among the living followed her as she nudged her horse forward. Her thigh burned where a *Tribor* sword had grazed her a few days back, and she shifted her seat in the saddle. For seventeen days they had camped in the cliffs above the valley, and her lungs still burned with death's stench.

"Any sight of our guests?" she asked as Sergeant Malcolm returned to her side.

"Not yet, Your Majesty, though they could be hiding as we are."

"Then we must move closer." Margaret urged her horse forward at a slow walk. The guards' hands remained on their sword hilts as the group neared the valley. They cleared the trees, and her skin crawled as if being watched. She could not help glancing over her shoulder as they proceeded. Despite the gory scene ahead, she brought the spyglass to her eye to search for evidence that any of the Little Dozen Kingdoms' rulers awaited her.

Ten minutes searching left nothing visible but corpses, and she gestured to her remaining guards. "Now is as good a time as any other to help the dead."

Most of the bones were sun-bleached and charred, though bits of shredded blue and green fabric accented the blackened earth. A large chasm split the ground, and Margaret dismounted. "We'll have to proceed on foot. Too many crevices make dangerous footing for the horses," she said as she handed off her reins. A guardsman led the horses back to a remaining tree while the other two followed her into the valley proper.

She donned leather gloves, as did the others, and they gathered remains as they passed. Whether they were Shadians or Alexandrian, Margaret and her guards worked their way through the valley, piling the remains into thirteen cairns. Scavengers had picked most of the remains clean, though a few bodies held fast to their rotting flesh, and she gagged as she and Sergeant Malcolm carried a particularly rotten torso.

Nothing remained to mark their ranks or names, and every body lay indistinguishable from another. Somewhere lay her Grand Marshall, and Margaret paused at the edge of another chasm, her gaze drawn towards the darkness below. Only shadows answered her, and she stepped back as she heaved the remains of a meager breakfast across the barren ground. The sun had long since passed midday, and Sergeant Malcolm handed her a waterskin, though nothing rid her of the bile and dust coating her throat. By the time they had gathered what remains could be reached, sweat dripped from her forehead, and the muscles across her shoulders and back ached.

"I am no member of the Holy Few, so I lack access to the

materials necessary to burn these remains down to ash," said Margaret as she glanced at the thirteen cairns. "But perhaps a small burning will allow their spirits to pass into the afterlife."

Sergeant Malcolm lit and distributed several torches, which they used to light the cairns in silence. Despite her sore muscles, Margaret returned to the valley's edge and waited.

"Will we wait the full thirteen candlemarks?" Sergeant Malcolm asked, and she shook her head.

"Without the Holy Few's special oils, the fire's too cold to sustain the burning, but we will remain as long as the fires last to honor those fallen."

As she spoke, one fire dwindled to a few glowing embers beneath the bones. She could pray, but to whom? The Thirteen who murdered the soldiers in the first place? Margaret pursed her lips as she watched the flames falter.

When the last one ceased delivering its smokey souls to the sky, she returned to her horse and accepted a leg up from a guardsman. She pointed to the cliff overlooking the valley. "If the others are waiting on us to be visible, our honoring the fallen should have been visible enough. But in case it was not, that cliff is easily viewable from all sides."

"Hard to defend though," said Sergeant Malcolm.

It was, but if she wished the other rulers to meet her under a banner of truce, she would have to show them she trusted them enough to meet at all. "We will make our new camp atop the cliff," she said. While the three guards followed her lead, they flinched at every bird call or wind gust. Margaret focused on the cliff ahead, which helped her ignore the bits of bone, blood, and dust that clung to her leather armor.

Once atop the cliff, the whistling sound of an arrow forced her to dismount as she dropped to a crouch, sword drawn. A rustle of pale purple moved in the brush, and a woman stepped out with a bow in her hand. The silver in her hair nearly matched the silver thread on her tunic, and Margaret sheathed her sword. "Queen Catia, I'm honored that you have agreed to meet," she said.

The woman lowered her bow, though she scanned the area thoroughly before doing so. "Cousin," said Catia as she inclined her head. "I apologize for shooting at you, but we weren't sure if you were friend or foe."

"Did you face difficulties in your journey here?" asked Margaret, and the woman nodded. "You're the first one to arrive, I believe—"

"It's her," Catia called out, and tree branches snapped as multiple people stepped forward into the clearing. All of them were well guarded, but if she counted the colors, eleven kingdoms now circled her. One face in particular, that of King Havin Bajit, scowled as the Little Dozen Kingdoms' rulers drew their weapons.

"Welcome to the meeting, Queen Margaret of Alexander."

BEING MET BY A FEW RULERS, weapons drawn, would not have surprised Margaret—it was to be expected—but to find herself surrounded by the swords of every ruler of the Little Dozen Kingdoms, including those she counted as allies in the potential civil war, made her insides scream with fear. Though honestly, she could not blame them for wondering if they walked into a trap, and she motioned for her guards to lay down their weapons.

When she touched her sword's hilt, King Havin Bajit's sword tip gently touched her hand, and she froze. "I'm going to unsheathe my sword and lay it on the ground. We mean you no harm."

The other rulers' gazes never left hers, and when she made no move to attack, several of them sheathed their weapons. Havin was the last to do so but only after encouraging her to remove the hidden daggers on her person.

"I-I'm glad you have accepted my invitation to meet."

Queen Catia said, "It's not every day that someone proposes a war against the Boahim Senate. Perhaps you care to explain?"

"Yes, I'd like to hear what reason you have to propose such madness, or is this merely an attempt to rid yourself of the army at your border?" asked King Marco of Halelind.

Margaret allowed them to mutter their complaints, but after a minute or two, she raised a hand to silence them. The moment her hand was in the air, Havin resumed his defensive stance with his sword aimed at her.

"Please, there is no need for weapons. I brought you here to discuss the evil in our midst. There is no need to fight with each other when a true enemy seeks to end us," she said.

"And how can we trust you?" asked Havin.

Rather than respond, Margaret strode into the clearing where her guards had made a fire and gathered near it to warm her fingers. "Please, come join us," she said and turned her back to them. One of her guards raised a brow at this, and she shrugged. The only way to gain their trust was to appear nonchalant about any potential threats the monarchs posed.

Guards wearing a variety of colors moved about, laying down pillows and mats on the ground. As the Little Dozen Kingdom gathered together for the first time since the fall of Boahim, Margaret smiled. They might never again be united as one kingdom, but perhaps they could unite in their purpose.

"Tell us why you imagine the Senators to be a threat to us." This from a wiry man of short stature who sat on a stack of pillows. His brown mustache twitched as he spoke, giving him the look of a beaver rather than a king.

Margaret inclined her head in his direction. "One has only to look at the Meridi Pass to understand why they are our enemy. While murder is against the Thirteen, the battle between my kingdom and Shad is not the first dispute to arise.

The evil committed against our peoples stretched far beyond anything King Havin or myself could have done. They slaughtered indiscriminately, and then raged quakes that killed innocent people across all of our lands."

"One could argue that you were deserving of such punishment."

Margaret's eyes narrowed. He was not a beaver but a weasel, a sneaky rodent ready to sabotage the meeting. She would have to be careful with him. "And your people? Were they deserving of punishment? What did they do to deserve to have their homes destroyed and families killed by falling debris or gaping holes in the ground?"

When he didn't answer, Margaret continued, "There is more to this than the murders at the Pass. The Senators use magic. *Real* magic. The very magic supposedly removed from the world centuries ago by the original Boahim Senate. In Alexander, we spent a great deal of time researching Senate members and discovered that they...they aren't human. Those we thought of as representatives are much more than that. They're gods."

Some of them laughed at her, including King Damiano Carrasco of Monpoli, but one face remained still as stone. Havin looked upon her as if seeing her for the first time. Was it respect she saw in his eyes? The moment the thought crossed her mind, his features changed to impassive, and he glanced away.

"You expect us to believe this?"

"Your mind is addled, cousin."

"Children often lie to gain attention. It's no wonder you would do the same. Someone of your age lacks the wisdom to rule."

The disparaging remarks continued around the fire as if Margaret were invisible. King Adir of Sadai stood from his small stool, his tall frame casting an eerie shadow about them, and all talk ceased.

Had Margaret stood, no one would have noticed. She repressed a sigh.

"I believe Queen Margaret. While it is an understandably difficult concept to believe, my own research and that of Grand Master Bredych of the Order of *Amaska* has led to the same conclusions. Those we call the Thirteen are alive and ruling over us from the Boahim Senate. This would explain their use of magic, and the Senate's ability to appear all-knowing."

Havin stood, his frown casting wrinkles across his brow. "I, too, believe this. There are many unanswered questions I've had over the years, and this...this would explain much."

Beside Margaret, Catia paled as she clutched her hands together. "If this is true, I have no interest in fighting them. To fight the Thirteen is utter madness. We have no hope of winning a conflict of that nature, no matter what the reason."

"You say there is evidence they are the Thirteen?" asked Damiano, and when she nodded, he added, "Then show us. Prove it, or this meeting is finished."

Margaret snapped her fingers and her two guardsmen approached carrying several saddlebags filled to bursting with scrolls, parchments, and more than a few books.

"The oldest of documents, a book known only as *The Circle*, confirms that the Senate's creation was intended to *help* the Little Dozen, not harm it. Every document we found points towards the truth that our Senators are the Thirteen. Even the very number of them. Why would twelve kingdoms need thirteen representatives? Why not stop with twelve? The power they have...have any of you been down to the Pass itself?"

When no one nodded, she continued, "The very earth is split asunder. Gaping chasms swallowed our people, chasms opened and controlled by these Senators. Have any of you ever known anyone with such power? Who else would but the Thirteen themselves?"

Margaret pointed at the parchments before her. "Look at them. Decade after decade, the same faces. The same Senators. No familial appearances are that strong across so many years."

No one made move to study the documents, but they listened as she recounted everything her research had uncovered. By the time she finished, no one spoke. No one needed to.

"They really are the Thirteen then." The weasel's mustache remained still on his face, the corners of it down-turned in disappointment. "I...I think I need to return to my kingdom posthaste."

When others nodded in agreement, Margaret held up a hand. "Please wait. Nothing has changed. Yes, our Senators are gods, but they possess an evilness that needs combating if we are to survive."

"What they possess is power, Queen Margaret. The kind that smotes anyone willing to go against them. I realize your family is dead, but mine is not. I value growing old enough to see my grandchildren born," said Catia as she brushed dried leaves from her skirts.

Havin was the last to stand, but even he turned to his guards and made to leave.

"We are lost then," whispered Margaret. "Lost."

CALLING upon the name of Sharmus meant the potential of healing or protection, though sometimes people called upon him solely to call upon anyone at all. Sharmus did his best to listen, but as his siblings drained Boahim of its magic, his ability to hear the people of Boahim wavered.

Even now, as he walked among them, their words mushed together into a garbled mess he could barely hear, let alone understand. Maybe magic's fading had stolen his hearing and comprehension, or maybe he had lived too long amongst his siblings to decipher the mass of words.

The group split from each other, leaving one woman to stand alone on the cliff. Below her, death painted the ground crimson and ebony, death brought about by his siblings, and Sharmus sighed. It was long past time for he and his kind to fade from the world.

A woman with long, dark hair stood a short distance away from a group of people, and while her face was turned away from him, Sharmus would know her anywhere. His veil kept him from view, though Queen Margaret turned in his direction, her gaze searching for something that wasn't visible.

Her eyes narrowed, and she gave the air a brief sniff before she shook her head.

"Please, don't leave," she called to rest of the group. "If you do, the Senate wins. The Thirteen will continue their destruction until nothing remains."

Her words rang with truth, a truth he could hear. He focused on her with complete concentration. The Little Dozen Kingdoms' rulers shuddered at the sudden chill when Sharmus gave a long exhale, rooting them in place.

"What have you done?" cried Damiano as he tried to lift his foot and failed. "What evil have you cast to keep us in this place?"

She raised both hands. "I am not responsible for your predicament. Perhaps it's the Thirteen you cling to in fear."

Sharmus grinned at her gumption. "No wonder they fear you," he whispered.

Wide eyed, they glanced at one another until Havin said, "Something walks among us. Be you friend or foe?"

Sharmus removed the cloak from his head first, followed

by his shoulders and body. Havin tried to kneel, and finding his feet still stuck, he bowed deeply at the waist. "Senator Raj, w-what brings you to the Meridi Pass?"

Margaret noted the deep green of his cloak and his lack of weapons. "Sharmus, you honor us with your presence."

While Damiano nearly fell over himself in his attempt to curry favor with the god, the others paled and fell on their rears as they attempted to flee.

"Why am I not surprised that you would be the one to recognize my true identity?" said Sharmus to Margaret. "How could you tell?"

"Your cloak is green, a color long synonymous with healing, and I recognized your picture from older sketches in a variety of notes about the founding of Boahim. Also, when your cloak moved, I could see your hooves beneath them. You mentioned someone feared me. Who?"

"The Senate, or the Thirteen. Whatever you wish to call us." Sharmus rubbed his thumb and index finger together, releasing the rulers' feet. When several made to leave, he wagged a finger at them. "Please stay."

"Excuse me, Senator Raj, but you admit to being He, Sharmus, and one of the Thirteen?" asked Catia.

Sharmus nodded and pointed to the fire. "Let us sit and talk."

While their expressions ranged from disbelief to outright fear, they reclaimed their seats about the fire and waited for him to speak. When he didn't, Margaret interceded. "My God, please tell us why you are here."

"The Thirteen have marked you for death, young queen. You who have outed them and marked them as enemies of the people. They sent me here to warn you to stop this foolishness. A battle against us will only end in death—yours and those you love."

She opened her mouth, but he shook his head. "I'm not going to kill you, Margaret, fear not."

"Then why are you here?"

The god closed his eyes. For them it was the briefest of moments, but for him, a lifetime as Luthia's prophecy resounded in his head. If he chose the humans' side in this, the prophecy would surely come true and the Thirteen destroyed, but if he didn't...

Sharmus smiled. "I was sent with a different purpose, but it was my own that brought me here. No one could force me to walk where I am not wanted, so I say to you, I am not here to harm you, not intentionally."

He turned to face Havin. "You know she speaks the truth, and yet you don't trust her."

The King flinched and said, "She's responsible for my son's death."

"She is no more responsible for it than her sister was. Your son was responsible for himself, though I would say he learned much in the ways of torture from watching you. You would do well to cease blaming her for your incompetence. Besides, it was Itovah who took your son."

"You would go against your own family?" asked Catia.

"When they are determined to be wrong, I would. Besides, we grow tired. The world no longer needs us, and we no longer need each other. It is time for us to rest now."

Havin laughed. "Beings that can live forever, with magic and power, and you wish to rest? I don't believe it."

"Just because you would use such powers doesn't mean you should," said Margaret.

Sharmus nodded. "We've long had the power some of you seek, and what did we do with it? We frightened the very beings who made our existence worthwhile. Then we set to slaughtering them. The time for gods is past, as the prophecy states. It is time for us to be at peace with our coming mortality. The longer we live, the closer we draw to death."

Margaret tilted her head. "Is that why Senator Montero...I mean Asti died?"

"And my brother, Diomus. I've spoken too much. I came here only to confirm what Margaret said."

The fire popped, and twelve sets of shoulders flinched. When no one else magically appeared, nervous laughter scattered across the clearing. Havin stood and with a glance at Sharmus, strode away.

Following him to the cliff's edge, Sharmus said nothing to allow the king a moment with his thoughts. When the king spoke, he did so at a whisper. "I'll not help you die, you nor the rest of the Thirteen."

"You would rather fight a civil war against the Alexandrians?"

Havin nodded. "At least that fight makes sense. What would it gain me to attack the Thirteen, other than my people dead?"

"You're approaching this all wrong. Rather than seeing what could be, you're looking at it this in terms of what it will gain you, which matters not at all."

"It matters to me," King Havin hissed as he kicked a rock over the cliff's edge. "I'll not have my people dying for nothing."

Being the God of Healing, Sharmus was used to people thinking of him as a benevolent deity, but healers fought daily. The body was no less a battlefield, and when Sharmus turned his gaze on Havin, the man's confidence drained from him like a mudslide. "I did not say you had a choice, Havin. You are mine to command, or have you forgotten the treaties between your people and mine?"

"Y-Yes, Senator Raj, I mean Lord Sharmus."

Sharmus allowed his eyes to spark a moment longer before

returning them to a peaceful green. "Withdraw from Alexander. They are not your enemy. Focus your efforts on uniting the Little Dozen Kingdoms for the battle to come."

The man before him squirmed, but in the end, he acquiesced before returning to the summit. Sharmus draped his cloak about him and remained long enough to see what he wanted. What he needed.

It would have to be enough.

His aching joints reminded Sharmus of how much magic he had used to travel to the Pass and how much would be used returning to the island. He rubbed his shoulder with the palm of his hand.

It was far past time to rest. But first, he would face whatever punishment his siblings deemed necessary for failing to kill Margaret.

2

One moment Sharmus stood at the cliff's edge, and the next, a bright ball of light shot up into the sky. By the time the light faded and Margaret's eyes ceased burning, the God of Healing was gone. Of those at the gathering, most sighed with visible relief, but Margaret bit her lip. Now that one of the Thirteen wasn't present, would those gathered agree to her terms?

She glanced up to find eleven people staring at her, and she resisted the urge to leap on her horse and ride home. This is what she had wanted—a united Little Dozen Kingdoms—united against the Boahim Senate. So why did she feel as if she were walking through a forest full of *Tribor*? Margaret forced a smile out of thin lips. "I guess we have their attention," she said.

"In this case, I don't see that as a positive," said Catia. The silver in her hair sparkled in the firelight, much like Sharmus's had. The Little Dozen Kingdoms' rulers remained seated around the fire pit. Damiano refused to meet her gaze, as did Havin, and the rest met her with a mix of consternation and outright fear.

"I believe this should serve as confirmation that the Senate are the Thirteen. In fact, it appears that some of them wish to rest and leave us be. I see this as a positive," said Margaret.

Catia rubbed her gloved hands together near the fire. "So how do we do this then? We all come to some sort of agreement? How do we kill gods? You said you've killed one before?"

At this, Havin's face paled. "How? How could *you* kill a god?"

"Senator Whitlen...Itovah...threatened me. We were speaking through the orb in Alesta, and when she tried stepping through it, I panicked and smashed it. When the glass broke, it beheaded her. Killed her."

"Itovah's not the only one dead." Havin's hands clenched into fists in his lap. "At the Meridi Pass, when the quakes began, Senator Ammons died. Don't ask me how because I don't know. He sent a bright light towards the front line of fighters and then collapsed."

Margaret nodded. "Senator Montero came to Alesta during that battle to deliver a message to me. Afterwards, he died, though his wound wasn't fatal. Something about their use of magic is draining them of their life force, but how is that possible? They're gods."

"How did the orb kill Senator Whitlen?" asked Catia.

"That at least makes sense. The orbs use magic so perhaps her casting such a powerful spell left her vulnerable in some way, weak enough for the orb's destruction to kill her. I certainly meant her no direct harm, and yet I did. With three of them dead, ten remain."

"Ten is ten too many," said Damiano.

"If everyone here were to return home and call their senators, give them a reason to come through the orbs, then maybe everyone could shatter them. Maybe it would kill a few more. It would certainly make future battles easier."

Havin cleared his throat. "You're asking us to murder them."

"That should be easy enough for you," said Catia.

"I kill when it's needed and nothing more."

"Is that why you killed my father with your pet?" Once the words started, Margaret's heart refused to stop them. "What did I ever do to you to deserve death? Admit it, you kill when it suits you, and you enjoy it!"

Damiano shot up from his cushion like it had sprouted thorns. "Enough arguing. Whatever we need to do, we will do it. Agree here and now, before all."

Margaret ground her teeth but nodded in agreement. There would be plenty of time for Havin to pay for his crimes. "Agreed. Those of you with representatives remaining will attempt to kill them. You will send messages to the rest of us on what occurred. We will make decisions on the next steps from there."

"Why do I need to agree?" asked Catia. "My senator, the goddess Itovah, is already dead."

Queen Beleviar of Nicen raised her hand. "As is mine. I'm not certain why all of us must be in concordance."

"What we are doing—the destruction of not just the Boahim Senate but the Thirteen themselves—will have wide stretching implications across all of the Little Dozen Kingdoms. The Thirteen laws will no longer be enforced by the Senate. Our every action will no longer be observed and weighed. Our actions will change everything. We will be free," said Margaret.

At first, no one spoke. Then one by one, they swore agreement. For the first time in hundreds of years, the Little Dozen Kingdoms were unified.

It should have lifted her spirits to see them agree to work together, but something lurked beneath their words—something dark, something disparate. When the last ruler avowed to destroy the Thirteen, a tightness settled over her shoulders.

"What's that?" asked Catia.

Margaret wrapped her hands around her shoulders. "You feel it too?"

"Like an itch I can't scratch," said Havin. "Sharmus?"

The others glanced around the circle, but the god wasn't visible. Damiano opened his mouth to speak, then closed it.

"We swore before those we intend to destroy. I suspect this...feeling...will persist until we do that which we've sworn to uphold." Havin pursed his lips. "I suppose the details of this revolt should be determined."

King Ermen Clavine, a quiet man of slight stature, cleared his throat. "Naribor is the furthest journey from this Pass, meaning we would need to agree upon a date at least twenty days from now, if not longer."

"We should attempt to break the orbs on the twenty-fifth of Anurus. That would give everyone enough time to travel home and plan their attempts in more detail," said Margaret.

"On the Feast of the Thirteen?"

Margaret nodded at Catia. "They won't expect an attack on their holiest of days. It will pique their curiosity and concern them if the rulers stop their thanks to cry out for help."

"After all, why should we leave offerings for those who have continually lied to us and are actively trying to kill their believers?" Havin scratched his chin as he thought. "The twenty-fifth of Anurus is perfect."

When the rest agreed, Catia sighed. "Since you all have agreed to this madness, I can do naught but follow along. At what time should we focus our efforts?"

"High noon," said Margaret.

Ermen cleared his throat again. "The sun is not highest

everywhere at once, cousin. Deciding a time is not as simple as that."

To have forgotten such an early lesson...warmth spread to Margaret's cheeks.

A time chart was produced and the candlemark upon which each ruler would attempt to contact their senators was decided. By the time they had finished, Margaret's back ached from sitting still for so long, and she stood to stretch.

"One more question, if you don't mind, cousin," said Queen Catia as she, too, stood, one hand massaging her back muscles. "There are twelve of us to their thirteen. Agaia represents no kingdom, though she will need to be...dealt with as well. Perhaps you could call on her? Since you have experience in killing a god."

"I have no way to contact any member of the Boahim Senate as my orb is broken. However, your orb is intact, as is Nicen's. Either of you could call on Agaia. Honestly, we have no way of guaranteeing that any one of us will be answered by our representatives. I say that those who have orbs attempt to make contact with the Thirteen, ask for help, and do what is necessary to harm them. It's unlikely that our plans will kill all of the Thirteen. The best we can hope for is lessening their number."

Havin nodded. "I say Beleviar and Catia should both try. It does no harm and if we're lucky, perhaps it will help us in our attempt."

When the other rulers nodded, the two queens agreed, though Catia sighed heartedly in response. Before anyone could comment further, Margaret gave a single nod and strode past her guards toward the horses. She led hers out of the clearing and into the surrounding trees. In the privacy of the forest, she allowed her shoulders to slump forward as she bit back a sob. Her guards ignored her moment of weakness as they followed.

The plan was in place and yet something lay unsettled in the pit of her stomach.

It wasn't until she was mounted and galloping towards Alesta that she remembered the look on Havin's face as he had learned she had killed a god.

The glee in his eyes...

Her bones trembled all the way home.

The City of Alesta

LEOLIN STARED at the old man and forced himself to take a deep breath. By the time the walls had been breached, most of Margaret's council had fled to safety, the exceptions being Her Holiness of the Holy Few and Lord Cornish. It was the latter that drove Leolin to insanity this morning as he stood inside the new council chambers, the previous having been appropriated for those injured or seeking shelter inside the safety of the castle.

Somewhere outside, Captain Fenton held off the Shadian army while the queen's physician patched up whoever still had limbs to use in the fight. All while Leolin was stuck inside with a poor excuse of a vassal. He glanced up at Lord Cornish, and the man's cheeks were flushed as he opened his mouth to speak.

"Most of Her Majesty's council is dead, young man, and with the queen off galivanting through the Pass, the likelihood of her return is slim. As slim as us winning this war. *Someone* must step forward and rein in this battle. Considering my friendship with Her Majesty's late father, the Thirteen bless him, I am privileged to accept this duty myself. Her Majesty would want this, of that I'm sure."

The man carried on with a list of reasons why he should

make the necessary decisions, which included everything from his vast intelligence to his lengthy experience giving advice to the royal family, which they "always considered helpful." It was everything Leolin could do not to drown out the old man as nothing Lord Cornish said was helpful in the least.

So far as Leolin knew, Margaret had planned to retire Lord Cornish to his estates when the Shadians attacked, but nothing Leolin said could convince the man of *that* truth. Her Holiness sat silently at the end of the table, her face still despite the magical quakes that shook the walls around them. There were fewer quakes since the battle at the Pass. Not that it mattered with the Shadian army emulating them with their trebuchet.

"Are you listening to me, young man?" asked Lord Cornish.

Leolin ceased pacing to glare. "Listening to what? You say nothing of consequence. There's an army outside our walls, walls I might add that have been breached twice now. Unless you wish to take up sword and join in the fight, I can't see how you'll help. It's Captain Fenton making the real decisions—"

"Now just a moment, young man. I'll have you know I fought—"

"Yes, yes, we know—in the Little War of Three—but that was quite a while ago, Lord Cornish. It would be wise to leave the fighting to those more able bodied. I ask again, what decisions do you think need making outside those of military consequence?"

Lord Cornish rose from his chair, standing tall and stiff in his outrage. Before he could protest, Her Holiness broke the silence with a simple tap on the table. "Her Majesty would wish those of us remaining to work together. Fighting like children over who leads misses the point entirely. Are we not her council? What is our purpose but to work together?"

Heat spread across Leolin's cheeks, and he bit back a curse.

"My apologies, Your Holiness, for my behavior. I should know better than to participate in squabbles, especially when we are at war." He waved his hand in Lord Cornish's direction and waited for an apology that would not come.

As expected, Lord Cornish merely cleared his throat.

"Has there been any word from Her Majesty?" asked Her Holiness.

Leolin shook his head. "Not since the message she sent when she arrived at the Pass."

"Why was she allowed to go to the Pass in the first place?"

It was a genuine belly laugh that escaped Leolin as he stared at Lord Cornish. "Would you seriously propose to tell the Queen what she can and can't do? Not even *I* can do that."

"That's the purpose of this council. To advise her and make her see reason."

Here we go again. Leolin glanced at Her Holiness to see the polite mask had returned.

There was a light knock at the door before it opened, and Bredych stepped through. Lord Cornish frowned as if something foul dangled from the tip of his nose, but the *Amaskan* paid him no mind.

"Has there been any word?" asked Bredych.

"That information is necessary only to those *official* members of Her Majesty's council, of which you are not." Lord Cornish jabbed a finger in the *Amaskan's* direction. "Why are we allowing a murderer into this room, let alone this Kingdom? This is why someone needs to be making the important decisions in Her Majesty's absence..."

"Someone like you?" Leolin's cheeks flushed as the words escaped him, despite his promise to maintain civility with the old fool. He inclined his head. "My apologies, Your Holiness. It seems the late candlemark leaves my tongue uncivil."

Bredych claimed the empty chair beside Leolin with a

heavy sigh. "I will assume then that no word has come from the Pass. What word from Captain Fenton regarding the city walls?"

"The walls have been fortified and should hold for the time being, but our army's comprised of those with little training and those so injured they shouldn't be fighting at all. Somehow Fenton has managed to hold the Shadians off, but if Margaret doesn't return soon, we won't last the season."

The moment Leolin ceased speaking, Lord Cornish shook a finger at him. "You leave me no choice, Lieutenant. If events are as dire as that, *someone* must lead. As the highest ranking member of this council, I will step up in Her Majesty's absence. Several surrounding cities could send fighters to our aid. I'll have messages sent at once so that we might strengthen the city's defenses. Those who can't help should be sent away. We have no time to protect the helpless..."

Her Holiness frowned. "My lord, that is the sole purpose of this city—protecting those who need it most."

"Pulling fighters from the smaller towns will only leave them defenseless. For now, I suggest we all make decisions *together* until Her Majesty's return. I would also add that you are not the highest rank present. That honor would go to Her Holiness," said Bredych.

Lord Cornish worried the inside of his cheek. While he said nothing, Leolin watched as the man jotted down notes on a scrap of paper—probably his plans for seizing the crown— and Leolin made a note to ensure no messenger birds were sent without full council approval. "I agree that removing support from our cities—"

"Our?" asked Lord Cornish.

"Yes, our as in Alexandrian. I meant no slight, nor did I intend any assumptions."

Bredych sighed. "My lord, you may be one of Her Majesty's vassals, but it is no secret that Her Majesty values

Leolin's insight more than yours. Should their relationship continue to develop, you might well be speaking to your future king, a fact you should remember when choosing your words."

The wine in Leolin's mouth burned as it tried escaping through his nose. While it was true that he loved Margaret and shared her bed, two facts that were not secret throughout the city, he had never envisioned a future where he wore the crown. While his guts churned at the idea, the reminder silenced Lord Cornish, a fact for which everyone seemed grateful.

"As I was saying, these towns you speak of have been sacked by the Shadians on their way to Alesta. Those who have not are safe only because of their fighters—those same fighters you wish to remove. I have no doubt Margaret would be against such actions. We'll have to find other means of keeping the city safe."

When no one responded, Leolin continued. "I suspect we all want the same thing—for Queen Margaret to return posthaste, and for the Shadian army to retreat. My recommendation is that Her Holiness and the other healers continue to help the wounded while we three do what we can to aid Captain Fenton and our fighters. Perhaps we should meet less to talk about what to do and spend more time with the doing."

Lord Cornish remained silent though the other two nodded their assent. After they left and only Bredych remained behind, the *Amaskan*'s brows furrowed as he stared at the unlit fireplace. Crammed into what had once been King Leon's sitting room, the room felt smaller than Leolin remembered, a feeling that doubled as Bredych began to pace.

"If the queen doesn't return soon, she won't have a crown to return to."

Leolin studied the *Amaskan* as he wore footprints into a

small blue rug on the floor. In the short while Margaret had been gone, Bredych had aged. Well into his seventies, every wrinkle was more pronounced as worried. "I fear you're correct. Lord Cornish will do everything he can to steal control from her."

"Leaving her people behind during a war could be seen as abandonment. Some might argue she's abdicated her crown."

"Who would listen to his complaint? The Senate?" Leolin laughed, though his shoulders hitched up as they tensed. If someone *did* complain to them...

When he sucked in air between his teeth, Bredych nodded. "A new king, someone not directly of the Poncett line means the Shadians wouldn't have a reason to attack. The war would end, not to mention any conflict with the Senate themselves, and everything would return to normal. The people of Alexander would be hard pressed to find fault in that."

"Oh gods," whispered Leolin.

"We can prevent him from sending any messages from Alesta, but how do you stop someone from talking with their gods?"

"I-I didn't think of that. We can't. There's nothing we can do but hope Margaret returns soon." When Leolin glanced up, Bredych's face was shadowed in deep in thought. Whatever the *Amaskan* was planning, he wanted none of it. Leolin finished his wine and fled the room.

3

Stone slabs and lumber stakes shored up most holes in the city walls. Every day brought another weakness in the city's defenses as the Shadian army broke through another portion of wall, Leolin sighed. Perhaps Lord Cornish had been right—maybe it was time to abandon the city as lost —but as he paced across the castle battlement, his gaze hovered on the corner of wall where Margaret had fled Alesta. His gaze shifted towards a tree where he had kissed her one evening during a leisurely walk. Memory after memory rolled across his mind.

There was no way he could leave the city. To abandon it to the Shadians would be sacrilege. Besides, Margaret would never forgive him, so he continued pacing as he waited for some miracle to save them. Queen Margaret's troops were scattered across the city and by their slumped shoulders and dull eyes, even Leolin had to admit that the soldiers had given up.

Men and women leaned against heaps of crumbled stone as they caught sleep when and where they could. Some drank water or nibbled on stale bread and cheese as the sun rose. Once the sky was light enough, the fighting would resume and Her Majesty's people would continue to die.

Someone's footsteps skittered across the stone floor in a hurry as they approached Leolin, and he swore. What fresh hell would this messenger bring? Would it be a summons from Lord Cornish or worse, a report on how many had died the day before?

"Lieutenant, a message for you!" the boy called as he approached. "From Her Majesty!"

Leolin's heart leapt in his chest and for a moment, it forgot how to beat. *Let the news be good. Thirteen knows we don't have it in us for another sustained battle.*

The boy handed him the scrap of parchment and waited while Leolin unfolded it.

L,

We are united.

M.

He didn't stop running until he reached Captain Fenton. He could hear the messenger boy running behind him over his own breathing, and when Leolin stopped, the boy wasn't even winded. "I've been too long in the castle," he said to the captain as he passed him the note.

"If you're huffing like that then yes! Grab your sword, Lieutenant, and I'll put you to work." The captain unfolded the parchment and scanned the message. "Great news for the future, but who's going to tell this to the lad out there convinced he's tasked with killing us all?"

Leolin grinned. "I would guess that's your job, Captain."

"Without his father here, he won't stop. Shadians hate like *Tribor*; they're relentless in their killing."

"Then perhaps we send that fool home in pieces."

Captain Fenton glanced down at the note before passing it back to Leolin. "I never thought I'd say this, but let's hope she brings King Bajit with her."

"Lieutenant Leolin, sir, do you have a return message for Her Majesty?"

Despite the messenger boy waiting near his elbow, Leolin had managed to forget his existence until the lad spoke. "I'm sorry to keep you waiting, but no, no return message," he said, and the boy scampered off towards the castle.

"I'm surprised he followed you out here. Brave boy. Perhaps he might be interested in joining the royal guard in the future." Captain Fenton directed a group of men bearing a piece of the city wall towards the last gap, and then turned back to Leolin. "Meet me outside the walls. Let's give our queen a proper welcome home."

It wasn't until Leolin was at the city gate that he paused. His Queen wouldn't relish a blood bath as a welcome, especially after returning from the Meridi Pass. What had this war done to him—to them all—that they could think cheerfully about bloodshed?

The message burned in his brain. A united Boahim. Too bad Prince Amar of Shad wouldn't care. When the gate opened, Leolin's sword was ready as he led the charge towards the Shadians.

One voice shouted, then another, until the Royal Army took up a chant. Leolin stabbed a man to his left and added his voice to the cry.

"For Boahim!"

PRINCE AMAR TOWERED over people with his impressive height, but astride his horse, a halfling born of a stolen battle steed out of Sadai, he sat like a god stepped down from above to lead his people to victory. Rather than his wiry and lithe build, he pictured himself to be more like Anur, God of War and Justice, with a warrior's frame and beautiful enough that warriors would weep to be near him.

That is, he pictured all of this until one Alexandrian shot a bow at his horse, nearly hitting her in the flank. The archer missed, but that wasn't the point. The arrow's close proximity worried the horses around him into bumping his lady until she bore dust and mud instead of her beautiful golden coat. They'd ruined Amar's boots as well, and he scowled when his fingers failed to remove the scuffs.

Instead of the picture of perfection, his dirty self sat upon a dirty horse upon a pile of dirt rather than a proper hill as he watched his troops fight to regain footing after yesterday's battle. Something had given new life to the Alexandrian Army as they had renewed the battle with vigor. "No sight of their queen?" he asked one of the *Tribor* beside him.

"No, Your Highness."

Dust kicked up as a rider approached the "hill," and Amar raised a brow. "Perhaps this is word now."

A simple Shadian guardsman, he dismounted in a hurry and bowed low to the ground before offering a piece of parchment to Amar who gestured for the *Tribor* to take it first. When the assassin began to open it, Prince Amar slapped the man's hands. "That message is for me."

To the guardsman, he gave the briefest of nods to dismiss him.

"If it's for you, why'd you have me take it?"

Amar scowled. "Why should I sully myself by touching him, hmm? Proper etiquette dictates that someone of your station receive it for me, then pass it along. Don't they teach you anything in that cult of yours?" The *Tribor* frowned but remained silent. When Amar opened the parchment, he let out a curse before throwing it to the ground. He bit his lip to keep from kicking his horse and when that did not cool his temper, he dismounted and scuffed his boots further by kicking a large rock.

"Bad news?"

"I'd ask you not to assume, but your kind excels at nothing else."

The *Tribor* laughed, a grating sound that gave Amar a headache. Why his father kept these pests around escaped him, though they had proven decent enough at fighting when attacking the Alexandrians.

"Are your men ready?" he asked the *Tribor* beside him.

"They are. They await your word, Your Highness."

"My father wishes us to withdraw." He wasn't sure why he said the parchment's message aloud, only that doing so gave him a perverse sense of joy. "As long as my father has his way, there will be no justice for my brother. Would you follow me into battle, even if it means defying my father?"

The *Tribor* laughed again, but this time the pitch was deeper, more serious as the man nodded. "Soon your father will pass like all the others, and you'll be our King. Young though you are, you understand that there's no Justice to be found in peace."

"Then at sunset, we attack."

"At sunset."

The *Tribor* urged his horse forward to spread the word, and Amar smiled as he patted his lady on the neck. Without their queen, the Alexandrian Army would stretch itself thin fighting both the Shadians and *Tribor*. If their queen showed up, they would divide her up as well.

⚔

THE MAN POSSESSED A NAME, though it was unknown to Prince Amar. No *Tribor* gave their name to anyone as their existence became only *Tribor*, but even if the man had given it to the conceited prince, the prince was too careless to recall it. *He* was the only one that mattered.

He and the Queen of Alexander.

He lusted after her death the way one lusted after their first woman. The *Tribor* snorted as he approached his brother who sheltered beneath a tall tree. "He wishes to attack at sunset," he whispered, and his brother nodded. "King Bajit sent a message. Did you read it when it came through?"

Another nod.

"Then you know we can't allow the fool to attack."

His brother glanced to where the prince had returned to his horse, his dirty armor clean of anything that mattered. "Let him attack, on his head be it. We'll be halfway to the Pass before he realizes we're gone. Maybe the fool will get himself killed in the process and save us the trouble."

"Perhaps. Still, we must report the defiance to the King."

His brother nodded. "The message will be sent. Be ready to leave before sunset. Itovah's honor."

"Itovah's honor."

The few *Tribor* nearby retreated further into the woods as word of the peace treaty spread. The man would join them shortly, but first, he needed to alert those *Tribor* hidden within the Shadian army.

Personally, he was never a believer in peace, but the *Tribor* followed King Bajit. If he ordered it so, it would be done. Justice would find a way no matter now or three weeks from now. When the fool prince attacked tonight, he'd be waiting for a second attack that would never come.

Good riddance to spoiled brats. Itovah's honor.

4

How many are there?" asked Margaret as she tugged at her horse's reins.

"More than I like." Her guardsman held a spyglass to one eye as he scanned the city walls. Mostly bare of Alexandrians, the outer walls were pierced with holes and some parts were little more than crumbled heaps of gray rubble. "The way the Shadian army's set, I don't think the battle's stopped."

That was Margaret's assumption as well, and she shook her head. "How far behind us is King Bajit?"

"A day. Maybe half-a-day if we're lucky."

Neither side fought at the moment, as the barest of yellows and pinks painted the horizon. Ahead of them, several guards paced back and forth in front of the city walls, though they wore Shad's purple rather than Alexander's blue.

Something glittered atop a parapet as someone crouched down, their sword drawn. On a whim, Margaret removed her short sword and held it aloft. A couple of calculated tilts signaled to whomever was on the wall that assistance was needed.

Beside her, the guardsman scowled. "Your Majesty, that could be the enemy. You've given them our position!"

"Captain Fenton would never allow the enemy inside our walls."

"My apologies, Your Majesty, but what if Captain Fenton's...gone? Look at the walls. Alesta's probably overrun with Shadians at this point. I can't protect Your Majesty if we're discovered."

She did not bother reminding the man of her position. It would not have solved anything as he considered his orders from Bredych to be above her own. It was one thing to protect her and another to stifle her. A cry at the gate distracted her from figuring out how to transverse the army outside, and the sounds of metal on metal reached them.

Margaret crouched behind the grove of maquis shrubs that served as their hiding spot. "What do you see?"

At first, her guardsman remained silent, and then a muttered oath passed his lips, followed by an apology to her person. She didn't have to wait long to decipher his concern as the sounds of hoofbeats approached. A small group of fighters in blue pushed their way through the Shadian army while a black horse carried a man towards them at a gallop. For all his hair had grown in, she'd recognize his sharp nose anywhere.

Bredych urged his horse forward as bodies fell to his sword. With the Shadians engaged with her army, only a few minutes passed until Bredych reached her. "Your Majesty, your presence is quite welcome to these eyes."

He removed a knot of clothes from his satchel and tossed it to her. "Drape this cloak over you. When you hear the whistle, ride for the walls at all speed."

A million questions plagued her, but she did as she was

told. There would be time later to ask what had occurred in her absence. The cloak reeked of horse sweat and manure, and she breathed through her mouth to keep the stench from her nostrils.

The whistle came sooner than she'd expected, and she pulled herself into the saddle as Bredych swatted its croup with the flat of his hand. The horse leapt forward, bolting in the Shadian's direction, and she unsheathed her blade. Beside her, Bredych did the same.

Someone made a grab for her horse, and she kicked the Shadian in the jaw. Another man stubbled into her mount's path, his cries lost as her horse trampled him. The cloak disguised her identity, but the Shadians cared little as they saw her only as Alexandrian and thus, their enemy. A sharp whistle cut the air and combat ahead cleared a path for them.

The whistle repeated and beside her, Bredych pointed at a dark-haired man leading a second group of Alexandrian fighters towards them. The man turned, giving Margaret a clear glimpse of Captain Fenton. In the moment she took to urge her horse in his direction, a Shadian grabbed her horse's reins.

Her sword slid down into his chest where it caught on his ribs. After a second tug, she abandoned the blade to the dust. Daggers would do little in a major battle but it was better than no weapon at all. Margaret grabbed one from her waist while Bredych urged his horse closer to hers.

The Alexandrian fighters formed a tight circle around her and her horse danced, eyes wide with fear. Like a wave, they carried her inside the city gates, though the fighting around her continued until a gap allowed them to close the gates. Captain Fenton held out a hand to help her dismount, seemingly ignoring the steady stream of blood trickling down his cheek.

"Did my messages arrive?" she asked, and when he

nodded, she frowned. "Let me guess, Prince Amar doesn't believe a pact has been made?"

"No, Your Majesty, though I'm not sure he cares either way. I don't suppose you brought King Bajit with you?"

"We believe he is a day or two behind us."

Murmurs traveled through the fighters, and she glanced around the entry courtyard. Not a single person lacked wounds, some more than others, and when she gave them a second look, more than fatigue carved its way through every wrinkle and line. Fear hovered in their posture as they flinched at every noise as the Shadians renewed their attack on the city. "How many are left?"

"Not here, Your Majesty."

His brevity was all the answer she needed. Beside her, Bredych winced as they walked. Somewhere between the bush and the gate, someone's sword had left a gash in his leg. It would be better for him to ride to the castle but with her army packed near the gates, horses would crowd an already tense situation.

Margaret glanced a second time at his wound. She was the only one without injury. Her people bled to keep her safe. *Had* bled to bring her home. Prince Amar would pay for every drop of Alexandrian bloodshed.

A shout rang across the courtyard and before she could do more than blink, she found herself in Leolin's arms. He clung to her for a moment before releasing her, though he left one hand resting on her waist as they walked.

The city walls shook as another volley of stone hit them, and part of the city wall slid into a crumbled mess at the road's edge causing Margaret to flinch.

"You'll grow used to it eventually," said Leolin, though his hand tightened around her.

She had no wish to grow used to the sounds of war, though she kept those thoughts to herself. As they passed through her city in silence, she used the opportunity to study him. Though she had been gone little more than a month, the lines around his eyes had multiplied. Fresher wounds and scars marred his normally tan skin, and deep circles spoke of his lack of sleep.

War had aged him. It had aged them all. "Has anyone sent a message to Prince Amar?" she asked.

"No point in doing so. He's determined to overrun Alesta."

Margaret stopped. "You did not attempt to stop the war?"

"Margaret, there was no need. We discussed it but with our army outnumbered, we can't afford to lose anyone. Who would carry that message? We need every fighter we can get."

Her skin grew warm, though not with embarrassment. Anger grew inside her belly, anger that her orders had been ignored by those who thought they knew best for her city. For her people. "Allow me to guess. This decision came from Lord Cornish."

Leolin nodded. "Though he wasn't alone. Captain Fenton and I agreed with him."

"And you?" she asked Bredych.

The *Amaskan* shrugged. "I disagreed, though in your absence, my opinion has mattered about as much as a turnip's. I do not think Amar would have ceased his attacks, but we won't know until we try."

Margaret kicked a loose stone in the road, and it bounced a few times before landing gently against an abandoned home. For all that her city was full, it was empty of that which made it Alesta—its people. Those who were able-bodied carried weapons now, drafted into a battle no one wanted, and here she was about to ask them to fight the Thirteen.

Goose pimples spread across her flesh, though no one but her noticed cloaked as she was. As she walked through the city streets, her fingers trailed along abandoned merchant carts, baskets, and signs. No business was open, not even the public houses, and her city's change left her empty.

With all of her escort injured, a candlemark passed before they reached the castle proper. While it showed no damage to its exterior, its insides were overrun with the injured. Almost every hallway and room had been requisitioned for war. Most of the wounded lay on makeshift cots on the first floor, but the second floor was where she found those Alexandrians who had remained in Alesta. Children played quietly in the halls while the elderly watched. No one who could walk and hold a sword remained inside. Leolin prodded her elbow towards the stairs and the third floor, but she shook off his grip.

"Your Majesty, with so few members comprising your council and so many injured, the council room has been...relocated," said Captain Fenton as he held his hand in the stairwell's direction.

She frowned but followed him directly to the fourth floor and her royal sitting room. Someone had removed the furniture burned in the fire, with the exception of her grandsire's chair, which had been repaired. An oval table had been crammed into the room, surrounded by half a dozen chairs of varying colors and styles. Margaret recognized one as having been purloined from an audience chamber on the second floor and a second as having come from her bedchamber. An arm's width of space between the chairs and wall left little room to sit, giving the room an overly stuffed feel. The few guards escorting her remained outside as Leolin, Bredych, and Captain Fenton claimed their seats in a well-practiced motion.

"Where is Lord Cornish?" she asked as she chose her grandsire's chair.

A brief knock answered her, and the old man strode into the room as if it were the Great Hall and not a modest room. He paused when he realized she had claimed her grandsire's chair, and she bit back a grin. The fool had thought to claim it as his own. The remaining chair—the one from the audience chamber—was notoriously uneven and intentionally so as her father had used it for those guests he wished a hasty retreat.

"Welcome back, Your Majesty," Lord Cornish said as he poured himself a glass of wine from a pitcher left on the table.

Decorum dictated a glass should have been offered to her first, though she ignored the slight. Beside her, Leolin's eyes narrowed as he all but wrenched the pitcher from the old man. He poured Margaret a glass before offering one to Bredych and Fenton before filling his own.

"I see my council has made themselves comfortable in my absence." Margaret sipped her wine while Lord Cornish squirmed in his chair. "Captain—forgive me, it should be Field Marshal now—if you would give me a thorough update on the state of our army."

If Fenton was surprised by the promotion, he did not show it as he gave a brief nod. "After you left, our fighters from Monpoli and a few more from the Pass arrived, as did some Shadian stragglers. We recruited every able bodied person within the city walls. At present, the Alexandrian army stands at 210 fighters, of which fifty cavalry and twenty archers remain. From what we can tell, the Shadians number a few dozen more than our numbers. They constructed their trebuchet last week, though our walls have withstood most of the damage."

"How many injured are being treated within the city?" she asked.

"Ninety fighters are too injured for battle, Your Majesty."

Margaret finished her glass of wine in a quick swallow. At the time of her father's death, the Alexandrian Army had been six hundred strong. While some of her people had died against the Shadians, so many lives had been silenced by the Senate at the Meridi Pass. "What are our numbers if we include those recruited from the populace?"

"Those *are* our numbers including the townsfolk. All those who could hold a weapon."

Her vision darkened around the edges, and the sitting room swam as her wine threatened to claw its way out of her stomach.

Lord Cornish reached out and took her hand. "The news is grim indeed, Your Majesty, but I've sent news home to Brussell to see if any more able-bodied people might be spared. I suggested to Captain Fenton—"

"Field Marshal."

"Yes, of course, Your Majesty. I suggested to your marshal that if the bordering towns in Alexander were to send more people to Alesta, perhaps we could overrun the Shadian army, though I fear my suggestion was outvoted."

Her faintness passed and when she turned her gaze on Lord Cornish, his fingers fidgeted with the hem of his shirt. "I would know the reason why my most recent orders were not followed," she said as she stared at him.

"W-Which orders would those be, Your Majesty?"

"Orders to cease fighting and notify the Shadians of the pact reached at the Pass."

Lord Cornish cleared his throat, his jowls shuddering. "It wouldn't have mattered, Your Majesty. Prince Amar is determined—"

"I believe Lord Cornish has mistaken his role in this council," said Margaret as she poured another glass of wine for herself.

"He wasn't alone in his decision, Your Majesty," said Leolin.

The formality from him caught her off guard and she frowned. "Then he is not alone in his presumption to know my mind. If I give an order, I expect it to be carried through."

"The council—"

Margaret held up a hand to cut Leolin off. "This council

exists to council me. It does not exist to make decisions *for* me or in my absence. I was quite clear in my directions."

"Yes, Your Majesty."

Fenton repeated Leolin's words, though Lord Cornish remained silent, his face a deep purple.

"You have more to add, my lord?" she asked.

"I do, Your Majesty." He stood and had there been space, he would have set to pacing. Instead, he gripped the chair's backing. "Your father would have understood the futility of such actions. He would have finished what was started and sent for the support of his vassals—"

"My father is dead, Lord Cornish. What he would or would not have done is irrelevant. Besides, I am not my father. My vassals have need of their fighters to protect them and their lands. I'll not call on them to send more than they can spare any more than I would expect you to take up arms. But since you all have seen fit to make my decisions for me, against my orders, I will do what I should have done at my father's passing. You are dismissed, Lord Cornish."

"Y-Your Majesty?"

"You are dismissed, my lord. You may return to your holdings where you can better defend them and make appropriate decisions better suited to your ranking."

"But who will council—"

Margaret set her wine glass down too hard, and the glass stem cracked. "This council is no longer needed. There is little three people can provide for me that I can't gain elsewhere. Her Holiness and my physician are busy treating the wounded. The rest are...elsewhere." She bit her tongue against saying the word aloud.

Dead. The rest were dead.

If she thought about all those gone, the tears would begin again, so she pushed the thoughts aside. "If I should need guidance on the state of my military, my field marshal can provide such information. Master Bredych and Lieutenant Leolin are also available to discuss tactics. I feel it wholly unnecessary to seek the advice of nobility for nobility's sake."

"I fear Your Majesty is distraught. Allow us to help you while you recover from your trip. That is our purpose, Your Majesty," said Lord Cornish.

"You make it sound as if I journeyed on a pleasurable trip around my Kingdom. While you played King, I was securing our very lives, my lord." She picked up the bell from the table and gave it a single ring. A guardsman entered a moment later and bowed. "My Lord Cornish will be returning home to Brussell. Please escort him to his rooms so that he might prepare for the trip."

The color rushed from her former advisor's face and his hands trembled as he released the chair's back. He gave a short bow, too short for her status, but she allowed it if it would remove him from her sight all the sooner.

"He'll need a few guards to escort him if he's to reach home alive," said Fenton.

Margaret nodded. "I hate to lose the fighters, but we would not slight him by having him arrive home in ashes."

A slight squeak escaped Lord Cornish, and he fled the room, the guardsman following shortly behind.

"I meant what I said. This council is dissolved as I have no more need for it. If I should require any advice, I will ask who I wish without the formalities."

Fenton gave her a proper bow. "By your leave? I should return to the city walls."

When she nodded, he exited the small sitting room, leaving her alone with Leolin and Bredych. Her vision clouded a second time as the room tilted, and she grabbed hold of the table.

"Maggie, what is it?"

She closed her eyes until the world settled. "Perhaps too

much wine...and too much death. A good night's sleep will help, I'm sure."

While Leolin patted her hand, Bredych watched her. Whatever he saw worried him as his eyes narrowed and his brows bunched together. Margaret poured herself a glass of water and gave it a sip. "On our way through the city, I noticed everyone has fled their homes and businesses. I assume that includes whatever contacts you had with the Order, Master Bredych."

"Not at all. We Amaskans are good at remaining hidden."

"Good. Our...our borders have been closed to the Order for longer than I've been alive, but with the coming fight, I would change this. I'll have the parchments drawn up for something official, but for now, I say to you as the Grand Master of the Order of *Amaska* that Alexander holds no grievance with the Order. In fact, I would welcome whatever support your Amaskans might provide in our fight with the Thirteen."

Leolin snorted. "No wonder you dismissed Lord Cornish."

"Indeed. I imagine the man would die of heart failure at the idea," said Bredych.

"Bredych, I will admit I'm surprised to find the Order *not* here. I would have thought you to have called for them the moment the city was attacked."

Like her father, Bredych paused before he answered her, but unlike her father, he held something back. She could see it in the way his gaze did not meet hers but settled slightly above her head. "In order to return here, I renounced my place as leader of the Order. It was the only way since I'm no longer there to ensure their safety."

"Surely they could continue without your immediate presence?" she asked.

"They could, but I would be doing them a great disservice

in remaining their leader while away. It was better for them if I stepped aside."

"Is that what you would have me do?"

Bredych shook his head. "Not at all, Your Majesty. Your visit to the Pass was a short trip and not intended to be permanent. The situations are not the same."

"So the Amaskans are not in Alesta because you are no longer their leader?"

"It's not that simple. I can ask them for help, but it would be one member of the Order asking another. I can't require them to help. Not anymore."

Still the man held something back. Something he worried would upset her, perhaps. Margaret made a mental note to ask him again when they were alone.

"Who leads the Amaskans now?"

At this, Bredych smiled. "A woman named Miriam. She reminds me of your mother, Leolin. Certainly in temperament."

"How long has she been with the Order?" asked Margaret.

"A year or two longer than I have, Your Majesty. She came to us from the Holy Few."

Chill bumps scattered across Margaret's skin. "I was not aware that one could leave the Holy Few."

"It's exceedingly rare, but it can happen. She was a child when she was given to the Holy Few and as a teen, decided the path was not hers, so she left."

"I will make it a request then to this Miriam."

Bredych nodded. "I think Miriam's knowledge about the Thirteen and this prophecy can only aide us."

"I could certainly use the allies, especially after sending that onerous lord home."

"Speaking of Lord Cornish, Maggie, I didn't mention it when he was present, but I don't think you realize how close you came to losing your kingdom. The man is set to seize whatever power he thinks he can however he can."

It was Margaret's turn to laugh, though when Bredych's face paled, the sound died on her lips. "How could he possibly take the crown?"

"It's an older law, but one that remained after the Fall of Boahim. Leaving your city without its ruler during a time of war could be seen as abdicating. Whether the Senate would bother to uphold it with a possible war is unknown, but Lord Cornish would have been within his rights to file the complaint." Bredych's face remained pale after he spoke. "It's critical that you remain in Alesta."

"My father left this castle during the Little War of Three! He led his army in battle, and no one dared accuse him of abandoning his people!" Margaret's face grew warm, and she lifted her water glass to her cheeks to cool them. "No one would dare."

"Your father was leading his army into battle. You left your army and your people. I understand why you left—securing peace with the other kingdoms and gaining the Little Dozen Kingdoms' support against the Thirteen might save us all—but that's not how it appears to everyone else. As your city walls fell, you rode away. Alone."

"I had my honor guards."

"In your people's eyes, you fled, Your Majesty. They do not have the necessary information to understand the why. They see only the action and the consequences—the deaths of many."

By the time Bredych finished, Margaret's fingernails dug into her palms. Every action she took was judged unfairly and inaccurately. Every decision she made failed to be as correct as her father would have done.

"Enough. I'm here. A pact has been formed amongst the

Little Dozen Kingdoms, a pact that would not have been possible without me, I might add. I am tired. Leave me."

Bredych held up his hands before him. "I might ask a boon of you, Your Majesty."

"Speak your piece."

"When the Shadians broke through the city walls, they did so along the outer circle. The hardest hit areas were those of the public houses and inns. Those without the means to rebuild as easily as the merchants and tradesmen with a guild behind them."

"There are city funds that could help with that," she said.

"The first of the townspeople to take up arms in the city's defense were those public workers. Illegal though it may be, public houses have always operated throughout Alexander. Despite being treated as maggots in rot by those who ruled before you, these men and women fought to defend not just their homes but yours, Your Majesty. I would ask you consider that as queen. Consider their sacrifice when deciding if their existence is any less than your own."

She swallowed hard. The Thirteen spoke of their work as akin to taking one's own life, a sin against the flesh and the soul, but the Thirteen spoke of many things, many sins that upon reflection, mattered little to those living in the Little Dozen Kingdoms. "I...I will give it some consideration," she said, and with a slight bow, Bredych retreated.

"Would you really grant them legality, Maggie?" asked Leolin, and she shrugged.

"They were as willing to give their lives in service to the kingdom as any other citizen. Perhaps once the Thirteen have fallen, it will be time to reconsider the laws of our lands. Nothing remains the same, Leolin. If you don't mind, I would like some time alone."

If the sudden dismissal caught him off guard, Leolin gave

no indication as he left her sitting room without another word.

Margaret rang the bell that sat on her table, and when a page entered, she said, "I would ask my physician to attend me." The boy bobbed his head when she held her hand up. "Never mind. He has more important tasks than me."

Once she was alone again, she stood gingerly, giving her muscles a slow stretch before retreating to her bed chambers. What she needed was rest, she was sure of it.

Her lady-in-waiting had left a light chemise on the chest beside her bed, though a slight layer of dust covered it. When it appeared Margaret was not returning anytime soon, the young woman had stopped worrying about such niceties. For all she knew, her lady-in-waiting was among those fighting.

Or perhaps she lay among the dead.

Margaret gave the chemise a good shake before she set it down again. Alone, she shed clothes dirty from travel, donned her chemise, and crawled into bed before the sun touched the horizon.

5

257 Anurus 1st

Something about the royal gardens spoke to Bredych; it was a pocket of nature in an otherwise cold castle. Bredych ran his fingers along the trailing ivy that curled its way around the stone bench before it stretched halfway across the walkway. His home of Sadai was mostly desert and grasslands, though pockets of green appeared around the seaside cliffs near the Order. Between spots of ivy, roses and orchids bloomed in ignorance of the death around them.

Bredych rubbed his right knee as he inhaled the garden's sweet fragrance. He supposed he should be thankful for King Bajit's arrival before dawn that morning. His knee was certainly grateful for the relief from battle. Despite the momentary respite, knots tied up his guts. Not even the beautiful gardens could keep him from worrying about whatever battle lay ahead with the Thirteen.

His thoughts spun round, so much that he didn't notice Leolin's approach until the lad was almost upon him. When he gestured for him to sit, Leolin shook his head before he set to pacing.

"You too?" asked Bredych.

Leolin nodded. "The battle's stopped. I should be happy for it, yet...this battle was nothing compared to a fight against the gods. How are we to win? Is it even possible?"

"That is the question."

For all that the boy disliked—even hated—Bredych, the past few weeks of battle had formed a truce between them. There was nothing like watching a seventy-two-year-old man fight the enemy with vigor to give one a healthy dose of respect, and Bredych bit back a grin.

"I mean, we knew this when we began walking this path, but there's knowing and then there's *knowing*." Leolin barely paused for breath as he spoke. "Margaret bought peace with Shad with the promise of freedom from the Senate. The threat of them, it changed all our courses, but we still don't have a solid plan."

Bredych sighed. "Margaret spoke of a plan to the other rulers."

"Yes, but what is that plan? As far as she'll tell me, she encouraged them to try and kill the gods with those orbs. That'll only work once maybe twice before they catch on. They're gods, not imbeciles."

"If you pace any harder, you're going to crack the cobble-stones," said Bredych. He had sought out the garden's silence to think, yet Leolin's persistent worry left the place too crowded. "The orbs are a beginning step. Margaret left Alesta to gain the other kingdoms' trust. Now that she has it, proper plans can be made."

When the boy continued his pacing, Bredych growled, a sound of half-frustration and half-understanding. "What do you want, Leolin? What do you need from me?"

"From you? Nothing. From her, answers. Something. Anything. An indication that she knows what's she's doing."

"Why not ask her yourself? Why pester me with this?"

Leolin kicked at an uneven cobblestone whose corner poked up crookedly in the path. "I tried. She ordered me to leave."

Laughter erupted from Bredych as he stared at the boy. "Either you trust the queen or you don't. In any case, pestering her won't endear you to her."

"I trust her." Leolin's voice hesitated, and he kicked again at the loose cobble.

"You trust Margaret."

"That's what I said."

Bredych shook his head. "You trust the woman but not the queen."

This time when Leolin kicked the stone, it uprighted and skittered across the path a few feet. When the boy did not respond, Bredych continued. "You need to trust both, or neither, otherwise your relationship will be little more than two Amaskans laying stones."

At this, Leolin frowned. He picked up the loose cobblestone. "What does this have to do with Margaret?"

"Most Amaskans don't keep close relationships—"

"Maggie's not *Amaskan*."

Bredych arched his brow. "Close relationships complicate matters. Anyone important to us becomes a target. When those of the Order need to leave a message for another member, we use stones to signify our need, so the saying is that two Amaskans laying stones are little more than two people passing messages in the night."

"I trust Margaret with my life."

"If you did, you would trust the decisions she makes for her people. When you look at her, Leolin, you see the woman you love, a woman in need of protection. When I look at her, I see a fighter who is capable of defeating the Thirteen. Therein lies the difference between us."

Leolin set the stone back within the path and resumed pacing. At first, Bredych thought that to be the end of it, but a few minutes later, Leolin sat on the bench beside him. "Do you have someone you love? I know you said that *Amaskans* don't foster attachments, but *Amaskans* don't tend to live long lives either. I figure someone who's lived as long as you have has loved before."

"I have loved more than most, but yes, there is someone." Miriam's blue eyes nestled in his mind a moment before his vision returned to the gardens. She would love Margaret's orchids. "Back at the Order."

"Do you worry about what'll happen to her without you there?" asked Leolin.

"I worry about her always, yes, but I don't worry for her safety. Not as you mean. Miriam is a strong, capable woman who can take care of herself. I have no worries about her ability to make the correct decisions. If I did, I would not have left the Order in her hands."

"Maggie didn't grow up like her sister. She was raised to rule alongside someone else."

Bredych glanced at the boy. "She has learned far more than her father intended, and quickly. You discredit her with your lack of confidence."

The boy's shoulders hitched up as he scowled. "You don't understand. We're talking about a war against the gods! She's going to get herself killed, and I—"

"Boy, we may all get ourselves killed. You're correct—these are gods—but they're weakened. They're mortal. A fact now known because of Margaret." Bredych placed a hand on Leolin's arm. "Everyone dies sometime, Leolin. If we're to die, better to do so seeking Justice than cowering in fear."

"And if your Miriam dies in this war? Will you still feel the same?"

"As I said, we may all die. When I left the Order, I made peace with that," said Bredych as he reached out and plucked a rose from a nearby bush. "Take this rose for instance. It's beautiful and worthy of enjoyment. If I sit here long enough, it will die, especially now that I've separated it from the bush. Knowing that it will wither and die, does that mean I should forgo the enjoyment of it now?"

The boy remained silent, though he stared at the rose in Bredych's hand. When the silence unnerved Bredych, Leolin spoke. "I understand what you're saying, but it doesn't rid me of this chill in my heart. It's as if the entire world will collapse without Margaret in it. How do you do...what you do knowing that someday Miriam will be little more than dust?"

Bredych picked a few petals from the rose and allowed them to scatter across the cobble. Leolin feared too much for love, and Bredych wrapped his hand tightly around the rose. "I have smothered this flower," he said and as he opened it, more petals fell to the ground. "In doing so, I can no longer enjoy it as it was meant to be enjoyed. You are like my hand around this rose, Leolin. You are smothering Margaret. If you can't believe her capable and trust her completely, then let her go. You'll only damage the both of you if you continue in this manner."

With this, the *Amaskan* stood and gave his muscles a gentle stretch. He dropped the remaining bits of rose in the soil. Either the boy would figure it out or he wouldn't, but for Margaret's sake, Bredych hoped it was the former. Besides, her people needed her more than the boy did, especially if they were going to battle the gods together. He left the boy sitting on the bench alone, a dozen rose petals strewn about him.

Gods help those who loved. What a mess it made.

Outside the Alesta City Walls

KING HAVIN BAJIT rubbed his brow with sweaty fingers. He missed the cool mountains of Drehsma, capital city of Shad, he missed his mistress and the way her fingers curled through his hair, but most of all, he missed Gamun, his youngest son. Tenacious and fierce as he had been, Gamun should have been his heir. Instead, his son's remains lay somewhere between here and the Boahim Senate, food for whatever worms and insects inhabited the soil of Alexander. Soil made richer by the death of a Shadian prince.

Instead, an impetuous hot head would rule after Havin died. This son glared at him, eyes frozen with hate as he asked for a third time, "Why would you sign a pact of peace with the Poncetts? Another day and the city would have fallen, especially with your arrival and fresh soldiers." Amar kicked up a cloud of dust with a booted heel.

Summer approached, bringing with it a heat that left them all a sweaty mess as they stood within Amar's tents. With no mountain breeze, the sun radiated through the silk fabric, and Havin sighed. "It's not your place to question my decisions. Rather you should learn from my example on how one plans for a longer game. There is winning, and there is *winning*, my son."

"How is this winning? Margaret might as well have murdered Gamun herself. To let her walk free—"

"She will not escape her crimes, Amar. That I promise."

His son sent up another cloud of dust. "She would pay all the sooner if we ended this now. Why the sudden change? Since when did you side with the Alexandrians on anything?"

"Since the Boahim Senate declared war across the Little Dozen Kingdoms. Think, son! With the other kingdoms' help, we could rid ourselves of not one but two thorns in our side."

Amar's brows furrowed as he sank into a small chair in the tent's corner. "How do you propose we do that?"

Had Gamun been that insipid? Havin could not help the second sigh that escaped him. "Our enemies become allies with a united threat. If we are fortunate, perhaps Queen Margaret will die in this battle with the Senate. Either way, it will appear that the Senators killed her and not us. We become the heroes who saved the Boahim people, placing us in a position of power. Think of the favors that will be owed to us."

"And if the queen survives?"

"Then we will have plenty of time to ensure she pays for Gamun's death, time without the Senate watching over us. Once her guard is down, a well-placed *Tribor* would serve well."

"What if I desire to kill the woman myself?" Amar asked.

"That way is fraught with danger. You are my sole heir now, and I'll not lose you."

He supposed he should have been honest with his heir. It was not as if the knowledge of the Senators' true identities was a secret, but something about the way Amar lusted after vengeance left Havin unsettled. It was not *lust* exactly, but an unhealthy obsession with Alesta Castle and Margaret herself. If he did not know any better, Havin would think the boy in love with the queen.

Gamun would have been a better heir, he thought as he closed the tent flap in hopes of stifling the heat. Outside, his army packed their supplies and made ready to return to Shad. "Amar, once we are returned home, I promise you we will plan for the Poncett family's end, but for now, we leave Queen Margaret off guard. She thinks us newfound allies. Let her believe it."

Amar spit in the dirt, an action picked up from the *Tribor* as they carried an unhealthy need to rid their mouths of the

Poncett name. "Allow me to stay. A few *Tribor* with me and we could make our way into the castle—"

"No."

"We could watch the queen and her pet *Amaskan*."

"No."

"Father, I wouldn't harm her. Not physically. But think of the information I could gather! Information helpful once you deem it time to take care of the problem."

Havin had to give the boy credit as his son did nothing to dodge the hand as it connected with his jaw.

Instead, Amar tilted his head upward, his teeth clenched together in anticipation of the blow. The last time Havin had struck his son, the boy had been a child, but now he wore the body of a man. Red flashed across Amar's skin, warring with the light blue of his eyes. "Father, I may not have your head for strategy, but you made sure I understood the ways of vengeance. You sent your *Tribor* to instruct me on what you could not, and the rest I learned in the streets of Drehsma."

"What would you know of the streets? You have lived a life of luxury and comfort inside my castle. Until this war, you were lucky to know hardship at all."

"Where do you think I was all those times you were busy playing favorites with Gamun, hmm? Rajami and I would venture into taverns on the West side until it was too late to see your hand in front of your face."

"I told him to watch over you and teach you to fight, not galivant through town like some peasant. You are heir to the throne of Shad, not some drunkard in need of a woman."

"Why can't I be both, Father? Or are you worried I might embarrass you or sully your reputation?"

Havin resisted the urge to slap his son for a second time, though Amar caught the slight movement of his hand.

"Six months ago, my father wouldn't have hesitated to

strike me for my insolence. A year ago, my father would have gutted me as easily as any rat in the street." Amar crossed the tent's distance with ease and held a dagger to Havin's neck. "Who are you? And do not say 'your father.'"

Havin grinned and waved his fingers casually. A bead of sweat froze on Amar's brow as magic touched him, and the fingers that gripped his dagger opened, allowing it to tumble to the dirt below. "I'm the father who could flay the skin from your bones with nothing more than a thought. Did it ever occur to you that perhaps I have knowledge you do not? Knowledge that leads me to make the decisions I have made?"

Amar stepped back, his eyes wide. "So share that knowledge with me! How can I learn to rule if you don't trust me enough to tell me these things?"

"I trust you as much as I trust anyone—not at all. You will learn the same way I did, with your feet before the fire. Once I'm dead, you can play king all you wish, but for now, you will do what I say, when I say it."

When his son strode from the tent, Havin bit back a laugh. His son thought him weak, but the boy would piss himself if he knew the Boahim Senate was the Thirteen. Havin glanced about the tent, his eyes searching for evidence of being watched. Did they need an orb to see or were the Thirteen watching him now? Maybe the same weakness that rendered them now mortal diminished their sight as well. Either way, he pressed two fingers against his brow to ward off evil.

He couldn't help the laughter that bubbled up in him at the reflexive action. The Thirteen certainly wouldn't protect him. At best, he might hope to escape their notice until they all lay dead.

Dead like Gamun.

Let others do the work of war for him. The moment the thought escaped, he swore. Perhaps the heat *had* addled his drive. It certainly had his son's. Somewhere outside the tent, his servants packed up his belongings. Come tomorrow, he would lead his people home.

6

Thirteen blackened spires decorated the top of the wooden staff, and each tip bore a fleck of gold, making each spire appear lit. Leolin stared at the spires as they swayed before him until they blurred together, forming a single golden flame. Mystic Shai Hauman said something, and while Leolin's brain acknowledged the words, he heard nothing but the low hum released by whatever magic held him enthralled.

Like dozens of times before, the memories snapped into his mind in a wash of color and sharp sound. His mother, Ida, shouting as his father's fingers dug into his shoulders. Lightning arched through Leolin's mind, followed by another scene: his father telling him a story about saving a deer from drowning as the candles in their home burned late into the night. Another flash, another memory.

His father, Samuhel, stood over Ida, every line in his face etched in anger. "He's not safe, but I'll make him safe. The

Order will save him." The words ripped from his father's mouth as another streak of light tore across Leolin's mind.

Somewhere in the distance, Shai whispered a single word and the wooden staff's thirteen spires danced before him again until Leolin's head ached with the effort of merging them into a single point.

More scattered memories: a birthing day, the town of Tarmsworth during a festival, his mother laughing at a joke they shared. Each moment grew shorter than the next until one last light—a mere flicker this time—left Leolin blinking against present day's sunlight.

Shai leaned his staff against the wall behind him. The man's tall frame folded easily into the couch in his guest quarters, though the cushions dwarfed his slightness. "Anything cohesive this time?" he asked.

"The memories are there, I can tell. I'm eight years old and could swear my father's hands are pressing against my collarbone as he's pulling me away from my mother. The moment's real enough I could smell the sweat on my father's brow, but when I reach out to grab hold of it, it's gone."

"What happens if you don't reach out?"

Leolin shook his head as he propped his feet upon the oversized footstool. "No matter what I do, there's always that light I told you about. It tears me from the scene and tosses me into another before I can even blink. Speaking of which, my head aches with the power of the sun."

The mystic passed him a small packet. "How frequently are they coming now?"

Leolin tipped the packet's crushed herbs into his glass of wine and gave it a slight stir with one finger before swallowing down the contents. The wine cut the herbs' bitterness slightly, though not enough to keep the grimace from Leolin's face. "Only when I try to remember."

The words turned the herb's bitter aftertaste into a sour

bile at the back of his throat, and Leolin poured himself another glass of wine. "I don't feel that this meditation is working, Shai. I'm no closer to understanding what happened to me and my father. If anything, the headaches prove it."

The man nodded as he stood from the couch. "What was done to your mind is not something many mystics would attempt. It's dangerous for one, not to mention being against the Thirteen. We who follow Sharmus are tasked with the healing of Boahim's people. This...this is not healing."

Shai inclined his head to Leolin as he held out his hands. "May I?"

When Leolin nodded, the mystic placed his middle fingers on each of Leolin's temples. He didn't meet Leolin's gaze, but rather stared through him as if looking at something inside of him. After a moment, his hands dropped to his sides.

"There's a reason we broke away from the Order so long ago. Though I suppose some mystics would argue it folly, we couldn't remain among those who failed to worry about the consequences of their actions. For any mystic to riffle through another's mind like this.... I'm sorry, Leolin. I've tried everything I know, and yet your mind resists."

"We have to try something. I'm losing my past with each headache. It's not just these snippets of memories that cause them but more recent times too. I...I can't think of my own mother anymore."

The mystic pursed his lips together for a moment. "I didn't want to mention it because I didn't want to give you false hope, but there may be someone who can help."

His breath caught in his chest as his heart kicked up a beat. "Who?"

"The man who did this to you."

How he found himself on his feet, he did not know until he was already pacing the small guest room's length. The real question Leolin wanted to ask was why the mystic had wasted

Leolin's time and energy on fruitless meditations when someone more powerful could have fixed him long before now. Instead, he merely asked, "You know who did this to me?"

Shai sighed. "I understand your frustration with our attempts, truly, but to send you to him is not a task taken lightly."

Leolin flinched and the mystic smiled.

"I didn't read your mind, Leolin. I would no more do that than use my skills to erase your memories. That's a skill set of one man in particular, one Mystic Doughal Nilesh of Sadai. The only mystic to have changed anyone's memories, at least that we know of. But it didn't take much of a leap for me to figure out what you were thinking." The mystic lowered himself onto the couch again, this time much slower than before. If anything, he moved like the very action aged him, and Leolin frowned. "You needn't worry about me, Leolin. Working magic is tiring work, and that's all I am, tired."

"I'm sorry."

Shai shook his head. "Whatever for?"

The heat spread across Leolin's face, and he glanced away from the man. "I confess I know nothing of the mystical arts, but I feel like I was the one doing the work today."

The man's hearty laugh caused Leolin's flush to creep down his neck. Shai was laughing at him! Closer to Ida's age than Leolin's, the man reminded him of what his father might have been like had he lived. His father definitely would have laughed at him.

"While you were doing the work of focusing your thoughts, I was using Sharmus's blessing to stitch together those memories for you to walk through. Doughal's magic is not one known to many, but if I understand it correctly, he changes the way your brain works."

Leolin frowned. "I don't follow."

"Have you ever seen a brain before?"

"I've not had that pleasure, no."

Another laugh, this one softer. "It wouldn't have to be a human brain. Even an animal brain would do."

"I've seen the brain of a deer once. My father showed it to me when he was claiming the skull from a deer he'd killed while hunting."

Shai nodded as he picked up an embroidered pillow from beside him. The pillow's blue flange was almost coil-like in shape, and the man pointed at it. "A brain is like one long rope all wound around itself in some bizarre pattern. Inside of that 'rope' are smaller ropes that connect everything together, including our memories, yes?"

"If you say so."

"Rather than using those pathways to find the memories you want, Doughal convinced your mind to avoid those memories altogether." When Leolin frowned, the man waved his hand in the air. "If you were traveling to Sadai, which direction would you travel?"

"Depends on where in Sadai, but for the most part, I'd head west."

"Exactly. Now imagine if someone convinced you that the only way to Sadai was south. What would happen?"

"I'd never reach it."

"Exactly. Doughal has convinced you that Sadai is not only south but visiting would mean sudden and painful death. Your mind is utterly convinced that if you recall the memories you seek, something horrible will happen to you. It's why those memories are in fragments and touching them leads to these horrible headaches."

Leolin took another swallow of wine as his head throbbed. Usually the herbs helped dull the pain, but this time his brain threatened to pry its way out of his skull, and he rubbed his forehead. "If this Doughal is the only one who can...convince my brain that Sadai is west again, why haven't I already seen him? You mentioned it wasn't a decision to make lightly, so I assume he is with the Order of *Amaska*?"

"He is."

"Then how did he do this to me? My mother wanted nothing to do with the Order. She would've no more taken me to the Order than returned to them herself."

"I don't know. My discipline among the mystics is focused solely on healing. We rarely work with the Order if we can help it. That would be a question for your Bredych. Perhaps he can point you in the direction of Doughal as well. Otherwise, I'm afraid there is nothing more I can do to help you."

The man handed him a second packet of herbs. "Don't take these just yet. Wait another candlemark at least, longer if you can manage it. If your head continues to ache, send word to me, and I'll see what we can do to dull it."

Before Leolin could take another sip from his wine glass, the mystic had ushered him from the guest room and closed the door. Whatever magics were involved in trying to piece together Leolin's mind, the man had appeared almost gray by the end of their conversation.

Either that, or this Doughal fellow was more dangerous than Shai had let on... Leolin put a hand above his eyes to shade them from the sunlight streaming in a nearby window. Whatever conversation needed to be had with Bredych would wait for another time. For now, Leolin had an appointment with a dark room and a bed.

257 Anurus 15th - City of Alesta

MORE OFTEN THAN NOT, Leolin could be found pacing in the royal gardens or hidden in a dark room with no windows. The headaches' frequency had increased while Margaret was at the Pass, and since her return, Leolin spent more days than not struggling to be present. Worried about him, Margaret searched most of the castle before finding him in a storage closet, a bit of silk cloth thrown over his head to block out any candlelight that seeped in from underneath the door.

When she woke him, he shielded his eyes until she set the candle on a shelf behind him so the flame was not directly in sight.

"How did you find me?" Leolin asked.

"By searching room by room for the past two candle-marks, but if I'm honest, I'm glad for it. Your headaches are growing worse." She sat at the cot's edge and dust tickled her nose. "How can you stand it in here with all this dust?"

He sneezed, then winced. "Some days I can't."

"What does Shai say about your head?"

Leolin closed his eyes for a moment before answering. "There's nothing more he can do. The damage done by magic has convinced my brain that Sadai is south."

"I don't understand. What does Sadai have to do with it?"

"Everything apparently."

When Margaret frowned, a small laugh escaped Leolin, and she said, "I missed the sound of your laugh."

"It's difficult to laugh when most of your memories cause you physical pain. Even walking around the castle is a visual reminder of the cost of this *magic*." He said the word as if it were a bitter poison on his tongue. "If the Thirteen hadn't used their magic to kill Adelei, where would we be? Would my mind be this damaged? Would you be so ready to fight gods?"

His voice rose as he spoke, and Margaret reached out to place a hand on his shoulder. "Leolin, we can't change what has happened, only what path we take moving forward. I can't undo what has been done to your mind, but if there is something I can do to help you now, name it. I will do whatever I can for you."

The corners of his mouth turned up as he glanced at her. "Whatever you can, eh?"

Her cheeks grew warm at his meaning, and she leaned forward to kiss him. The moment her lips brushed across his, fire roared across her skin. One month had been one month too long since Leolin had held her, and her lips pressed harder into his.

With all the pain in his head, she thought he might break away from her, but he smiled against her lips and drew her into his arms.

"I missed you," he mumbled against her lips as he pulled her close. "I never properly welcomed you home, did I?"

"What about your head?"

Leolin kissed her again, his tongue dancing with hers. A sneeze ripped through him and he almost slammed his forehead into hers.

"Maybe this is not the place—"

He silenced her with another kiss. "It's dark and secluded. Sounds perfect to me. No one would think to look for their queen here."

When he pulled her down to the cot, her skin tingled in anticipation. Her heart sped up as his hands untied the laces of her shirt. In that moment, her only thought was that the walls could fall down around them as long as they were together. The warmth of his fingertips reminded her that they were alive, and she pushed aside all worries of war and gods as he welcomed her home.

257 Anurus 25th — Drehsma, Capital City of Shad

"Do you trust her?"

King Havin Bajit pursed his lips together and shook his head at Rajami's question. Head of the *Tribor*, the man was critical to Havin's plans, particularly those of this morning. "Trust is not a word I'd use to describe my thoughts regarding Queen Margaret, but we all agreed that the Boahim Senate poses a threat that can't be ignored."

Rajami leaned closer to Havin. "But to go against the Thirteen? What you ask is madness, Your Majesty."

Five men gathered with them in a room that could be described only as an afterthought of a closet. Much like the room in Alesta, this one held more dust than Havin thought possible, which was not surprising considering how few times the king had used it. What good was there in calling upon what he perceived to be a useless group? Especially when he had the *Tribor* at his beck and call.

The *Tribor* remained silent, though their curiosity about the orb obvious in the way they stared at it. When one man reached out with a finger to prod it, Havin swatted his hand away. "You don't want to do that."

"What is it?"

"Magic like nothing you've ever seen," said Havin. He glanced at Rajami, who kept his distance from the orb. "The Boahim Senate is a threat to every kingdom and every people. While I do not care if they destroy all of Alexander, our allies would mind it greatly if I did nothing while the Senate marches across all borders with their magic."

"Were they responsible for the ground quakes?" asked one of the men, and Havin nodded.

"So we're here to do what, exactly?" asked Rajami.

A grin spread across Havin's face. "To do what the *Tribor* do best...kill. These orbs exist in every kingdom, known only to those of royal blood and the Holy Few." At the mention of the holy order, the *Tribor* spat on the floor, and Havin made a mental note to have a servant scrub the stone when the day was done. "Queen Margaret threatened Senator Whitlen—"

"You mean Itovah," said Rajami.

"Yes, Itovah. She attempted to step through the orb to reach Queen Margaret. Apparently, the Senators or the Thirteen can use these to travel long distances in a heartbeat as well as listen and spy on people."

At this, the five *Tribor* stepped back until their backsides pressed against the room's stone walls. Unlike the others, Rajami leaned closer. "You say they can walk through this thing? They can use it to travel in a moment?"

Havin pushed the man away. "Unless they come through, stay in the shadows. They can see us even now."

"I would assume so being gods and all." Rajami grinned as he poked the orb, though it remained silent. "Could be a useful weapon."

The damned fool had always been drawn to anything that he believed would give him power, especially if it involved magic. Havin glared at the man until he returned to the shadows.

"Once the orb is awake, we'll see which senator answers. Perhaps our Senator Raj but perhaps not. Either way, I will do my best to encourage the senator to pay us a visit. Once he begins to step through the orb and his head is on this side of it, we need to break the orb by whatever means necessary. Stab it, hit it—whatever it takes."

"Why break the orb? Powerful device like this could be useful. Can't we just stab the man?"

Rajami shook his head at his man's question. "It's the only way to make sure he dies. Despite what ya learned, the senators are the Thirteen." He leaned closer to Havin and whispered, "Are the orbs really necessary to kill a god?"

"Yes."

"Shame. Damn shame."

It had been a risk telling someone as greedy as Rajami the truth, but Havin needed at least one fighter beside him in the room. Just in case.

"If these senators are the Thirteen..."

Havin sighed. "There's no *if* about it. They are the Thirteen."

In the shadows, it was impossible to see Rajami frown, though Havin could all but hear it in the man's sigh. "So when you say that queen killed Itovah, you mean it truthfully."

"Yes."

Several men muttered, and Havin stepped closer to them with the candlelight. "I understand you have sworn an oath to Itovah, but the goddess is dead. Your oath has as much meaning as mouse droppings."

They trusted his words as much as they trusted anything, which was to say not at all, but it would have to do. King Havin returned to the orb and whispered, "*Ta'asor Ley.*"

At first, nothing happened. The orb remained dark. Havin opened his mouth to repeat the words when his candlelight flickered, and the dust coating the orb swirled through the air as the orb pulsed once, then a second time before a face appeared.

The *Tribor* gasped as they withdrew their swords. Despite his warning about what to expect, he could hear the *Tribor* whispering as they took in the deep green cloak the man wore about his shoulders. Senator Raj, or Sharmus, stood before them, his frame slightly warped by the orb.

Standing beside Havin, Rajami bowed. Havin couldn't help the trembling that ran the length of his body. Unsure of how to proceed, he dipped his knees briefly.

"King Bajit, what may the Boahim Senate do for you?" said Sharmus.

He swallowed hard as he raised his gaze toward the god. Despite Queen Margaret's assurances that the gods could be killed, something about Sharmus's green eyes promised it would not be as easy as promised, and Havin's mouth dried around the words he'd planned to say.

"I assume you called on me for a reason."

"My apologies, this room is rather dusty, and my throat is dry. I called because I'm concerned about the *Tribor*'s reaction to the agreement signed at the Meridi Pass. They clamor outside my castle as they feel they were promised a battle with the Alexandrians." Once he began, the lies fell easily from his tongue. "I feel I need your assistance to rid myself of these vermin."

Behind him, someone hissed. Whoever had dared make a sound would lose his head once he finished this coup, and Havin forced his shoulders to relax.

Sharmus's brows furrowed as he leaned closer to the orb on his end, but he didn't lean through the glass or pass through it as Queen Margaret had described. "If my information is correct, and I am sure that it is, the *Tribor* have been your pets for the entirety of your reign. I would think it rather simple to send them away."

"I will admit to having had dealings with them, as my father did before me, but once the war with Alexander ceased, a united Boahim has no need for those who would break it apart again. I...I need your help, Sharmus."

He hadn't intended to name the god, but something about the orb required the truth and in that moment, everybody in the room stilled. Even the air froze in place as something cold swept over them. Havin tried to inhale and found his lungs as still as the rest of him, and his eyes widened as a woman older than the oldest tree in Shad peered at him over Sharmus's shoulder. Swords clattered around him as the *Tribor* scrambled to leave the room.

"He-l-p," Havin whispered, though the word came out a choked stutter.

Sharmus spun around and pushed the old woman aside. A gust of wind rushed into the room, and Havin gasped in the sudden air. His limbs hung weakly at his side, though he could move them again.

"King Bajit, I came to the Pass to warn you. I encouraged you to band together as only united do you have any chance of defending yourself against the dangers to come. Calling me in an attempt to kill me, your one ally amongst the Thirteen, was not the brightest of decisions—"

Someone shouted in the background, and Sharmus ducked as lightning erupted across the room he stood in. A deep rumble was the only warning Havin had before the ground trembled beneath his own feet.

"He's coming," Havin whispered as he withdrew his dagger. How had the god known the truth about why Havin had called him?

More shouts erupted from the senate rooms, and Rajami stood shoulder to shoulder with Havin, his grin too wide for his face. "I'm gonna kill me a god."

There was no time to chastise the man as the ground gave a hefty buck, and a crack split the tile floor beneath them.

"...damn fools..." A few words made it through the orb, though Sharmus remained hidden from view. "...dead?"

At this word, sweat broke out across Havin's brow. Had the plan worked? Had someone else managed to kill one of the Thirteen through the orbs? A woman with wild hair that stood on end as if she had been struck by the earlier lightning pressed her face against the orb. Her eyes flashed as blood flushed her face. "Are you the one who deemed us unnecessary? Was it you who planned to hurry the prophecy?"

She screamed at Havin, who grabbed hold of the orb as the ground gave another shake.

"You're too close!" yelled Sharmus.

Havin stumbled backward into Rajami, whose short

sword almost impaled him. He widened his stance to gain better balance against the ground's quaking. As the woman pushed herself through the orb, he managed to bring his dagger up.

It was not like Margaret had described. Whichever goddess this was, her entire torso leaned through as she grabbed for Havin. Her hands blocked his dagger, now bloody from the defensive cuts on her hands. While her focus was on Havin, Rajami slammed his sword's hilt against the glass orb, shattering it in one blow.

The ground continued to sway for a moment longer, and Havin fell to his knees. Someone stepped forward and when he glanced up, the woman's upper-half lay on the ground before him, her eyes blinking slowly as life fled from her.

Several heartbeats thumped in his chest as she stared at him before her eyes lost focus, leaving only a corpse beside him. Her body shriveled and aged until it became dust, and he released the breath he'd been holding.

"Did I do it? Did I kill a god?" asked Rajami.

Several of the *Tribor* who'd fled the room had pushed their way back inside. They glanced between the body, Rajami, and their king in confusion. With the orb shattered, the results of their experiment would have to wait until messenger birds could be sent to Alesta, but for now, the Thirteen were two fewer in number.

Havin's bruised knees ached as he stood, though he kept the pain from his face. He clapped a hand on Rajami's shoulders. "If I recall correctly, that was Echana, Goddess of Chaos who just disintegrated before us. You have indeed killed one of the Thirteen. I'll not forget this," Havin said as he toed the orb's glass with his booted feet. Such a waste.

"Wait for me in my study," Havin said to Rajami. He waited until the *Tribor* were gone to ring for a servant. If the servant was surprised to see a hidden room connected to the storage room, she kept the thoughts to herself as she gave a brief bow.

"Clean this up."

The servant nodded and reached out to grab a piece.

Havin grabbed hold of the woman's hand. "The glass is sharp. Take care in handling it."

"Toss it, Your Majesty?"

He almost nodded when he noticed the way the candlelight glinted off the glass. Almost as if it were alive, the glass shimmered, and Havin shook his head. "Pick up every piece, including those still attached to the pillar. Place them all together in a box or basket, something lined to keep the glass from falling out, and have it left in my chambers."

If the glass could be saved, it would be. Perhaps the orb could be reassembled.... As Rajami had said, it seemed such a waste to destroy so much potential. He left the woman to her duty as he set off for the messenger birds.

This was a message he would send himself.

7

aiting for messages from the Little Dozen Kingdoms' monarchy was a test in patience that drove Margaret to pacing. When she tired of pacing, she stretched tense muscles before she resumed wearing a hole in the rug covering the stone floor of her sitting room. Not that it was a particularly large rug, nor a large room for that matter, but with the table pushed against the fireplace, it gave her enough room to fret.

Rather than join her in impatience, Bredych sat in one of the room's few chairs, a book open in his lap. He rarely turned the pages, and if Margaret had to guess, she thought him as worried as she was. Leolin waited in the messenger tower, where he probably wore a path in the stone with his own restlessness. Her orders had been for him to wait for all eleven messages to arrive before joining them, and as time dragged past, she gnawed at the side of her cheek.

"What could be taking the messages so long to arrive? We're well past the agreed upon time to…"

"Kill the Thirteen?" asked Bredych.

Margaret closed her eyes for a moment. "We knew the risks of such a coup, but they left us no other choice. Do you think the Thirteen would…of course they would. They snapped their fingers and murdered innocent people at the Meridi Pass. Oh gods."

The room spun, and she reached out a hand to grab the table's edge, digging her fingernails into the wood. "This was a mistake," she whispered.

Bredych set his book aside before he rose and crossed the room. When he reached her, he laid a hand upon her shoulder. "For as long as words have had meaning, the Thirteen have guided us towards a future of their making. After the Fall, they deemed it necessary to take a more active role in our world through the Senate's creation. Their intentions may have been good in the beginning, but power can be a dangerous weapon. The more they used it, the more they needed it. The gods we worshiped changed. *We* changed."

She shrugged off his hand. "I do not need a history lesson."

"And I'm not giving one. The Thirteen no longer serve us. They are neither needed nor wanted. For them to make quick decisions about the people of Boahim without a care for how the world has changed is irresponsible. Their actions since the death of your sister have been abhorrent—"

"Since they murdered her, you mean."

"Yes. By the Thirteen laws that they created for us, they should be punished. What you and the other rulers are choosing is survival. No one would fault you for that."

"Fault?" she asked, and a laugh escaped her. "I encouraged these rulers to kill, Bredych. I made murderers of them."

"You told them the truth. The decision of what to do about it came from all of you, correct?"

"Yes, but—"

Bredych shook his head. "You gave them the tools necessary to keep their kingdoms and people safe. Many would consider that a heroic feat."

Nothing felt heroic about encouraging the death of others, even if they were gods, but Margaret kept the thought to herself as she resumed pacing. Bredych returned to his chair, though he left the book set aside as he stared at the door.

"Margaret, do you think these monarchs have hands clean from bloodshed? I guarantee you that they don't."

"Neither do I. I'm no better than Adelei in that regard."

"Your sister served Justice."

Margaret ground her teeth. "What does that mean when the gods themselves are corrupt fools who would kill us all? Justice? There's no such thing."

Whatever Bredych might have said was lost when a guardsman knocked on the door. He opened it to allow Leolin entrance, and Margaret slid into a nearby chair, her limbs trembling. Mistake or not, the success or failure of their plans would be revealed momentarily.

A stack of parchment lay in Leolin's hands, though she thought it would be thicker, and her heart tried to erupt from her chest. He set the stack neatly on the table before he claimed a third chair, one facing the door. Like Bredych, Leolin stared at it as if he expected the Thirteen to break into the room at any moment.

"Did you read any of them?" she asked.

Leolin shook his head. "I glanced at them long enough to confirm we'd received all the messages."

The stack of parchment lay beside Margaret, though she hesitated to pick them up for a few minutes. Her fingers trembled as she opened the first message, from Marco in Halelind, her neighbor to the East. "'It worked. Atlina is dead,'" she read, and her stomach churned. The Goddess of the Sea was not a deity Margaret felt any affinity towards but her death weighed on her nonetheless.

While Bredych nodded, Leolin let out a whoop. "One down."

Margaret set the message aside to move on to the next. "Adir reports his orb was 'dead' and responded not at all."

"That's odd," said Bredych as he frowned. "I've watched him use the orb on two separate occasions."

"Do you believe him to be lying?" she asked.

"Unlikely. Maybe the Thirteen caught on to the plan and rendered the orbs useless."

"I sincerely hope not." Two more messages, these from Naribor and Monpoli. "Ermen and Damiano's senators broke the orbs upon contact. Damn."

Leolin winced at the swear, though he tried to hide it behind a faked yawn, and Margaret resisted the urge to repeat the word. The message from Delia in Ethenium was lengthier, though it puzzled Margaret.

"'Broke orb. Nothing happened. Scared myself silly. You owe me a bottle of wine.' During the meeting at the Pass, Delia spoke very little, though she struck me as a stern woman. I have a difficult time picturing her frightened of anything."

Bredych laughed. "The woman's a sycophant and a drunk. She probably knocked a wine bottle into the orb on accident."

"Did she activate the orb before breaking it?" asked Leolin.

Margaret turned the parchment over but nothing else was written. "It doesn't say. I truly hope so." The next three king-doms all reported their orbs unresponsive. When she opened the next to last message, the one from Shad, her throat dried. "Havin reports Sharmus threatened him before Echana tried to force her way through the orb. They destroyed it and beheaded her, but he reports a struggle occurred between the Thirteen."

"So it's possible others have died," said Leolin, who glanced at Bredych before his gaze returned to the door.

"I suppose, though I wish I knew for certain. The last message is from Merriwynne. King Lizana's orb went dark a few heartbeats after he activated it. We will assume his senator is alive."

"So two."

Margaret glanced at Leolin. "Yes. At least two more gods are dead. Eight remain living." She held up her hand as she counted. "Cerci, Agaia, Anur, Farimun, Adlain, Sharmus... Delorcini, and Luthia."

Leolin's hand rested on the hilt of his sword. Beside him, Bredych's fingers twitched at his side. She set the stack of messages on the table, and then retrieved a small basket from a shelf on the wall. There was little need to contact those rulers whose attempts failed, at least not yet, so she scribbled a few brief words to Havin and Marco before sealing both messages.

She strode towards the door and when both men rose, she gestured for them to sit. Only a moment passed between her ringing the bell and a servant's appearance. Margaret passed the messages through the gap in the doorway. "Take these to the messenger tower and have them sent with all haste."

When the door closed, Leolin asked, "You would trust a servant to deliver those messages to the tower?"

"I asked for more details about what was seen in the background, though I took care to be vague in my phrasing. Without knowledge of what we planned, someone reading my messages would have little understanding of what matters I referred to. Besides, I need you both here."

Margaret turned her chair to better face both men and sank into it, grateful not to be standing on trembling legs. "We knew there was the possibility that this plan wouldn't rid us of the remaining Thirteen. Two additional dead gods is better than none, though I wish more had succumbed to the orbs."

"I think the problem lay in the execution," said Leolin.

"How so?"

"That many rulers calling for aid at the same time? Once one of them died, it didn't take much thought to understand the trap. If you'd used the orbs at different times, staggered across days, perhaps the plan would've gone differently."

Bredych shook his head. "It's likely they would have caught on sooner. If one of them dies, they are all on guard."

"Agreed. This way, we carried the element of surprise with us," said Margaret as she rubbed her fingers together. "This was the best plan possible for the information at our disposal. Before today, I was the only one who had managed to murder a god."

When her hands continued trembling, Bredych poured a glass of wine and passed it to her. "Drink."

She swallowed it quickly before setting the glass on the table beside her. Her stomach lurched in response, and she stumbled from the sitting room and into her private chambers. Leolin called after her, his voice warped by the sounds of her retching as she emptied her stomach into a chamber pot.

When his hand touched her nape, she flinched, one hand landing on a dagger's hilt before relaxing once he spoke.

"Should I call for Roland?" asked Leolin as he rubbed her back.

"No. He has more pressing patients to attend to."

"He's your physician first, Maggie. Everyone else can wait."

"But they can't. Who am I to be more important than anyone else, especially those with critical wounds?"

"You're their queen."

Margaret rocked back to sit on the stone floor, the cold seeping through her skirts. At that moment, she did not want to be their queen. Let someone else take the heavy mantle for a time. She resisted the urge to lay down and press her cheek against the cool floor, instead pressing her palms against it. "Do you ever feel as if you are trapped beneath the surface of a lake, staring up at the rest of the world above ground? That you struggle for each breath while everyone else makes it look effortless?"

"I'm not sure I understand."

"I *did* this, Leolin. Me. I asked these rulers to partake in a scheme that was not only dangerous but potentially foolish. What guarantee did we have that this would work? None." Her stomach roiled in response to her emotions, and she closed her eyes for a moment. "Who do I think I am to ask them to risk themselves and their people like this? Eight remain. Eight gods. The plan failed. The Thirteen won't give us another chance and now... Leolin, how can I keep my people safe?"

He claimed her hands in his and helped her stand. "You fought your way through your own city, twice, spent five days on horseback and another seventeen days camped on a battle-field of corpses where as I hear your guardsmen tell it, you hauled the dead's remains into funeral pyres. You presented your rationale to eleven strangers, any of which could have killed you before you could blink, only to ride home and fight your way into the castle. Maggie, you're exhausted."

She allowed him to lead her to her bed, where he helped her undress down to her underclothes before tucking her in like a child.

"Honestly, I don't know how you're standing. What you need is a good night's sleep and proper rest. Then you can debate the wisdom of your plans and how best to keep your people safe."

He drew her window curtains before retreating, though the light penetrated the lightweight material. Outside, her people worked to rebuild while she curled up in her room, safe. What right did she have to rest when most of them had no means to join her?

So many homes destroyed and lives lost.

If it wasn't war with the Shadians, it was the earthquakes that ripped the land in two.

Margaret bolted upright, and her stomach protested. Every time the Thirteen used magic, the ground shook. Was it the use of magic or the strength of it that heaved the ground? Thoughts chased themselves in her mind as she wrapped a robe around her shoulders and tied it at the waist. When she opened the door to her sitting room, Bredych and Leolin were still there, the latter with his mouth open.

Leolin swallowed back whatever words he wished to say as he glanced at her. "Maggie, you need rest—"

"What if magic is why the Thirteen are dying?"

Bredych tilted his head in thought. "Magic has been since the beginning. It's neither life nor death as we understand it, but power. Energy."

Rather than explain, she picked up the small bell and gave it a ring. When the servant entered, Margaret said, "Have the Mystic Shai brought here at once."

"Maggie, surely this can wait. You're near gray with exhaustion. When's the last time you had a restful sleep?" asked Leolin.

"Time is against us, Leolin. I will sleep this evening."

He rubbed his temples with his fingers but remained silent as they awaited the mystic's arrival. Margaret poured herself a glass of water, ignoring the concern on Leolin's face as he watched. Out of the corner of her eye, she glanced at Bredych to find a similar expression on his face.

The silence stretched into minutes as Margaret waited. Another sip of water, and the servant returned to announce their visitor. For all that his years counted in their fifties, he moved through the room with a smoothness that spoke of well-conditioned muscles. He bowed to her, then lowered himself cross-legged to the floor. "What knowledge may I offer you, Your Majesty?" he said.

"Mystics have continued to use magic since Boahim was split asunder, despite it being forbidden by the Thirteen, correct?" She paused only long enough for him to briefly nod. "What do you know of magic's source?"

His gray eyebrows shot up as he shrugged. "It's always been assumed that magic comes from the source of all things, the Thirteen."

Margaret frowned. "Yes, but does magic have a limit? Can the world run out of magic? Or can a person? How does it work?"

It was the mystic's turn to frown. "Some magic is driven by intent. If one wants something, they will it into being. Other magics are more ritualistic in nature, using herbs and spoken words. I don't think any one person truly understands magic in a definitive way. If I were to try and will myself into a frog, I'm fairly certain I wouldn't succeed. Is that because there is a limit to magic's source or how much magic I can control? I don't know. I'm not sure anyone does."

"So how do you know if your magic will work?" she asked.

"The simple answer? I don't. Not until I try. I believe that the Thirteen will bless me with the power if it's their will."

Bredych shook his head. "I've seen mystics try and do things they shouldn't and almost die in the trying. The world is made of order and so must magic be."

Shai chuckled. "I'm sure you're right, but as I said, I have no way to define that which has no definition. We might believe it to be structured because all things must, but I can't tell you what that structure looks like."

"So magic is a matter of will, blessed by the Thirteen."

"As all things are."

Margaret pursed her lips. "I have information that might change the way you view magic." Both Leolin and Bredych opened their mouths in protest, but she ignored them. Shai remained silent as she recounted what had once been only theories about the Boahim Senate. Halfway through the telling, his eyes unfocused only to dart about the room.

"I would assume they can see and hear all, being gods, but so far, they have done little with whatever knowledge they have gleaned," she said as she passed him an empty glass and the pitcher of wine.

He continued to look about as she recounted their discovered information, ending with the meeting at the Pass and the death of two more gods. Margaret retrieved the evidence she had taken with her to the Meridi Pass and passed it to him. "Any proof you need of this, you will find here. Some of these documents are very old so take care in handling them."

Shai spread the documents across the table, reading first one and then another. By the time he'd finished, the pitcher of wine was half-empty. When he found the words to speak, he asked, "How is it possible that the Thirteen can die? They're gods. Immortal beings."

"And yet I killed one."

"Your evidence is clear. I see no reason to doubt that the Boahim Senate is in fact the Thirteen, but—"

"That's why I brought you here," said Margaret as she held up her hand. "I know you have many questions but they will have to wait. When Senator Whitlen used magic to pass through the orb and come to Alesta, she did so with ease. She stepped between the Senate Isle and this castle like one puts on a pair of shoes. Her attempts to control Gamun and whoever stood with him, weakened her. I could see it in the lines across her face. Each time they have used magic, the magic's been more powerful than anything I have ever believed possible.

"Two senators appeared at the Meridi Pass without the

orbs to support them. The carnage they left..." Her skin chilled, leaving a blotchy red and pale pattern behind. "I spent seventeen days burning the dead, or what remained of them. The Thirteen accomplished this feat within a heartbeat. If magic is will, they willed the death of hundreds."

"As brutal as that is, I would expect nothing less from a god," said Shai.

Margaret took a sip of water. "Agreed, but when they released their magic, the ground shook and it was not intentional."

"How do you know?"

"I was speaking to Senator Whitlen, or Itovah, when the ground first quaked. When the Meridi Pass was set aflame. The shock on her face couldn't be faked. Pieces of the Senate Hall fell. One almost hit her in the head. Is it possible that in using magics of such power, they damaged the very land itself?"

Bredych sucked in air between his teeth. "You think in damaging the land, they damaged themselves?"

Margaret nodded. "If the Thirteen are the creators of everything, including magic, maybe forbidding its use so many years ago limited its existence or made it less powerful. Or maybe there has always been a limit and when they tried to do more than they ought, it drained both the land and them. Maybe that weakened them enough to become mortal again."

The mystic poured himself another glass of wine, his cheeks flushed. He drank it without much thought to what it was, and when he set about pouring another glass, Leolin slid the pitcher across the table and out of reach.

"Honestly, Your Majesty, y-you seem to be more informative—informed on these matters than someone like me. I'm not sure what I can contribute to the discussion," said Shai, and he pressed two fingers to his forehead as his gaze wandered the room.

"I need to know if this is plausible. Your people are the only ones I know still using magic, other than the Holy Few."

The mystic's foot jiggled as he rolled his fingers against his palms. "A candlemark ago, if you'd told me the Boahim Senate were the Thirteen, I would've c-called you a liar. What I think I know and what I actually know are too far apart for me to think straight, let alone answer a question like that. I—" He gave one last glance about the room before he rose to his feet with a wobble. "By your leave?"

She nodded, a frown on her lips as she watched him depart.

"Well, that was useless," said Leolin.

"Not exactly. I'd always had the impression there were laws and rules to magic. Learning that there aren't might give us an advantage," said Bredych.

Margaret tilted her head. "How so?"

"If all that limits magic is willpower, then perhaps we have more power at our disposal than we originally thought."

Leolin asked, "What's to keep us from just wishing the gods dead?"

"Indeed. I doubt it's that simple but the point is that we've possibly learned two things today: one, the more magic they use, the weaker they grow, and two, we have magic users ourselves who stand every chance of successfully combatting their magic. We have only to try."

"You mean we might actually have a chance," said Leolin.

"Exactly."

Margaret stared at her fingers, which she clasped in her lap. Weaker gods would be easier to kill but they were still gods. "If their use of magic ripped the ground apart, what will our use of magic do?"

No one answered.

No one needed to.

8

Despite needing the rest, Margaret slipped in and out of a light sleep until the predawn hours, when she gave up all pretense. Careful not to wake Leolin, she crawled out of bed and tossed a robe about her shoulders before quietly entering her private study. It was odd thinking of it as hers when every piece of furniture still bore the wear and tear of her father's use. Moonlight streamed in from the room's lone window, and she used it to see by as she used a fire striker and flint to light the room's lone candle.

She doubted any of the books in her study discussed magic, but the conversation the day before left her mind whirling. If the very use of magic was weakening the gods, why wasn't it also weakening the mystics and healers who used it? Or the Holy Few? Was it the magic's strength that resulted in the loss of the gods' immortality? Margaret held the candle closer to the bookcase as she skimmed their titles.

Maybe the Thirteen asked for too much, but how did a god ask for more than what was allowed? That implied there was someone else to ask. Several histories on Alexander, followed by the Poncett royal family were crammed on several shelves, along with a treatise on government, but nothing stood out as overly helpful.

Rather than put out the candle, Margaret carried it with her as she left the study. She could pull tomes from the castle's library or her private library, but she did not recall seeing any books on magic itself or the Thirteen when she had sought answers about the Boahim Senate. Between her childhood studies and the search for answers prior, she could list the title of almost every book in the castle.

Which left outside sources.

Margaret set down the candle long enough to tie a cloak about her, slide her feet into her slippers, and grab a bundle of papers before setting out for the small building that housed the Holy Few. Several guardsman followed in her wake, and she ignored them, much like she ignored her stomach's complaints about the early hour. The way the moonlight struck the words engraved on the simple wood door made them sparkle, an oddity considering the words were from Itovah. Nothing about her had been beautiful, and Margaret suppressed a grin at the knowledge the god had died by her hand.

When she raised her hand to knock, the door opened. It was not an acolyte who answered, but Her Holiness. The woman wore her usual crimson robe and her cheeks were flushed. "How can we help Your Majesty so early in the morning?"

"I have questions that I believe only you can answer."

The woman ushered Margaret inside where dozens of candles burned, lighting the room like fire. The cots lay empty as the followers of the Holy Few crowded on benches around the room's few tables as they dipped quills into inkwells. Whatever they wrote was important enough that they all but ignored Margaret's entrance as they continued their work. Her Holiness gestured for Margaret to follow her towards a corner where a desk stood covered in several open books. The woman claimed a hard, wooden stool behind the desk, leaving Margaret to claim the one on the opposing side.

If the hour weren't so early, she would have bristled at the informality of it all, but when she had set out for the small building, she had expected to be turned away. Only Her Holiness could refuse an order from a queen, at least with the Boahim Senate in place.

Where did it leave the Holy Few if they succeeded in their plans to destroy the Thirteen? When Margaret glanced up from her hands, she found Her Holiness watching her with absolute calm.

"How are you that patient?" Margaret asked, and the corners of the woman's lips turned up in response.

"Life is waiting, especially if one is a member of the Holy Few. I find that others are more willing to speak if I provide silence for them to fill."

The desk was narrow in depth, placing Margaret an arm's length from Her Holiness, a fact that gave her pause as she recalled the woman's use of magic. Her brows furrowed at the word.

"Something is troubling you enough to come to me this early. Would Your Majesty care for some hot tea while we talk?"

She pitched her voice higher, keeping it light to disguise the mistrust in her belly. "No, thank you. I appreciate the offer, but I hope to return to the castle soon. I came to ask you about magic."

At this, Her Holiness frowned. Like before, the woman waited for Margaret to fill in the silence.

"From my understanding, the Holy Few use magic, much

like healers and mystics as well as others across the Little Dozen Kingdoms—"

"The Holy Few are nothing like mystics, heathens that they are. We use only what powers are given to us by the Thirteen."

Margaret opened her mouth, then thought better of it and closed it.

"If you wish to use magic to solve your troubles, I'm afraid we cannot help you." Her Holiness stood and when Margaret remained seated, she stared at the queen with such intensity that Margaret's skin crawled.

"Do you know who the Thirteen are?" asked Margaret.

"Of course. They are the gods."

The bound parchment lay heavy in Margaret's robes. It was a risk to share the information but without it, The Holy Few would remain as secretive as always. Margaret withdrew the papers and untied them. "These documents have been amassed by myself and others since my late father's passing, documents showing that those we know as the Boahim Senate are the Thirteen."

She passed the parchments to Her Holiness and waited as the woman flipped through them.

"These are your handwritten notes?"

Margaret nodded. "I have the books referenced in them in the castle library or my own private library, should you wish to read them, but the information within my notes was detailed enough that every ruler of the Little Dozen Kingdoms agreed with my conclusions." She decided not to mention Sharmus's visit at the Pass as it was likely the woman would not believe her. "This is why we all agreed to a pact and why the Shadian army no longer attacks."

Her Holiness held a candle closer to the pages as she read and when she reached the end, she held the parchment's corner into the flames. The parchment caught quickly, but the woman held them in her hands until the flames reached her palm. While her skin pinkened, the fire no more marred her flesh than it would the sun.

Margaret gasped. "And the Thirteen deemed it necessary to use magic just now?"

When the pages were nothing more than charred ash, Her Holiness dusted off her hands. "This is not the first time someone has thought to share this information with the world, which is why the Holy Few keep control of certain books, a few of which I believe your father had taken from this very room. I expect those volumes returned to us, Your Majesty."

"You knew?"

"Knew what, Your Majesty?"

Margaret glanced down at what remained of her notes. "You knew that the Thirteen walked among us? That they served as the Boahim Senate?"

Her Holiness allowed a small laugh to escape her. "I wouldn't be much of a believer if I didn't believe the gods were among us, Your Majesty. Of course I believe it. They are here in this very room with us, listening to us as we speak, and guiding us along the paths we are meant to trod. I'm sure that they guide our senators as well in the same way they guide you now, but I must caution you against sharing this information with others. While you may have the discernment to fully comprehend how your words will impact others, most people do not."

"You do not rule over me, Your Holiness. I will share this information as I see fit, with or without your permission."

"Surely you see the folly in such actions. The panic that would rip through the Little Dozen Kingdoms if they thought the gods were truly among us."

Margaret frowned. "I thought we were supposed to believe them among us. Is that not the point of the Holy Few?

To spread word of the Thirteen and teach us how to live by the Thirteen laws?"

Again the woman laughed, a rich sound that caused her eyes to dance. "It is, but it is only one of our many purposes. Most people in Alexander, let alone the Little Dozen have no patience for gods. They seek them out only when their crops do not come to yield or their child has taken ill. Through us they learn to be good citizens, but few *truly* believe. Times were different in your ancestors' time, even in your great-great-grandsire's time, but as seasons pass, fewer give thought to the Thirteen."

Her Holiness made a sweeping motion with her arm as she stared out across the room. "Times were, this building would be one of many in Alesta to house those pursuing a closer relationship with the Thirteen. Now, we're fortunate if one or two acolytes dedicate themselves in any given year."

"Maybe that's why the Thirteen are mortal. I thought it was the use of magic draining them of their livelihood, but maybe it's belief, or the lack of it. How can the Thirteen live and breathe if they are but an afterthought in our world?"

Fire danced in the woman's eyes as she stared at Margaret. "The Thirteen are immortal. They are the creators and destroyers, the very breath that we take, and the—"

"The Thirteen are not *guiding* the senators. They *are* the senators, and they are mortal. Whether you believe it or not, matters little. We won't acquiesce to bullies who would ask us to follow their laws while they commit those very sins against us."

Whatever sparked the indignation in Her Holiness fizzled as the blood drained from her face. She reached out and grabbed Margaret by the wrist. "What have you done? Explain what you mean."

Margaret tried to wrest her arm free, but the woman tightened her grip. "Unhand me," Margaret shouted, and several acolytes glanced up from their research. When none came to her aid, Margaret's stomach dropped. "Release me at once!"

Her Holiness pressed her other hand against Margaret's forehead and the sensation of ants dancing across her skin returned as it had done before. Rather than a room full of people sitting at desks, the past year's incidents flowed through Margaret's mind as if she were experiencing them again, only faster. Her father's death, working with Bredych and Leolin to find out the truth, Itovah's death, the meeting at Meridi Pass, the appearance of Sharmus... If there was anything she had intended to keep from Her Holiness, it fluttered into her foremost thoughts. Even her concerns about her relationship with Leolin passed on to Her Holiness.

The last information gave Margaret the strength to wrench herself free of the woman's grasp. She staggered back, bumping into an empty stool. "That's twice now you have used magic to steal information from me without my permission. Holy Few or not, that does not give you the right to rifle through my mind. Who are you to assault the crown so?"

Rather than answer, Her Holiness fell back, missing her stool completely and landing on the ground with a thump. Her hands shook as she reached out toward Margaret. "Y-You killed Itovah?"

Margaret nodded. "It was not done on purpose."

"Yes, but the others were. You hatched a plan to destroy them all. Do you know what remains without the Thirteen? Evil. Evil is the gods' absence."

"The Thirteen have outlived their usefulness. They signed their deaths in blood the moment they killed my sister."

Her Holiness remained seated on the floor, her body trembling. At first, Margaret thought it fear, but the spark returned to the woman's almost clear eyes. An acolyte rushed to her side and helped Her Holiness stand. She rubbed one hip as she glared at Margaret. "I misspoke. Evil is already here."

"You would call me evil? A queen who has done every-thing that has been asked of me, even when it cost me everyone I love? Evil is watching people suffer and doing nothing about it."

"I appreciate the information you've given me, Your Majesty. I would appreciate it more if you were to leave. Now. The Holy Few is not yours to command, nor will we be party to the destruction of this world. Rest assured the Senate will know of your plans."

"If they are the gods you believe them to be, they already know." Margaret swept the ashes off the desk with one hand. "Those notes were not my originals. Burning them served no purpose, rest assured. Because my great-grandsire gave your order the land beneath this building, I'll allow your acolytes to remain, but it is you who will leave, Your Holiness. This is still my city and my kingdom, and I won't allow those who would take others by force to seek refuge here. Return to your Holy Order or do not, but you will leave Alesta by daybreak."

It was a risk to turn her back on the woman, but Margaret did so, trusting that whatever faith the woman held would prevent her from attacking Margaret outright. As she strode through the room, the trainees found reasons to bury their noses deep in their notes. The entire walk to the door, Margaret waited for a knife in the back or the feeling of ants that meant magic was being used against her, but nothing happened.

When she passed through the entry door unaccosted, all she wished to do was to collapse against the door frame in relief. Instead, she squared her shoulders as she pulled her cloak tighter about her. The guardsmen waiting outside trailed behind as she crossed the small courtyard between the Holy Few's buildings and the castle itself. Morning dew on the flow-ering shrubs along the path glistened in the light cast by her candle and the predawn light.

By the time she returned to her bedchambers, hints of pink decorated the horizon. Leolin remained asleep, oblivious to her absence, and she removed the cloak and her robe before crawling under the bed covers. When her cold feet brushed against his legs, he pulled her against him until his lips neared her ears.

"How are you so cold?" he whispered, and she turned her head to look at him. His eyes were still closed and his face relaxed.

Rather than answer him, she feigned sleep until exhausted, her body drifted into an uneasy sleep.

DESPITE THE ODD dreams that plagued her rest, Margaret awoke fully alert. Nothing moved in her bedchambers, nor in her sitting room that she could tell, but something had caught the attention of her sleeping mind, so she remained still in her bed and listened.

There.

Something moved in her bathing room, and she slid the dagger from beneath her pillow. Leolin slept and for a moment, she considered waking him, but he needed to catch up on his rest as much as she did, if not more. She stepped out of bed, and holding the dagger before her, tiptoed towards the room.

Water dripped along with a scuffing sound, and when Margaret swung the door open, a handmaiden screamed. Her eyes darted between the dagger and the door before settling on Margaret.

"You startled me, Your Majesty!"

Margaret noted the drawn bath and lowered her hand. "My apologies. I was not aware of how late the hour." Leolin all but smacked into her in his rush, startling the handmaiden a second time and setting off another round of screams. This time, Margaret left the bathing room and closed the door on the cacophony.

Shortly after, Leolin followed, his hands holding a small towel about his waist to cover himself.

"New servant?" she asked.

He returned his sword to its scabbard and leaned it against the bed frame. "Most of the castle staff fled when the Shadians breached the city. More return every day, but in the meantime, we make do with what and who we can."

"Someone should have warned her that I'm armed."

Leolin's smile faded as Margaret returned her dagger to its home. "Especially if you're sleeping with a dagger beneath your pillow. When did that begin?"

"It became habit when I was camped at the Pass."

"Habit that stayed with you once home?"

Without answering, she strode across the chilled stone floor towards the bathing room, this time unarmed. She dismissed the servant with a hand, and shut off the taps overhanging the tub. Few rooms in the castle had access to the water pipes, let alone to water already warmed by fire before it was piped in. As she stepped into the stone tub, the warm water relaxed her muscles, and she was grateful hers was one such room.

Several bottles of oils sat on a nearby stool, along with a small amount of soaproot. Margaret grabbed a bulb and rubbed it between her hands until it mixed with the water to create a lather, which she used to wash her skin and hair. As she finished, Leolin stepped into the room fully dressed.

"I meant to mention, I woke up during the night and you'd gone. Was there anything you needed to tell me?" he asked.

She dipped her head below the water to rinse her hair, and when she surfaced, he sat on the tub's edge, waiting.

"You avoided my question in there, so I'd hoped a little time relaxing would help shake whatever's bothering you. Why are you avoiding my questions this morning?"

"Not every question deserves an answer." She removed the stopper from the tub's bottom to allow the water to drain and stood.

When she reached for a bottle of oil, Leolin held it out of reach. "Perhaps if I were a servant, that excuse would be valid, but I'm not. If nothing else, I'm your friend, Maggie, so I would expect an answer."

He passed her the oil, which she rubbed into her bare skin. "Some habits persist because they are worthy habits for one to have. As to where I was this morning, I visited Her Holiness. I wished to know the origins of magic."

"Did she know?"

Margaret shook her head. "I told her who the senators are. At first she did not believe me, but...she's done this before, Leolin, that is, used magic on me—"

Leolin dropped the glass bottle, which shattered against the stone floor. "When? Why?"

"It was before the Shadians attacked. I think she thought I knew more than I would tell her, which I did, so she pressed her fingers against my forehead. It was as if ants marched across my skin, both fire and rain at the same time. She wanted inside my mind, Leolin. I've never felt anything like it before..."

"I have," he whispered as he stared at the broken glass.

She chose a blue robe from a peg on the wall and donned it, tying a belt around her middle. He had not talked much about the mental barriers placed on him as a child, not since the mystics had tried to correct whatever damage had been done. At least he hadn't talked about it with her. When she touched his arm, he flinched.

"Sorry," he said as edged around the glass on the floor. He

followed her out into the bedchamber and watched her dress in silence.

How Adelei would laugh to see the change as Margaret dressed herself. Besides, it meant fewer people to judge the fighting muscles that had developed across her frame.

"Gone is my Maggie who would've had a dozen servants busy fitting her into some contraption of a dress."

She frowned at Leolin as she glanced at the pants and tunic. Both fabrics were lightweight, yet heavily adorned with silver embroidery. "Gone is the woman who would have hidden away from the conflict ahead of us. Besides, what I'm wearing is both fitting to my station and allows me to arm myself."

He waved a hand at her. "I know, I know. None of us are the same anymore. Tell me more about this meeting with Her Holiness and why she dared touch you."

How he managed to remain silent through the retelling of it both concerned and amazed her. She watched his brows furrow and his fists clinch, but he said nothing, even after she finished speaking. "I have possibly sent away one who could have been an ally, but in the end, she serves her own purposes, I think," she said.

"The Holy Few always have. They've built up this wall between the Thirteen and the people, one only surmountable through their order. Then they wonder why so few people come to them for guidance."

Something in the way he said it reminded her of her sister, Adelei, particularly the exhaustion and grudging acceptance that came with her surrender to the Boahim Senate, and Margaret strode over to where he sat. Upon her return from the Pass, his presence in her bedchamber had been a foregone conclusion, but the way he hunched at the bed's edge, he looked out of place. Uncomfortable.

"We have had several opportunities since my return to

speak, yet we do not," she said as she lay her hand against his cheek. "Something weighs heavily on you, Leolin. If you do not feel you can unburden yourself with the mystics or the Holy Few, please share with me. What worries you so?"

"Much." He took her hand in his and traced circles around her fingertips like worry stones. "You and me...when this is done and the Thirteen are gone..."

She opened her mouth, and he pressed his index finger against it.

"You always say we will talk about it when the danger has passed, but be honest with me. Be honest with yourself. You're the Queen of Alexander. Danger will always be a part of your life, especially with the Bajit family alive. Sometimes I think you'd prefer we never talk about our future."

Her stomach flipped in response as she glanced at her hands. "We will talk about it, I swear, but it is impossible for me to make decisions about a future that is shrouded. This plan we have to destroy the gods might not work. It could end in the destruction of us all. How can I make plans knowing this?"

Leolin's lips pursed together as he frowned. "You asked what was bothering me."

"I did, but there is more to it than our future. I do not doubt your love for me, yet the way you look on me at times... The death around us has left me little choice but to adapt, to make decisions I know you don't approve of—"

"Maggie," he said as he lifted her hands to his lips. "I haven't always been as supportive as I should've been. I know this. It took time for me to adjust to the woman you've become, but I understand."

"Do you?"

He nodded. "Many people's lives depend on you. While you were away at the Pass, I heard the way Lord Cornish tried to diminish your abilities, the way he belittled your decisions.

To him, you're nothing more than a dewy-eyed fool who should abdicate so he can rule. I can't help but miss the friend I grew up beside, the one who'd hide from a spider and allow me to play hero, but I know that's not you anymore. People grow up, even princesses."

"So you understand why I went to the Pass?"

"I—" He swallowed hard, his throat convulsing. "I know why you went, though I still think you shouldn't have gone alone."

"I was not alone. Several guards died protecting me, Leolin, and while I'm sure their families would disagree, I would rather them die than you."

"You could've taken Bredych."

She pulled her hands away from his and stood. Her legs itched to pace, but she resisted as she turned her back on him. This was the *real* wall between them, his hatred of everything *Amaskan*, but particularly Bredych.

"I'm leaving."

The words were little more than a whisper, and at first, Margaret thought she had misheard him. She turned to face him, mouth open to reply but he shook his head.

"You talk of the Thirteen and Amaskans with such calm, much the same way you speak of magic, and I can't, Maggie. There's this piece of my life that appears in fragments, and everything I thought I knew is skewed. It's like what you mentioned before. I feel like I'm underwater. How can I expect you to trust me when I don't even trust myself?"

He allowed her to touch him as she straightened the collar on his shirt. Lately, his every movement ran like a taut wire, and even now, as she rested her hand on his shoulder, his muscles quivered in response. "When I returned from the Pass, there were rumors...about you," she said and he flinched. "They say you relished killing the Shadians, too much perhaps. I worried that rather than answers or justice, you would seek revenge."

Leolin leaned his head against her stomach and wrapped his arms about her waist. She tried to meet his gaze, but he closed his eyes.

"For every day you were gone, I made it my goal to end that many Shadians. If I couldn't protect you, I would protect Alesta to my last breath."

"Where do you intend to go?" she asked.

"The Order."

It was her turn to flinch. "We need the Amaskans to defeat the Thirteen—"

"I'm not going there to kill them, Maggie." He released her as he stood, nervous energy carrying him across the bedchamber. "I may have made a mess of the Shadians, but even I know we're going to need the Order's help. I don't like it, but it doesn't make it less true."

She paced with him, waiting for him to fill the silence.

"Bredych tried to get me answers about what was done to me, but my mother didn't tell anyone. She shared none of this part of her life, not even with your father. The timing is horrible, I know, but if I'm to be of any use to you, I need answers. I need my memories back. I need to find the mystic who did this to me, this Doughal Nilesh."

"How will you find the Order?"

Leolin smiled. "For all that I hate the man, your Bredych's already agreed to grant me passage to their home. He's written a note for the new Grand Master, Miriam, to ask them to help me as well as help the Little Dozen Kingdoms. If this Doughal's still alive, maybe he can fix me."

Margaret touched his hand. "You are not broken, Leolin. Besides, Bredych already promised they would help us with the Thirteen."

"But can he guarantee that? He's no longer their Grand Master."

She shrugged. "I think they would help if he pressured them to do so. Perhaps they have reason for not leaving Sadai. Besides, if he had no sway, they would not be required to help you either."

"That's true. I guess once a Grand Master, always a Grand Master? You realize that if they do come here, the Amaskans bring that prophecy of his closer to coming true?"

Margaret nodded. "It can't be helped. If we're to destroy the Thirteen, we need every ally we can manage...and here I've sent away Her Holiness. Damn."

"She tried to violate your mind, Maggie. No one needs any ally like that."

She swallowed the lump in her throat. "How long will you be gone?"

"As long as it takes. If the Order decides to travel to Alexander, the Amaskans may beat me back to Alesta."

Tears prickled along her eyelids, and the room blurred. She stopped pacing and snatched his hand, pulling him to her. Leolin wrapped his arms around her shoulders, his lips brushing across her hair.

"Take what time you need and find your answers," she whispered.

The irony of his embrace was not lost on her. When she needed to leave for the Pass, he would have locked her in the castle if he could have. Her leaving was a point of contention between them, whereas now that *he* needed time, she would release him to find his answers.

Even if she never saw him again.

Something in him recognized the finality of her thoughts, even if she did not speak them, and he held her tighter. "I will return, Maggie, I swear to you."

She nodded against him. "When will you leave?"

"As soon as I can."

When he released her, it was to kiss her, not with the fervor she had expected but tenderly, almost hesitantly.

"I need to see Bredych. Will you be all right...?" he asked.

Margaret nodded, and then watched as he left the bedchambers they shared. As the door closed behind him, she hardly noticed as the tears fell. The kiss was a promise, but would she still be alive when he returned? By the Thirteen, they could all be dead by the time he had his answers.

Margaret allowed herself a few moments' weakness before she swallowed the grief and pushed it aside. There was no time to be Leolin's lover...not yet. For now, she must be queen.

And a queen had no time for tears.

9

257 Sharimus 2ⁿᵈ — City of Alesta

A few days had passed since Leolin's decision to leave and yet he remained firmly in Alesta. It was not that she minded his company, but his existence in her bedchambers forced her to think on topics she would rather avoid, especially considering the very real threat of waging war against the gods.

This morning her lieutenant was helping her field marshal and Shai train her army in defending themselves against magic. The idea that any of them had any idea what they were doing made her giggle, though the emotion was quickly followed by a sense of despair.

Everything in her world oscillated between joy and terror: joy that she was home with those she loved, especially Leolin, and happiness that the Shadians were gone and her city could rebuilt. Yet fear for the future slashed any hopes to tatters. Everything could be undone if the Thirteen deemed it so.

Margaret sat alone in what was originally her sitting room but had been converted temporarily to a council room, though now that she had no council, it served once again as her sitting room. A small array of fruits, dried meats, and nuts lay on the small table before her. She picked at the offerings, but the desire for a midday meal receded as did her dreams.

She rang the bell beside her and when a servant entered, she said, "Ask Master Bredych to attend to me please. He should be with Fenton in the field."

The boy scurried away, leaving her alone again with her thoughts. Perhaps it was stress that left her emotions to wander. Who in their right mind would take on the gods? She spit out a piece of pear that had soured as she stared at the empty chair across from her. Leolin might as well be gone for all that he avoided her of late. Maybe that was the root of her troubles.

If Leolin ever reached the Order, would he find this Doughal? Would the mystic still be alive or even willing to help? Or would Leolin's mind continue to unravel? A pang sharpened in her chest for a moment. If Adelei were here, at least Margaret would have someone to talk to, another woman who would understand... A laugh escaped Margaret then. Adelei had cared very little for romance, at least as far as Margaret knew. She would have been downstairs with Leolin, helping to ready the army for what was to come. Even her father would have chided her for self indulgence.

A brief knock and the servant announced Bredych's arrival. She gestured for him to have a seat, but he shook his head. "If Your Majesty doesn't mind, I'd rather return to the Fenton as soon as possible."

"Of course. I...I wanted to ask you why you have not sent my message to the Order, asking for their assistance against the Thirteen," she said.

His fingers rested lightly against the back of a wood chair, the one Leolin would have claimed had he dined with her at midday. "With Leolin heading there, it makes sense to send your request along with the boy. Better the message is seen only by eyes we know we can trust."

Margaret cocked one eyebrow. "I thought you trusted all your Amaskans."

"To a degree. We never know what dwells inside someone's mind. At least the boy can be trusted to go where he's led."

"Leolin will leave when it suits him, and we do not have the luxury of waiting."

"You could order him to leave."

She opened her mouth, a retort on her lips, but sighed instead. "I could. I probably should. But that's not the reason you dally."

"Oh?"

"Bringing the Order here means we are closer to potentially fulfilling that prophecy from the Holy Few. I know what you think it means, and it frightens you." Margaret reached out to rest her hand on his. "For all that you are not my father, you carry yourself like him at times, especially when you are afraid. You think in delaying my message, you might delay your own death, but the truth is, we might all find our end at the hands of the Thirteen."

Bredych sighed, his shoulders slumping as he gripped the chair's back. "The longer I'm here, the more of myself I've lost. Some might see it as a boon, but now when I need my bravery the most, it fails me. The man I used to be was unafraid to do what was necessary to serve Justice, but there's more than myself to lose."

He reached up to touch the side of her face. "You are your own person, Margaret, yet you have become so much like your sister. You say I have become like your father, but in truth, you have become a daughter to me. So much like Adelei was. If I have to die in order to serve Justice, I do it gladly, for I'll not see you burned to ash."

Tears gathered at the corners of his eyes, and Margaret found her own vision blurred by tears. "My emotions have their way with me of late, though apparently yours have as well. Perhaps we are all more aware of this war we've started. There will be more casualties. Too many, in fact."

"I feel my age in more than my bones these days," he said.

"If age is your excuse, I worry about living so long."

He gave a brief smile though it did not reach his eyes the way it should have. "If I may, I would return to practice."

When she nodded, he all but fled the room. Margaret stared at her hands, calloused by swordswork rather than the softness of her life before.

Before her sister came home and changed the world.

Bredych did not believe he would live to see the Thirteen's end. The sadness in his eyes just now had confirmed it, but more, he did not believe she would survive either, and the knowledge left a sourness in her stomach.

If she were destined to die, she planned to take as many of the Thirteen with her as possible.

She stood and followed Bredych from the room.

BETWEEN THE CASTLE proper and the barracks near the castle gate lay a small field where the Royal Army practiced and trained. From the castle's rear doors, Margaret could see what remained of her army as they, backs to her, faced Fenton, Leolin, and Shai. Bredych's bald head bobbed up and down as he strode through the soldiers on his way towards the front. A small light in front of the mystic faded as he called out something. Whatever he said was lost in the noise as the soldiers stood and gathered their weapons and shields.

She was never without her blade or her daggers these days, even when sitting court. Not that there was much of that to do these days with the city rebuilding, not to mention most of her courtesans having fled when the Shadians attacked. A few candlemarks prior, her field marshal, along with Bredych, had disclosed the truth to her army about what they faced, and in retrospect, she should have been here, not up in her rooms worrying about Leolin.

Not only should she have been here, she should have been the one to tell them the truth. Yet another mistake in a long line of mistakes made, but she would set it right beginning now.

At first, no one paid her any mind as she moved through the soldiers. Halfway through the crowd, someone recognized her enough that a murmur spread through the army until it caught the ears of those up front. Leolin's gaze sought and found her, his frown visible from across the field. By the time she reached the front of her army, the soldiers had straightened their shoulders and lifted their chins with what Margaret only could assume was pride. A soldier with a shock of red hair stood beside her and stared a moment before his manners caught up to him.

Her field marshal cleared his throat. "Is there something your army can do for you, Your Majesty?"

Margaret held her sword in front of her like an offering. "Teach me."

"Your Majesty?"

"If we are to win this war, we need every tool at our disposal. I killed Itovah, but it was by accident." Murmurs spread throughout the army as she stared at Shai. "We can't defeat gods by accident alone. Teach me...teach *us* everything you can about fighting magic."

If Fenton or Leolin had any objections, they were lost in the cries of the men and women around her. The shouts of her name shook her bones. On the short dais where those who led her army gathered, Bredych inclined his head at her, a slight smile on his lips.

"We spent some time discussing the earth-shakes that occurred during the attack at the Pass," said Shai as he glanced down at Margaret. "The truth is, the Thirteen's magics are far beyond anything we mystics know. We used to have some of their knowledge, but no longer. When it comes to an uneven fight like this, it is about defending oneself rather than attacking."

Much to the surprise of those in attendance, Margaret raised her hand, and when Shai nodded, she said, "There are no promises, but we are investigating how mortal the Thirteen are. We know they can be killed, but are there any limitations to that? If they can be killed with a sword, then the fight is less one-sided than originally thought."

"Until then, we will focus on defense," said Shai, who raised his arm in the air.

Beside her, the soldiers unsheathed their weapons and began to pair up. The red-haired man beside her said, "We're pairing up to practice defense, Your Majesty. I'm Philip."

She nodded. "Today, I'm just another soldier in the army. Please call me Margaret."

"The mystic can't make the ground shake, so we're supposed to spar until it rains."

Margaret glanced around at the clear sky. "We might end up sparring for a lengthy stretch of time."

Philip laughed, his shaggy red hair shaking. "Mystic's gonna bring the rain. Then we're supposed'ta pretend it's a quake."

As Philip tapped his sword against hers, she relaxed her stance to better shift from one foot to the other. For her, it was a dance more recently learned than the soldiers around her, but fighting as close together as they were was completely new. Each time Philip came at her and she stepped away to avoid his attack, she bumped into several soldiers around her. Rather than be irritated by it, they smiled to see her trying, though she grew frustrated at her clumsy attempts.

"In close combat, ya can't rely on avoidance alone. When possible, it'd be better to fight back to back so you're protected," said Philip as he parried her attack. "When ya can't do that, ya gotta be better at deflecting attacks than evading them."

"Both of my teachers have worked with me on this, but it's different to experience it with more than three fighters. There are some skills that can't be practiced with a teacher."

He nodded. "There're some things you hafta learn by experience."

Leolin, Fenton, and Bredych moved through the army, changing pairings or making comments of approval or disapproval as they walked. As Leolin corrected a soldier nearby, Margaret watched him. The distraction left her open, and Philip gave her a light swat on the thigh with the flat of his blade.

As she stepped forward, her focus returned to her "foe." A droplet of rain splashed against her cheek, followed by a second and a third. In a perfectly clear sky, rain began to fall, and when she glanced up at Shai, his eyes stared off at nothing in particular as he focused on whatever spell brought rain.

Philip tapped her on the shoulder. "Your—Um, Margaret, this's when we're supposed'ta pretend the earth's shaking."

"What do we do when that happens?"

"Watch."

All around her, soldiers moved to huddle together in the field's most open area. It was then that she noticed the stones that formed a circle around the area where her army huddled. Whereas she would have sought shelter under a tree or overhang, her army pulled away from any objects and crouched. "They are pretending to avoid falling objects?"

"Aye. That's our 'safe area' though nothing's safe when the ground shakes like it did at the Pass."

"In a thunderstorm, we are instructed to take shelter, but when the ground's shaking, we're to do the opposite?" she asked. Her wet tunic chilled her even in the warm sun, and she glanced up at the mystic. Was he adding some cold to the rain, or was she unusually sensitive to it?

The rain stopped as quickly as it had begun, and before Margaret could react, Philip lunged forward. She brought up her sword at the last minute, the metal clang ringing in her ears.

"If we'd been fighting instead of sparing, you'd have a nasty neck wound 'bout now."

"I didn't know we had begun sparing again."

From behind her, Bredych's deep voice rang out. "If you are surrounded by people with weapons, always assume the fight continues. Do not drop your guard, or you'll be dropping more than that."

Heat rose to her cheeks. This time when she attacked, it was Philip's turn to be distracted as Bredych studied his grip. Philip brought his sword up too late to block, and Margaret's blade nicked his palm. Much to his credit, he did not drop his sword. Instead, he feinted to the right and managed another swat with his blade, this time against her hip.

"Are all in my army this skilled?" she asked.

Bredych repositioned her back foot with his leg, giving her a better stance to defend from. While she bumped against another soldier, Philip glided around his fellow fighters with ease.

"Neither," said Bredych as he shifted her foot again. "You are woefully out of practice, Your Majesty. Though Sergeant Philip is one of your best instructors and fighters. You'd best pay attention."

Her thigh stung as Philip's sword left a scratch across it.

Sweat tickled her back and stung her eyes as it began to rain again. This time she moved with her army towards the marked safe area. This time, Fenton blew a sharp reed whistle and fighting broke out across the field.

Philip grinned at her shock. "Just because the ground's shaking doesn't mean the enemy's gonna stop attacking."

Trying to stay inside the safe area while fighting added a complexity to battle that she had not expected. When the rain stopped again, she held up her hand. Giving Philip a momentary break, Margaret walked up to Shai. "If the ground opens up to swallow us like it did at the Pass, huddling together will only protect us if we are nowhere near the chasm. What we need is a way to stop the ground from opening up," she said.

"Your Majesty, if the Thirteen can be killed by a sword, as you suggest, that makes them easier to kill, but you still have to get close enough to do it. Unless you can detect magic or use it, there is little you and your army can do to prevent it or its effects."

He turned away from her, ready to make it rain for a third time, and she grabbed his hand. When he opened his mouth, she shook her head. "Cast your spell."

At first, there was nothing but the sounds of soldiers fighting but a few breaths later, her skin tingled. It began as a slight itch and by the time it was raining, a thousand ants marched across her flesh. Margaret tried and failed to release her grip on the mystic. Until the rain stopped, her skin would burn with whatever she felt when she was part of the magic.

After a time, she no longer felt the rain, nor could she hear the sounds of practice fighting around her. Even the painful way her skin crawled faded until she stood in the rain, tears pouring down her face.

When the rain stopped and Shai's magic ceased flowing through her, she crumpled to the ground with a gasp. Leolin ran over to her as Shai crouched to rest a hand on her shoulder. "You could feel it?" he whispered, and Margaret nodded.

"Feel what? Magic?" asked Leolin.

"I noticed it when Gamun died, when Senator Whitlen and King Bajit struggled. It was a mild hum in the back of my head—not exactly uncomfortable but noticeable. But when Her Holiness tried to...read my thoughts, I guess, it hurt. Like needles were being driven into my skin."

"She was touching you then, yes?" asked the mystic.

"Yes. The second time as well."

"Which is why you grabbed my hand just now."

Margaret nodded. "I wondered if it would be the same experience. Only this time was more intense and painful. The power you were using to create rain..."

"Creating anything takes energy."

"Does it hurt you?" she asked as she noticed the almost gray pallor of Shai's skin.

"Every time."

With the help of Leolin's arm, she stood and watched the relief spread across the faces of her soldiers. "Does this mean I'm a-a mystic?"

"I'm not sure. You could be more sensitive to magic than others, or yes, you could have the abilities needed to do magic," said Shai.

Leolin frowned. "What abilities would those be?"

"No one knows for sure."

"Then how does one know if they can do magic at all?" she asked.

"If one can make their will into action, then one can do magic."

The answer that lacked any real answers reminded Margaret of the same language used in the *Book of Ja'ahr*. Knowing that the mystics split away from the Order of *Amaska*, it made an odd sense that they both spoke in tongues meant to say as little as possible. Rather than press further, she turned to Leolin. "Have every soldier join hands with each other until we are all linked."

Word spread fast through the group, and soon every Royal Army member was linked hand in hand to her. Even Bredych joined in. She held out her hand to Shai and said, "Please bring forth the rains again."

He took her hand and then a deep breath.

The space between dry air and rain stretched longer this time, and when Margaret glanced up at the mystic, sweat dripped down his face. After this test, they would break for the day or at least he would. They needed him alive and able, not overextended. The thought had barely left her brain when the tingling began.

Rain poured down, and before she lost the ability to hear, many soldiers cried out in pain. This time, the sensory deprivation only lasted a few breaths before the magic and the pain stopped.

As loudly as she could, Margaret said, "If you felt any pain, tingling like needles, or even humming, step forward towards the dais. If you felt nothing, group together towards the castle doors."

People shuffled around each other for a moment or two until finally two distinct groups formed. Of the 210 soldiers in her army, one third had stepped forward to form a group of those who reacted to the touch of magic as she did. Beside her, Shai gasped.

"I don't know if this means any of us have your abilities, Mystic Shai, but seventy of us have something different. Perhaps we can use that in some way."

The mystic nodded. "I believe so, Your Majesty. But not today, for I believe myself exhausted beyond the ability to call even a droplet of water."

"Go rest. This can wait until another day." *I hope.* For all that the man needed rest, the Thirteen might not. "Thank you, soldiers, for your help today. Your work with Mystic Shai will continue on the morrow."

She turned to Leolin as a sense of lightheadedness slammed into her. "Lieutenant, I believe I shall take my leave as well."

He leaned close to her ear and whispered, "You don't look well. Do you need help up to your rooms?"

Margaret straightened her back and shook her head. As she passed through her soldiers, most bowed. Many more gave well wishes for her health, and the few that did not, stared at her with wide eyes as they gave her wide berth. Whether it was her involvement and reaction to magic or the knowledge that she had killed a god, fear held them at a distance.

Before she reached the end of her army, a young boy ran up to her and bowed, his face almost touching his knees. She would have believed him a page or perhaps a squire, but he wore the uniform of her army. When she raised her gaze from the boy to the soldiers around him, their eyes softened. He was too young, and yet they needed every fighter they could scrape together.

She touched his shoulder, and he looked up at her, his eyes shining. "Y-Yer Majesty, thank-ee for helpin' us fight good."

"You are welcome, ah..."

"Stefan, Majesty."

She smiled at the young lad. "You are very welcome, Stefan. Are you Alesta born and bred, or do you hail from somewhere else in Alexander?"

"Hersh, Yer Majesty."

"Lady de Gant is a family friend. You do her proud, Stefan." Margaret nodded to him and turned to leave when he made to grab her hand.

His manners caught up with him and he stopped, his

hand hovering before him. "Yer Majesty, we're gonna win, right?"

For a moment, she worried her legs would give out from under her. She wanted to believe they would save Boahim and defeat the Thirteen, she *needed* to believe it, but there would be a cost. There would be casualties.

And Stefan would likely be one of them.

Rather than share her worries with the boy, she turned to face him, a bright smile upon her face. She took his outstretched hand in her own and gave a slight nod. "Stefan, you will help us defeat the evil that walks upon this land. All of us together will unite the Little Dozen Kingdoms under a banner of peace. So yes, sir, we will win."

She turned away from him before he could see the doubt in her eyes.

Cheers and roars of approval sounded behind her, and she closed her eyes a moment before striding through the castle's doors.

She had lied to the child, and somehow, she would need to get used to it. The thought sickened her as she fled to the safety of her rooms.

10

Despite Margaret's worry that the Thirteen would attack them all at any moment, Shai's ability to use his magic remained exhausted. He claimed that it would return, but only time and rest would allow for that, so Margaret swallowed down her doubts and fears, choosing instead to focus her time on encouraging the rebuilding efforts.

Every trip through the city of Alesta meant promising her people that they were safe, that they could rest easy at night, and that the Shadians were gone and would remain gone. It meant holding the hands of people older than her twenty-one years as they cried about the loss of a family member or their home, and dividing up food supplies for those working to rebuild. But mostly it meant being surrounded by guards who treated everyone as the enemy, even her own citizens, and Margaret chafed under the constant supervision.

She was a capable fighter, but still her honor guard treated her as a string of delicate twine that could break with the slightest tug. Fighting her way to the Pass and back again, without Leolin or Bredych beside her, had left a taste of power in her mouth and carried a hint of freedom she had not experienced before. Nor since as her guards believed it their job to keep her secluded and safe from dawn until dusk. A few days prior, she had dressed in simple fighting clothes and attempted to sneak out to the stables without drawing attention.

By the castle's first floor, a dozen guards followed. Some nearly nipped her heels in an effort to protect her, while others trailed behind and watched, hands on hilts. She had ordered them to leave her only to find them pretending to guard empty rooms or "passing through the area" as they guarded her.

While it was their job to ensure her safety, it chafed knowing her father would have had a moment's respite if he had ordered it. Thus far, her ability to send her guards away had been as successful as her attempts to rid the world of the Thirteen.

Margaret sighed, and the woman before her paused mid-sentence. "Your Majesty, is something wrong?"

Mid-seventies judging by her wrinkles, yet the old woman stood before her with more energy than Margaret carried in her smallest finger. Rather than evacuate when the Shadians had threatened Alesta, the woman had set off for the castle and offered her services as an herbalist and healer. Now, she walked house to house through the city, ensuring that its residents' wounds were healing as they rebuilt.

Today, as the old woman walked through the city's upper circle, she had expressed a concern to her queen about their dwindling supply of *perin*, an herb used to lessen pain and inflammation. The herb was grown in the mountains in Southern Alexander, and the woman was concerned about the lack of a recent shipment.

"It's likely the rains have delayed travel from the south."

Margaret patted the old woman's hands. "If you would check the supplies in the city's upper district, I'll return to the castle to check when the last shipment left Roue."

The weak excuse left her kicking herself, but the thought of listening to more complaints about a missing roof tile or a damaged basket caused another sigh to escape her. Margaret did not mind the lower circles—those people needed her help in rebuilding—but the wealthier citizens had means and opportunity the others did not, and it galled her that it was the latter that demanded so much of her time.

She itched to don the black silk wraps the seamstress had made for her and escape to the city's lower circle. With her guards keeping watch over her, Margaret had taken to escaping through a storage closet's window, which gave her a straight path to the servant's gate. A coin or two in the right pocket had given her silence as she fled the castle under the darkness of night. Besides, one could hear more useful information on the streets of Alesta than curled up in bed.

Her silks, unlike Adelei's, fit her curvier frame as she had hips and a chest where Adelei had not. Sometimes, Margaret would flee her responsibilities during the day. Though not as often since the more risks she took, the greater the chances were she would not survive to see the Thirteen killed.

The return to the castle was uneventful and once returned, she paced her study for a candlemark. Waiting inside made waiting to attack the Thirteen or waiting for them to attack her much less tolerable, so Margaret grabbed a small bag that held her newly sewn silks. She held it for a moment as her heart beat in her chest, and then set it aside.

Maybe it was the need to control something in a world out of control, or maybe it was grief that caused her to grab her sister's silks, but Margaret fetched a different, more worn bag before leaving her suite of rooms. Several guards followed behind her at a respectful distance as she walked down the stairs and towards the kitchens. When she opened the kitchen door, she acknowledged them with a nod. They would remain guarding the kitchen doors, firm in their belief that she remained inside and safe. Though what they thought she did inside for several candlemarks... She hid a grin behind her hand as she closed the kitchen door. If the servants were shocked to see her again, they hid it well as she sought out a nearby storage closet.

She had taken the idea from Leolin, though it would disconcert him to know he had helped her. His use of several closets throughout the castle when his head ached, put it in her mind to use the closets for another purpose. Escape.

Once inside, she set the bag she carried aside and wedged a chair beneath the door's handle. Secure in her privacy, she shed her clothes and stuffed them in the bag before donning her silks. Staring at the clothes, Margaret pursed her lips together.

She had promised, not only Leolin and Bredych, but herself that she wouldn't don the *Amaskan* gear anymore. She didn't need to be her sister to accomplish her goals and honestly, she didn't want to be. Adelei was a strong woman, a believer in justice, but she was not Margaret. She didn't know her home country and its people like Margaret did. But with the never-ending trail of people following her every movement, there was no other choice.

It was disguise herself or be hidden away from potentially critical information.

With practiced hands she changed into clothing of stealth, though she tied a blue sash about her waist. She used the head wrap to cover her hair, but not in the way of the Order. Now, she looked less *Amaskan*, which suited her until she reached the castle's first floor. When she crawled through the window, a servant yelped in surprise. Margaret held a finger to her lips and the girl gave a nod before running into the castle.

Walking from the castle proper to the city's lower circle took the better part of a candlemark, and once there, she found an alleyway properly shadowed from the afternoon sun and crouched behind a stack of wood. With the efforts to repair the city proper, more people had returned. Watching them gave Margaret a better handle on how her people were doing than the official reports that landed on her desk.

After a bit, she settled down in a tavern and caught a few rumors that folks believed the war between Alexander and Shad wasn't finished. The number of guards in Alesta rather than at the border made her people uneasy. Not that she could solve that issue in the foreseeable future, but it was information she had previously lacked. She left the tavern feeling like the task had been fruitful and as the sun approached the horizon, she returned to the alleyway from before. This time, she removed the blue sash around her waist and used the hair wrap to better cover her hair.

The types of folks who walked the streets at night were different than those out and about in the daylight. Most who passed her alleyway were people on their way home from their place of employ, and she relaxed her stance until she sat on her butt. Half a candlemark passed with nothing more than the chatter of evening meals when someone around the corner said the word *Tribor*.

Margaret tried to roll up on her feet, but her muscles had stiffened and fought to move without protest. She crept around the wood stack until she stood at its edge, her head poking above it. Ten feet away, two armed men stood facing each other, their gazes shifting as they spoke. She could not hear every word, but bits and pieces reached her, including a second utterance of the word *Tribor*.

When they turned their backs to her and set off towards the tavern she favored, Margaret followed behind them at a distance. Rather than go inside, they headed down the alley beside it until they reached the door of a shack. She stopped when they ducked inside.

If the *Tribor* were here, she needed to know, but there was no way to know what awaited her inside the shack. Rather than follow, she approached the door on tiptoes and leaned her ear to it. If the two men had continued their conversation, they did it deeper within the building as no sound reached her. She pressed her ear harder to the dilapidated wood.

One moment, she leaned against the door and the next, she tumbled inside as the door was suddenly opened. The loss of balance sent her sprawling across a dirt floor. The earthen taste of it and a bit of blood greeted her, as did the sound of laughter.

"Looksee-like we caught us a-maskan."

The way the man slurred the words together tickled Margaret's brain. Maybe he was someone she had heard talking before in some tavern while seeking information. She rolled up on her feet to find herself facing one of the men she had followed. Now that she was closer, his mustache split an average nose from an otherwise average set of lips. He could have been anyone. While she couldn't see the blood on his black clothes, she could smell it and her heartbeat quickened. "I'm not *Amaskan*," she said as she met his gaze.

His dirty hands reached for her chin, and she leaned backward out of his reach. When the man behind her moved, she partially pivoted, giving her a view of both men. This one's looks expressed his misdeeds: multiple scars across his flesh spoke of fighting while piercing blue eyes watched her with all the warmth of a winter day. His clothes were worn but high quality as they bore their wear well. With another glance between the two, she stepped closer to the wall behind her.

For all that she did not intend to be cornered, being pinned between both men would leave her too vulnerable. Besides, if her back was to the wall, maybe she could scoot close enough to the door to flee. No blades had been drawn yet; that meant there was still a chance to escape unharmed.

"I thought I saw someone I knew come this way." Margaret held up both hands in front of her. "I meant no harm."

The man with blue eyes tilted his chin at the other man, then turned his gaze to the door, which he guarded. The man with the mustache scurried toward it and slid out once the other man opened the door. Margaret stepped forward to follow him when the man with blue eyes pulled it shut.

"We aren't finished," he said as he dropped a wooden latch in place, locking the door. "No one wears *that* who isn't *Amaskan*."

"But I'm really not."

He reached out and grabbed her before Margaret could think, let alone react. He pulled her close to him, his breath stinking of onions and garlic. As he ran a finger across the black silk, his touch set her skin on edge. She tried to twist down and out of his grasp, but this caused him to tighten his grip around her forearms.

"I've seen this cut of cloth before. These aren't just fighting clothes, my dear, but special ones the Order makes for their cult. They do not hand these silks out to anyone. Either you're *Amaskan* or you killed one, and I highly doubt it's the latter."

When he released her, he did so with a shove that sent her stumbling in the opposite direction from the door. Margaret reached for her short sword and he erupted with laughter. "Go ahead. Show me how you killed someone for your silks."

Rather than draw her blade, she held her hands up in front of her again. "If I'm honest, these were my sister's clothes. She died, and I miss her. Sometimes I walk around in them to remind me that at one point in time, she was alive. Foolish perhaps, but my mistake and mine alone."

He made a *tsk*ing sound as he wagged his finger at her. "No use lying to me."

"Please, sir. I'm not looking for trouble." As she talked, she unwrapped the silk about her head. "Look, what *Amaskan* would have hair?"

"Then you killed one."

She shifted her weight to her right and prepared to feint left in the door's direction. "If you allow me to leave, I'll—" She darted left, but so did he.

He moved into her space like water flowed into the smallest of crevices. Her momentum carried her into him, and he wrapped his arms around her, trapping her in his embrace. "As I said, *Your Majesty*—" He dragged out the honorific, "—we aren't finished yet."

Margaret stared at him. His speech marked him as educated and the way he spoke of the Order, made him more knowledgeable about them than most. "Who *are* you?" she whispered.

"The name's Till."

She resisted the urge to squirm and met his gaze instead. "Release me then...Till."

He laughed. "You're in no position to make demands, little queen. While I have your attention, a bit of advice. Since you enjoy playing the *Amaskan* so much, perhaps you should learn to fight like one."

The way he wrapped his arms around her meant she could wiggle her fingers but nothing else, certainly not to reach any weapons on her body. When she tried to lift a knee towards his groin, he squeezed hard enough to knock the wind out of her, and her heart fluttered with her panicked breaths.

"Rule One: Never get into a fight with someone unless you know you can defeat or escape them. Take me for example," said Till as he relaxed his hold enough for her to fill her lungs. "I outweigh you, probably double. I've got no worries about my ability to disarm someone with...your level of skill. But you on the other hand... You've got no business picking a fight with the likes of me."

"You mean a member of the *Tribor*."

He inclined his head a fraction of an inch. "If you need to assign me a label."

Margaret glanced around the room, and other than a single, rickety stool in one corner, it remained empty. Nothing she could use, or hook with her leg and use as a weapon or means of escape.

Till chuckled, his lips turning up in a sneer. "Rule Two: If you're not sure you can hold your own in a fight, never walk into some place blind. Especially not alone."

"What are you going to do to me?"

"Rule Three: Women have no place carrying a blade."

Heat flooded her cheeks, and she dug her nails into her palms. To draw his own weapon, he would have to release her. Any opening would give her more of a chance to escape than currently standing in his grasp. "I asked you a question. What are your plans for me, or do you plan to hold me all day?"

"I'm going to kill you, little queen, but I'm going to savor it—allow the taste of your fear to linger as long as I like—but first, perhaps we can enjoy ourselves."

As close as his face was, she could see the slight wrinkles at the corners of his eyes as well as the puffy scar beside his nose, so when he parted his lips, his eyes on her mouth, she leaned back and slammed the front of her head into his nose.

Till shrieked and release her as he tried to stem the flow of blood pouring from his now broken nose.

Before she could do more than blink, her vision grew hazy. When she stepped towards the door, her body kept moving as if pitched forward. The vague feeling of landing on the hard, dirt floor greeted her before blissful darkness swept in.

WHEN MARGARET WOKE, it was to the rhythmic pounding of her head along with the feeling that every meal she'd ever eaten wished to make a quick exit from her stomach. Opening her eyes brought on more nausea and the sense that the world was awry, so she closed her eyes again as she sagged against something hard beneath her.

Was she sitting on the floor? Margaret unfurled her fingers to better touch the hard surface.

A wooden stool sat beneath her and when she explored it further, she found her hands bound to the chair's legs. *That* sharpened her thoughts, and she opened her eyes again, this time fighting to ignore the way the world spun before her.

Before, the shack's front room had been lit by whatever light poured in from its single window, but now three candles burned on a small table. Their flames burned her eyes with their brightness and she retched.

"She awakens!"

Till's voice pierced her skull, and she winced as her stomach threatened to revolt.

"I would apologize but after the way you broke my nose, I'm not sorry you've given yourself quite the knock on the head." Blood tinted the skin of a swollen and purple nose on the man standing before her. He chuckled briefly before he strode from the room.

Wherever the second door led, a fireplace roared inside as the heat swept into the front room where she sat. Flexing her wrists, she found the ropes binding her loose enough for some movement, but that was all. Unless she found something sharp, she would remain tied to the stool while the room spun.

The *Tribor* returned with a hot poker in his hands. "You keep too much with Amaskans, so we'll make you one, little queen. Then you can die like one."

Margaret's eyes widened as he strode up to her chair. With one hand, he gripped her chin to tilt it away from him, and her head pounded in her ears with the motion.

Hot metal touched the spot where her jaw met her ear, and she screamed as he used the poker to carve a small circle into her flesh. Pain drove her to tug at the ropes keeping her in place, but they would not give. As Till stepped back to admire his handiwork, she stood, taking the stool with her and charged him. Rather than hit him with her head, she angled her body so that her shoulder connected with his stomach.

He had not been expecting her to move, let alone attack, and he dropped the poker.

Somewhere, a door slammed open, though whether it was to Margaret's left or right made little difference. Moving caused the room to tilt, and she pitched forward before vomiting along a nearby wall. Till grunted as someone punched him and after sounds of a brief scuffle, he landed on the floor beside her. She tried to face whoever had barged in through the main door when rough hands turned her away.

"Hold still," said Leolin as he cut through the ropes binding her to the stool.

"Leolin?" Her voice cracked, and she ground her teeth in frustration. While she was grateful for his appearance, his rescue lent more encouragement to his idea that she was incapable of wielding a sword, let alone risking herself for her kingdom. Being free of the stool did not rid her of her pounding headache, nor the way everything pitched and swam around her, both of which multiplied when he turned her to face him.

"When I saw you duck in here, I waited. I could hear you screaming down the road."

His blue eyes were almost gray, though whether it was from worry or the dim lighting, she couldn't tell. Till moaned from his spot on the floor, and the cloudiness in Margaret's mind cleared at the sound.

Till was *Tribor*. He was a threat. The pounding surged when she bent over to grab her dagger from her ankle, so she held out her hand. "Give me your dagger."

Leolin frowned. "What do you need it for?"

She kicked Till with her foot. "This man's *Tribor*."

Rather than hand over the weapon, Leolin grabbed the assassin by the armpits and dragged him upright until he leaned against the wall. Blood poured from his nose where she had broken it. "I don't care what he is. He tied you to a stool," Leolin said as he rolled up the man's pant legs. On his left leg, a single triangle tattoo marred Till's skin, and Leolin swore. "He'll stand judged for his crimes."

"Hand me your dagger," said Margaret. She needed to hurry before both her resolve and her stomach betrayed her.

Leolin shook his head. "You can't kill him. It's—"

"Against the Thirteen? You mean the gods who are trying to kill me? I find this man guilty of crimes against me and my kingdom; now hand me your dagger."

This time, he touched her hand gently with his own. "I'll take care of it, Maggie."

She shook off his touch and thrust her hand out before her. "Now, Lieutenant."

Another moan escaped Till. When Leolin relinquished the weapon, Margaret grabbed the assassin by his hair and tilted his head back.

"Maggie, you don't have to—"

The glare Margaret gave Leolin silenced him and without pause, she slit Till's throat. Leolin leapt backwards a second too late to keep the blood spatter from his pants. She wiped off the dagger on Till's shirt before handing it back to Leolin.

"I could have dealt with him." His voice carried bravado, but Leolin's face bore a sickly pallor.

Margaret pursed her lips. "*Tribor* are a danger to the

crown, and their mere existence is punishable by death. Besides, he was *mine* to kill."

Leolin tilted her head to the side, his gaze falling to the blood on her jawline, and his features softened. "You're hurt."

"I'm fine." She wrested her chin from his grasp, the motion sending a herd of horses thundering through her head, but rather than succumb she stepped towards the door. "We need to leave."

"Not in that." Leolin stepped between her and the door. He opened it a crack and reached outside to retrieve a small satchel. Inside were a set of clothes Margaret recognized as those she used to practice her swordswork.

When he tried to hand it to her, she said, "We don't have time for this."

He grabbed her forearm to stop her forward momentum. "You can't go back out into the city in those clothes. Think about it. You've been championing the Amaskans as worthy of your trust, but if you flee the scene of a crime in that outfit, people will think him dead by *Amaskan* hands. Fear will spread through the city. People will question your wisdom in bringing the Order here to Alesta. This should have been an official execution by their queen, not something done in a back alley shack, but what's done is done. Now we live with the consequences."

Removing the *Amaskan* wraps proved difficult with her dizziness, and the task required more of Leolin's help than she desired. He was correct in his worry about the Order's honor, but it stung nonetheless to have to be reminded of it. Her brain refused to think clearly, and it rankled.

"Did you bring a change of clothes for you as well or was it only me you were expecting to rescue?" she asked as he tucked her sister's wraps into the bag. At least he did not try and leave them behind, as much as he probably would have liked to do.

When he made no move to answer, she asked, "Why were you following me?"

"Bredych's orders."

The curt answer of a soldier to his superior. Perhaps some time away from Alesta would do them both some good. Margaret untied her hair to allow it to better cover her jaw. As she reached the front door, Leolin muttered something she did not quite hear. "Did you need something else?" she asked.

"Did he mark you? Or did you do it?"

Fire scorched her insides at the idea that she would mutilate herself, but when she faced him again, her gaze fell on Till's corpse and the blood spatter. "He said he wanted me to die like an *Amaskan*. Now I have killed like one. Let us leave."

She did not wait for him. He would follow behind her or he would not, but either way, he would have to make peace with the fighter in her. Margaret made it ten steps from the shack before the ground rolled up to meet her, then everything faded into a blissful silence.

11

Someone held a cold cloth against Margaret's head, something she appreciated as it both blocked the room's glaring candlelight and soothed the throbbing pain in her skull. When she turned toward the shadow to her left, the woman holding the cloth *tsk*ed as she pulled it away. Woolen, brown skirts swished across the wooden floor, and when Margaret tilted her head to better see the woman, she winced at the bright candlelight.

"Candles'll be the bane of ya for the next few days, I be thinkin'. How'd you come to such a knot on yer head anyway?"

Her eyes watered as they burned, yet Margaret kept them open. Wooden crates of various sizes were stacked around her in a small storage closet. Someone, perhaps the woman in the revealing bodice, had managed to prop her up in a chair with enough cushioning that she had awoken thinking herself abed.

"Can ya hear me?" the woman asked.

Margaret nodded. "Where am I? Where is Leolin, the man who was with me?"

"Yer at Mademe Pouffaur's public house. The lad's with Mademe. Do ya recall how ya came to this state?"

"Someone attacked me. You said a public house?" Heat rose to Margaret's cheeks. It was not as if she were ignorant that such houses existed but to be inside of one.... The location certainly explained the low cut of the woman's blouse and the undercut style of her bodice.

The scrap of cloth used on Margaret's head lay on a nearby crate, a variety of pinks and reds tinging the rough linen. She raised a shaking hand to the top of her head, and when she touched it, she hissed.

"I told ya you've got quite the knot. Better to not bump it around or touch it. I'd like t'say we're a safe city, Alesta bein' the capitol and all, but since them Shadians ran us through, we've got all manner of folks wanderin' 'round, though I'm sorry ya 'ad to run inta one of the surlier types. I'm Jessa, by the by."

"M-Maggie," she said. Not that Jessa would automatically assume someone named Margaret was her queen, but Mademe Pouffaur was a recognizable name in Alesta, even to her. Bredych had used the woman on several occasional to send messages to the Order. Jessa might not recognize who she helped, but it was almost certain that Mademe would. "I appreciate your help, but I should leave you to your evening."

When she stood, the closet grew smaller as her vision darkened. Margaret held out her arms for balance, and Jessa seized one to help steady her.

"I don't think it wise for ya to be settin' out anytime soon. I think you should wait for Mademe."

Margaret gripped the crate closest to her. "I...I have to leave," she muttered as she stepped towards the door. If the nausea did not upend her, the double vision surely would. She opened her mouth to speak, but her mind stumbled through a haze that left her speechless. When Till was still breathing, the pain in her head had faded to an annoyance she could push aside until danger passed, but now she paid for that decision.

The door opened easily, though the hallway appeared at an angle contrary to her steps. Jessa trailed along behind her in silence. By the time they reached the hallway's end, Margaret's head threatened to rip itself in two. At least the public house's main room was cloaked in shadows as few candles filled the space. Panels made of sheer linen subdivided the darker areas and a stairwell led up to another hallway of rooms like the one she stood in.

Between the world spinning and her pounding head, no sounds reached her from any of the dozen or so rooms, nor did any sound from behind any of the panels. "It's quiet," said Margaret as Jessa stepped in front of her.

"I cleared the place out when Jessa found you two." The woman behind a small bar bore a wicked smile as she glanced in Margaret's direction. Long, black hair wrapped the shoulders of a voluptuous woman whose tight-fitting clothes left no doubt as to her line of work.

Bredych had never described the woman, but there was no one else this woman could be other than Mademe, esteemed lady of pleasure and a woman whose reputation curried favor in the lower circle of Alesta. Margaret's mind whirled. She had hoped to avoid stumbling upon the only woman in the place who might recognize her, but that wish was too late in the making.

"But I-I've put you out of yer earnings for the night. You didn't have to do that." Margaret attempted to mimic Jessa's speech patterns as best she could.

"The best part about being Mademe Pouffaur is that when I speak, people around here listen." The woman shot a pointed look at Jessa, who reached out to take Margaret's arm and guide her.

By the time they reached the bar, Mademe had fetched a

chair considerably more comfortable than a stool and placed it within Margaret's reach. She gestured for Margaret to claim it, which she did just as Leolin appeared from behind a closed door. He carried a bowl of something that smelled of herbs, which he brought directly to her.

"You were supposed to remain in back," he said as he set the bowl on the small table beside her. His gaze settled on Jessa, who flushed before scuttling through the door Leolin had passed through a moment before. Once the woman had retreated, his shoulders relaxed, but only a fraction as he stared at Margaret.

"I get that you've no reason to trust me, but Jessa won't say anything without my say so. None of my girls or lads will. Their survival depends on it," said Mademe Pouffaur, who nodded at the soup. "Eat that before it gets cold."

Once Margaret picked up the spoon and began eating, the woman left the two of them alone. Leolin remained silent while she sipped a few spoonfuls into her mouth. With her head aching, the idea of food sent her stomach into knots, and she set the bowl down. "We need to leave," she whispered with a glance at the back door. "Why did you bring us here?"

"I needed somewhere...safer to clean you up. When you fell, you cut your hands and your jaw started bleeding again. You can't walk through the city looking like you've fallen in the wrong side of a fight without eliciting the wrong questions."

Margaret arched a brow at him. "How did you know this public house would be safe?"

Leolin's face flushed wine red. "Bredych mentioned the place. I figured anywhere he considered safe probably was. Even still, I don't like us being here. We need to be careful what we say."

She gave the barest nod of her head. Any more than that and she would have decorated Mademe Pouffaur's floor with what little remained in her stomach. Not that she needed the reminder to watch her words. Rather than say it out loud, Margaret lifted the spoon and forced herself to resume eating.

The soup held more flavor than she had expected of a place like this, though she could not identify the ingredients. If anything, she would have called it herb-filled and left it at that. With a few more spoonfuls in her, the knots in her stomach relaxed enough for her to enjoy the soup's taste. While she ate, Leolin paced, his gaze locked on the front door.

While Jessa seemed unaware of who she had helped, something about Mademe Pouffaur's furrowed brows hinted that the woman knew whom she served. If so, Margaret would finish her soup and be a gracious guest though her brain cried out for her to return swiftly to the castle. She ate as quickly as her stomach and head allowed, all while keeping her gaze on the door where the two women had retreated.

As she finished the last of the soup, Mademe Pouffaur returned, arms full of various fabrics, including a simple head scarf. Sky colored fabric was embroidered by simple flowers along its edge and when the woman placed it in Margaret's hands, the fabric was softer than she expected.

"Even cleaned up, your...mark is oozing and you've a knot the size of an egg on your head. You'll be stopped by every guard between here and...where you're headed. It doesn't match your current clothing but we can fix that," said Mademe Pouffaur.

The woman worked with an efficiency that surprised Margaret as she wrapped Margaret's head with the wrap before tying a matching belt around her waist. A small, leather pouch was added, followed by another scarf around Margaret's neck. The clothing transformed her from a fighter to someone of middling status. Mademe Pouffaur pulled out a small set of wooden pipes from her pocket and handed it to Margaret. "If anyone sees any bruises, they'll think you yet another bard who picked the wrong song to sing in the wrong tavern. Have the lad carry your sword when you leave."

Margaret nodded. "I will return all of this to you when I can...and thank you. I won't forget the kindness shown to me here."

Looking nothing like the woman who had left the castle earlier in the day and nothing like the woman who had entered a public house covered in dirt and blood, Margaret rose with care, handed her blade to Leolin, and stepped outside.

Night had fallen in their absence, punctuated only by the occasional torch light. In the city's lower circle, the darkness swallowed most signs of life, a fact that Margaret was grateful for as they stepped away from the public house. Beside them, Jessa placed an iron lantern on the steps before retreating back inside.

"It didn't take long for Mademe Pouffaur to return to business," she said. A single narrow road led away from the public house and into a residential area. The quiet unnerved Margaret, and she felt for a sword she did not carry. "How much time passed while we sheltered?"

"A candlemark or two." Leolin's hand rested on the hilt of his sword. "Even with folks rebuilding, the city is quieter at night. People seek their homes sooner and businesses close earlier."

"The Shadians are gone."

Leolin frowned. "You've been outside the castle at night enough times to know that more than the Shadians have the city afraid. Tonight's events are proof enough of that."

She mumbled an affirmative as they walked. Once, Alesta had been the pinnacle of prosperity, but now, newer buildings were punctuated by rubble, signs of a city in distress. How many *Tribor* lay in wait in her city? How many of the Thirteen watched her every movement? Margaret shivered.

Perhaps sneaking around the city without an escort had been a bad idea.

At least the darkness gave them cover. They passed so few people that there was no need to lie about their identities or purpose to anyone. When the packed dirt roads gave way to cobblestone and the third city wall loomed before them, Margaret sighed with relief. Walking from the castle to the city's edge was a good forty-five minute walk as long as one did not dally, but with her head pounding with each footstep, the trek threatened to take twice that.

The guardsmen at the gate studied them as they passed but made no move to stop them. More light did not mean more townspeople shuffling about, though it did mean more city guards. They passed a dozen as they traveled down several roads. Margaret stumbled twice, and her cheeks burned with frustration. Leolin grabbed her hand, bringing her stride to a halt.

"Maybe I shouldn't leave. If I hadn't been there…"

"I would have freed myself, even if it meant running out the door with a stool strapped to my rear." She giggled at the imagery, and Leolin shook his head.

"It's not something to laugh at, Maggie. Till was going to kill you."

A nearby guard lifted a lantern to better see them as they passed, and Margaret waited until they were out of earshot to continue. "Leolin, I was there. I know what Till's intentions were. The knot on my head did not happen by accident. My breaking his nose was something *I* did in my attempt to escape. Am I glad you arrived to help? Of course, but this doesn't change anything."

"I can't believe you think you had the upper hand in that fight."

His words were too loud, and the guardsman from before called out to them.

Margaret pulled Leolin around the side of a brick home and into a small garden area. They ducked behind a small shrub, and Margaret muffled a slight giggle with her hand.

Once the guardsman passed, Leolin whispered, "Now what's so funny?"

"You remember that time we hid from your mother in my father's gardens when we were kids?"

Leolin grinned. "You must have been seven maybe? I thought we'd never get the stench of the Valerian out of our clothes." When she laughed and pointed to the pale, pink petals on the ground, he groaned. "Why doesn't it stink?"

"We haven't disturbed the roots enough yet. I think if we move carefully, we should be able to avoid the sweaty odor. The last thing we need is to arrive at the castle with me wounded and smelling of stink."

When they escaped the shrub, the guardsman who had sought them was nowhere to be seen. The smile fell from Leolin's face as he caught a glimpse of the wound on Margaret's jawline. He pulled the head wrap forward to better hide it before setting out again.

"Something on your mind?" she asked.

"One moment, we're children again, laughing at the most ridiculous of plants, but then I wake up and realize that we have enemies, you more than me. Multiple groups of both people and gods are actively trying to kill you, and I don't think you take it seriously enough."

"I'm aware of the threats."

Leolin stopped, his face full of shadows. "Are you? Do you know how many people have died to protect you?"

Margaret gave a brief incline of her head. "We should keep moving. We're too exposed out here. To answer your question, yes. I haven't counted but I know."

"Yet you continue to place yourself in risky positions so

you can dress like Adelei and…I don't know, pretend to be something you're not?"

For a moment, the urge to order him to leave Alesta threatened to overwhelm her. Instead, she imagined his words as water that flowed around and over her, but not through her. He lacked the ability to understand the battles she fought, a fact she would forgive him for later, when she could afford to do so. "Wars are bloody, Leolin. They are difficult. To stop the Thirteen, everyone is expendable, right down to me. If I need to move about my city without people knowing who I am, so I can gather the necessary information to defeat them, then I'll do it. I can take care of myself. I did so for many days at the Meridi Pass."

He remained silent for a moment as they passed a small group of guardsmen gathered at a cross street, then he said, "I know you can, but you shouldn't have to. It's my job to protect you. How can I do that when you're determined to get yourself killed? You aren't Adelei."

"Stop trying to use my sister against me. Despite your beliefs on the matter, I'm not trying to be her. Am I using her knowledge to gain what a queen can't? Absolutely, and I will continue to do so if it serves my purposes."

"Even if it kills you? Then who will defeat the Thirteen?"

Was it wounded pride speaking or inexperience? Margaret sighed. "Maybe you *should* leave."

"What?"

"Seek out your answers and learn what it means to truly sacrifice. Understand what it means to make difficult choices. Maybe then you can be of use to me again."

Even in the near darkness, Leolin visibly paled. "Is that all I am? Useful?"

The gate to the castle proper lay ten paces from them, and while Margaret needed her physician and a bath, in that order, she paused in sight of her guards. "You may be a lieutenant in my army, but sometimes I question whether you should be. You speak of your job of protecting me, but can you allow me room enough to do *my* job? I'm—" She glanced away from Leolin long enough to note that the four men stationed at the gate where actively listening. "I'm trying to save us all. The choices I must make are ones only I can make. My father understood this. So does Master Bredych. If we are...together, this is something you must understand. Would I rather you be more than just useful? Yes, but if you don't stop smothering me, that is all you will be to me. Useful."

She turned to the nearest guardsman who bowed deeply before she had a chance to remove the scarf around her head. "I require my personal physician to meet me in my chambers. Alone."

The man bowed once more before ringing a bell at the gate. At a slower pace than she had used walking through her city, Margaret walked towards the castle doors. Her heart begged her to wait for Leolin or glance behind her to see if he were following, but what the woman in her wanted, the queen would not allow.

12

257 Sharimus 5ᵗʰ — The Senate Isle

An image of Alesta Castle's interior hovered in the air as sweat dripped down Anur's face. There was a time when using such magics was no different from drawing breath, but now every minute he watched the Alexandrians rebuild was one minute too many. His hands trembled as he waited.

Seeing the young man leave the queen's chambers without her raised many questions in Anur's mind, questions he filed away for later. He could open a picture into her private rooms, but he held back from the intrusion. At least for the time being...

When Margaret stepped into the hallway, she held parchment before her like a shield. Anur lifted his hands and tilted them, cutting the space between them until the parchment floated before him.

It was blank, and he cursed.

His legs quavered, forcing him to lean against the shelf behind him, and when his heartbeat quickened, he released the image. The magic's rush to return to him knocked him to his knees, a position he remained in as Agaia rounded the corner.

Anur knelt in a hallway much like the one in Alesta Castle, though its stone walls were much older. Formed by magics long lost to the Thirteen, they too showed their age in the cracks and lines that worked their way from floor to ceiling. A single row of brick ran along the bottom of the wall, and a few stuck out at odd corners.

"Humbling, isn't it?" Agaia asked.

Rather than use her offered hand, Anur stood, his knees protesting audibly. The ligament alongside his knee throbbed, and he bit back a wince as he eyed one of the loose bricks. "I refuse to believe this theory that we are dying. I am not one of these bricks to crumble to dust."

"When death herself is gone, one has to wonder how much longer we have."

The reminder of Itovah's loss curdled his stomach. "Everything comes down to that family. Before them—"

Agaia laughed. "Before them magic was still fading. We were still aging, still weakening. Perhaps it's our time, Anur. Nothing lives forever." She plucked a hair from his head, a white hair so thin he squinted to see it, and she stretched it out between her two index fingers. "Our lives have been long, my brother, but not infinite."

"You pulled a hair from my scalp to tell me that?"

"Upon first glance, this single thread is smooth and strong. Easy to navigate, much like our lives these many, many years." Agaia pulled the hair at both ends, not enough to break it but stretch it and when she released one end, the hair crinkled into a loose ball of spirals. "With enough complications, even something straight becomes wrinkled."

"How does one family complicate the very fabric of existence enough to destroy us?"

Another laugh, though this one held a sharpness. "For all that the Amaskans honor you and speak of your Justice, you have a very skewed idea of it. Think of it this way. We set our feet upon this path the moment we decided to involve ourselves in the lives of mortals. Itovah always said it was a mistake to remove magic from the world and hoard it for ourselves. At the very least, we never should have created the Senate."

When she gestured for him to follow, he did though both knees ached with each step. Another Fall season meant the rains approached on their temperate island. While parts of the main continent would be scoured in snow, the Thirteen would be buffeted by seemingly nonstop rains and pressure shifts that left Anur cranky on the best of days. He followed his older sibling outside through a single door and onto a path that led towards the cliffs. The ground beneath his bare feet shifted from green grasses and moss to rocky sediment, though the rough callouses protected him from any jagged edges.

Agaia gestured at the sea below. "When I was born, Adlain said I brought light back into the world with a promise that life would always endure. If I were to fall from this cliff and die, would that promise still hold true?"

Anur shook his head, and she stepped closer to the cliff's edge. "You speak in riddles. Come back before you fall," he said.

"Do I? Think on this. When beings beyond us first walked these lands, they stumbled. They crawled and fell and rose again. Our magics shaped the world around them, but their lives were driven by their own desires. They succeeded or failed on their own merits. But when we became the Boahim Senate, we wrested away their agency and in some ways, their free will. It wasn't enough that they live by the *Thirteen* laws, but we became active enforcers of those laws. We watched their every movement in search of fault."

"And what of it? Isn't that what Justice is about? Ensuring that everyone lives rightly?"

"When Itovah died…"

Anur frowned. "Was murdered."

"When she ceased to walk in this realm, I watched for I was curious. Would death cease to be without the Goddess of Death?" When he rolled his eyes, she wagged a finger at him. "That's the problem with you, little brother. You see life as a series of absolutes. Right or wrong. Just or unjust. But the world is never that simple."

She spread her hands out before her and touched them to the rocks below. A tendril of light snaked its way from her fingers into the ground, and it trembled before a green sprig shot up between a crack. A few leaves erupted from strong limbs, and Agaia's arms shuddered in response. Her normally youthful skin roughened as each new branch carved lines across her face, and her breath grew haggard.

"Stop!" shouted Anur, but she shook her head.

"Look at it."

He glanced at the plant as its growth slowed. "It's alive."

Her skin grayed with the loss of magic, and she pointed a finger at the blossoming sapling. "Really…look."

Anur leaned in until his nose nearly touched the tree's trunk. The energy she poured into the plant had created it, but her light stopped at the root. Nothing of Agaia flowed through the sapling itself. When he lifted his head, she cut off the magic and crumpled to her knees. It was his turn to offer his hand, though she no more took the offered assistance than he had. Stubborn fools they all were.

"Without Itovah, I had expected death to cease, but people, creatures, and even plants continued to die. This tree will continue to grow long after I am gone." She dusted bits of rock and dirt from her skirt with shaking hands. "We may have created this world, but it no longer needs us. It no more needs our magic or our wisdom, and *that* is why we are dying."

"We taught them too well."

This laugh was a light chuckle as she smiled at him. "That we did, my brother. That we did."

"So all is lost then? We are destined to die and leave the world we created behind?"

Agaia wrapped her hand around the sapling and snapped the trunk in half. The top half rolled over the cliff and into the ocean below. "I have no intention of leaving this realm empty handed, my brother."

When he met her gaze, her green eyes sparked as she smiled. It was a cold smile of fury and contempt and nothing like the life that normally warmed her features. She gave a small tug, uprooting the sapling in one go.

"All that wasted energy," he said as she tossed it over the cliffside. "I think this is why we die."

"Like most things in this land, it served its purpose. I have no doubt that I am destined to die and probably soon, but you were correct about one thing. When Itovah made the Poncett family her little project, she opened the door for our lives to shift. Margaret beheading Itovah hastened whatever path we were meant to tread. It was never going to stop with one death. How could it? But if I'm to die, I will take that spoiled princess with me."

"How do you plan to do so? Every magic we use only weakens us further, and with the orbs destroyed—"

"There are many ways to walk a path, Anur, but all of them are traveled by Farimun."

Anur gasped. "He'll never help you. He's wanted nothing to do with this war from the start."

Agaia wagged her finger at him again. "Perhaps, but he also loves being alive. What would any of us do to keep breathing?"

"Assuming he'll help you reach Alesta, then what? How mortal are we, sister? Are you willing to be run through with a guardsman's sword to find out?" he asked.

"Better than sitting here comparing myself to crumbling bricks."

She strode past him as if she were thirty and not many eons in age. While his body wanted nothing more than a hot bath and a nap, her rage fueled her in a way he couldn't replicate and he swore.

"What will we do with Sharmus? He failed to kill the queen," he called out, and she paused at the stone archway leading indoors.

The Goddess of Life disappeared into the shadows as she strode inside, but her voice carried to his ears as if she stood beside him. "What does one do with traitors?"

The words sent goosepimples across his skin, a reaction he couldn't remember ever having before, and he shivered beneath the sun. When it ceased to warm him, he trudged inside where he found one of the loose bricks had been pried out of the wall and set on a nearby table. Anur picked it up, bits of dust coating his hand. For all its rounded edges, its center was strong and he cursed again.

At this rate, the brick would outlive them all.

Anur shuffled down the hall in search of that bath...

Drehsma, Capital City of Shad

KING HAVIN BAJIT ground his teeth as he resisted the urge to throw another cup across his audience chamber. The orbs had managed to kill two more of the Thirteen, but not as many as Queen Margaret had implied, nor had the attempt killed Sharmus.

The god had grown to be a reminder that Havin controlled less of his kingdom than he wished. Every time he thought to rid himself of the Poncett family, Sharmus's face would appear in a mirror's reflection in the hallway or the god's shadow would cross the room as Havin settled into bed.

Healing was never all that important to Havin, being a man of pain and control. Prior to the meeting with that Poncett woman, Sharmus meant nothing to him. A senator meant even less.

But now...

He flung his arm out to sweep the mug and several papers from the table beside him. As they landed on the stone floor, the woman who waited before him flinched but remained silent. A nearby servant retrieved the cup and returned it along with the contracts he'd unsettled to the table before blotting up the spilled wine.

"You're still here?" asked Havin, and the woman paled. Her red hair lacked luster, probably because of her dependence upon *perin* if the dark, hollow circles under her eyes were an indication. He shook his hand in her general direction and stared at the wall behind her.

The woman gave a brief bow. "Your Majesty, I come before you in hopes your mystics can help me. The pain in my...."

Movement towards the back of the room caught Havin's attention as a shadow took form. At first he thought it Sharmus again, but when the form stepped closer to the light, Rajami's scraggly beard and blue eyes came into view.

"Leave," Havin said to the woman. She uttered a few more words, and when his gaze met hers, she stumbled from the room.

He snapped his fingers in the direction of a servant. "Clear the room. Except for Rajami."

The line of people waiting for a moment of his time

followed the servant from the room without complaint, then the servant and guards followed. Alone with the *Tribor* leader, Havin refilled his cup but made no move to offer any to Rajami.

The bulky man strode toward him and stopped an inch short of insulting before he gave the briefest of bows. "Your Majesty."

"What brings you before me, Rajami?" Whatever it was had better be important.

"It's this truce, Your Majesty. This deal with the Alexandrians."

Havin sipped his wine and scowled. "Go on."

"I-I get the pact with the rest of the Little Dozen Kingdoms, but when your father pledged his support to the *Tribor*, certain promises were made, promises not being upheld by…Your Majesty."

He pursed his lips together but said nothing. Better to make the man say it.

Rajami shifted his weight from one foot to the next. "My people have sent me here to ask if Your Majesty is planning to keep his word to rid us of the Poncett family."

"And I told you that with this pact, that is now your task to fulfill."

"We can't get close to her! She's protected at all times—"

Havin grinned. "Now we get to the true purpose of your visit. Whether or not your people can succeed in killing someone is a reflection on you and your leadership, isn't it? Last we spoke, I explained to you why this task falls on you. You swore to me you could handle the responsibility. Has that changed?"

"No, Your Majesty, but I can't kill someone I can't get close to! My men die in the trying. Many would rather let her live than toss body after body on what many new recruits see as a fruitless task. They don't understand the history—"

"It sounds as if you have a problem with your recruitment techniques. If you can't keep your men in check, that is a problem. A *you* problem. I take it your people are displeased with *your* inability to keep *your* promise, great god killer?" When Rajami flinched, Havin's laughter filled the empty room. "Did you think word wouldn't reach me of your new proclaimed title? What was it, 'The Great God Killer of Shad'? I would think eliminating a queen would be simple for someone with such a grand title."

"You said I killed a god—"

"And you did, but only because of the orb's magic. The servant in the hallway outside could have risen to such a task with the same conclusion. Rajami, you succeed because I allow you to succeed, because I provide you with the means of success. Without me and mine, the *Tribor* would have dwindled into nothing more than rumor, dark tales told at night to keep children from misbehaving. My father's money put food in your belly and weapons in your hands, but it was me that guided and united the *Tribor*, not you. Do not think for one instant that I can't replace you. Every last one of you is expendable, understand?"

For all his great frame, Rajami shrank in on himself as he cowered before Havin. "Then help me, Your Majesty. Help *us*."

Bajit sighed. The man had outlived his usefulness if he could no longer find his way to a plan or idea, but replacing him would wait. At least for now. "I can't harm Queen Margaret. She is an ally in our fight against the Thirteen, and I am sworn to protect her as well as any member of the Little Dozen Kingdoms—" When Rajami opened his mouth, Havin held up his hand. "However, if I were wishing to gain an *audience* with Her Majesty, I might begin by *observing* her movements."

"We've done that, Your Majesty. She's never alone."

"We both know that to be false, do we not? Was it not last year that she began moving about the city in her sister's clothes?"

"She's not done that since your army attacked Alesta."

"We both know that's a lie as well. Lying to me will get your neck strung up in a noose, Rajami, if you're lucky."

"I…I wasn't aware."

"But you were. Your man, Till."

Rajami winced. "He failed. I didn't realize he'd caught her about the city."

"To be taken down by a woman so easily. What happened to the mighty *Tribor*?" Havin shook his head. "Does the queen not help with the rebuilding of her kingdom? Does she not still walk among her vassals?"

"With your magic, you could—"

"No." Havin slammed his cup on the table, its contents sloshing on his fingers. He brushed them across his silk pants, leaving wet fingerprints across the fabric. "I cannot break the pact."

Rajami shook his head. "It wouldn't be the first time you've broken a promise."

Heat gathered in Havin's eyes, turning his vision slightly red as he stared at Rajami. Greater men had fallen before the look he gave, but the god killer stood his ground, and Havin lifted a single hand which glowed, sickly green flames flicking across his skin. The magic wouldn't harm its user, but the *Tribor* recognized it for what it was and stumbled backward.

Rather than allow it to dissipate, Havin stood and with a blink, closed the distance between them. "I will put this simply since your brain can't conceive of why the little queen's death falls to you. Sharmus has bound me, bound all rulers of the Little Dozen into this pact. Bound by magic. By the words of a god. If I so much as think an ill thought in her direction, he is here. In this castle. I can't break the bonds upon me.

Believe me I have tried. If you want a specific someone dead, you will have to do it yourself."

The man glanced around the room, his eyes wide with fear. "He's here now?"

"Not currently, you fool." At least not to his knowledge. Havin refrained from glancing at the mirror that hung on the wall to his left. "Once the Thirteen have been dealt with, I have no qualms about dealing with those still plaguing me, as well as rewarding those who have been loyal. Do not mistake the boon you are owed as an opportunity to treat me as an equal. The *Tribor* exist only because I allow them to exist."

He held his glowing hand before Rajami's as sweat trickled down the *Tribor*'s face. "If I decide it, the *Tribor* will fall into memory and nothing more. Understand?"

"Yes, Your Majesty."

The glow faded, and Havin pointed a finger at Rajami. "If you watch someone long enough, they will always betray a weakness. Sometimes eliminating the weakness is where to begin."

"The *Amaskan*'s boy."

"Perhaps. As I said, the job falls to you, 'Great God Killer.'"

Rajami gave a final bow, this one properly repentant and solemn, before he retreated. A moment later, Havin's servant returned, and he gestured him over. "Send word to my field marshal. I wish to speak to the *Tribor* known as Shandar."

Perhaps it was time the *Tribor* had a new leader. Someone capable of more than a single thought.

When he glanced to his left, light green eyes stared back at him from a face full of disappointment. The way it flickered, it could have been his father's face, but the chin's curve was wrong. Magic hummed briefly as he found himself unable to move.

"Harm no one." It was a mere whisper in his ear, but the words left Bajit covered in a cold sweat.

Once motion returned to his body, he fled the room for a small guest room down the hall, one that had been stripped of all furniture and decoration, the exception being a single, simple bed. Havin crawled into it like a child and hid beneath the covers until his body stopped shaking.

If anyone wondered where their king was for the next few candlemarks, they didn't wonder it aloud. Had they, magic would have flowed through the castle.

He couldn't kill anyone, but Sharmus had said nothing about torture....

13

When Margaret sought out the *Amaskan*, he was not in the gardens, nor in his rooms. No one in the castle had seen him since the day before, and a tight knot gripped her stomach. Had he decided to return to the Order? Perhaps travel there with Leolin? If Bredych had left Alesta, she would be on her own, and the thought both terrified and thrilled her.

She strode through each of the castle's four floors, making mental notes of her plans as she walked. Eight of the Thirteen remained. Shattering the orbs should have killed more of them, but she had planned for the inevitable. Messages sent between the other rulers meant her contingency plans had contingency plans. She reached into the pocket of her pants for the slip of parchment and brushed her fingers against it. One messenger pigeon from her, and each ruler would send messages directly to the Boahim Senate.

Knowing that a full third of her army could detect magic

and possibly use it created more possibilities with regards to battling the Thirteen.

The Shadian army's withdrawal meant more people returned to their homes. This freed up space for the wounded to obtain the privacy of one of the castle's guest rooms. Despite this, a few wounded lay in cots across the castle's first floor, and she still found her walks hindered by folks who sought a moment of her time.

If only that privacy applied to her time as well.

People still stared at her jaw when they spotted the brand Till had given her. He had joked that he was marking her an *Amaskan*, and while the circle still smarted, she slept better at night with her new "tattoo." Of late, she felt closer to Adelei and Bredych than she did those around her. Bredych saw the potential in her and recognized the skills she possessed. Few in Alesta did, though the new mark certainly made them think again about their knowledge of their queen.

Once clear of the castle interior, she continued towards the castle walls until she reached the stables, where a wrinkled hand grabbed her arm. Margaret leaned into the motion, bending her body sideways at the hips and twisting to wrench herself free. She held her dagger in front of her, gaze traveling from the wrinkled hand that grabbed her to the face connected to it.

The corners of Bredych's mouth twitched in response, and he said, "Next time, don't wait so long to arm yourself."

Margaret nodded towards the saddle bag on the ground at his feet. "Are you leaving?"

A shadow darkened the doorway, followed shortly by Leolin. "It's mine. I'd hoped to be on my way by now, but Bredych had some suggestions on where to look for the mystic, Doughal Nilesh, if he isn't still with the Order." He scooped up the saddlebag. "I'll carry Bredych's letter with me, Your Majesty. With hope I'll return with more than just information and memories." His gaze settled on her jaw for a moment before he gave a short bow and ducked back through the stable doors.

Part of her longed to follow him, to make up an excuse why she needed *his* help and not Bredych's so he might not leave her, but his leaving was for the best. What they both needed was time and distance. Instead, she said, "When you have a moment, Bredych, I need your assistance."

When his footsteps followed hers, she strode away from the castle proper and into the small garden near the castle's rear walls where she claimed a seat on a small, wooden bench. Bredych sat beside her in silence, though his fingers tapped an odd rhythm along his thigh.

A variety of vegetables thrived in the garden beds, despite some charred rubble ruining an otherwise perfect garden, and she frowned. "Even the smallest garden was marred by the Shadian army. That they were able to breach so close to the castle...it's a wonder they didn't overrun us completely."

"It was a very near thing, Your Majesty."

She bent over to run her fingers along the round stones that lined the garden, and her fingers came away dirty with soot. "When the rulers of the Little Dozen met at the Pass, we discussed what to do if breaking the orbs wasn't enough. I think we knew it would not solve our problem and rid us of the Thirteen."

When he didn't praise her for her estimations, she suppressed a frown. Perhaps it was good for Leolin to leave as she had grown too accustomed to his small encouragements and empty platitudes.

"The problem before us is the same. How do we kill a god? Our known means of doing so is lost to us, so we must find another method to destroy them."

Still he remained silent, choosing instead to continue drumming his fingers on his leg.

"We need a way to measure how mortal they are. If you were to stab one with a sword, would they bleed and die like we would, or would it take something extreme such as a beheading? Or does it require a magical catalyst, like we had with the orbs?" This time, when he said nothing to answer her, she pursed her lips together. "Say something."

"What would you have me say?"

"You could begin with your thoughts."

Bredych shook his head. "You aren't interested in those, Your Majesty." When she furrowed her brows and stared at him, he sighed. "During your time at the Pass, you tasted what it was like to carry power. To hold information that others needed and use it in a way that gave you some semblance of control over the future. It's intoxicating, that control. Not just that but being able to direct others as you see fit, knowing they have little choice in the matter if they wish to live."

"That's...that's not what it was like—"

"The Little Dozen Kingdoms are facing an unprecedented future. A world without the Thirteen. If they refuse to defeat the Thirteen, these rulers will die and likely their families with them. You traveled to the Pass under the guise of seeking their help, but what you really needed was for them to do as they were told. You needed them to murder the Thirteen for you through the orbs."

Margaret's face grew hot. "I gave them a choice!"

"But was there a real choice to be made? Your people fought for their lives so that you might tell these rulers the truths you'd learned, truths that left them no choice at all. Kill or be killed. I'm not saying it was the wrong decision, Your Majesty, not at all. If it had been me, I would have come to the same conclusion, but I'm no king. I'm *Amaskan*."

He touched a single finger to the brand on her jaw, and she flinched. It had ceased hurting weeks ago when the scabs had fallen off to reveal the circle that would forever mark her skin.

"Perhaps you are closer in your heart to my Order than you are to the crown you wear," he said. If it was intended as a compliment, his face gave no indication.

"I spent my morning roaming the castle in search of you, my *sepier*, for advice, for your assistance as I have need of your particular skills on this day, and instead you assault me with guilt." She pointed at his fingers that lightly strummed against the fabric of his pants. "You obviously have something on your mind, so please, say it."

Bredych's fingers stilled. "Why did you seek me out?" he asked.

"For your help."

"Leolin's leaving today and depending upon how your plans proceed, you may never see him again, correct?"

She nodded, but when she opened her mouth to speak, he claimed one of her hands.

"Queen you may be in name, but name alone. While you were gone, your own citizens planned to maneuver your throne out from under you, and the first opportunity you have now to make decisions for your people, you come running to us for what you claim is aid, but in reality you wish for us to reassure you that your plan is the correct path. To absolve you of the guilt that comes with possibly sending folks to their deaths. I saw the look in your eyes when that boy in your army...Stefan, when he asked if we would win."

"You mean when I had to lie to him? To pretend he isn't going to be one of the first to die?"

"Exactly that, Your Majesty. Leading is *hard*. You are absolutely sending that boy to his death and yes, if need be, you will lie to him and do it again in order to make him believe that he is dying for a lofty cause."

She shook her head. "That's unacceptable."

"And that is why we are losing this war before it has begun. You have to *believe* we will win. You have to make *us* believe we will win. Your father sent many men and women to their deaths in the *Little War of Three,* and he did it without pause. Leading others requires you to *lead* them. Stand by your decisions and all that comes with them."

Margaret leapt to her feet, wresting her hand away from his. "The gall of you all. I don't wish for others to tell me what to do—I certainly don't need another man presuming to know my mind—but your counsel is something I'm wise to seek, am I not? My own father shared his mind with his advisors daily, so why am I not given the same courtesy?"

"If you were that man, I would agree, but you are not your father. You are a young, untested queen who has a history of relying on others to point her in the direction she should go. Leolin's leaving and your first action is to seek me out. I only ask that you examine why, Your Majesty. If you truly need advice, I will give it, but not in this."

She turned away from him so he would not see her bite her inner cheek.

"Leading others can be a very lonely path, Your Majesty. One fraught with second guessing oneself and the guilt that comes with the consequences of one's actions."

"If anyone would know guilt, it would be you," she snapped.

"Indeed."

When he touched her shoulder, she shrugged off his hand. "You are my *sepier*. If I order you to return to the Order, you will do so. If I order you to stay, you will do so. If I ask your opinion on something, you will give it. If following my orders is a problem for you or anyone else, you are welcome to head for the border. Perhaps another ruler will be more accommodating."

She glanced over her shoulder to see his reaction, but he was already gone, and she frowned. It wasn't until she reached the castle proper that both his meanings hit her.

Looking for his reaction made him correct about her ratio-nale, and second, by ordering him to do what she asked, he had caused the very shift in her he had wished to see.

"Damn," she whispered.

257 Sharimus 7th

IF ANYONE HAD questions about why their queen resembled a storm cloud that midday, they kept their tongues in check as Margaret roamed the hallways, alternating between checking on the wounded and muttering to herself. Once she had exhausted her temper, she returned to her private study and sent for a stack of parchment.

The first document she wrote left her hand shaking and her face flushed warm as it was a letter asking a favor of the Amaskans.

> *I know not your name, only that to the Amaskans, you are called Miriam. Though if I listen to Master Bredych, your title is now Grand Master. I hope this letter finds you and your Order as well as can be expected during these complicated times. In the seasons I've spent with your former Grand Master, I've come to better appreciate your Order's purpose and why such a group was created.*

> *The Boahim Senate's measure of justice leaves much to be desired. Since learning that our senators are indeed the Thirteen, I've found myself wishing for someone to hold them accountable for the many deaths and atroci-ties they have caused through the years.*

The Little Dozen Kingdoms' rulers, myself included, have agreed that the Thirteen is a threat that cannot be overlooked, and as such, we have sought to rid our world of these gods we no longer need. We have discovered that the Thirteen are mortal, but how mortal, we have yet to determine. This is where I must beg a favor of you and your Amaskans.

I know Master Bredych has asked you to aid us in our fight by sending your people to Alexander. In the past, your people have not been safe in my kingdom, but I promise you that your people are not only welcomed but needed. Your people will be as safe as I can provide. I would ask for one more boon before you send Amaskans into my kingdom.

I do not know the location of your Order, only that it is coastal in Sadai, but being coastal, your home is nearer to the Senate Isle than Alesta. This makes you doubly qualified to do what I cannot.

Send two Amaskans to their island with all haste.

While only eight gods remain, we don't yet understand exactly how mortal they are. If two Amaskans were to sneak into the Senate halls with the purpose of killing one of the Thirteen, we might gain vital information about whether or not human weapons might injure or kill them. Knowing that we might be able to defeat them in a fair manner is critical to the future of all the Little Dozen.

I understand that whoever you send will likely die. Sending two increases the likelihood that one might escape with the information we need. If anything were to serve Justice in this world, I believe it to be this plan. The Thirteen must be stopped. Should your people kill more than one, the Little Dozen Kingdoms would be beholden to you.

I realize what I am asking, but the Book of Ja'ahr states that "When Justice hides, so must we all." Anur has done nothing to give Justice to those who have suffered at the hands of his brothers and sisters. If he is unwilling to do what is right and just, then it falls to us to uphold all that we hold sacred.

If this plan is amenable, you may send word through Master Bredych here in Alesta before traveling for our borders.

May you walk the way of the warrior.
Signed by my hand,

Queen Margaret Poncett of Alexander

After folding the parchment closed, she sealed it with wax and stamped her emblem on it before setting it aside. A messenger pigeon could deliver it to the town of Menoir for Leolin to carry to the Order. She paused long enough to steady her hand before setting her quill upon a second piece of parchment, this one addressed to the eight remaining members of the Boahim Senate. This was the letter that should have set her knees to wilt and her breath to catch. Instead, the faces of the dead flashed through her mind with each pen stroke, fueling her anger and granting her the strength to write it.

While it is my hand that writes these words upon this parchment, it is with the united voices of Boahim that I pen this.

As children we are made to memorize the Thirteen laws meant to guide our every action. We are taught that our souls are bound in this agreement, as the Thirteen themselves made us to be so. We are made to believe that the Boahim Senate, a group created and blessed by the Thirteen, will ensure Justice is made available to all who seek it and that no one can act poorly without consequence.

But these are tales made for simpler minds. Stories made to keep the people of Boahim reined in by lies and deceit.

No longer shall we be ruled by callous gods who believe themselves to be above reproach and act without care for the very people they claim to protect.

The Thirteen are mortal, this we know. You may have lived as gods once, but no longer. Rather than rip Boahim asunder a second time, we would ask the Thirteen to think of the people they once created and the love they once held for them.

We, the rulers of the Little Dozen Kingdoms, do emancipate our kingdoms and our people from the Boahim Senate. We require that the remaining Thirteen surrender to us at the Meridi Pass on 257 Luthian 28th. Those that surrender will be granted a swift, merciful death. Those who refuse can be guaranteed a punish-

ment befitting those crimes committed against Boahim's people.

By our hand,

Queen Margaret Poncett of Alexander

Having penned it, she was the first to sign, though she would not be the last. By the time this letter reached the shores of Merriwynne, it would bear the signatures of all twelve rulers in a document calling for a change not seen since the split of Boahim. With the last signature, it would arrive back in Alexander where Margaret would send it to the Senate Isle... assuming they were still alive to receive it.

If the Amaskans agreed to send their people first, there might not be a need for this portion of the plan, and she sent a silent prayer that the Order would be successful. A sigh escaped her lips when she realized what she had done. Praying to the very gods she hoped to kill felt absurd.

This message would go unsealed until it reached her again, so she moved on to writing a short note to King Adir Monsine of Sadai, who would be the first to receive this letter. He would then send it on to King Damiano Carrasco of Monpoli. The message would travel the continent until its inevitable delivery to the Thirteen.

Rather than resume praying to gods who no longer cared, she pressed two fingers to her forehead and hoped her plans succeeded. If the Thirteen lacked the magic to travel to the Pass, then the job was already done as they were likely too weak to do more harm to the people of the Little Dozen Kingdoms.

Or so Margaret hoped.

When she stood, the room tilted slightly, and she grabbed

hold of the table for support. Her stomach threatened to empty itself, and she fell back into her chair. For weeks her appetite had been off, not to mention the headaches and the slight sense that something was wrong.

At first, Margaret had believed it to be nothing more than fatigue and worry, or symptoms left over from the mild concussion she had received in her fight with Till, but the longer the sickness remained, the more it concerned her. If Leolin were here, he would have everyone from her personal physician to the mystics in her chambers in his quest to discover what plagued her.

What if she were being poisoned as her father had been?

With all the people moving about the castle these days, it would be easy enough to gain access to her person. She stared at the glass of water on the desk. After a few minutes, she picked it up and gave it a sniff.

As far as she could tell, it was only water.

But would she know if it were something else? Something sinister?

This time when she stood, she moved slowly until she reached her bedchamber. Once there, she settled onto her bed and rang the bell for her handmaiden.

"Have Roland attend me," said Margaret as she closed her eyes.

If she were being poisoned, better to know now before it was too late. Images of her late father rippled across her mind, and her eyelids flew open. This was his bed, the place where he spent the remainder of his days in brutal agony. Now she lay upon it in the throes of something unknown.

She leapt from the bed, her bare feet standing on the cold stone floor. Whatever this was, she would confront it as she planned to confront the Thirteen: on her feet.

"You think you're being poisoned?" Roland's gaunt features were pulled tighter across his face as he frowned at Margaret.

For all that he had been her father's personal physician, close was not a word she would use to describe their relationship. She trusted that the man understood the body and how to treat a great many illnesses, but something about the way he tilted his head when he stared at her gave her the distinct impression that he did not believe her. Or perhaps he did not accept that she was a grown woman now, a woman in charge of an entire kingdom. Some days, she did not believe it herself, yet the more she thought on it, the more she was convinced that something was wrong.

"Leolin was convinced it was fatigue and the stress of the battle with the Shadians, but there's more to it than that. Nothing I eat tastes as it should, and everything makes my stomach turn. I can barely keep down water, let alone mulled wine. Fruit tastes sour on my tongue, and I wake with my head pounding like I spent the night before drinking until the sun came up. The headaches have lessened some, but some of these symptoms remind me of when my father grew ill..."

"Any dizziness?"

Margaret nodded. "Mostly when I move too quickly."

"Is there a time of day when the symptoms are worse? Morning? Night? Do they ever fade or are they constant and steady?"

"I definitely feel better as the day progresses. By night fall, I could say I almost feel normal again, though my appetite is not all that improved by the time I retire."

"Open your mouth please," said Roland. His face remained impassive as he looked at her mouth and her teeth. He raised her eyelids and then looked at her fingernails before he released her hands. "The poisons used on your father left signs on his body as the they amassed in his blood. Things like darkening and pitting of his fingernails, discoloration of his gums, and sores in the mouth. You have none of these signs."

When she opened her mouth to object, Roland wagged a finger at her. "I'm not finished, Your Majesty. I have a question for you of a personal nature. When was the last time your body cleansed itself?"

Her cheeks warmed, and she glanced at the floor. "I'm not sure what you mean."

"I realize I'm a man and that this might be the sort of information you would prefer to share with your lady in waiting or handmaids, but your body's monthly cycle is part of your health, Your Majesty. Did your body cleanse itself in Anurus or Atlinas?"

"N-no, I do not think so. It was a hard road to the Pass and back. Sometimes stress can delay such things."

Roland nodded. "It can, as can illness."

"Is it possible I'm being harmed by something different than what was used on my father?"

"Your Majesty, I suspect the reason is simpler than that. A more mundane reason if you will."

She stared at him as her thoughts ran rampant. When nothing came to her, he gave a patient, yet pained smile.

"It's not a secret that you and Leolin are close, Your Majesty. I suspect that what you are suffering from is not a poisoning but pregnancy."

Margaret glanced at her stomach. Her clothes fit more snugly than before, a fact she had attributed to her increasing swordswork and horseback riding, but the idea of being with child felt like a far off possibility, one so remote she almost laughed.

"Have you experienced any tenderness in your breasts? Fatigue after a good night's rest? Think carefully, but how many times have you missed your cleansing?"

She resisted the urge to touch her breasts, both of which

ached. The fact that she could not recall when she had last bled left her speechless.

"I thought as much." He turned to get a better look at her abdomen and nodded to himself. "What you are experiencing is normal, Your Majesty, though the nausea and dizziness should start to pass as your pregnancy progresses. If they don't, let me know immediately. Being your first child, you'll experience a host of bodily changes. If they grow too uncomfortable, let me know as there are a few herbal teas that can help soothe you. Is there anything else I can do for you?"

Pregnant. The word lay heavy on her tongue. With the Little Dozen Kingdoms' fate on her shoulders, she was somehow supposed to bring new life into the world. At any moment, the Thirteen could strike her down for her insolence, and she would never hold her child. Nor would the father.

Leolin.

He would still be within the borders of Alexander, close enough to call home with the news, but to do so would prevent him from gaining the answers he so desperately needed. No, she would bear this news alone, at least for the time being.

"Your Majesty?" Roland's hand rested on her shoulder as he studied her face. "I didn't realize this would be such a shock to you. My apologies, Your Majesty. Is there anything I can get for you? Perhaps a calming tea or—"

"No, Roland. It was a momentary shock, but I'll be fine. Women have babies every day. Some of them while the walls were falling down around Alesta. If they can manage, so can I."

"If you're sure."

Margaret waved a hand in his direction as she walked toward her bed. "I think what I need is some rest," she said as she crawled underneath the massive quilt.

She waited until the door closed behind him to rise, her

steps taking her towards the chest at the foot of the bed. The top layer held all manner of robes and scarves, which she pushed aside until she reached the thin wooden panel near the bottom. With trembling fingers, she lifted it out to expose the hidden compartment beneath.

After killing Till, her sister's silks had been cleaned as best as they could, but as Margaret lifted them from the chest, the earthy smell of blood wafted towards her, and she set them on the bed. Bredych had once told her that she didn't need to wear her sister's clothes in order to be strong, but as she wondered about the child within her and the future, the desire to be close to Adelei overwhelmed her. Margaret untied the belt that cinched her silk dress closed and allowed it to fall from her shoulders before she shed her chemise.

Naked, she saw the slight bump of her abdomen. It could be explained by bloating or any number of natural events, but when she lay hand against it, something buzzed beneath her skin. Similar and yet different from when Her Holiness had touched her.

Much closer to the feeling of peace that had settled over her when Asti had blessed her in the forest, and Margaret smiled. If she lived through this mad plan of hers, perhaps she could have the life promised to her as a young child after all. Her gaze shifted to the black clothes, and she allowed her hand to fall away from her stomach.

The Order's clothes were meant to fit tightly, to move with the body, but as Margaret pulled them on, the fabric strained across her abdomen. Adelei's frame had been leaner, lither than Margaret's, even before Margaret found herself pregnant. Fighting muscles rested on a curvier body, and she tightened the pants waistband with a strong tug. Various strips of fabric bound the wraps across the waist, ankles, and wrists, and she tucked her dark hair into the cowl on her head.

Standing before the slim mirror, a different fighter stared

back at her. She would never be Adelei, not that she wanted to be anymore, but the eyes reflected back spoke of a wisdom and strength hard won.

"Gamun would not recognize the woman before him."

His name on her lips almost soured the moment. She pushed the thought aside. He would not recognize many things about this future, a world where his former wife had killed a god... Margaret tucked her throwing knives in the *Amaskan* wraps before adding her short sword at her waist.

Mentally, a part of her strode towards the door, ready to face whatever came her way, while in reality, her feet remained rooted in her bedchamber. She walked over to the window to stare out across the rooftops. How Adelei had navigated across them with ease was a mystery to Margaret, but then, much of Adelei remained a mystery.

Her father had raised Margaret to be a queen similar to her mother, Catherine, to be the kind of woman who allowed others to think and act for her. As Margaret stared across the rooftops, she marveled that she and Adelei were so different from their mother. If their parents had lived, perhaps Margaret would still resemble the kept princess her father had wanted her to be.

But if she were going to lead the Little Dozen Kingdoms in their defeat of the Thirteen, she must be capable and strong. If she were going to be a mother, she must be able to stand on her own.

Slowly, she removed her sister's silks and tucked them back into the chest. When she returned to her dress, she placed a hand on her abdomen. Though she was marked like an *Amaskan*, an *Amaskan* she was not. She was a queen.

Adelei's silks would remain in the chest until they could be burned.

14

Traveling to the Pass to observe the Little Dozen Kingdoms had left Sharmus exhausted in ways he had never known before. It wasn't just that his knees ached while walking as if he were some infirm mortal, but every joint in his body throbbed as if the very bones inside of him were crumbling like dust, one speck at a time. It was agonizingly slow, and a part of him wished that if he were dying, his body would hurry up and do it.

At first, he had spent days abed, hiding in a small cave on their island. At one point, the small hideaway had been a place of solace for him, a space to escape the cacophony that was life in his family's hall. Something about the cave muted all the voices and gave him peace from all the ants that crawled their way across what was once Boahim.

He supposed it was unfair to think of them that way. They weren't ants but people, yet the exhaustion that weighed upon his mind left him uncharitable. When he had enough energy to rise from his bed and come out of hiding, the return to his family's hall weighed as heavily upon him as the lack of magic within him.

If he had needed to heal a someone's wound, he could... probably, but anything more than a person or two was beyond him, and the knowledge both scared and saddened him. Anur had been the one to warn Sharmus that his sister, Agaia, searched for him, and after a moment or two in his personal library, the planning had begun. Very little in his room would fit in his satchel, so he limited himself to two sets of clothes, a necklace Luthia had made for him eons ago, and two books. Everything else would remain behind.

Every other Luthday, a ship arrived at their dock to deliver supplies sent from the Little Dozen Kingdoms. For now, those deliveries continued, but as word spread about who the senators were, some kingdoms, if not all, would stop their dues, so Sharmus needed to act quickly if he were to escape.

Three days prior, Sharmus had "taken a walk," one that had just so happened to lead him to the docks. Once there, he stowed his satchel inside an old basket in the small hut nearby. Task one accomplished, he remained as hidden as possible, eating alone long after the others had gone to bed for what passed as sleep these days for the Thirteen. The fatigue in him grew as he only slept a candlemark or two a night, and by the time Luthday arrived, he walked on sharp knives of pain and fear.

For many years, food was little more than a curiosity or indulgence, certainly not something required to nourish them, but as their immortality waned, Sharmus found food a necessity, as did the rest of the Thirteen. While his brothers and sisters broke their fast, he sneaked into the kitchens to stuff dried fruits and jerky into a smaller bag he carried. Enough for a picnic if anyone were to stop him and ask. No servants dared, and with his family in the dining hall, there was no one to stop him.

His hand rested on the back door when the scuttling of shoes on the stone floor stopped him. When he turned around, expecting Agaia, it was Luthia who stood in kitchens. As usual, she said nothing, only looked on him with her dark brown eyes. Her normally bright smile was gone as she spotted the satchel he held. When he opened his mouth to explain, she rushed forward and pressed a finger to his lips.

"Go."

In the eons of time they had existed in the world together, she had never spoken a direct word to him. It was said that she whispered dust into form and sang Adlain into being, but time had once again taken her voice and returned her to the silent being she once had been. To hear her speak was to hear the world sigh, and Sharmus rested a hand against her face.

Her skin was parchment, yet he would miss the touch of it, and she gave him a sad smile, followed by a small push towards the door. He opened it slowly to keep its hinges from squeaking, and when he glanced over his shoulder, Luthia was gone.

Without another look back, Sharmus walked down the rear steps as quickly as he dared and out the gate to the trail that led to the coast. He would need to reach the ship before it docked so that he might stow away on board before the sailors rang the bell to alert the servants of their arrival.

Throughout all of time, there were moments when one of the Thirteen had hidden away in some place of their own, but each stay had been brief. Delorcini had even walked among her people now and again. Not one had left the island with the intention of never returning, and a few tears trickled down Sharmus's face.

Since when had he been one to cry? When had any of

them? Each day meant another step into mortality, and with it, aches and emotions anew. By the time Sharmus reached the docks, the ship was casting ashore, its captain on deck. Sharmus waved at him before he stepped inside the hut to retrieve his satchel.

"Senator Raj! We weren't expecting you down here," called the captain.

"I'm taking a small trip to Lavi, if you don't mind having me on board on your return sail."

The captain shook his head. "Having you aboard would be an honor, I'm sure. Will anyone else be joining you?"

"Just me, I'm afraid, though please don't say anything to the others. I have a surprise in mind, and I would not have them know and spoil it." Sharmus forced himself to smile at the captain. The man had no clue the irony of his words, and Sharmus hoped his family would not seek retribution against the good captain for ferrying their brother to the mainland.

Sharmus held out his bags for a young lad to take. The captain barked an order, and the lad scurried off to tuck his belongings somewhere below deck. When Sharmus walked across the gangway and onto the ship, his knees shook, and the captain held out a hand to steady him.

"Getting your sea legs can take some time. You'll have 'em just in time for us to reach land again." The captain let loose a hearty laugh, and Sharmus joined him to keep the man from realizing it wasn't the sea that shook him.

"If you don't mind, I have quite the headache. Perhaps too much ale last night. I think I might see myself to my quarters while the supplies are unloaded."

The captain nodded and ordered a sailor to guide Sharmus down into the ship. Sharmus had lied about the headache, but being below deck, relief flooded through him. Being away from peering eyes meant he could release the magic disguising his hooves.

With frequent trips to their island, unloading would take a candlemark or two, and then he would be *safer*. In no way did Sharmus believe his leaving made him *safe*, not with his siblings ready to destroy all of Boahim in order to remain living. But being away from them would help. They would not necessarily know where he was going or why. They might think him sulking in his small cave.

They would never think him capable or willing to seek asylum with the Amaskans.

257 Sharimus 17th — Sadain Desert

TRAVELING to Sadai meant following one road if the traveler wished to remain alive, at least once over the Sadai border, for the Sadain Desert washed half the kingdom in seemingly never-ending sand. The heat alone could make one hallucinate, and without a well-marked road as a guide, a traveler could die of thirst before reaching the capital city of Aruna.

If an actual road had ever existed, shifting sand had long since buried it, but round pillars as tall as a small building were interspersed at regular intervals between the border and major cities of Sadai, set in place long ago when the Little Dozen Kingdoms were still united as Boahim.

How they remained in place after so many years had baffled many scholars, and as Leolin touched one with a gloved hand, the barest hint of magic sent a tingle through his hand. Or at least Leolin assumed it to be magic as his hand warmed like he held it over a fire pit.

Much like Adelei had done, Leolin traveled alone, but unlike her, it was a journey he had never taken. He relied heavily on notes from Bredych as he journeyed not toward Aruna but to the Order itself. Various shrubs and dry brush had begun to appear the day before as he approached the desert's edge at the foot of the Sadain Mountains. His horse remained stabled in the last town he had passed where it would remain until his return. Rather than a horse, he had crossed the desert on a *gachia*, a pack beast native to Sadai and well versed in traveling the desert. He nudged his *gachia* forward with the promise that soon they would reach the Anan River and with it, fresh water. While the beast could make it across the desert without water, Leolin could not. Squeezing water from Mayai plants left his arms sore and his temper sorer, not to mention how it slowed down their progress.

Before crossing the border, Leolin had stopped in Tarmsworth, the hometown of his late father. While the mayors had changed, some documentation stored in the town hall noted a few details about Leolin's family. His father, Samuhel Banach, had run the town's inn before his death, presumably while reporting back to the Order. Population records show that his mother, living under the name of Shara Baudin, had lived with Sam for a time. Sometime after Leolin's birth, Shara ceased showing up in the records. It was thought that she had left town, leaving Leolin in the care of his father.

The records were the same ones Bredych had found, including those eight years later stating that the woman named Shara had returned. The town guards were called one evening after a struggle at Sam's room at his inn. Shara was reported to have defended herself against Sam, who had beaten her for trying to leave. She had claimed that Sam had beaten her and Leolin regularly, though Leolin had no memories of it. When she pushed Sam away, he fell and hit his head, which killed him.

His body was discovered with a triangle on his ankle, a known mark of the *Tribor*. While the guardsmen were surprised to find it, they admitted that Sam was a quiet man. It was noted that he could have been *Tribor,* and no one would have known.

Two retired guardsmen still living in Tarmsworth remembered Shara and Sam, though they couldn't speak to whether the relationship was as volatile as Shara claimed. They figured Shara had another man and was looking for an excuse to leave again, this time with her son. Other than that, they remembered little, and Leolin left the town with no additional information.

With both parents *Amaskan*, any information as to their real names and family details would be at the Order. With hope along with details as to what the mystic had done to erase Leolin's memories.

Leolin's thoughts shifted from his mother to Margaret, and he pursed his lips as his mount continued picking his way across the sand. He wanted to trust in Margaret's abilities, but the way she threw herself into danger was enough to drive anyone mad.

In the distance, the air shimmered, and Leolin thought it the river's mouth until the effect moved closer to him. It grew in size as it approached, and Leolin dismounted and drew his sword. Whatever it was moved swiftly until ten paces before him where it stopped, *it* being a good choice of word as he stared at the creature whose movements had stirred up the sand.

Much taller than a barn cat, its head would easily reach Leolin's chest, and he was a tall man. The size of a small melon, its head featured large, intelligent eyes that blinked at him with a calm Leolin didn't feel. Other than its size, it moved like a cat as it sat on its haunches a stone's throw from him.

Then it smiled.

Or that was what it looked like if a cat could smile. With

canine teeth as long as Leolin's thumb, he gripped his sword's hilt all the harder. Beside him, his *gachia* snorted but did not bolt or rear. Head held high, the mount was alert but not as concerned as Leolin.

"You can put down the swo*rr*d," said the creature.

Leolin took a step backward but did not return his sword to its sheath. This creature was something magical, something of myth if it could speak to him, and he pressed two fingers to his forehead in brief prayer. The gesture was futile considering he had no one to pray to, but he made it just in case.

"Have you neve*rr* hea*rr*d of the g*rr*eat *Chathula*?"

"The what?" asked Leolin.

"Dea*rr* Alishe*rr*, save us from the two-legged beasts who blunde*rr* th*rr*ough the wo*rr*ld so igno*rr*ant."

"Who's Alisher?"

"A goddess of many g*rr*eat things, none of which you would unde*rr*stand. But you waste time. I b*rr*ing a wa*rr*ning. You a*rr*e about to be attacked."

Leolin shook his head. "Wait, I've never heard of Alisher. Is she one of the Thirteen?—"

Before he could blink, the creature reached out and swatted Leolin's leg. "Pay attention! You a*rr*e about to be attacked! You need to *rr*un fo*rr* the wate*rr*s, I think you call it a lake?"

"What are you? Why—"

Another swat, this one with a claw which left a tear in his breeches and a light trail of blood across his skin. With trembling hands, he pointed his sword at the cat-like creature. "Wound me again, and I'll repay the favor." Leolin glanced around him but the sand remained sand. Nothing moved nearby that he could see.

Before he could respond, his *gachia* snorted, a sharp, explosive sound from his nostrils as he pulled on the lead in an attempt to draw closer to the mystical creature. Leolin leapt on the *gachia*'s back and urged him forward with a swift kick. Whatever or whoever was hiding worried his mount enough that he set off at a full-out run, his wide, furry feet sending sand flying.

The *chathula* dashed ahead of them. It should not have been possible, but the cat-like creature easily outpaced the *gachia*. When Leolin tried to lead his mount in the direction he thought the lake lay, the *gachia* ignored him, obediently falling in line behind the *chathula*. Something whizzed by Leolin's ear and he ducked, leaning as close to the saddle's pommel as he could. When the second object flew by, it embedded itself in a nearby rock. Thundering hoofbeats echoed nearby, and he risked a glance over his shoulder where two men whipped their horses nearly bloody to pull up alongside Leolin's mount.

Leolin released his hold on the reins and moved to unsheathe his sword when one man tossed another blade at him.

It should have hit him.

He would have placed odds that the blade would hit him square in the chest, but instead a green mist sprang up in front of him, and the blade fell to the sand below. A moment later, the mist dissipated. One of the men pointed at Leolin and shouted something in the old tongue.

Bhaghodi. Traitor.

Either that or an evil doer, but it mattered little as the intent was clear. If they had not wanted to kill him before, they certainly did now as one man slowed his horse enough to drop back and ride around to Leolin's left. With both men flanking him, he glanced ahead to see they were attempting to drive him back out into the desert and away from the lake.

You must get to the lake.

The voice in his head was calm if not a smidge out of breath. Leolin blinked as he tried to steer his *gachia* to the right. Who had spoken? Was it one of the Thirteen or this Alisher the *chathula* had spoken of?

Stop worrying about that and outrun these fools!

With a smirk and a small pinch of fear, Leolin glanced back and forth between the two men. Neither carried a sword, just the small throwing blades. *Whatever you are, I hope you can do that green misty thing again*, he thought while the man on the left readied to throw one. It was a risk, but Leolin stabbed at the man. The blade tore a nice gash in the man's arm, but he did not drop the throwing knife. Instead, he grinned and threw it directly at Leolin's head.

Leolin twisted in the saddle and felt a sharp sting as one sharp edge left a small cut across his cheek. No green mist appeared, and Leolin's heart beat in rapid count with the *gachia*'s hoofbeats. If he hadn't dodged, Margaret would be lacking a lieutenant.

He could smell the water before he saw it and thought the lake lay further ahead, but as his *gachia* crested a sand dune, the lake was almost within reach. The *chathula* stood at the shore, her body emitting a green glow as she hissed. Leolin's mount didn't stop. He kept running until his feet met water, stopping so abruptly that Leolin slammed his chin against the *gachia*'s tall neck.

Despite the pain that shook him, he sat up, sword in hand, but the two men remained on the desert sand as they muttered.

The word *bhaghodi* popped up, as did *chathula*, though the remaining words were lost to the wind.

Whoever the two men were, they knew more about the cat-creature than Leolin did. When he stepped forward, his outstretched foot stopped short. Something blocked him from leaving the river. He turned to face the cat. "Are you doing this?"

The cat didn't answer so much as snarl. Beads of sweat were sprinkled across the cat's fur.

Leolin had thought it moisture from the lake but most of the cat's fur remained dry. This was perspiration. "If you release me, I can kill these two men and save you from...the effort of whatever you're doing," he whispered to the *chathula*.

No. I can't protect you outside of the water.

More speaking in his mind. Leolin shook his head as the sensation was akin to a mild buzzing, almost like a bee bounced around in his skull. "If you keep me here, we'll slowly starve. We can't stay in the water forever. Speaking of this lake, if it gives you more power, why don't you take care of these two?"

Gladly.

The glow surrounding the cat doubled until the buzzing in Leolin's mind audibly filled the space between the river and the men, both of whom flinched as it reached them. One turned tail and ran, though his steps numbered only three before he fell to the ground like a plank of wood. Once down, he remained still. Rather than run, the second man faced the *chathula* as his body froze, his mouth open to speak. His eyes glazed over, and he fell to the dirt below.

"Inter*r*esting," the *chathula* said as the protective barrier faded. "The second human faced his death b*rr*avely *rr*athe*rr* than flee. I thought them both cowa*rr*ds."

Leolin approached their bodies slowly as he watched for any indications that they lived. When neither chest rose to draw breath, he crouched down and held his hand over the second attacker's mouth. No warmth tickled his palm. He pressed two fingers against the man's neck and felt nothing. The man who had run was as dead as the first, and Leolin turned to face the creature. "What are you?"

The creature's fur bristled as it hissed. "I will fo*rr*give you the slight, especially after taking ca*rr*e of you*rr* p*rr*oblem. I am Avishai the Fie*rr*ce, Daughte*rr* of Avi the G*rr*ave and membe*rr* of the Geutha T*rr*ibe of the Nine. I am a *chathula,* one of the g*rr*eat c*rr*eatu*rr*es f*rr*om ac*rr*oss the G*rr*eat Sea."

"Across the Harren Sea?"

Avishai blinked once and stared at Leolin. "No, the G*rr*eat Sea."

"I'm not familiar with a sea by that name."

The *chathula* blinked again, slower. "I am not su*rr*p*rr*ised. You*rr* kind is not familia*rr* with many things. We should leave this a*rr*ea."

Leolin led the *gachia* closer to the lake. "Agreed, but first, the *gachia* needs a drink." Besides, doing so would give Leolin an opportunity to better question the magic wielding creature. "I apologize for not recognizing what you are. I've never heard of your kind before. Most magic is long gone from the Little Dozen Kingdoms. I'm Leolin...of the Kingdom of Alexander, in service to Her Majesty, Queen Margaret Poncett I." The fewer details given, the better. "Why were you talking in my mind before but now you're not?"

Avishai's eyes faded from their normal blue, a shade similar to the lake in color, to a blue almost the color of the sky as she answered. "We p*rr*efe*rr* to speak silently, as vocalizing aloud is cumbe*rr*some, but it uses magic to do so. I ti*rr*ed afte*rr* such combat. You*rr* mount is sated. We must leave."

The way the creature stared at the shifting sands made Leolin's skin crawl. He mounted the *gachia* and set off at a steady pace towards the mountains ahead. Again Avishai kept pace with Leolin's mount, her tongue hanging out of her mouth. The trait was more dog-like than cat, giving Leolin the feeling that this creature was something quite unique.

Unlike the Meridi Pass, through the mountains that led to the capital city of Aruna, this road was less road and more like a trodden down dirt path. While it led to the city of Inbarr, it was also the path heading in the Order's general direction. They moved quietly through the foothills, neither speaking to the other until the elevation changed enough for Leolin to dismount and lead the *gachia* through the mountain pass.

Question after question danced in Leolin's mind. Why had Avishai warned him of the attack? Why get involved at all, and if she had magic enough to kill the two attackers to begin with, why not do it immediately? How much magic did she have, and would she be willing to help the Little Dozen Kingdoms wage battle against the Thirteen? He frowned as another thought occurred to him. Was she an enemy sent to catch him off guard? As another thought popped into his mind, Avishai let out a massive sigh.

"I'm not you*rr* enemy. I wasn't sent he*rr*e by anyone. Honestly, I came down from these mountains for a d*rr*ink at the lake when I hea*rr*d the noisy, stupid minds of those two fools. Then I hea*rr*d you," she said as she sat on her haunches long enough to scratch behind one ear. "If I had wanted you dead, I would have killed you too. Is it possible fo*rr* you c*rr*eatu*rr*es to silence you*rr* minds at all? Must you all yamme*rr* as loudly as possible at all times?"

"I-I'm sorry. I wasn't aware I was thinking particularly loud." How did one think loudly anyway? Leolin snorted as he released his hold on the reins. He could see the trail marker ahead but to reach it, he would need both hands as the path grew steep. Better to let the *gachia* find its own footing. Beside him, Avishai sighed a second time. "I'm sorry. I know I already apologized, but I'm not sure how not to think."

"Sometimes I find humming a good activity," said Avishai, and with that she set to humming a tune Leolin had not heard before—an eerie tune that set his nerves on edge—though it distracted him as much as the mountain as they climbed.

The sun descended towards the horizon as they reached a natural plateau in the path. To the north and south, snow-capped mountains rose in the distance. For all the work it was to climb, this pass that traveled from east to west crested nothing more than an annoyingly large hill. The plateau at the top made for a natural stopping point, and Leolin said, "This would be a good place to stop for the day."

"You have walked this path befo*rr*e?"

He shook his head. "Not personally, though I know those who have. They gave me detailed notes about this mountain range, including where to find water, where to stop, and areas to avoid."

"I have lived in these hills for seve*rr*al seasons."

It was as polite a rebuke as the creature had given, and Leolin inclined his head. "If you know somewhere better, lead on."

Avishai walked a stone's throw from where Leolin had stopped and curled up near a shrub. "He*rr*e would be a good place to settle fo*rr* the night."

At first, Leolin frowned. As far as he could tell, where the cat lay was no better or worse than where Leolin stood, but as the *chathula* stared at him, occasionally blinking as she smiled, Leolin sighed. Perhaps the creature knew something he didn't, or perhaps she was closer to a cat than mystical being.

Bredych's notes made it clear that while this was an area not prone to landslides, because it was a good place to rest, it was occasionally struck by bandits and the like. Leolin removed the saddlebags from the *gachia* and stowed them in the nearby brush. Once free of its burden, the beast curled up under a bush and began to snore, the sound a mix between a trill and a hiss.

Domesticated *gachia* were well trained, much like hunting hounds, and while the beast would happily sleep through the night, its sensitive ears would detect anyone approaching well before Leolin would. He rooted around in the saddlebag for some ointment to slather inside his nose. While it was unlikely a sandstorm would reach them in the foothills, his skin still burned from the constant chaffing of a trip through the desert.

Watching Shai use magic had demonstrated how much energy magic expended, so when Leolin turned away from the saddlebags to find Avishai curled up in a tight ball, her fluffy tail tucked under her chin, he was not surprised. The *chathula* was still, the only movement being the slight rise and fall of her chest.

Rather than risk a fire, Leolin wrapped a blanket around himself and chewed on dried meat until his eyes grew heavy. He leaned his back against a small tree and fell promptly asleep.

AFTER COUNTLESS DAYS in the desert, Leolin thought he would be grateful for a short stint in the mountains. While beautiful, the rough terrain and colder temperatures made the passage in many ways more challenging as winter approached. Even in the foothills it snowed at night, and twice he woke to a whitened landscape. The change in elevation meant a bit of a climb, which warmed him and his travel companions but not enough. The *gachia* shivered as it walked, and on the second night in the foothills, Leolin braved a fire. Despite the risk, everyone needed the warmth.

When the sun rose without any attacks, he breathed a sigh of relief. Another a few candlemarks later as they descended into the plains. Out of the mountains proper, three days would see them at the Order.

After a stretch in the saddle, the *chathula* asked, "Wherre are you trraveling? This isn't the path Levi."

"It isn't. I-I'm traveling to see friends." The creature tweaked its whiskers at him but kept following. When they stopped for a short rest, Leolin frowned. "I appreciate you warning me about the attackers, probably *Tribor* if I had to guess, and I appreciate you taking care of them, but I'll admit to being curious. Why are you following me?"

Avishai grinned, her canines visible. "I'm t*rr*aveling to see f*rr*iends as well. The*rr*e is g*rr*eate*rr* st*rr*ength togethe*rr*, yes?"

The creature was as elusive with her answers as Leolin had been. For the time being, he would allow the *chathula* to follow along, but within a day or so of the Order, he would have to part ways with Avishai. The fact that she didn't ask who the *Tribor* were was curiouser still, and Leolin tucked the information away.

Unlike the desert, no trail markers would lead Leolin to the Order. He followed the sun as he traveled due west through the grasslands, which stretched the length from the mountains to the coast. Bunches of tall grass whose stems varied from blue to purple stood as tall as Leolin as they grew at random intervals amongst shorter, more manageable grasses. Trees, first sporadic and then more numerous, grew amongst the grasses as they neared the coast.

On the third morning after leaving behind the foothills, Leolin turned to Avishai with a sigh. "I...I appreciate your willingness to accompany me, but where I'm going, you can't follow. This is where we part ways, I'm afraid."

If a cat could snort, Avishai would have as her nose and muzzle twitched. "My new f*rr*iend, it's no sec*rr*et that you a*rr*e seeking the counsel of the shadow-walke*rr*s."

"Shadow what?"

"The shadow-walke*rr*s. It's what my t*rr*ibe calls you*rr* assassins."

Leolin slowed his *gachia* to a stop. The *chathula* stepped as close as she could get to the *gachia* without touching it, her head reaching the *gachia*'s shoulders with ease. Avishai stared at Leolin, her blue eyes almost clear as she waited. When he said nothing, she asked, "Did you think you*rr* people the only ones to know of the Amaskans?"

"At first I thought you were talking of the *Tribor*, but you know the Order?"

Avishai blinked. "My fathe*rr* met one of thei*rr* membe*rr*s while indebted to one who t*rr*ades in slave*rr*y. This membe*rr* bo*rr*e you*rr* featu*rr*es, in fact."

Leolin's heart pounded in his chest. The Order had plenty of female members but something in the creature's story tickled in memories, which flickered away the harder he tried to grab hold of them. "When was this? And where?"

"Many yea*rr*s ago, nea*rr* Tovias. My mothe*rr* told me that my fathe*rr* was a b*rr*ave *chathula*. He helped this woman and he*rr* b*rr*othe*rr* defeat evil. Without his help, they would su*rr*ely have pe*rr*ished."

As far as Leolin knew, his mother and Bredych were the only sibling members in the Order, at least in Bredych's lifetime. He narrowed his eyes as he leaned closer to the *chathula*. She bore no wrinkles or graying fur, nothing to note her age or her life expectancy. "How old are you?" he asked.

"I have seen the seasons change twenty-fou*rr* times, and will see them change fou*rr* times that numbe*rr* if Alisher is willing."

The timeline fit, if what Leolin knew of his mother's life in the Order was true. "I...I think your father helped my mother."

"That's what I said."

Leolin furrowed his brow. "You said your father met an *Amaskan*. You didn't say which one." He would have remembered.

Avishai leaned forward and touched her nose to Leolin's hand. It was cold and damp, and when he stretched out his fingers to touch the *chathula*'s fur, it was surprisingly fluffy, closer to rabbit than cat fur. When it was slicked back and unruffled, it appeared thinner than it was. He ran his fingers through it until he reached the creature's ears.

She leaned into his touch. *Oooh, right there, please.*

He scratched behind her ear as she twisted her head to lean into it more. It was cat-like enough that he couldn't help but laugh.

When he smiled, she gave a toothy grin in response and asked, "Better*rr*?"

"How did you know what I was feeling?" He drew his hand away from her.

"I did not intend to hea*rr* you but you speak so loudly. The loss of you*rr* past mind bothe*rr*s you g*rr*eatly. Why? Is it not the past?"

"Past mind? You mean memories?"

"Yes."

Leolin urged his *gachia* forward. There was little point in splitting up now if she was acquainted with the Order. Besides, being a magic user, perhaps she could help if Mystic Doughal Nilesh could not. "For humans, our past is what makes us who we are now, in the present. Without my memories, I don't know who I am."

When she didn't respond, he glanced down to see her eyes had darkened a touch, so he remained silent as they traveled. They came upon a small pond before her eyes returned to their pale blue color, and when he cocked his head, she said, "Someone else moved nea*rr*by. They a*rr*e t*rr*aveling the opposite way. Oh, this is ti*rr*ing, may I—" —*talk this way? It's more civilized.*

"You've already heard thoughts you shouldn't, so go ahead. Everyone else has been in my mind so what's one more?"

She trotted closer to the *gachia* again so that she might touch her nose to his hand. *I'm sorry that others have done what no one should without consent. I would never, and I'm sorry I can't help but hear you.*

"It's fine. It hurts to try and remember, but it's all I can do."

For chathulas, *past us is no longer relevant. We've grown and learned and moved beyond that stage, but if your past matters so, then you do right to seek it. I'm not sure how the assassins will help you find it, but I hope they can. You hurt too much for one so young.*

"Since you know about the Order of Amaska, why are you heading there?" Her eyes darkened almost black as a tear slid down her fur where it left no trail. Had he imagined it? A few more left her eyes before she closed her outer lids to blink them away.

My outer fur is waterproof and hides my weakness well.

Leolin shook his head. "There's no weakness in crying."

For your kind, perhaps, but for mine, it often leads to great harm for the tribe. This is why I seek the Amaskans. My father... he was captured along with my mother. Because my mother was carrying me, she was sold while my father was enslaved. He was found near death and indebted for many years before he died, but my mother never saw him again. My people come from across the Great Sea. The only chathulas *in this land have been brought here by force. Since the Amaskans had dealings with the one who held my father, I hope to find answers."*

"You hope to know who you are."

Yes.

"So you do understand the desire to know one's past."

Avishai sighed. *I am young. My mother called this quest of mine silly and unbecoming of a mighty Geutha Tribe of the Nine, though I admit to knowing nothing of this tribe. She spoke of a place and people I've never known. I would trade all of my magic to know my home. Perhaps she is right. This is a foolish quest.*

He reached out and patted Avishai on the head. "If it is foolish, may we both be fools."

The bigger fool is the person who knows everything.

Leolin stared out across the grasslands, *chathula* at his side. He squeezed his legs on the *gachia*'s sides, encouraging the beast to speed up.

Perhaps knowing the answers would gain them nothing, but even a fool was right sometimes.

15

257 Sharimus 22nd — City of Alesta

Waiting for a plan was much like waiting for a storm to break, the air thick with promise and the hope of relief. While the moments before a storm might smell pleasant, a storm could bring cities and farms to ruin. Like a storm, Margaret promised she had a plan and that the wait was necessary, but inside, Bredych itched for action.

As Grand Master, Bredych would have counseled a fellow *Amaskan* for patience, to allow time for the Order to make the necessary proposals to best serve Justice, but now... What was the purpose of Justice if the Thirteen were as corrupt as anyone else?

He dug his hands into his tunic's pockets. Walking around the castle, he spent more time in the Alexandrian Army's blue uniform than the Order's, and the alteration saddened him. Leaving the Order meant change, of course, but a part of him had hoped to remain in Alesta serving in a role more fitting to an *Amaskan* than that of an advisor.

Or maybe he had hoped Margaret would see him more as a father and fill the aching hole in his heart that Adelei used to fill. The queen cared for him, but it was not the same. Bredych rubbed at his hip. Winter was soon upon them, the worst time for an army to fight and a certain reminder of every previous injury he had suffered.

Maybe he was too old for this. War was a young man's folly, and Margaret was certainly more than capable. He stared out across the city from the castle parapet. Guards stood by idly as the city citizens below rebuilt what had been lost to the Shadians.

Life continued in spite of his morose mood. If Shendra were alive, she would have kicked him in the seat of his pants, and he sighed. Then he frowned as his skin tingled.

Bredych had been among those in the field who had felt the touch of magic when Shai had called the rain, but up here, no one physically touched him. He glanced at the nearest guardsman, but the lad appeared nonplussed as he yawned.

The feeling intensified until he thought his skin would burn off. An audible pop sounded inside his ears, and the sensation dissipated. Someone had cast powerful magics. There was no other explanation.

Margaret.

His footfalls echoed loudly on the floor as he ran towards the queen's rooms. He was halfway there when he saw her. Her blonde hair was longer than it was in her portraits, falling nearly to her ample hips, but there was no doubting those green eyes or the childish face, especially with the man standing beside her.

Possibly the fattest man Bredych had ever seen, Farimun's multiple chins bounced as he spoke. Whatever was said was lost to the sound of servants chattering as they came around the corner.

Agaia spotted the two girls at the same time Bredych did and snapped her fingers. The first girl crumpled into a pile on the stone floor. The second, seeing her friend collapse, glanced at Agaia, then at Bredych.

"Run!" he shouted, and the girl bolted down the hallway.

"You didn't have to kill the lass," said Farimun as he stared at the body.

When Bredych unsheathed his sword, Agaia laughed. "You know who I am, yet you hope to defeat me. I could snap my fingers again, and you would be but a puddle on the floor."

Bredych shook his head. "You know as well as I do that magic is fading. The energy it took you to kill that girl has you drained. I can see it in your face."

"Magic may be fading from the land, but not from the gods," she said, and it was his turn to laugh.

"If that were true, Farimun wouldn't be with you." Bredych nodded at the God of Journeys. "You were her only way here. With the orbs broken and magic dying, you're the only god with the ability to travel quickly, am I correct?"

Farimun stepped away from Agaia and raised his hands up. "I agreed with your plan to kill the queen, but not this girl. If you want the *Amaskan* dead, do it yourself."

When the god blinked, a sharp pain like thorns being driven into his skin caused Bredych to double over. It passed a moment later, and when he righted himself, the God of Journeys was gone.

Rather than panic, Agaia smiled, her green eyes sparkling with amusement. She reached into the thin gauze that served as her skirts and when she withdrew her hand, she held a sword of her own.

Bredych kept the surprise from his face through the practice of experience alone. Considering her pale legs shone through her skirts, there was nowhere for the sword to have been hidden, leaving magic as her only means of having hidden it. He strained to hear the footfalls of guardsmen running up the stairs and heard none.

The goddess smiled. "No one's coming to help you," she said as she stepped toward him. For all that she was a curvaceous woman, she moved lithely, her gaze never leaving him or his sword.

"If you came to kill Margaret, I'm surprised you didn't have Farimun bring you directly to Her Majesty. You could have rid yourself of her in a heartbeat and been gone before anyone noticed."

Her brow furrowed. "Perhaps I enjoy the chase as much as the kill."

"I think even Farimun's magic must be waning. Perhaps you planned just as I said, but his magic brought him to this hallway instead of to the queen. Or perhaps the Thirteen are poor planners. You've had ample opportunity to rid yourselves of the little rodents in your midst, yet here we remain."

"I think rodent is a good word for you, and rodents shouldn't talk so much."

The space between them folded in on itself as one moment she stood twenty paces away and the next, her sword tapped against his. She could have run him through, but instead she smirked at him as she waited.

She had spoken truly then. This was a game to her, and she wanted the chase. Bredych needed to kill her and do it fast if for no reason other than she had killed the servant. But could she be killed? There were no more orbs, and he certainly was no mystic, for all that he could sense magic's use.

He rose to the balls of his feet, muscles flexing in response to age-old memory and experience. Agaia might be a god, but she could not see what he could. Worry lines gathered at her eyes and her skin held a pallor that spoke of fatigue. All these magic tricks had exhausted her while Bredych was ready for a fight. Besides, god or not, he was *Amaskan*.

He would kill her and send her to the Thirteen Hells for her trouble. When he shifted his weight to his right, she parried but his sword was not there. Instead, he hopped to his left foot and stabbed at her exposed side. It was not a hard jab as he was testing the reflexes of his opponent, but the sword cut her, leaving a wound behind.

Blood. Red blood, just like his.

She was mortal, or close enough to it to be killed. "When we still worshipped you and believed you were gods, we followed your laws, the Thirteen, but since you are nothing more than dying plagues upon this earth, I believe it's time that we rid ourselves of the fleas upon us."

Agaia sidestepped his attack as if she were taking a casual stroll. While she could use magics that shook the earth, one look at her ample frame, and he had assumed her a novice fighter, an assumption that almost cost him as she lunged at him. He parried the blow at the last moment. She tightened her grip on her sword's hilt and feinted a few times before driving her sword in front of her like scythe.

Bredych brought up his sword to block, and Agaia's eyes glowed green as she snarled in fury. Her sword radiated as she drove it forward into his. As his sword neared his body, he shifted his weight to duck and roll away from her.

With the clanging of metal, her sword met his three more times and yet still she fought him. Considering that magic was fading, where did her energy come from?

"I think you believed me tired, but you forget, little *Amaskan*. I am the earth. I am life itself. My bounty is infinite so long as life remains in this world."

"And you accused me of talking too much." While holding his sword in his right hand, he pulled out his dagger with his left. If she spoke the truth, she would outlast him and he would die, along with Margaret and countless others. He sighed, and Agaia smiled in response.

He stepped to his right and pulled back his sword as if preparing to lunge, leaving his side exposed. She saw the opening, as he knew she would, and stepped forward.

The sword was sharp like Miriam's humor, as he thought of her in that moment when Agaia's sword slid inside him. The goddess's eyes sparkled as blood stained his blue tunic, and her sweet breath tickled his nose. Before he stopped too long to think on the wound, he slashed her bare throat with his dagger.

She opened her mouth to speak, but only blood came out. Agaia dropped her sword as she stumbled backward before falling. She glanced up as Bredych approached, her green eyes glowing.

He may have wounded her, but she was still a god. Still one of the Thirteen.

Bredych swung his sword at her neck, then twice more as he beheaded her. As the light faded from her eyes, footfalls sounded on the stairs nearby as many people found themselves suddenly able to enter the hallway.

The hall tilted, or perhaps it was Bredych who moved—he could not tell—only that his vision dimmed around the edges and sound faded to little more than an annoying buzz. He thought he spotted Margaret's face among those who stared at him from his place on the floor.

When had he fallen?

It did not matter. The floor seemed an appropriate place to sleep.

Bredych closed his eyes.

257 Sharimus 22nd - Outside the Order of Amaska

THE SMELL of sea water was Leolin's first clue that he neared the Order. His second was a crooked tree marked in Bredych's notes. The third and most important indicator that he had followed Bredych's instructions correctly was the whistle in the air, followed by an arrow that planted itself firmly in the ground in front of him. His *gachia* snorted and bucked until Leolin gave a tug on the reins.

Someone watches.

Leolin gave the *chathula* a brief nod, his gaze searching the trees for signs of the *Amaskan*. The fact that they had warned him surprised him. Rather than give them a chance to change their minds, he called out, "I'm Leolin, and I mean no harm. Master Bredych, former Grand Master of the Order has sent me."

At first nothing moved. He was fairly certain that neither he nor Avishai breathed. His heart pounded in his chest at least a dozen times before something moved in the brush. The leaves parted way as a young man stepped forward. For all that he wore complete black, his clothing did not match the wraps Adelei or Bredych had worn, nor did the young man bear the circle tattoo at his jaw. His long, black hair reminded Leolin of his mother's.

"My name is Kellen. I would ask your business on this path." If the young man was surprised by the appearance of a *chathula*, he did not show it as he kept his gaze firmly on Leolin. His eyes were muddy in color, but they held his attention as sharply as Bredych's blue.

"I have stated my intent. I see no tattoo on your jaw, so I can only assume you have no business being here." Leolin urged the *gachia* forward, but Kellen reached out a hand, which he placed firmly on the *gachia*'s nose. The creature immediately stopped and lay down, leaving Leolin to leap off the saddle. "How did you do that?"

"While I bear no tattoo, I'm a member of the Order all the same. Not all of us are *Amaskan* by trade, but all of us serve Justice. You claim to know Master Bredych, yet you have an Alexandrian accent. *Amaskans* aren't welcome in Alexander."

Leolin squatted down beside the *gachia* to open his satchel and withdrawn the initial letter from Bredych. The one from Margaret was for Miriam directly, so it remained in the bag. He handed the initial letter to Kellen, who paled to see the Master's mark. He gave it a quick read before handing it back. "We have to be cautious, especially now. Come."

"Wait, how did you make the *gachia* follow your commands?" asked Leolin.

Kellen smiled. "Easy. I trained him. Good to see you again, Cyrui."

The *gachia* hummed as he stood and began following Kellen. Leolin glanced at Avishai before he trailed along. If the *chathula* could hear his thoughts when she didn't mean to, Leolin could only assume the creature could when intended. He concentrated on the words as hard as he could, trying to shout them in his mind. *WHAT ARE YOUR THOUGHTS ABOUT THIS KELLEN?*

Avishai hissed. *Ouch.*

"Sorry," Leolin whispered.

The shadow-walkers are known animal trainers and traders. Perhaps this Kellen is one of the many there who train and breed such creatures, especially since he seems to know your mount.

They had taken a dozen steps when Kellen froze, his bow in hand before Leolin did more than blink. The young man loosed an arrow at a clump of bushes, which shook before a tall, elderly man in a green cloak stepped into the clearing. "State your business," said Kellen as he readied another arrow.

"My apologies, young Kellen. I did not mean to startle you."

Kellen frowned. "How did you know my name?"

For a moment, the old man's eyes widened as if surprised. Then he smiled. "I overheard your conversation with Leolin." His gaze shifted to the *chathula*, and his smile deepened. "Though I did not realize you traveled with so awe-inspiring a companion."

Be wary.

At the *chathula's* thoughts, Leolin unsheathed his sword. "Who are you?"

The old man threw back the hood of his cloak, his green eyes sparkling with great humor.

Leolin bristled. "What humors you?"

"My apologies, it has been a long time since I last visited this area. I realize now that I've startled you all and not even given you my name. Many call me Senator Raj of the *Boahim Senate*."

Kellen gave a brief nod. "To my knowledge, the Senate has never visited this area. How can I trust you are who you say you are?"

Leolin pointed at the man's feet where his hooves stuck out from beneath his pants. "He is more than a senator. This is Sharmus."

"All the Thirteen Hells, I swore I covered those up, and here I have gone and startled you again."

At first Leolin thought the god spoke to him, but when he glanced over at Kellen, the young man was white beneath his tan and trembling. For all that the old man could have been lying, the firmness of his voice paired with hooves where feet should have been left no doubt in young Kellen's mind about who stood before him.

Kellen dropped his bow, and then dropped to his knees, his face buried in the dirt. Sharmus stared over the young man to meet Leolin's gaze. "He is afraid of me, but you are not. You could only be Lieutenant Leolin in service to Queen Margaret of Alexander. Strong woman, that one. Seems fitting you would love a woman like that after having a mother like yours."

Leolin tensed at the mention of his mother but kept his sword trained on the god. "Why are you here?"

A weariness rushed over Sharmus as his shoulders drooped. "I fear I've nowhere else to go." He glanced down at the young man still prostrate on the ground. "Please, young Kellen, do not give worship to the unworthy. Stand up."

The young man raised his head but remained on his knees. "U-Unw-worthy? But you are one of the Thirteen!"

Sharmus sighed. "Would you do me the honor of taking me to your Grand Master, young Kellen? I have been standing near this tree for quite some time waiting for someone to pass."

"Why did you not *trr*avel to the O*rr*de*rr* on you*rr* own?" asked Avishai.

Kellen scrambled to his feet, bow at the ready. "It talks!"

"I am most definitely *not* an it! I am Avishai the Fie*rr*ce, Daughte*rr* of Avi the G*rr*ave and membe*rr* of the Geutha T*rr*ibe of the Nine."

Leolin placed a hand on the young man's shoulder. "Avishai is a magical creature and worthy of respect. I know this is *a lot* to digest, but please, we need to see Grand Master Miriam with all haste." When Kellen rushed ahead, Leolin gestured for Sharmus to walk before him. Thus far, the Thirteen had sought to harm Margaret. As far as he was concerned, the Little Dozen Kingdoms would be better if he ran Sharmus through in the forest and left his body for the scavengers.

Sharmus paused to glance over his shoulder. "You are probably right, Leolin," he said and then continued following behind Kellen.

Heart pounding like he had run from Alesta to the Order, Leolin continued onward with Avishai and the *gachia* beside him. He sincerely hoped this god was on their side.

16

A large gray and white stone building loomed ahead, ivy trailing its way across the walls. "Wait here...please, my lord...God," said Kellen before running inside the building. While Leolin did not see any Amaskans around, eyes watched him. He could feel their judgment and curiosity as easily as if they were standing out in the open. Whatever Kellen said once he was inside brought a hornet's nest of activity as many Amaskans poured forth from the building's double doors, including an older woman whose hair would certainly be long gray if she had any, but her head was as smooth and shaven as every other person in sight. Her dark, tanned skin carried many wrinkles and scars.

"It seems we have some interesting guests among us," she said, her blue eyes studying Sharmus as if she stood before a trap.

Sharmus merely inclined his head. "Master Miriam, though I suppose it's Grand Master now. I never believed

Bredych would willingly step down from that position, let alone pledge his support to the Alexandrians."

"Grand Master will do." Miriam turned toward Leolin, and her gaze slid to Avishai. Only then did her mouth part and her eyes widen. "A *chathula*. I thought them only a myth." She strode forward with a slight limp and held out her hand for Avishai to smell her fingers, as she would a domesticated pet.

Avishai hissed. "I am not a cat for you to stick you*rr* finge*rr*s in my face."

"They talk? Lieutenant, you bring the strangest of guests to these halls. What other surprises do you have in store for us?" She turned and strode toward the door and once there, called over her shoulder a single word. "Come."

Murmurs spread throughout the Amaskans loitering outside as they admired the *chathula*. Sharmus they ignored completely.

"I do not think they believe I am who I say I am," Sharmus muttered in surprise as he glanced around.

"Were you expecting them to grovel at your feet?" asked Leolin, and the god blushed.

On the other hand, Avishai squared her shoulders as she stood tall and lifted her nose high in the air. Her tail twitched as her ears pivoted to take in all the chatter.

A younger *Amaskan* in gray stepped forward to claim the *gachia*'s reins, and Leolin removed his saddlebag and carried it with him through the double doors. Miriam led them down a lengthy hallway. Sharmus's hooves clopped as he walked and more than a few bald heads poked out of the numerous doorways to watch the procession. Finally, they passed through a single door leading to a room with a single dais. On it sat a single chair. Blue and green painted walls with flecks of gold reflected the candlelight, and framed paintings of the Thirteen decorated the walls.

Sharmus found his portrait, turning his head this way and that. "Do people truly believe me to look like this?"

Leolin glanced between the painting and the god. "They painted your nose too narrow."

Miriam snorted as she gestured for them to follow her. Bredych had warned Leolin about the blue arch, but even with the warning, the prickling sensation that coursed through his body unnerved him. His muscles relaxed and the desire to smile washed over him. He turned as Sharmus passed beneath the arch.

The god's eyes widened as it held him in place. He placed a hand on the arch's frame. A hum filled the air, and the smell of earth tickled Leolin's nose, followed by a loud pop. Before, the stones had glowed a light blue, but now they retained only their normal, gray color.

"What did you do?" asked Miriam as she touched the arch.

"No one placates me."

Avishai sniffed the stone before walking through. "It is a door*rr*way, yes?"

Miriam scowled and pointed to the door on the left. Inside the second room were a dozen Amaskans, all of them much older than those who stood outside. A few of them stood when they saw Sharmus, but the majority remained seated. Although they had passed through the same arch as Leolin, many clenched their jaws as the group entered.

It was a feeling Leolin understood. He had sheathed his weapon once they had arrived at the Order, but he kept his hand ready. They still did not know how easily the gods could be killed, and here one walked amongst them.

Leolin claimed an empty chair as did Sharmus. Someone had thought to bring an overly large pillow, presumably for Avishai, but she ignored it, choosing instead to claim one of the empty seats. She folded her limbs into a chair with silver embroidered pillows and waited. Miriam gave a longing glance at the chair claimed by the *chathula* before choosing one of the less comfortable seats remaining.

"I—"

Miriam rested a hand on Leolin's arm and shook her head. "The *chathula* is an esteemed guest and welcome to my chair."

Leolin retrieved the letter from Bredych as well as the one from Margaret and passed both over to her. "I come seeking knowledge, but Master Bredych and my queen have a boon they wish to ask of you."

She opened the letter from Bredych first, moisture gathering at the corners of her eyes as she read it. Having also read it, there was nothing personal that Leolin could see in the letter, but she sniffed once while she read it, her fingers hovering over the inked parchment.

"He misses you," he whispered, and she gave the smallest nod of her head before she picked up the second letter. Miriam lingered on this one less and set it aside with a deep sigh.

Before responding to Leolin, she turned to Sharmus. "I know who you claim to be, though I'd be foolish not to believe you considering your imagery decorates these halls and the halls of many others, though I'm curious why you're here and not on your island."

Sharmus brought his hands together in front of him. "My brothers and sisters value their godhood greatly. With Queen Margaret's beheading of Itovah, it was decided that she should die—"

Leolin stood and grabbed the hilt of his sword. The calm he had felt before was gone as fury swept through him.

The god furrowed his brows. "Please, Lieutenant, return to your seat. If I wished the queen dead, she would be dead."

"And if I ran you through right here and now, would you be dead?"

"The child-god means no ha*rr*m," said Avishai.

Leolin returned to his seat, but he did so only because he trusted the *chathula*. While he seemed able to read people's thoughts, did the same apply to gods? And why had he called him a child-god? He tucked that information away to ask later, but then Miriam asked.

"Alishe*rr* is the creato*rr* of all and has been since the beginning, long befo*rr*e Luthia's silence and Adlain All-Fathe*rr*. You a*rr*e but a child among giants, though in the g*rr*ande*rr* scheme of all, I am but a flea."

For the second time that day, Sharmus was stunned into silence as he stared at the *chathula*. Miriam rapped her knuckles on the table. "So the Thirteen wish Queen Margaret dead. If that is so, why are you *here*?"

"I am old, older than you can imagine and a weariness rests in my bones that I cannot explain. My brothers and sisters feel it as well, and our magic fades from us as it fades from the world."

"Wait, magic's fading from the world?" Leolin's heart thumped in his chest. "The mystics are still capable of magic. I've seen it."

Sharmus nodded. "For now. But soon, that too will die. I think perhaps the time has come for the world to be without the gods' gifts. I know not of this Alisher, only that there was Luthia and then the silence was broken that there were more. But even my knowledge is fallible these days.

I was tasked with killing Queen Margaret, but when I arrived at the Meridi Pass, I found a capable young woman with veracity and strength worthy of existence. End her life? I would rather end my own. This is why I sought out the Order's help."

Miriam gasped. "You came here to die?"

"Yes. I am tired. If my brothers and sisters were truthful with themselves, they would admit to the same. The time of the gods has passed."

"You're a coward," said Leolin as he shook his head. "You're a *god*, one of the mighty Thirteen. You don't want to kill Margaret? Fine, don't, but use your powers! Help us fight against the rest of them." The look Sharmus leveled on Leolin made him fidget, but he refused to yield. "You say the time of the gods has passed. If so, help us bring that to fruition."

Sharmus stared at the long, wooden table that divided the room's occupants. The other masters whispered to each other as the god thought. When he glanced up, his face was pale. "I have too little magic to help. Not even enough to cover my hooves. What help could I possibly give?"

"You have a little, which is more than me," said one of the masters.

"I used most of what was left in me to travel to the Pass and back to the island. Small amounts expended here and there. I even sailed aboard a ship to reach Lavi. I..I sold a book most precious to me in order to buy a horse, though the beast threw me a few miles from the Order."

Leolin snorted. "People are dying, most by the hands of the Thirteen, and you're worried about selling a book? Do you have any idea what happened at the Pass before you arrived? Did you see the death and destruction wrought by your 'brothers and sisters'? Spare me your concerns as they are nothing."

"The god-child is like any other child. He sees not the full sto*rr*y. Pe*rr*haps help is what he needs to unde*rr*stand the b*rr*eadth of you*rr* conce*rr*n, Leolin," said Avishai as she flicked a single ear.

Besides, you need his help.

Leolin glanced around, but no one else reacted to Avishai's last sentence. He held up his hands in defeat. "Tell us more, oh, Sharmus, about how awful it is being a mighty god."

Sharmus released a deep laugh that rang in Leolin's head. "Oh, I like you, Lieutenant. Before the Little Dozen

Kingdoms, when this land was Boahim, we had fire such as you still. Perhaps if we had kept it, the Little Dozen would still see us as worthy and relevant."

A pitcher sat on the table and when Sharmus snapped his fingers, it began pouring its wine into an empty glass. Several jaws dropped at the casual use of magic, and Miriam's eyes narrowed. "I thought you said you had no magic."

"This?" The glass floated into Sharmus's hand. "This is but a parlor trick. A tiny magic that is meaningless."

"Our mystics can do similar...tricks, but their magic is little enough that they don't waste what they have on trivial displays," said Miriam as she poured a glass of wine, which she offered to Leolin. "Do *chathulas* imbibe?"

"No, but I would gladly take a small dish of wate*rr*."

Before anyone could move, a dish of water appeared before Avishai, whose fur bristled in response. "If you*rr* kind a*rr*e *rr*unning out of magic, pe*rr*haps you shouldn't be using so much of it," she said before taking a single lick of water.

"You are wise beyond your youth, young Avishai, as are you, Lieutenant." Sharmus swallowed the wine in his glass in a single gulp. "I can't promise to be of much help, but perhaps you are correct. Maybe my knowledge can be of some help to you."

The corners of Sharmus's mouth twitched with amusement as he picked up the pitcher with one hand and poured himself another glass of wine. This one he sipped.

Miriam held up the letter from Bredych as she glanced at the other masters. "Our former Grand Master has several requests of us, but we'll begin with the one involving Leolin. Many of you knew his mother and Bredych's sister, Shendra. Before she fled to Alexander, she bore a child with another *Amaskan* named Samuhel Banach, that child being Leolin. For reasons unclear to any of us, Shendra brought Leolin to the Sadain border, where she met Doughal Nilesh. At her request, he hid Leolin's memories from him. Leolin would like to meet with the mystic about this. Is this correct?"

When Leolin nodded, Miriam added, "The second request from Master Bredych is for our help. All twelve rulers of the Little Dozen Kingdoms have signed an agreement to fight for their right to rule themselves without oversight from the Boahim Senate."

"From the Thirteen," said Leolin.

Miriam nodded. "Queen Margaret and Master Bredych have asked for the Order's help. They wish us to journey to Alesta and help with whatever fight they're all planning. It's a discussion to be had in private, but it is one we must agree to unanimously."

"I would like to add something to that conversation," Leolin said.

"As would I," said Sharmus.

When Miriam nodded to Leolin, he took a swallow of his wine before speaking. "Many of you probably believe that this isn't your battle, that this is a problem created by the Alexandrians and thus, a problem for them to solve. I understand. Amaskans have been forbidden from the Kingdom of Alexander. They've been beaten, tortured, and killed—"

"By your queen!" said a frail woman with a nose as sharp as her tone. "My grandson was slaughtered by Queen Margaret because he crossed over the border to see his brother. Why should we help her now?"

"Queen Margaret is not alone in making mistakes. Master Bredych tried to kill his own sister, my mother, as a matter of pride. He kidnapped Margaret's sister, Adelei, to hurt King Leon. It certainly wasn't to serve justice. A long and bloody history stands between us now, but it doesn't have to. People like him—" Leolin pointed at Sharmus, "—have told us what we can and can't do for too long. They tell us not to kill, then kill indiscriminately. If we can put aside the past, we can create a new future, one where we can live as we choose, where Amaskans don't have to hide, and maybe justice is available for everyone.

My queen is willing to make a pact with the Order. She has detailed it in her letter to you all. There has been death enough already. I beg of you to consider the future, if not for yourselves, then for those who come after you. That's all I ask."

He did not mention the prophecy. Not that he believed in the power of such things, but he figured if it had been important, Bredych or Margaret would have mentioned it in their letters. It was possible Margaret did, as Leolin had not read it, but somehow he doubted it. She was nothing if not succinct.

The frail *Amaskan* pursed her lips together but remained silent. Miriam gestured for Sharmus to speak.

"I do not wish for anyone to believe my words to be what *has* to be or *should* be, only that it is my belief. You are all free to make your own choices and decisions with regards to these matters. It's long past time for that. That said, I believe that dividing the Little Dozen Kingdoms was a mistake. United as Boahim, the people were stronger. While I do not foresee a time when the land will be unified again, if the kingdoms were to come together for a common purpose, perhaps to defeat a common enemy, maybe the future will not appear so grim to these eyes. Groups like the Order, and yes, the *Tribor*, arose from unhappy people who wished to see change, but you can't see change through inaction. Allow the Amaskans to become the change they fought for in the first place." With that, the god crossed his arms across his chest and closed his eyes.

"We will consider all of this information, I promise," said Miriam.

"I, too, have something to ask," said Avishai as her tail flit back and forth. "I wish inforrmation on Lady Essia of Tovias and the evil man who did her bidding. You had dealings with them both, I believe."

Miriam nodded. "I believe we can accommodate your request, Avishai the Fierce. There was one last request Queen Margaret asked in her letter. A concerning request."

"More concerning than asking us to come rescue the Little Dozen Kingdoms again?" This question came from a man Leolin could only describe as older than the oldest man he had ever seen. His hand trembled as he pointed at Miriam. "What else could she possibly want?"

Leolin frowned and opened his mouth in protest. One moment the room was quiet and the next, a slight hum sounded as something whizzed by Leolin's ear. Not close enough to be a danger but near enough that his muscles tensed. A triangular throwing blade vibrated in the wall to Leolin's right where it had embedded itself when the old man had thrown it.

"Did you think me too old to be of use, child?" the old man said as he smirked. "We are each still here for a reason. If I take issue with your queen, then I do. Defending her won't ingratiate yourself with this Order."

Miriam rapped her knuckles on the table. "Thank you, Master Orin, for your council. To the request, while Margaret managed to kill Itovah, we still do not know how mortal the Thirteen are. Can they be killed by sword or does it take magical means to do them harm?"

"You know one way we could find out," said Leolin, with a glance at Sharmus. Miriam gasped, and Leolin held up a hand. "What? He did say he wanted to die. We wouldn't have to kill him, just wound him."

Sharmus opened his eyes. "The young lieutenant's not wrong. I did come here hoping to die. This would give you answers to many of your questions."

"While young, the child-god could be helpful against his

b*rr*othe*rr*s and siste*rr*s. Pe*rr*haps the*rr*e is anothe*rr* way," said Avishai.

"Queen Margaret has suggested that the Order help with this job. She would like to hire the Order. Officially." Miriam glanced around the table at the other masters. "We would send two Amaskans to the Senate Isle. They would attempt to kill one of the Thirteen, the idea being that with two, one could escape and report back to the Order, giving us the details needed to help the rest of the Little Dozen Kingdoms defeat the Thirteen.

"That's a mighty ask, I know, but having the Queen of Alexander hiring the Order officially would go a long way to changing the past and healing the wounds between her kingdom and our Order."

Leolin dug through his satchel and withdrew a smaller bag that clunked when he set it upon the table. "My queen didn't know how one goes about hiring the Order, whether payment is involved or not, but she sent this as an offering. If you help us and require more, it will be sent to you at once. If you choose not to involve yourself in this fight, you may keep the gold and do with it what you will. Either way, she sends her thanks and well wishes to you all."

Miriam left the bag on the table and stood. "One of the trainees outside will see you all to our guest quarters. Food will be brought to you when you require it, but I would ask that you not leave your quarters unescorted."

While Sharmus left first, Leolin trailed closely behind him. The god spoke like someone weary of life, but he was one of the Thirteen. Besides, he had been tasked with killing Margaret. Nothing he said could be trusted, at least not yet.

Avishai strode up alongside Leolin. *I agree. We will watch him together.*

THE GUEST QUARTERS were an entire building rather than a set of rooms. It stood near the horse pastures and housed a living and bathing space, along with several private bedchambers. The beds had left much to be desired when it came to comfort, but the space was ample enough that Leolin, Avishai, and Sharmus could claim private space if they desired. Avishai had settled on a couch in the living area, her entire body stretched out across it as if it were made for her. Several minutes later, light snores punctuated the silence.

So much for watching the god together.

Sharmus, on the other hand, had frowned when he claimed a lounging chair in the same room, which creaked in protest. "You would think the Amaskans more capable of a comfortable seat."

"They're killers, not furniture makers," said Leolin.

"Killers or furniture makers, treating one's guests as one treats their family is the mark of greatness. Besides, we are not *normal* guests."

"Did you expect them to magic up some nicer accommodations because a god walked into their home? Because we humans can't do that." Leolin pursed his lips. "For a god who claims he wants to die, you sure do expect everyone to treat you like spun glass."

The god laughed. "I suppose I do. Your life is so short and you so early in it. Next to you, I am ancient. I have seen many kings and kings before that in the times before Boahim was a mere thought. I've spent my time shaping the world, safe in the knowledge that I would continue long after people like you are gone. Now I am dying. My magic is fading from this world, so yes, I suppose I am 'spun glass.'"

Uncomfortable chair or no, the moment Sharmus closed his eyes, the god was asleep. Leolin wished he could join them, but he dared not lose track of Sharmus, so he settled down in a wooden chair with no cushion, which he angled to face the god. Even with the wood poking into his thighs, he caught his eyes drooping, and he shook himself awake.

Outside the room's lone window, the sun shone brightly, and Leolin frowned. Why was he sleepy? While he had been traveling for some time, it was not like him to fall asleep midday. Leolin stood and paced, but even then, his limbs grew heavy. He touched Sharmus's arm, and the god snorted awake.

"What is it?"

"Why are we all fighting sleep?"

Sharmus shrugged. "I traveled a lengthy distance to get here. I suppose my old age is catching up to me."

"And the *chathula*? Me? Neither of us are your age, and yet even pacing I can't keep my eyes open."

When the god closed his eyes, Leolin gave him another shake, and Sharmus waved a hand at him. "I am not sleeping but *seeing*. Give me a moment."

Leolin had no idea what he meant but waited until the god opened his eyes. His ears popped at the same time, and he glanced over to see Avishai awake. "What did you do?" Leolin asked.

"Something about this building...is much like the room with the arch. Did you know the arch was magic? Not the stuff those mystics use but *old* magic, my kind of magic. I do not remember laying such a spell here, but it tasted like my work. Perhaps it has been so long that I forgot."

"How does magic have a taste?" asked Avishai, and she stretched first her front legs, then her rear legs, before settling down on her haunches.

"It matters not. The arch's purpose was to read intentions and placate those who passed beneath it, but this building is one, giant arch. Rather than encouraging one to be truthful, it encourages sleep. Rest. Tranquility."

Leolin ground his teeth. "These damn Amaskans and their

need to control people. I've had enough people playing in my brain without more of it. How did you get it to stop?"

"I broke the spell," said Sharmus.

He gave no explanation as to how, though Leolin supposed a god would not need to do so. Instead, the god returned to his inclined position, closed his eyes, and fell asleep.

Turning to Avishai, Leolin asked, "Are you still tired?"

"I am, but we *chathula* sleep much of the day."

"You didn't while we were traveling across the mountains."

Avishai yawned. "I was being polite. Not eve*rr*yone sleeps when I do, but since we have nothing bette*rr* to do, I will *rr*est while I can." *Assuming you are capable of watching the child-god.*

Leolin nodded. With the spell broken, he felt no need to rest and settled in the wooden chair once more.

THE ROOM'S SHADOWS SHIFTED, and Leolin started awake. When had he closed his eyes? Avishai and Sharmus still slept, and he glanced out the window to see sunset upon them. The door opened, and a trainee in gray entered carrying a tray heavy with food and drink. He set it on the table before them and left without speaking.

Hints of savory roast pig and fresh baked bread wafted up from the tray, and Leolin's stomach growled in response.

Avishai licked her chops, her blue eyes flashing between light and dark. "They have given us a feast," he said.

Sharmus snorted. "A snack at best but much appreciated."

Despite the noises made by his stomach, Leolin stared at the food. When he did not move to eat it, Avishai paused, one claw hooked into a slice of ham.

"Is something w*rr*ong?"

He turned to Sharmus. "When you rid us of whatever spell made us sleepy, how do you know it worked?"

"Magic is energy. The energy ceased."

"And yet we all fell asleep soon after...during the daytime." Leolin pointed at the food. "How do we know that the food isn't tainted?"

The guest building's door opened, and Miriam stepped inside. "Because it isn't. We don't make a habit of poisoning or drugging our guests."

"But you make a habit of using magic on them? How can we trust what you say is true?" asked Leolin.

Miriam walked over, picked up a piece of pork, and stuck it into her mouth. She licked her fingers and then tore off a small hunk of bread. "This is the same food the rest of the Order has just finished eating. As to the spells in this building, they are older than the Order itself. We could no longer remove them than change them. Their sole purpose, from what we understand, is to relax the occupant. If relaxation helped your fatigued body to sleep, then that's what happened. Nothing else. Now, do you wish to know what the Order's decided or would you rather argue some more?"

Sharmus gestured to an empty chair. "Please join us and share your words."

The *Amaskan* glanced at Leolin and when he nodded, she sat. The stiffness with which she moved and the way she rubbed at her hip made Leolin frown. Perhaps their magics were not as strong as he had assumed if they could not fix whatever pains ailed their leader. He reached across the table for a piece of bread and popped it into his mouth. The bittersweet flavor of rye made his mouth water. A hint of sour and tanginess made him reach for a second piece.

"The decisions made by the Order's masters are traditionally made unanimously, so any decisions I speak of, know that they were made by all of us and that we're speaking as one," said Miriam. She met the gaze of each of them in turn before she continued. "The Order will send two Amaskans to the Senate Isle in order to determine if the Thirteen are mortal. While we could test whether they can bleed on Sharmus, if we're to help the Little Dozen, we need to know more than if a god can bleed. We need to know if magic must be involved, if it is the action of beheading, or if a mortal wound will do. Because Queen Margaret's favors are so great, we won't help the Little Dozen Kingdoms—"

Leolin stood. "Bredych asks this of you as well. Does that mean nothing to your Order?"

Miriam waited until he returned to his chair before continuing. "Please hear the Order out, Lieutenant. If you had allowed me to finish, I could've told you that we won't help *until* our members return from the island or enough time has passed to determine their failure. We *must* know what we're dealing with before we walk into such a fight."

Sharmus nodded. "It is a wise decision."

"There might not be time. Before I left, my queen had decided to begin the next step in the Little Dozen Kingdoms' plan."

"Which is?" asked Miriam.

"All of the rulers are declaring emancipation from the Senate. They are giving the Thirteen a set number of days to concede, or the rulers will form a united front and...deal with the problem."

"In other words, kill us," said Sharmus, and Leolin nodded.

Miriam shrugged. "It can't be helped. While I would ride for the Alexandrian border this instant, a few of the masters won't be swayed. At least not yet. They have agreed to helping if the gods can be killed by non-magical means, but only then.

I'm sorry. I did the best I could to convince them. Perhaps if Bredych were still here…

As to your other request, the Order has no issues with granting you access to the records you've requested, Avishai, though I suspect you won't find the information you seek. Not here."

"Is the*rr*e somewhe*rr*e else that might have it?"

The *Amaskan* nodded. "The lady you speak of was killed by two Amaskans, Shendra and her brother, Bredych. I assume that your request is regarding the *chathula* who was in her home when the Amaskans broke in."

"Yes, he was my fathe*rr*."

"Ah, both mentioned encountering a creature such as you, but most masters believed they spoke of a house cat, so no mention of the *chathula* was made in the Order's official records. Their encounter was brief, to my understanding. Shendra's dead, but her brother Bredych's still alive, as you've heard us speaking of him. Maybe he would have more information about your father."

Avishai's tail twitched as she tilted her head. "Pe*rr*haps."

"You are welcome to come with me to Alexander when I return and speak to him," said Leolin. "Besides, we could use someone with your magical abilities if we're to take on the Thirteen, or the child-gods as you put it."

"I will think on it."

Miriam stood slowly and walked towards the door. With her hand on the knob, she turned back to look at Leolin. "Doughal Nilesh will see you on the morrow."

The air rushed from Leolin as he released the breath he did not know he had been holding. "Thank you," he managed to say before the door closed.

Tomorrow he would see one of the most powerful mystics in Bredych's lifetime. When he glanced at Avishai, the *chathula* still stared at the door.

I don't trust her. Be careful.

Leolin nodded. Something about this visit felt off and had since they had left the small forest before the Order. Bredych might be decent enough, but Amaskans could not be trusted. There was a reason his mother left their kind and hid him. The thought of his mother sent a sharp pain through his head.

Rest. Let us hope this mystic has a good temperament.

Beside him, Sharmus continued eating, picking the bones clean and licking his fingers dry. Leolin put his head between his hands and sighed.

He needed his memories back, if only so he could stop his headaches.

17

Roland, Margaret's personal physician, rushed from Bredych's rooms a dozen times, which did nothing to calm Margaret's nerves as she paced outside. Shai remained inside, along with a few others trained in the arts of healing. While they worked on Bredych, several servants scrubbed the stone floor. Seeing the blood pooled on the stone twisted Margaret's stomach into knots, but Roland's pained face as he came and went from the *Amaskan*'s room left her trembling.

Bredych couldn't die. She needed him and not just his sword. The thought of losing another father... Margaret glanced at the closed door.

Only once had the *Amaskan* cried out, an anguished scream as they had moved him on a litter to his rooms, but the sound would remain with Margaret as long as she lived.

When Roland exited the room again, this time moving slower than he had before, Margaret ran up to him. "Is he...?"

"He lives, but I can't promise he'll remain so. I'm sorry," the physician said as he wiped his hands on his overshirt.

Margaret glanced down to see Bredych's blood on the man's clothes. She must have paled as he reached for her arms. He saw the blood marring his hands and stopped. "You should sit, Your Majesty. When did you last eat?"

"I-I'm not sure."

The physician leaned close to her ear. "Now is not the time to skip meals, Your Majesty. Please, go eat something."

"I must see Master Bredych first."

The door opened, and Shai poked his head out. When he spotted Margaret, he gestured for her. "He's asking for you."

With a nod to Roland, she followed the mystic through the door. She had been in Bredych's rooms before, guest rooms of a decent size, but with so many crowded into his bedchamber, they resembled a closet more than a proper room. The taste of dirt and iron coated her tongue as the smell of blood hit her nose. In the corner lay a pile of linen stained crimson, along with the clothing Bredych had worn when he had been stabbed.

Bredych lay in his bed, though he better resembled a shriveled piece of skin as he sank into the sheets. His skin was white, and his lips almost blue as he opened his mouth.

Her name was little more than a whisper as she walked over to the bed. A small chair had been placed beside it, which she claimed, and Bredych held out his hand to her. When she took it, his fingers were icicles against her skin. Everything about this man was shutting down, and she held back tears.

"How bad?"

She had intended to ask Shai, but it was Bredych who answered. "Bad enough I-I...dreamed of Adelei."

Margaret had to strain to hear him and patted his hand. "Don't feel you have to talk. Save your strength."

Shai pulled back the blankets to check the mass of

bandages wrapped around Bredych's midsection. Satisfied, he returned the blanket and added another one. "The stab wound missed the heart and lungs, but he lost a lot of blood before I was able to stop it. Even a few fingers to the right, and you would not be visiting Master Bredych."

She almost ordered them all to leave so she could speak to Bredych alone, but considering how small and weak he appeared, doing so would be a mistake. Instead, she forced a smile across her face as she looked at Bredych. "You killed Agaia."

Bredych nodded. "Had to."

"She may have claimed you in the process, you old man. What made you decide to fight her alone?"

"M-Magic. Kept me from...help. Was me or you. Chose me."

He closed his eyes then, and for a moment, Margaret thought him dead by the way her heart stopped in her chest, but when he exhaled, she breathed with him. She turned to Shai, who was grinding some herbs together with a mortar. "Will he recover?" she asked.

"If Roland was the only physician treating him, probably not, but I was able to use magic to stop his bleeding. Now it's just a matter of whether his body can heal. He's lost a lot of blood. I've seen a few folks recover from worse wounds but not many. I'm sorry."

Bredych squeezed Margaret's hand and when she turned her attention to him, his eyes were wide open and clear. "If I die, take me back...ashes...Order."

Tears blurred her vision as she nodded. "It will be a long time before that's necessary."

"Order must...be more. Help them be more."

She resisted pulling her hand away as he squeezed it hard enough to hurt. Something about the way he stared at her worried her, and she glanced at Shai, but the mystic's back was to her as he fussed with his medicines.

"Listen to me," whispered Bredych. "Time here has...made me different. The Order must...be more."

"They will, I'm sure, Master, and you will be there to see them...change." How the man wished them to change, Margaret did not know, but she patted his hand and nodded as if she did. His eyelids fluttered for a moment as a heavy sigh escaped his lips.

He inhaled sharply as he opened his eyes again to stare at her. "If I die, don't...mourn me. Use anger. Kill them," he said.

She nodded. "You're not dying, Master."

"Promise. Kill them."

"I promise."

When she swore, he squeezed her hand again. "You... Adelei, like daughters...to me. You have...filled...my heart."

Tears moistened her cheeks. "And mine. You are a great teacher, but more, a second father to me. I love you, though I could wish you less brave. Taking on Agaia by yourself."

He winced as a brief laugh escaped his lips. "Love you, daughter. Wasn't...alone. Far-far—"

"Farimun?"

Bredych nodded. "Helped...but left. Abandoned."

"He abandoned Agaia? Interesting."

Perhaps the Thirteen disagreed amongst themselves. That could be useful information.

He closed his eyes again, his chest rising and falling evenly. Rather than pray to useless gods, Margaret counted the ways she would kill them as she held his frail hand.

One way for every death since Adelei's.

257 Sharimus 23ʳᵈ - The Order of Amaska

IF LEOLIN HAD NOT KNOWN someone lived in the small cabin at the edge of the Order's lands, he would easily have overlooked the nondescript man sitting on the porch. Brown hair, brown eyes, and tanned skin blended Doughal Nilesh into the wooden hut. The mystic whittled a piece of wood, not even glancing up as Leolin approached, though he had no doubt the man was aware of his every move.

Leolin stopped before the porch steps. "Mystic Nilesh? Grand Master Miriam said I could find you here."

The man continued working his piece of wood. Leolin leaned forward and waved his hand in the air in front of the mystic, half expecting the man to catch it. When the mystic ignored him, Leolin frowned. "Miriam told me you would see me, sir. If you could put down whatever you're working on—"

The whittling motion continued as the man met Leolin's gaze. "The work never stops, young one." He nodded at the empty chair beside him and when Leolin remained standing in front of him, he frowned. "I've been waiting for you. If you want my assistance, sit."

Wood planks groaned beneath Leolin's feet as he climbed the steps to the cabin's porch. The chair was more comfortable than it looked and once seated, Leolin said as much.

"Carved it myself, much like this cabin."

"You built this?" asked Leolin.

"Many years ago. Long before you were born. Hells, long before your mother was born too."

Leolin studied the man's face. Wrinkles amassed across his skin but no more than Miriam bore. "Sir, if you don't mind my asking, do mystics live longer than the rest of us?"

"That's a good question. I wish I had the answer to it." Doughal paused in his carving to hold up a piece of wood as long as Leolin's hand. While pieces of wood had been removed from it, presumably with some care, to him the wood was little more than a twisted, gnarled root. "This wood came from a tree older than me, though you'd never know it by looking at it now. Like me, it's older than it seems. Perhaps we do live longer. I stopped counting after ninety."

"Winters?"

Doughal nodded. "I know you came to talk about more than wood. What can I do for the son of Shendra Abner?"

"How—"

"Did you think Miriam would ask me to meet with someone without telling me who I'm meeting?" The mystic laughed as heat crept to Leolin's face. "Not everything is magic."

"If you know who I am, then you know why I'm here."

"Indeed. At the time, I told your mother it was a bad idea. Using magic to convince someone that what they saw was a dream isn't right. The Order has been good to me, giving me a safe place to retire as it were, so I used my gift to do what they asked on the rare occasions they did, but your mother, she had a way about her. Never could say no to her."

Leolin sighed. "She's dead."

"I heard. Damn *Tribor*."

"What did you do to me and...and why?"

"Do you know who your father is?" asked Doughal.

"Samuhel Banach. He was an *Amaskan*."

The mystic nodded. "That he was and damn good at his work. The Order used him as more spy than assassin as he could charm his way into and out of any situation. Had a comfortable way about him so people talked to him. Your mother, she had it in her mind that Samuhel would be hers, but Samuhel lived on the road like any other *Amaskan*. With the Little War of Three beginning, Adir's father, King Arie, worried that the war would spread to more than a tussle between Alexander and Shad. He approached the Order, and they sent your father to Tarmsworth where he could keep an eye on things. You know your mother's role in that war?"

"I know she was sent to kill King Leon's daughters."

"She was, and she refused. She didn't know Bredych's intentions until it was almost too late, which is when she decided to leave."

Leolin nodded. "I know all of this."

"I see her impatience continued in her line." Doughal turned the wood in his hand until it was upside down. The portion he had been whittling held the vague shape of a human. "Bredych tried to kill her and thought he'd succeeded. Had her body dragged to the property's edge for the scavengers, but I found her. Wasn't right killing her because she wanted out. So I healed her as best I could. Well enough for her to bolt as soon as she could. Her brother didn't know it, but she was already with child."

"She said she never knew who saved her," said Leolin.

"She didn't. I shrouded myself so she wouldn't know. I didn't see her again until years later. I was in Tarmsworth visiting a friend when she showed up with you."

"But what happened? Why did she kill my father? And why erase my memories of him?"

"Your father had been called back to the Order. With the Little War of Three in the past, there was no reason for him to stay in Tarmsworth. Your mother was still in hiding, but Samuhel was going to take you back to the Order with him. Shendra didn't want that life for you, and they argued. Samuhel grabbed you, and your mother...well, she made sure you grew up safe—away from her brother—but you saw her kill him. You started crying, and she couldn't get you to stop, so she brought you to me." Doughal sighed. "I'm sorry, Leolin. Children are resilient creatures and with her there, you would've been okay, but she was insistent. She didn't want your early memories of her being ones where she killed your father."

Leolin was silent for a few minutes. He could understand the decisions his mother had made, especially the ones that kept him away from the Order, but erasing his memories felt like a step too far.

The sun glistened in the morning dew and as the wind shifted, he could smell the salt of the ocean. The trees around the cabin blocked any view of the sea from here, but if he walked into a clearing, he would be able to see the cliffside and the ocean below. This had been his mother's home. "I wish she were still alive so I could ask her why."

"Parents do what they think is best for their children. Sometimes they're right and sometimes they're not. Would you have preferred to grow up *Amaskan*?"

He blanched. "No. I don't know why it's not happening now, but lately, thinking of her causes these blinding headaches. Mystic Shai said it was because whatever magics you used to hide my memories from me are breaking down, that they're twisted wrong. Is there any way to undo what was done?"

Doughal stuck his knife into the wood in his hands and flicked a few curls away. "There is as I'm the one who did it. Is that what you want?"

When Leolin nodded, the mystic stopped whittling and reached out, offering the wooden figure to Leolin. What had been a rough shape now had structure. Curves and etch marks showed the figurine to be a woman. Was it his mother? When he picked it up, a wall of thoughts and emotions slammed into him.

His mother and father, holding hands as they walked.

Samuhel's laughter as he ran with a small boy across a field.

His mother standing in front of him as Samuhel shouted

at her, his face full of fury. This memory gripped him like a vice as it expanded in Leolin's mind.

The man who had represented shelter and love had grabbed at Leolin, tugging on him hard enough that Leolin's shoulder had popped. He had screamed as his mother cried.

Then Samuhel had unsheathed his blade. "You aren't safe, Shendra. He'll always be in danger if you're alive. Bredych should've done a better job."

A flash and then his mother stood over his father's body, her sword covered in blood.

The past sped up until Leolin could no longer see it, just a blur of white. Something dropped, and he was on the cabin's porch again. The figurine in his hands had turned to saw dust.

"She had no choice. He was going to kill her," said Leolin, his face damp with tears he did not know he had shed.

Doughal patted him on the shoulder. "I never saw what I erased—that's not how the magic works—but I'm glad you have your memories and your answers now."

Leolin glanced down at the dust in his hand. "I'm sorry about your sculpture. All that work. What happened to it?"

The mystic smiled. "Such is the way with work. Sometimes the work is not for you."

He shook his head. "I'm not sure what you mean—"

Leolin's words were interrupted as the mystic's eyes bulged, his mouth open as he stared at the sun. One moment, the man was sitting in his chair and the next, he curled in on himself, shoulders slumped and his chin resting on his chest.

"Mystic Nilesh?"

He shook the man's shoulder, and the mystic slid out of his chair to the ground. Leolin crouched beside the body and held a hand over the man's mouth. No air moved, nor did his chest rise or fall. Leolin held a few fingers at the man's neck. No heart beat beneath his skin.

Doughal Nilesh was dead.

IT DID NOT FEEL right to leave the man's body behind, so Leolin secured Doughal's body across the back of his borrowed horse and returned to the Order. He waited for the man to wake up and demand to know why he was tied to a horse's ass, but the mystic remained still.

As Leolin approached, Miriam spotted him and came out to meet him. When she rested her hand against Doughal's cheek, sorrow colored her face pale. "I'm sorry, Leolin," she said as she helped him untie the body. "I'd hoped old Doughal would live long enough to give you some answers. Looks like you just missed him."

"He was alive when I arrived at the cabin."

Her body tensed as she turned to face him. "And...?"

"I didn't kill him, if that's what you're thinking. He talked a lot about work, unlocked the memories in my mind, and then...it was like he went to sleep. He said he'd been waiting for me."

While she relaxed, Miriam kept her gaze trained on him. "If that's so, he waited a long, long time. We'll see to his remains." Several Amaskans picked up his corpse and carried it to a separate building nearby. "The burning will occur tomorrow. You are welcome to attend."

As she strode off, a trainee at his elbow took his horse and another gestured in the direction of the guest building. They were not taking any chances with their guests, and as he followed the trail to the building, his thoughts shifted to his mother.

She had been as cautious as the Amaskans here, long after she had left the Order. Her caution had possibly saved his life. Tears gathered at the corners of his eyes.

Now, he could think of her without wishing his head ripped from his shoulders. Now, her face in his mind did not cause his thoughts to mash together in a maelstrom.

Now, he could grieve his mother properly.

18

257 Itovan 1ˢᵗ - The Senate Isle

The sailboat's crew who saw the two Amaskans most of the journey to the Senate Isle had been rewarded handsomely for their silence. Once in sight of the island, the two had disembarked in a row boat. Both Amaskans had grown up in seafaring families, and while rowing towards the island at night had its challenges, both felt up to the task.

In the morning, the ship would dock properly in order to drop off supplies under the guise of good sails leading to an early arrival time. If fortune favored the Amaskans, the remaining Thirteen would be dead and the two could return to Lavi on the same ship. If their task failed, there would be no one to return. If their job fell somewhere in the middle, whoever survived would have to improvise.

Luck already favored them that the seasonal rains were nowhere to be seen. Slick grounds made for hard escapes, not to mention loud ones. Maya looped the rope around the pier beam. With hope they would not need the boat, but just in case, she tied a knot that could be untied in a hurry. Maya and her partner, Evoni, made use of the little shelter at the pier to change out of their clothes and into something more fitting.

Black silk covered them, wrapped tight and tied at the ankles, wrists, and waist. They both donned head wraps and smeared grease on exposed skin to blend in with the darkness.

"Do gods even sleep?" whispered Maya as she placed the lid on the grease jar and returned it to their bag.

Evoni shrugged. "No idea, but the masters said these gods were weak. Dying. Let's hope they need their rest like most elderly."

They returned to the row boat and exchanged one bag for another, a smaller bag that Maya slung across her body. The steps heading up the trail were old but stable and led to a large, stone building. Unlike most stone buildings that were built of stone bricks, this building was carved directly into the stone. Its smooth gray surface was cold, much like the air now that winter held the Little Dozen Kingdoms in its grip.

Maya pointed at the sole light shining down from a small window on the top of the building's three floors. Other than that, the building lay quiet like the rest of the island. A smaller building stood off to the side, which they would search if needed. Based on the information they had gathered from the sailors who delivered supplies to the island, the main building housed the senators. Perhaps the smaller building served as storage or housed servants. Either way, it was as dark as the main building.

It felt weird not to ask for Anur's blessing for their task—a change to the Order's traditions now that they knew the truth about the Thirteen—and Maya pursed her lips together as she tested the back door's knob.

It turned easily in her hands. Of course it was unlocked.

Besides being the only people on the island, what did gods have to fear from robbers or cutthroats? She tested the door's hinges, opening it a small amount at a time until she was sure it would open without giving them away.

They found themselves in a small antechamber outside the kitchens, which led to an empty dining hall on the right and a hallway on the left. Unlike the exterior, the insides showed the building's age as lines and cracks found their way across the walls. The hallway was lined in stone brick, a few of which were visibly loose. Maya pointed at the hallway, then up. Evoni nodded, and they stepped heel to toe as they moved. Candles lit the hallway every twenty paces, and she made a hand signal.

Servants.

He shook his head and made another sign, one all Amaskans memorized but rarely used. *Magic.*

Maya signed both, then continued forward. A turn at the hallway's end led towards the rest of the lower level and housed a stairwell. She stopped and glanced at Evoni, who gestured away from the stairs.

They would check the lower level before continuing up towards the lit room. One door led to a massive library with at least a dozen bookshelves lined in rows. Evoni shook his head, and she closed the door. If anyone was in there, a light would be visible. A room with a multitude of chairs and couches came next and was just as empty.

When she stepped into the next room, the hair on her arms rose beneath the silk, and she froze. Moonlight shone through several large windows, exposing a floor covered in broken glass. The windows themselves were not broken, though broken glass was strewn across the entire room. But from what?

Empty pedestals were spaced evenly throughout the room, and Evoni tugged at her arm. Something in the room made her skin crawl and when she glanced at Evoni, his eyes were wide as he signed again: *magic*.

Maya took a deep breath and something rank hit her nose, something foul mixed with a metallic, almost earthy odor. Somewhere in this room was blood. Something or someone had died here, of that she was sure. Her partner came to the same conclusion and signaled that they should leave.

Several rooms were locked and not even their lock picking tools would open them. A strong lock or perhaps magic kept the rooms protected. As the two Amaskans stood at the stairwell's bottom, they slowed their breathing. The second and third floors were likely to hold their targets.

Stairs were trickier than a regular wooden floor as they often creaked as the wood sagged, so they took one step at a time, pausing between each step to assess whether the wood was sagging. Other than the room full of broken glass, the house felt as if it had been built only a season ago, despite being hundreds of years old.

Every step was smooth and when they reached the landing, Evoni pointed at himself before gesturing that he would continue to the third floor. He was up the stairs before she could protest. These were not their normal marks but *gods*. Grand Master Miriam had expressly forbidden them from splitting up.

Typical of Evoni to not listen.

A hallway ran the building's full length with a dozen doors to check, and Maya swore under her breath. The third floor likely mirrored the second, which meant Evoni was facing the same challenge, only one of those rooms was lit. She swore again, then climbed the stairs to the third floor.

The Order's rising star, Evoni was very, very good at his job. He could talk his way into any building and move between nobility and the poor as easily as breathing. With a fine nose and high cheekbones, he could have been a lord somewhere had he not decided that killing others for Justice was a better path. Youth brought out a certain disregard for the rules in him, something the Order had driven out of Maya at an earlier age.

Unlike Evoni, she had been born to the Order. *She* understood why the rules existed.

Like the second floor, both hallways were lit with the same magical candles. Evoni stood halfway down the hallway as he approached the sole lit room. With no way to signal to him silently, she moved as quickly as she could down the hall.

He spun on his heels when she neared, throwing knife in his hand. He relaxed a hair when he saw it was her and not one of the Thirteen behind him, then he pointed at her and gestured down.

She shook her head and made two fists, slamming them together.

Together.

Evoni shrugged, his expression one of impatience. She spun a single finger around in a circle at the doors, but he shook his head again and gestured at the far door on the right.

Light flickered beneath it, but every few heartbeats, the lighting almost disappeared completely. Someone was pacing in front of the door. Maya unsheathed her dirk as they approached. They slowed their steps, almost on tip toe.

The footfalls inside did not drag or thump in a way suggesting any sort of limp or fatigue. If anything, they sounded normal. Maya made the signal again for servant, and again Evoni shrugged. They would not know without opening the door.

She gripped the door's knob and turned it as slowly as she dared. When it stopped, she nodded to Evoni. Three heartbeats later, she shoved open the door. The room was a bed chamber decorated in various shades of browns and reds, and at the center of it, a beautiful woman. Her umber skin danced in the candlelight as she pursed her lips together. The woman ran one hand through the tight curls cascading down her back.

"I wasn't expecting any visitors." She spoke softly, yet the words echoed oddly in the room as the house awoke. It was the best description Maya could think of as the sounds of multiple people rising reached them. "They won't be happy to see you here."

Evoni threw his knife at the woman who sidestepped it easily. Another was in his hands as quickly as the first, which he threw. This one she repelled with a wave of her hand.

"Why the need for violence, my child?"

As she spoke, he paused on his way to retrieving a third knife as his face relaxed. A goofy smile was plastered across his face as he swooned. A light hum filled the room as the woman smiled knowingly at Evoni. Whatever magics held him enthralled failed to infect Maya, and she pulled a small knife from her waist with her free hand.

Something loud crashed through the door behind her, and Maya used the opportunity to throw her knife. It landed in the woman's heart and she turned to Maya, the light fading from her eyes.

"Cerci!"

As Evoni stumbled backward, a burly man with almost white hair and a white beard rushed in. *Anur.* Even aged, Maya would recognize the God of Justice. He held Cerci, Goddess of Love and Joy, in his hands, which almost dwarfed her slight frame. Her body seemed to melt into the floor where it turned to ash. The knife that had pierced her heart landed on the wooden floor with a thump.

Anur spun to face them, his gaze shifting between their clothing and their faces. "You would dare! You, who I nurtured and protected, who I held most dear, would dare come into my home and...and *kill*? Amaskans serve Justice, serve ME!"

The last word rattled the glass panes in the window, and Evoni gave the sign.

Run.

Cerci was dead. The Thirteen could be killed, and that knowledge had to make it back to the Order. She was running before she was thinking, adrenaline driving her down the hallway.

A slip of parchment nestled in her pocket, which she would hide at the dock if she reached it in time. A sailor the Order had paid beforehand would take its message to the appropriate people in Lavi if neither of them escaped the island alive. It was her job to hide the parchment before attempting to rescue Evoni.

Assuming he was still alive to rescue.

The other gods were already running up their stairs. Maya opened the door to the nearest room and rushed inside. Other than the moonlight shining through the window, the room was dark and empty. No furniture, just a thin layer of dust on the window sill, which Maya disturbed as she opened the window. She removed the bag slung across her body and fetched the grapple and rope from inside.

Any other height, any other job, and she wouldn't risk it, but the stakes were too high. She wedged the grapple into the window's stone frame and ensured the rope was secured to it with a sturdy knot. The other end of the rope she wrapped around her waist several times before looping it around both thighs and tying it off. Shouting sounded at the hall's end as the others discovered the death of Cerci.

Maya climbed onto the window sill and wrapped her hands around the rope before lowering herself over the ledge. Dropping a body length at a time, she kept her feet plastered to the building's side. Just short of the ground, the rope stopped, and Maya glanced down. The drop was her height and survivable, so she removed a knife and hacked at the rope until it gave.

She dropped the remaining length and landed in a crouch. While the moonlight lit the area, the black clothing she wore hid her fair enough as she abandoned the rope and ran down the hillside toward the docks. Behind her, magic filled the air as a ball of light almost as bright as the sun hovered above the building.

They were looking for her.

Rather than take the trail towards the dock, she slid down the hillside itself. If they reached the docks before she did, she would be able to see them and hide. She was grateful for her thick gloves as she used the tall grass and even rocks to slow her descent. The docks were clear when she neared them, and she cut sideways across the hill to reach the steps.

She did not go inside the small shelter but stopped outside it, where she removed the piece of parchment from her pocket. Maya crumbled it into a ball, and then grabbed a rock the size of her hand. She set the stone between several shrubs growing near the shelter's door with the wad of parchment underneath it.

Even if the rains began and erased the ink on the message, the parchment's mere existence under the rock would be signal enough. The Order would know what it meant and that both of their Amaskans had died in the service of true justice. Duty done, Maya withdrew her dirk and began the trek back towards the buildings.

The likelihood that Enovi lived was low. If he had, he would have made his way to her by now. The thought chilled her more than the cold as her breath showed in front of her.

If Anur wished to know what real justice looked like, she would show him.

257 Itovan 8ᵗʰ - City of Alesta

SNOW FELL OUTSIDE THE WINDOW, which was frosted around the edges. Two weeks had passed since Bredych had been stabbed and Agaia had died. A flutter of pigeon carried messages had been sent to notify the Little Dozen Kingdoms of the death of another god, though news of Bredych's injury had been left out. His recovery crawled by as Margaret awaited news from the Order.

Roland and Shai believed it possible for Bredych to recover, though whether he would ever fight again or move without pain was another matter entirely. When Margaret was not at his bedside, she was in her study, pouring through books in hopes of better understanding magic and the Thirteen.

That afternoon, another batch of letters had arrived from across the Little Dozen Kingdoms, the first batch being agreements from the other rulers that the final stand with the Thirteen should take place at the Pass. Besides being a central location for all the kingdoms, the Meridi Pass lay at the heart of their conflict. It was the place where many had died at the hands of the Thirteen, and thus, it would be the place where they fought for their freedom.

While most of the messages had been positive, King Havin Bajit of Shad had sent his agreement by way of a scathing retort. "Alexander started this. I will help but only because I have no choice."

His comment about having no choice meant Sharmus had to be involved, though how, Margaret did not know, and she sighed. Once Sharmus died, Margaret would have another war on her hands. If she were lucky, the other rulers would defend her, but if not, Havin would have to be dealt with.

It was in the second batch of messages that Margaret

found the ones she had been hoping for. The first was from Grand Master Miriam.

To Her Majesty, Queen Margaret Poncett I,

I know former Grand Master Bredych would never ask the Order to do something this dangerous unless it was absolutely necessary. Because he has been keeping me apprised of what your people have discovered with regards to the Thirteen, my council and I have agreed that we must know exactly how mortal the Thirteen are.

It was with this in mind that we sent two of our best Amaskans to the Senate Isle. They implemented a plan similar to what Bredych and Your Majesty suggested. A day ago, our messenger brought us word of the results.

The Gods are mortal.

I don't know when this changed, but our Amaskans were able to kill one of the Thirteen using non-magical means. Unfortunately, I can't tell you which one as both of my Amaskans died in the attempt, but one of the gods was killed with a blade.

This changes much.

As such, the bulk of the Order's members have been recalled in order for us to travel to Alexander with all haste. Some council members too old to travel will remain behind with the trainees too new and green to help, but the rest of the Order will help in any way we can. Anur betrayed us, and we will have our justice.

I've got a strange visitor who will travel with us, but I truly think his help is needed.

We should arrive in time for the worst of winter. Next time you decide to declare war, perhaps we could pick spring time to do it?

Grand Master Miriam of the Order of Amaska

Margaret released the breath she had been holding. The gods might have fading magic at their disposal but so did the mystics. Being able to defeat the Thirteen in combat meant they had a chance. While it saddened her to know the Order had lost two of its members, far more would die without that information. Her stomach fluttered in response, and she set the parchment aside. The second letter, this one directly from Leolin, was much shorter.

Maggie,

I'm leaving Sadai tomorrow. Grand Master Miriam's message may arrive before mine, which includes details about the coup on the Senate Isle, so I'll skip those bits. Needless to say, I'll be returning with most of the Order with me.

I've picked up a new ally and friend named Avishai. She's a chathula, *if you can believe it. I'd never seen one before but apparently her father helped my mother a long time ago. I'll tell you the tale when I reach Alesta.*

Miriam's message to you might be vague about this as I've learned she has an odd sense of humor about her, but I didn't want this to be a surprise when we arrive. Sharmus is with us. He came to the Order seeking help to die.

Instead, we convinced him to help the Little Dozen Kingdoms. It's odd, but I think he really wants us to succeed.

Hopefully we won't get caught in any storms while at sea.

Luck be with us all and see you soon,

Leolin

Margaret glanced down at her stomach as it fluttered a second time. At first, she had thought it an anxious reaction to the messages, but the second time was stronger, more focused. Was it the baby moving? Roland had mentioned she would feel the baby move as she entered the fourth month...

There.

It was not a kick; more like being tickled from the inside. She rested her hand against her growing stomach. Marching in winter meant every estimate for travel must be doubled. A few more days would need to be added to that now that she was with child.

Three more messages sat in the stack, two of them concerning a raid at the port city of Lyon. The first from the city's portmaster regarding the missing crates and the second from Lord Cornish demanding to know what Margaret planned to do about the men who had attacked a supply boat. Lyon was not even a part of his holdings, yet his letter made it clear that he expected her to do something about the matter or he would. Margaret penned a brief response reminding the man that he was no longer her advisor and should he wish to keep his holdings, he should look to them and nothing more.

She frowned as she set the message aside. He was not completely in the wrong. The raiders had been plaguing Lyon as well as other port cities for some time, but with the Thirteen trying to split the Little Dozen Kingdoms apart, there was little she could do with her attention elsewhere. For now, she made note of it and set it aside to look into as she was able.

The last message was on parchment well-worn, and when she opened it she recognized it as the letter she had penned declaring the Little Dozen Kingdoms emancipated from the Boahim Senate. Her hands trembled as she unfolded it.

All twelve signatures marked the bottom of the letter.

Margaret folded it closed again and sealed it with wax. This message would be sent directly to the Thirteen on their island. Far away kingdoms like Merriwynne and Nicen likely were already moving towards the Meridi Pass. She picked up the bell on her desk and rang it.

Her lady-in-waiting entered and bowed. "Your Majesty?"

"I need to see the field marshal as well as the steward. Have them meet me in my sitting room in a candlemark, please, and send these to the pigeon keeper."

The woman nodded and left. It was one thing to ride to the Pass with a few guardsmen, but another to move the bulk of her army. That planning would be done by those more knowledgeable on the subject. Instead, Margaret left her study for Bredych's room. Rather than lying flat on his back as normal, he was sitting upright in his bed, several pillows behind him.

While his face remained waxen and pained, he smiled when she entered the room. Margaret claimed the chair beside his bed and nodded to a healer who ground up herbs with a pestle. "How are you feeling today?" she asked.

"It still hurts to breathe, but I'm upright. Better than the alternative." Bredych waved at the healer. "Could you...do that elsewhere, please? I feel like I'm waiting for you to grind my bones next."

The woman's cheeks flushed as she fled the room, and Margaret frowned. "You live because of women like her. Perhaps a bit more tact and politeness are in order."

Bredych wagged a finger at her. "Gretchen has been told numerous times that I'm better able to rest when I'm not forced to listen to her grinding away, both by Shai and myself. A little reminder hurts no one." He winced as he gave a slight chuckle. "Besides, I'm one of her better patients. Now tell me what news you carry."

"How did you know I had news?"

"I've spent a lifetime studying people, including the way they move. There was a lightness to your steps as you entered... and something else. Stand up!"

The order came at half the sharpness of his normal commands, but the tone was all him, and she was halfway to standing before she realized why he had asked. His gaze settled on her middle before rising to her face.

"You are with child." She returned to the chair without confirming, and he pursed his lips together. "You realize this complicates your plans."

Margaret shrugged. "It's not as if I planned this. Plenty of women were fighting and having babies when the Shadians attacked Alesta. I hardly will be the first or the last to lead an army while with child."

"Is Leolin the father?"

"Unless Gamun has risen from the Thirteen Hells, he is."

Bredych's face relaxed as his eyes lit up. "It's good to hear you speak that name without it poisoning your lips. Does Leolin know?"

She shook her head. "I didn't know I was pregnant until after he'd left, but this was not the news I was bringing to you."

The healer knocked at the door before entering, this time carrying a cup in her hands. "It's time for your tonic."

He screwed up his face like a child as he took it from her. While he drank it down, he gasped and coughed. "Besides muddling my head something fierce, it tastes like three rats died in a vat and were left there for several seasons. Whatever the herbs are, they help, but faugh!"

Once the healer left, Margaret scooted her chair closer to Bredych. "The Order was successful. They killed one of the Thirteen."

Bredych shot one arm up into the air in a cheer and then groaned as the movement tugged at his wound. Roland had done his best to sew the skin back together, while Shai had used magic to help the bleeding stop, but the wound was still fresh enough that sudden movements could disrupt its healing.

"We do not know which one, only that a weapon was successful."

"The Amaskans, did they escape?"

She shook her head. "The Order is on their way here though. From the sound of it, most of the Amaskans are coming to help fight. Sharmus is with them."

He stared at her and tried not to cough. "Sharmus?"

"Apparently he sought out the Order in hopes they would kill him. Leolin didn't give details, only that Miriam and the others convinced the god to help us instead. Leolin also has a... what did he call it, a *chathula*...with him?"

"I have not seen their kind since I was young."

Margaret nodded. "Leolin said that Avishai—that's her name—her father helped Ida long ago."

Bredych stared at the blanket covering his legs for a long enough stretch that Margaret wondered if he had fallen asleep with his eyes open. She touched his hand and when he flinched, she released it. "Are you well?" she asked.

"My apologies, Your Majesty, but the Thirteen must be playing a trick on me. When I was younger, Shendra and I were on a job together when we encountered a *chathula*. This one taught me quite a lesson about what constitutes intelligence. I assumed it nothing more than an overly large cat, but this creature was anything but. He saved our lives and helped us rid the world of a cruel, cruel woman."

The way he paused then, there was more to the story, but he did not elaborate and Margaret did not push. He would either tell it in his own time or he would not. The choice was his. "I guess this is the descendent of the one you encountered," she said.

"That would be my guess. Any other surprises coming from Sadai?"

"None that I'm aware of, though I need to return to my rooms. I'm to meet Fenton shortly."

As she stood to leave, Bredych reached out to grab her hand. "Send the army to the Pass if you must but do not follow. Remain here."

Margaret frowned. "You asked me to kill them."

"That was the request of a dying man. I still might be dying, but you are with child. I'll not have your child's death on my conscience."

"You speak as if I'm going to die in this fight."

Bredych squeezed her hand. "I thought... the prophecy... well, I thought I was the spark, that my death would bring honor to the Order and yield the freedom of the Little Dozen Kingdoms, but I was wrong, I fear. Younger people will fight this battle while I lie in this bed, meaning it's not me the prophecy speaks of. I fear it's you, Margaret."

"So you believe I will die and my child along with me?" When he nodded, she smiled and said, "I believe you may be correct, but I'm not afraid of death for it walks all around me. I may have killed Itovah's body, but her spirit is set on reaping as many souls as she can."

"Do not allow her to take yours as well."

She gave his hand a pat before releasing it. "We all play what roles we must in order to protect others. If that means my death, so be it, but I do not intend to die, Bredych. I intend to live."

ACT II

19

258 Luthian 18th - City of Alesta

T hey are late."

Margaret paced in the short space between the door and chairs in Bredych's guest suite. A little over a month had passed since his stabbing, and with Shai's help, the former Grand Master could move about, albeit slowly. In Roland's esteemed opinion, had it been anyone else, even with magical intervention the *Amaskan* would be dead. Her physician had spent the past month worrying for her and the baby while trailing behind Shai in hopes of learning more about magical healing. Margaret spent the month alternating between her worry about Leolin's return and Bredych's healing. Since she was not a healer, all she could do was fret about the former, so she continued to pace.

Her father would have lost money on any bet regarding Roland's willingness to work with a mystic at his age. Times were changing, and with hope Alexandrians would be willing to change a bit more assuming the Order of *Amaska* safely arrived in Alesta... She glanced at Bredych who sat in a stuffed chair in his room, a book in his hands.

"While sailing is easier than crossing the mountains in winter, it's not without its risks, Margaret, especially the Harren Sea. Baudwin Bay has a reputation for its storms, so it's likely they've been delayed."

"I know. As I said, they're late."

When she continued to pace, Bredych set his book aside and reached out to catch her arm. "The storms have delayed them, but I'm sure they will arrive in Alexander safely," said Bredych.

"The Thirteen will arrive at the Pass in fifteen days. Most of the other rulers have left with their armies. If I don't leave soon, I won't arrive on time."

Bredych frowned. "I've said this before, but you should not be traveling. Let your field marshal take your army."

Margaret shook her head. Since learning she was with child, he treated her as if she were incapable of feeding herself, let alone leading an army. "And I've told you before that I must be present for this fight. The Thirteen are coming to the Pass because of *me*."

"Because of *all* of the rulers. Everyone signed that letter sent to the Thirteen, did they not? Do you even know if they received it? Perhaps this entire idea should be reexamined." As he spoke, his shoulders slumped a bit.

He pretended he was stronger than he was, but healing was difficult; Margaret chided herself for sharing her frustrations with him. For all that he wanted to share her thoughts, he lacked the strength to do so. Besides, if she were to lead her people in this fight, she needed to worry less about his thoughts and more about what lay ahead.

Perhaps it was better he did not know that her army was already prepared to leave. All they waited on was for her to lead them to the Pass. Margaret resumed her pacing. "The

Order is coming here to help us fight the Thirteen, but if they do not arrive in time, we will have to fight the gods without them."

Bredych stood slowly, using a staff for balance, and stepped forward to take Margaret's hands in his own. "I can see it in your eyes."

"What?"

"The determination to leave."

She tried to release his hands, but he gripped hers all the harder, and she sighed. This was the man who had become a second father to her, the man who had trained her in blade-work and kept her safe as she found her own footing, but since his injury, the resolve had bled out of him.

Margaret pulled her hands from his. The way his eyes widened made her heart flutter, and she reached out to hug him. It was not an action she did often with him, but the difference in his frame was more than just demeanor.

He was old.

"I must, but I'll be careful. I was trained by the best, after all."

Bredych shook his head. "It's not enough. The prophecy —wait for Leolin, for the Order."

When she nodded, his piercing gaze followed her as she walked towards the door. Even with her back to him, she could feel him watching her. She had lied to him, and they both knew it.

She would lie again if it meant saving him.

The door closed softly behind her. What Bredych needed was time to heal and her worry would not fix his wound or his broken spirit. Her footfalls sounded overly loud to her ears as she walked towards the stairs.

While the thought of the Order being lost at sea terrified her, what sent her heart beat racing was the idea of losing Leolin, and she almost stumbled walking up the stone stairs.

There was no god she could pray to in hopes they would protect him. Rather, she took a deep breath and continued to her rooms in order to pack a small bag.

Her emotions had left her in a state of flux as she waited for others and for herself. She stopped a passing servant outside her rooms. "Tell my field marshal and steward that we leave tomorrow."

Margaret was done waiting. Besides, the Thirteen would wait for no one.

20

258 Luthian 21ˢᵗ - City of Alesta

How could you let her go?" They were the first words out of Leolin's mouth as he stood in Margaret's sitting room. Bredych sat near the fireplace with a stack of parchment on the table beside him. The *Amaskan* glowered but said nothing, and Leolin waved his hand in the air. "I know, I know. Telling Maggie what to do is like telling the snow not to fall, but at least I thought you would've gone with her."

"Shai was quite adamant that I not travel as my insides are still healing." Bredych stood and raised his tunic. A rainbow of reds and browns crept up from the edges of the bandages wrapped around the man's midsection. "Trust me, boy, if I thought I could sit a horse, I would've taken the first one for the Pass."

Albeit slowly, Bredych moved well as he sat, and Leolin sighed. "What do I tell the Order when they arrive tomorrow? I rode ahead to..."

"To see Margaret alone—I know—but when the Order arrives, you'll all need to ride for the Pass like you've had a month's rest. The Thirteen will be there in seven days. That leaves you little time to reach them."

Leolin groaned. "Miriam swore sailing here would be the better path but that storm! I will never set foot on a boat again so long as I live."

"I told Margaret you were likely delayed by a storm."

"More than that—two storms, but the one in the bay landed us in the Kingdom of Naribor. We had to wait until the ship was repaired before we could sail again for the City of Lyon. Luckily it's been warmer this week, so we didn't have to fight too much snow riding up through the southern forest."

"You'll be hard pressed to make it to the Pass in time. How far behind you are the rest?"

"No more than a day. Depending upon how many horses they could talk old Daryn out of."

Bredych groaned. "That man wouldn't sell a loaf of bread to a starving king!"

"Lucky for us, Sharmus was with us. That god could talk even you into laying down your sword," said Leolin. When the *Amaskan* frowned, Leolin tilted his head. "You haven't given up the way of the warrior while I was away, have you?"

"Fighting Agaia was...challenging. You've heard?"

"The tale of how you killed a god and were mortally wounded?" Leolin nodded. "Every page and soldier between the city gates and this room regaled me with the story."

"It makes for a lovely tale, I'm sure, but it was a reminder of how many years have passed since I swore to uphold Justice. Perhaps it's this injury or how close I came to holding Itovah's hand that has me a bit addled, but I'm tired, boy. Weariness is rooted in my soul."

Leolin poked Bredych in the shoulder. "Thirteen Hells,

you are wallowing like a pig. Maggie needs an *Amaskan,* not an old man."

"Then it's a good thing the Order's on its way."

His words had been in jest, but Bredych's response worried Leolin. The man was different. There were stories of fighters who had lost their nerve after a near fatal wound, but to see such a change in the former grand master left him speechless.

"Looking into the Thirteen?" asked Leolin as he pointed at the stack of parchment.

"No, King Bajit." When Leolin raised an eyebrow, Bredych shrugged. "The man's dangerous. He knows as much about magic if not more than Shai, probably more than old Doughal. Once the Thirteen are dead, that man will do whatever he can to ensure Margaret dies. You know that, yes?"

Leolin nodded. "There's not much you can do about that from here, though, is there?"

"No, but if enough evidence of his crimes can be gathered, perhaps the Little Dozen Kingdoms will agree to...do something about the problem. The rulers have grown to depend upon the Senate to ensure that Justice is served, but part of emancipation is rebuilding and reframing how one sees the world. Without Havin plaguing the world, I think the Little Dozen will finally have a chance to thrive."

Behind him, the door swung open and a page ran in. "There's a whole bunch of people here to see you, sir." The page gasped for air as he gripped the doorknob.

"Ran the entire way, did ya?" asked Bredych, and the boy grinned. "We'll be right with them. Go on."

He stood straighter than when he had shown Leolin his healing wound, but he leaned heavily on the wooden staff as he trudged towards the door. "I guess the Order managed to talk Lord Daryn out of enough horses."

Bredych led the way down to the first floor and the entry hall, which was empty of everyone except an old woman with sharp blue eyes. When Miriam spotted Bredych, her expression fell and her skin paled.

Perhaps it would have been better if Leolin had gone down first to warn her. As if she heard his thoughts, she glared at Leolin as the two men approached. Whatever she had planned to say was lost when Bredych pulled the woman into a tight embrace. He whispered something into her ear, and she nodded against him.

Leaving them in the entry hall, Leolin walked through the empty reception area and into the audience chamber to the right. Inside were most of the Order of *Amaska*, sans those masters too old or infirm for travel and trainees too young to fight. According to what Miriam had told Leolin, the Order had once been 200 strong, but now, the group before him numbered 112. Counting Bredych, 113, and he winced.

Avishai sat at Sharmus's side, but as she caught Leolin's thoughts, the *chathula* glanced at Leolin. *You're worried about their leader.*

He did not have to think as hard anymore for the creature to hear his thoughts, only to relax and think of Avishai, but the tension in his frame spoke more than his thoughts. Still, he gave brief nod. *Bredych is no longer their leader—Miriam is—but yes, I'm worried.*

Miriam may hold the space but this Bredych is who leads their hearts.

The thump of Bredych's staff announced his arrival and every *Amaskan* in the room bowed their heads. Avishai approached the man gently and offered his shoulder as a support. "Thank you," said Bredych.

As he stared across the mass of black silked bodies, Leolin noticed the man's eyes tearing up. Beside him, Miriam clapped her hands and as one, the Order raised their bald heads, tattooed chins held high.

"Welcome to Alesta, Capital City of Alexander," said Leolin. He gestured towards the empty dais. "Our Queen is already traveling to the Meridi Pass with great haste. Today and tonight, you should rest for tomorrow, we will ride for the Pass."

"Hopefully on fresh mounts!"

Leolin could not see who said it, but he laughed along with the Amaskans. If they had ridden their horses anything like he had, new mounts would be a necessity if they were to make it to the Pass in time. The steward walked into the audience chamber with a dozen servants trailing behind him. "With most of the Royal Army gone, our castle steward will show you to the barracks. Along the way, he will note where the dining hall and bathing chambers are. Rest up," Leolin said.

While the bulk of the Order gathered what belongings they carried with them, Leolin gestured for Miriam, Avishai, and Sharmus to follow him. With most of the wounded cleared from the castle, he led them to Margaret's sitting room, one that also served as an informal audience chamber and was large enough for them all to sit while they talked. By the time they reached the third floor, Leolin had expected Bredych to be pale and sweaty, but for all the man leaned on Avishai and the staff, he did not even appear winded. Perhaps the *Amaskan*'s wounds were not as severe as Leolin had been led to believe. The thought lasted until he noticed how tightly Bredych's hand gripped Avishai's fur. Another look revealed almost white knuckles on the hand that held the staff.

Leolin ushered them into the room where he ordered wine and a few refreshments brought in.

As he closed the door behind him, Miriam leaned

Bredych's staff against the wall. "Now that we're away from listening ears, tell me what in the Thirteen Hells happened to you," she said as she turned towards Bredych.

"I would like to hear this tale as well," said Sharmus.

"Pa*rr*don me, but if you do not mind, I would like to hunt *rr*athe*rr* than hea*rr* this tale. Is the*rr*e an app*rr*op*rr*iate place for such a task?"

"I can have food brought up for you," said Leolin.

"That would take all of the fun out of the task, would it not?"

Leolin rang for a servant, who knocked on the door before entering. "If you would take Lady Avishai to the Huntsmaster. She is hungry and would like to hunt." To the *chathula*, he said, "Our Huntsmaster will show you the best areas to flush out game." *And ensure no one hunts you.*

Avishai grinned. *Anyone who tried would find themselves serving as my meal.*

The servant, a short statured girl, stared at the *chathula* who stood above the girl's shoulders. "Sir, you want I should take a cat to the Huntsmaster?"

"I am not a cat."

Hearing the creature speak, the girl let out a squeak before giving a brief curtsy. "My pardons, your ladyship. Please follow me."

The *chathula*'s tail swished back and forth as she followed the young girl out the door.

"No more delays or distractions. Tell me," said Miriam.

Bredych sighed. "Agaia arrived at the castle with Farimun as her escort. She told me she was here to kill Margaret. I fought her. She injured me and I removed her head with my sword."

"I sincerely doubt it was that easy." Miriam tilted her head. "How long ago was this?"

"A month or so."

While Leolin relaxed, Miriam's frown deepened. "How did she injure you? And with what?"

"She stabbed me with her sword. Here." Bredych pointed to his side. "Mystic Shai and Roland, the Queen's physician, have been taking good care of me."

"Mystic Shai...he's of the Healing School of Sadai, yes?" When Bredych nodded, she straightened upright in her chair. "You were gravely injured, you fool. You're only upright because they've been throwing magic into your body every chance they get. Am I wrong?"

Sharmus stood and approached the chair where Bredych sat. "Rather than chastising him, perhaps I could take a look."

Bredych flinched, his eyes wide. Beside him, Miriam pressed a hand against his thigh. "I didn't trust him at first, being one of the Thirteen, but as we sailed for Alesta, we talked at length. I'm convinced he wishes us no harm. Besides, the *chathula* agrees."

"What will you be doing to me?"

"I don't know. I won't know until I look at the damage."

"I would rather you didn't."

Sharmus merely shrugged and returned to his seat. A servant arrived with a tray bearing a variety of dried fruits and pitcher of wine, which she set on the table at the room's center. The servant remained long enough to pour glasses for each of them before leaving. No one spoke until the door was firmly shut and they were alone again.

Miriam pursed her lips as she glared at Bredych. "Your distrust is understandable, but I have vouched for Sharmus. He's been nothing but helpful, including at the Pass when Queen Margaret needed to convince the others to participate in this revolt against the Thirteen. Let him look."

"We will discuss it later." In private.

The last two words were not spoken, but Leolin heard them in Bredych's tone. Rather than watch the two Amaskans argue, he cleared his throat. "I don't know how much you know of the *chathula,* but Avishai saved my life while I was traveling across the desert. Two men attacked me, probably *Tribor,* though I couldn't confirm it, and she used magic. She was able to kill them with seemingly little effort. I've already discussed this with Sharmus and Miriam, but with the Meridi River running straight through the Pass, she'll be able to use her water magic against the Thirteen."

"While our magic is fading, I have no explanation for how this creature can readily access magic by standing in water. She demonstrated it while we were at sea. There are limits to what she can do, but the Little Dozen Kingdoms has gained a powerful ally and should be made aware," said Sharmus as he picked at the fruit. "But magic does not come from water. What Avishai does is something new."

"Don't get any ideas. The last thing we need is the rest of you finding out," said Leolin.

Miriam withdrew a stack of parchment from the satchel beside her and handed it to Bredych. "This is everything our people could gather on the crimes of King Havin Bajit, as well as notes on the *chathula* tribes, which isn't much to be honest. You and Shendra's contact with Avishai's father was not the first contact the Order's had with the *chathula,* but prior to you two, the only other mention was a few decades after the forming of the Order."

"We were aware of their existence, particularly on the other continents, but not that they were capable of magic. Something about that land is hidden from us," said Sharmus, and he frowned. "Child-god. Faugh!"

"She mentioned a god not of the Thirteen," said Miriam.

Bredych arched a brow. "Interesting."

When he offered no more input, Leolin studied him. The lines around his eyes betrayed his pain, as did the way he leaned on his left side while seated. The man was more severely injured than originally thought. "You've overdone it. You should rest," he said to Bredych. "Honestly, we all should. The steward can show you to your guest rooms, which will be on the floor below this. You are welcome to remain here until you wish to retire."

As a yawn threatened to split Leolin's skull apart, he stood and left the room. All he wanted was the softness of a bed, preferably one with Margaret in it, but she was many miles from here. Leolin's heart panged in response as he took the stairs up to the fourth floor.

Margaret's suite was empty, but her rooms still carried the hint of lavender and wildflowers. When he entered the bedchamber, a vase sat on her desk. The flowers in it were wilted and dry.

BREDYCH REMAINED BEHIND in the sitting room. He thought himself alone when he stood, his knees shaking with the effort. His body ached in a way it hadn't before and even with the magical healing, his body refused to do the simplest of things. The weakness took him at the most random of times. He fell back into the chair, his breath coming in haggard gasps.

A footstep near the door startled him and when he glanced up, Sharmus stood in the corner. The god approached silently, moving with a fluidity that Bredych used to have, and knelt on the floor in front of the *Amaskan*.

"You are gravely injured still."

Bredych nodded. "Shai sleeps for a full day after a session spent trying to heal my wounds. They thought they stopped the bleeding inside, but something isn't right. I'm growing weaker, and I'm needing healing more often than before."

"Yet you persist."

"Aye. I have to go to the Pass."

"Why?" asked Sharmus.

"The prophecy. I am the spark. I-I have to be." The way the god's green eyes watched him unnerved Bredych. He looked away, his gaze falling on the god's hooved feet. "Margaret can't die, so it must be me."

Sharmus nodded. "But you are in no position to ride."

"This is the crux of the matter. I must ride. If for no other reason than to kill Havin myself."

"That is certainly a man who needs killing. May I?" Sharmus held his hand in front of Bredych's chest.

"Why?"

"Because I am still the God of Healing."

"I heard you have little magic left," said Bredych.

"It's true, I have very little left to give, but for this, I will try."

When Bredych nodded, the god touched him. Tingling, much like a bee sting, rippled across Bredych's body until a sharp pain lanced his wound. He lurched forward from his chair as tears ran down his face. When he screamed, Sharmus snapped his fingers and the sound disappeared, though it did not keep Bredych from crying out. The pain persisted for a few minutes as his muscles spasmed. His insides moved, and he howled his throat raw.

His vision faded, as did the pain, and from somewhere to his left, Sharmus patted his hand and said, "I am sorry for the pain."

For a time, all Bredych knew was the sound of his own whimpers and the taste of his snot as it ran down his face. When he opened his eyes, Sharmus was gone and so was the staff. Of course the god would take the one object of any help these days. Bredych took a deep breath and stood.

He had expected resistance and fatigue. Instead, his muscles held him easily.

With trembling fingers, he raised his tunic. The bruising that had peeked out from beneath his bandages was gone. Bredych untucked the bandage's corner and slowly unwrapped it until his wound was exposed. At first, he dared not look, but after the air failed to irritate the wound, he glanced down at his side.

Only a scar remained.

RATHER THAN RETURN to his guest suite, Bredych spent the better part of a candlemark roaming the castle, not because there was anyone in particular he sought out or anywhere he needed to be, but because he could. For the first time in over a month, he could walk without pain, so he meandered through Alesta Castle.

When he returned to his room on the third floor, Miriam's bags sat next to his favorite chair. He supposed the steward had shown her to Bredych's rooms at her request, and he eyed the room to his bedchamber. Even newly healed, his knees trembled at the thought of facing her.

With a heavy sigh, he reached out and paused, his hand on the door's handle. He loved her, but in that moment, fear held him apart.

The door opened without his aide, and Miriam stood in his bedchamber in nothing more than a short chemise, and he frowned. "How did you know it was me?"

"Who else would be entering your bedchamber?"

Bredych shook his head. "I've had all manner of healers and such coming in and out of my rooms for over a month. I could have been any number of people—"

The words stopped as Miriam's lips pressed hard against his before pulling away. "Let me see your wound," she said, and when he hesitated, she pulled up his tunic to look for herself. No bandages remained around his midsection, only a scar half the length of her forearm, and her hand fell away.

"Sharmus healed me." The Miriam he knew would have used that opportunity to help herself to his body, but she stood staring at him, her face a mask. "You told me to let him help, so I did."

A sob burst forth from Miriam as she reached for him. Bredych held her while she cried, and when small sniffs were all that remained, he tilted her chin up so he could see her face. When she met his gaze, tears remained in her blue eyes.

"You almost died."

Her words were a whisper that stung him more than her tears, and when a few more spilled from her eyelids, he brushed them away with a well-calloused thumb. "But I didn't. Besides, 'Death is nothing to an *Amaskan*, since when we are, we live and Itovah has not come for us, and when Itovah comes, we are not alive to be. Death is the cost of Justice.'"

"Don't quote the *Book of Ja'ahr* at me, not with this. Agaia could have killed you. The rest of the Thirteen still could."

Bredych tilted his head. "I know, but I can't stay hidden away in a castle while others do the work of freeing Boahim. Neither can you."

A small smile played at the corner of her mouth. "But we could. We could hide away here in your rooms until the world figures itself out. I could make you forget this silly prophecy and the Thirteen."

It was a half-hearted attempt at best, and they both knew it. Bredych kissed her fingers as he studied their wrinkles. Small lines and none-too-few scars covered her hands just as they did his. They weren't growing old, they *were* old. Bredych released her hand with a small sigh. "As much as I would love to run somewhere with you and allow others to fight this war, you know I can't. Besides, by tomorrow you would be bored with me."

She stepped back to allow him entrance to his bedchamber, and he spotted two cups on the small bedside table. No steam rose from either, and he nodded towards the brown liquid in them. "Cold tea?"

"It was hot when I made it, but someone took his time being healed."

Bredych chuckled. "Healing hurts, even when a god does it. Remind me to tell you about the experience some time. After that, I took a stroll. Had I realized you were waiting for me, I would have walked straight here."

"Of course I was waiting for you!" Miriam picked up a cup and handed it to Bredych. "I love you, you know."

They had each spoken those words many times through the years, but something in her voice was different, more fragile. But then, his words held more emotion these days, too. He was about to take a sip of tea when he noticed her cup sat untouched. "I love you, too, even when you're trying to distract me. What did you put in the tea?"

"Nothing but tea."

Bredych set his cup down, untouched. "You're welcome to mine then. I don't much enjoy cold tea."

When he sat on the bed and began removing his boots, Miriam swore. "I-I was worried you would try and ride for the Pass tomorrow with us while wounded."

"You put *valian* in the tea, didn't you?"

"Just enough to help you sleep through until morning. Besides, I was going to make it up to you tonight."

"I was too wounded for that. Besides, you can't make up for something in advance, Miriam."

She smiled at him as she untied the top of her chemise. "You absolutely can. But now that you're healed, would you like to find out how?"

"As long as it doesn't involve tea, I would love to."

Bredych pulled Miriam to him and kissed her. At some point, they would both need rest before riding for the Pass on the morrow, but for now, he would remind her of how much he loved her, because if the prophecy was true, he would not have the opportunity again...

21

258 Luthian 24ᵗʰ - Meridi Pass

Margaret's tent at the Meridi Pass leaked cold air worse than the castle's garderobes, and worse, the hard cot left her sore and out-of-sorts. With enough room for a small table, her cot, two chairs, and a small brazier, her tent was larger than those shared by members of her army but not by much. Her army had been at the Pass for barely a day, and already she longed for home. The Royal Gardens would be coated in snow, but with a proper fireplace to escape to, it would be better than the Pass in the winter. At least the tent allowed her the privacy to stretch out and pace without trudging through snow as her muscles ached. There was no remedy for the stuffiness of her mind, and she sipped now-cold tea Roland swore might help.

Most of the Little Dozen Kingdoms camped with her, leaving the Pass a rainbow of colors, though King Bernd Lizana of Merriwynne was late. Like everything these days, nothing moved on time. Not even Leolin and the Order were here, which set her nerves on edge.

For all she knew, they were lost at sea and dead. She shook the thought from her mind as she rubbed the muscles of her lower back. Curse Leolin for being late, if for no other reason than she could use a good massage.

There was no footfall or shushing of fabric, but something on the air hummed within her mind, and Margaret turned as she slid a dagger from its sheath. A portly man filled a significant portion of her tent, his jowls sagging as he frowned. There was no doubt that Farimun stood before her, and she tightened her grip on the dagger.

"How did you have the magic to get here?" she whispered.

"I am the god of journeys. No journey is beyond me."

Rather than call out for help, she asked, "So why visit me?"

"I assume Agaia is dead, courtesy of your *Amaskan*, and now Sharmus is missing. If he is gone as well, then five of us remain. So I come to you, Queen Margaret Poncett, to ask if there is something you want?"

Margaret shook her head. "What do you mean?"

"To stop this war—is there something we can provide? Name it, and it is yours." When she shook her head again, he reached forward and grabbed her by the shoulders. "What about your father returned to you? Alive and well?"

Her breath caught in her throat as a picture floated in the air before her. In it, she still wore the crown, but her father stood beside her. No longer sick, he smiled and waved at something she could not see.

"No."

Margaret pulled herself from Farimun's grasp. When he stepped forward, she waved the dagger before her. "Approach me again and you'll be taking one final journey."

"If not your father, how about your sister?" said Farimun.

The tent filled with fog, which parted slightly for a figure to pass. Margaret forgot to breathe as the figure took shape.

Adelei's lithe body draped in *Amaskan* silks stood before her. When Adelei's dark brown eyes opened, color returned to her cheeks, and she inhaled deeply.

"Margaret?"

Tears gathered in Margaret's eyes when her sister spoke, and she dropped her dagger to the dirt below. Unable to help herself, she reached out and touched Adelei's shoulder. She was real. Solid.

Alive.

"Farimun?" The fog cleared enough for her to see his face, and she asked, "You could do this? Bring her back? You have the magic still?"

"I could. I would do this for you, Queen Margaret."

Her sister, alive, had been her wish for almost the entirety of her childhood. They had found each other in time for Adelei's death, an unfairness that rankled her. If Adelei were alive again, *she* would know how to win the battle against the Thirteen.

She could be the strong one.

Margaret reached out again, this time to touch her sister's face. Her skin was warm to the touch, and Margaret's heart raced. *No.* This was wrong. For all that Adelei felt alive, she was not.

"Having my sister with me again...nothing would bring me more pleasure, but this is wrong. Adelei is dead, and Itovah is to blame. This is against the laws of...well, your laws! You should not tempt me so. How corrupt our gods have become."

Farimun waved his hand, and Adelei disappeared. In her place was a pedestal and on it, a small marble bust bearing Adelei's face. The angle of her nose, the width of her eyes—every detail correct. Coloring had been applied to the marble giving it the suggestion of life, and Margaret's heart leapt.

The god leaned close to her ear and whispered, "A reminder for you, of what could have been."

He disappeared, taking the fog with him, though the bust remained. Margaret touched it with a trembling hand, and then yanked her hand away.

The marble was still warm.

When she touched it a second time, the warmth had faded. Margaret swept the bust from the pedestal where it fell to the ground. A piece of Adelei's cheek broke off as it hit a rock, and she cried out as she fell to her knees beside it. The piece fit back in place if she held it against the bust, but the image was broken. No longer did it resemble Adelei in so life-like a manner.

Adelei was truly gone.

Sounds of people talking reached Margaret and when she glanced up, someone stood outside her tent. "Come," she called, and when Leolin entered, she burst into tears. He rushed over, taking her into his arms as she cried. Several moments passed after the tears stopped in which she was inclined to hold him close.

Leolin, here. Safe.

The child within her moved, reacting to her distress, and she clung to Leolin as she recounted the details of Farimun's visit.

"They're desperate," he said as she released him.

She turned toward the small table where a map of the Pass lay spread out and pretended to study it. "He knew exactly what to offer me, Leolin. I...I almost took it."

"But you didn't. You saw it for the feint it was. Your strength amazes me. Did I mention that I've missed you?" He reached around her middle from behind to wrap her in an embrace, but his arms froze part way through the motion. He spun her around, his gaze trailing from her eyes to her expanded middle. "You're...?"

Margaret nodded. "I assume that you have a reason for arriving this late to the Pass. Why are you in full armor? Was more than Farimun here?"

"No, just Farimun. It was easier to ride on the ready, but we'll discuss that later. Did you know you were pregnant when I left?"

"Not until after. Roland believes I'm halfway through the pregnancy." Leolin's eyes widened, and she added, "If you are about to order me to return to Alesta, don't. I need to be here, same as you."

Leolin shook his head. "I met Doughal, and one thing he said stayed with me on the journey. He said 'the work's never done.'" I know he wasn't talking about ruling a kingdom, but the message applies. You have duties and responsibilities I don't. People look to you, not just to settle disputes but to ensure they are safe and that they have a home worth fighting for. For you, the work's never done. You could be dying, and you would still be queen. You may not be the swordswoman your sister was, but you have an inner strength she didn't get to see."

"I think she did. She believed me capable of more than others saw. She's why I am queen." A few tears trickled down her cheeks, and she wiped them away. "It's why Farimun's offer was so tempting, though I will admit that having another ally in this fight would not hurt."

"Anything touched by the Thirteen is spoiled. You don't need an ally like that. Speaking of allies, I have a few surprises for you."

"I have one for you as well," she said, grinning. Margaret reached for Leolin's hand and placed it on her belly where their child lay. The baby gave another kick, and Leolin stared at her belly in awe.

"She's going to be a fighter like her mama."

The assumption that their child was a girl caused her to start, and she furrowed her brows. Leolin grimaced at her response.

"Maggie, I'm sorry that I haven't always believed you to be as capable as you are. I know I only want you to be safe, but it's no excuse for treating you as if you're incapable. I have a lot to make up for. But first, let me tell you about who I brought with me..."

A light rumbling sounded outside, like thunder in the hills. Margaret pulled a heavy cloak over her shoulders before exiting the tent, Leolin a step behind her. At first, Margaret thought her sense of balance off as the land shifted. A low rumble vibrated through her leather boots and swelled until the ground buckled in front of them. All around them, soldiers cried out as they tried to avoid the cracks opening throughout the Pass.

Margaret crouched beside Leolin to keep from falling over. "The Thirteen are here," she said.

"How do you know?"

"Why else would the ground be shaking?"

The buckling stopped. A soldier ran towards them, his eyes wide. When he reached them, his breath came in gasps.

"You must have run clear across the Pass. Fenton wanted you to tell me the Thirteen are here, yes?" she asked. He opened his mouth to answer, and Margaret shook her head. "Save your breath. Do we know where?"

He pointed up to the other end of the canyon, further down river. "He said...Shadians...lost some...to the...quakes."

Leolin handed the man a water bag. "Return to the marshal once you've recovered."

Metal clanging against metal reached them, and

Margaret's skin tingled. She stepped back inside her tent to grab her armor. When she exited again, hands full of leather, Leolin shook his head. "You can't—"

Margaret placed a finger over his lips. "Do not presume to order me about. I'm not infirm."

"No, but you are with child. You have more to think about than yourself."

She pulled the padded vest over her shoulders, followed by the leather cuirass and held her arms to her sides so he could fasten the buckles. "That's precisely why I must go, now help me with this armor," she said. The leather had been dyed a deep shade of blue and the chestplate bore two conjoining circles, the symbol of Alexander.

"Too much longer and you won't be able to wear this set," he said as he clasped the buckles on their loosest setting. He frowned when he spotted the row of circles running along the chestplate's bottom. Rather than Alexander's symbol, the armor bore the symbol of the Order of *Amaska*. "Interesting choice."

She strapped on her bracers and greaves before pulling on her gloves. Around her, officers shouted orders as she hurried for the horse pen. Leolin helped her mount, and she was astride and riding towards the combat when a large feline creature cut across their path.

"The child-gods a*rr*e he*rr*e."

When the creature spoke, Margaret slowed her horse and turned to Leolin. "Is this one of the allies you spoke of?" she asked.

"Your Majesty, this is Avishai the Fierce, Daughter of Avi the Grave, & member of the Geutha Tribe of the Nine. She is a *chathula*, a mighty warrior race from across the sea. She can also speak in your head so don't be startled if that happens."

"Magic user?"

"She saved my life. There's another ally. I was going to mention it..."

Leolin's words faded as Margaret spotted Sharmus riding towards them on one of the Order's battlesteeds, and she unsheathed her sword. How dare he kill an *Amaskan* for that horse. Anger welled up inside her. The burning of magic being used nearby grew, and she kneed her horse, prodding it in the god's direction. Avishai bumped her leg and when she ignored her, the *chathula* leapt in front of Margaret's horse.

"Shar*r*mus is an ally," said Avishai.

"He's one of the Thirteen." Margaret tried to push her way past Avishai, but her horse refused to move. "Are you using magic on my horse?"

"You*rr* hor*r*se is listening to *rr*eason. Put you*rr* swo*rr*d away."

Margaret glared at the *chathula*, and when the *chathula* did not move, she turned to Leolin. "Explain."

"Sharmus came to the Order seeking help to die. We convinced him to help us instead. It's a bit of a long story, but yes, he's an ally," said Leolin, his words coming out in a rush. The ground rumbled again but did not break open, and their horses snorted.

Her skin crawled, and she fought the urge to claw at it. Rather than run the god through as she had planned, Margaret rode ahead towards the command tent.

Later, when the battle was over, Leolin could explain how a god could want to die.

THE LITTLE DOZEN KINGDOMS' rulers stood around a large table where a map lay, though none of them looked at it. Instead, they all spoke at once, a cacophony of sound that amounted to no decisions being made. It was a scene of chaos when Margaret entered the tent, and she almost turned around and left at the sight of it. Instead, she remained near the tent flap to listen.

"The Amaskans are better equipped to fight the Thirteen and could do it directly," said King Monsine of Sadai. "They could slip in and out of our armies with ease. The gods wouldn't see them approach."

King Havin Bajit shook his head. "My army is the strongest in number. With the *Tribor*'s help, we can take the battle to the Thirteen directly."

Margaret bristled at the admission that the man had brought his pets with him. Queen Helena of Lorellyn who stood a few feet in front of Margaret, raised her hands in protest. "You would dishonor us all by relying upon murderers and assassins? Faugh, I would rather hand myself over to the Thirteen."

As the arguing continued, several rulers mentioned splitting their fighters to flank the Thirteen, while King Bernd Lizana of Merriwynne, who had arrived in the tent a few minutes before Margaret, wished to withdraw and regroup.

Everyone spoke their own ideas as how to best defeat the Thirteen and not one of them the same. Rather than try and shout over them, Margaret walked up to the table and grabbed the map with both hands. She crumpled the parchment into a large wad as the shouting around her stopped. "Arguing isn't helping anyone. The Thirteen are here *now*," she said as Sharmus, Leolin, and Avishai walked in, followed shortly by Miriam and an *Amaskan* Margaret did not recognize.

Seeing Sharmus and the *chathula* threatened to undo them all as the monarchies demanded answers to everything from why Sharmus was present to what was a *chathula* and could it kill the Thirteen for them. Margaret could not get rid of the sense of magic crawling across her body, and as the tent's volume doubled, she brushed through the tent's flap in time for her field marshal to run into her.

"My apologies, Your Majesty," said Fenton, and he pointed at the nearby hill. "There's something you must see."

She stepped over a few cracks in the ground on her way to the hill and noticed Leolin and the rest of her people doing the same as they trailed her. From the hilltop, she could see clear across the valley. Nearer to the bridge, the Pass proper, something ugly surged against soldiers from the various kingdoms as officers tried to direct them through the chaos.

Hundreds of soldiers fought against the Little Dozen Kingdoms and when she narrowed her eyes to better see, she gasped. "Are we fighting against each other?"

"In a manner of speaking, yes, Your Majesty," said Fenton as he pointed. Up on the cliffside where she had met with the other rulers to decide their fate, five figures stood, their bodies encased in a shimmering blue field. "The Thirteen have raised the dead."

Miriam pressed two fingers to the top of her brow and asked, "How is that even possible?"

"They're gods. I suppose anything is possible. Better question is how do we stop them." Leolin glanced down at Avishai. "I assume that blue shimmer is similar to the magic you used to protect me from the *Tribor* men?"

Avishai nodded. "Yes, though it's much st*rr*onge*rr* than anything I can make."

"It's worse than that. Those are our own soldiers—those that died at the Pass...before," said Fenton as he paled. "We're killing our own people, people we know, and...and then they get back up! How do you stop them when they just get back up and swing at you again?"

The panic in his voice worried Margaret, and she glanced behind her at Sharmus. The God of Healing's facial features drooped, as did his shoulders, but he said nothing. "Avishai, you mentioned using magic to protect Leolin. Is there a way through protection like that?" Margaret asked.

"Always. A st*rr*onge*rr* use*rr* would be able to push th*rr*ough it. If I was ti*rr*ed enough, the wall would weaken."

Margaret nodded. "So we need the gods to exhaust themselves. If we can outlast them, we'll have an opportunity to defeat them."

"Or perhaps we need a spark."

She spun around to face Bredych who stood at the back of the group. "You should be back in Alesta healing!"

"I guess I should have mentioned the last surprise," said Leolin.

"How are you standing?" she asked, and Bredych pointed at Sharmus.

"Having a god of healing on your side can be an unexpected boon. He healed me the day the Order arrived in Alesta, so I rode out with them."

Margaret swatted Bredych on his side, lightly enough not to harm him but strong enough to test whether the wound was truly healed. He did not flinch as he watched the fighting in the distance.

"We don't understand this prophecy, not completely. What does it even mean? We're just assuming there must be a catalyst of some sort," said Leolin.

"'Until the day of Truth, we shall remain in darkness, but on that day, we will be the Light. We will brandish our Light before us like an ever-burning torch and battle the corruption in our midst until everything before us burns. No corruption, be it man or king or god will destroy Boahim again,'" said Miriam as she took Bredych's hand in hers. "Word of the Boahim Senate's true identity is spreading. The prophecy makes it clear that the Order of *Amaska* must be here, as the instruments of truth and justice. While your asking for assistance was understandable, Your Majesty, we aren't here for Alexander. We're here for justice."

Miriam's gaze froze when she spotted the mark on Margaret's jaw, but Bredych shook his head. "The *Tribor* marked her as a warning," he said.

"They did, hmm?" Miriam pursed her lips together.

"Did Bredych tell you his interpretation of the prophecy?" asked Margaret, and Miriam shook her head. "He believes that someone must die in order to become this light—this spark—and that will unite us once again."

"I'm correct. You saw the chaos in that tent yourself, Margaret. How else will we unite a bunch of power-hungry nobles? They aren't even aware that the dead walk!" Bredych's muscles tensed as he pulled his hand away from Miriam's. He was running down the hill before Margaret could stop him. Avishai's tail twitched for a moment before she ran after him.

"He's going to get himself killed," whispered Margaret.

Beside her, Leolin squeezed her shoulder. "Better him than you."

When Margaret glanced over at Miriam, the *Amaskan*'s skin was pale as she glared at Leolin. "You were supposed to heal him, not convince him he's twenty again," she said to Sharmus, who merely shrugged. "Fenton, tell our soldiers to pull back. If the others want to fight their own men, that's their decision but this is madness. I'll not have our soldiers die for this."

Margaret followed Fenton down the hill and watched him ride off towards the battle. She took her horse's reins and knotted them with Leolin's horse.

When Leolin caught up to her and saw the knots, he asked, "What are you doing?"

She pulled him close and kissed him, taking in the smell of his sweat. When she released him, she said, "I love you."

Two battlesteeds trained by the Order stood nearby and

Margaret approached one. Hands out in front of her, she whispered, "*Shie-neah*." It was the word her sister had used when she had introduced Margaret to her horse, Midnight. When she reached for the reins, the horse stood perfectly still. Without a leg up, Margaret pulled herself into the saddle by the pommel and her arms ached from the effort. As she turned the horse in the direction Bredych had ridden, she caught a glimpse of Leolin approaching the other mount. "If you don't know the proper command, she will take your arm off. Be safe, Leolin," she called.

How Bredych planned to push past the Thirteen's magical wall, Margaret did not know, but she would not allow him to die in the attempt. There had to be some other way to weaken them.

She urged the *Amaskan* mount through the mass of soldiers as she rode after Bredych.

22

The shimmering blue magic between Bredych and the remaining Thirteen was warm to the touch, but his hand refused to move through it. No matter how hard he tried, it remained at the edges of his skin as the sensation of stinging nettles pricked his fingers. While Farimun and Adlain's eyes were closed, Anur stared straight at Bredych, his face a fierce mask of frustration.

Whatever kept Bredych out, appeared to also keep the God of Justice in. Avishai stood beside the *Amaskan*, the hairs of her fur standing upright. "Can you feel it as well?" asked Bredych.

Yes. This is a protection I cannot break.

"As long as they are protected, people will die fighting those already dead. There must be something we can do." Bredych pointed to the river. "What if you were in the water, like you were near the desert?"

Not even then. Child-gods they may be, but they are still gods.

Bredych swore. When he wrested his gaze away from the fighting below, he met Anur's gaze again.

The god was grinning.

While his hair and beard were nearly white with age and his blue eyes almost gray, he stood behind the magic with a warrior's stance of someone much younger. Bredych nudged Avishai. "Look at his stance," he whispered.

He's ready for a fight.

"But why? Unless their magic is almost gone, they have no reason to fear us."

The old one, he fears you.

Bredych nodded, though he did not need to be told. He could feel it in his bones. As he watched Anur, the *Book of Ja'ahr* came to mind. He had not opened his copy since he had left the Order, not that he needed to as the text was well ingrained in his mind. The softness of the worn leather and the smell of the pages, like sandalwood, tickled his memories, and the words came to him.

"'Truth is not a comfort, but a liberation, a resistance to falsities and corruption, for only those two have reason to fear.'"

He had not intended to speak the words aloud, although it caused Anur's eyes to widen. The god unsheathed a long sword, which glowed white as he approached the magical wall. Behind him, Adlain cried out, then grabbed Anur by the shoulders.

A calmness settled over Bredych in that moment, and he looked at the *chathula*. "Can you...talk to everyone here in the Pass at once?"

She flicked her tail as she cocked her head. "Maybe? I have neve*rr* t*rr*ied. Fo*rr* that, I will need the *rriverr.*"

Bredych turned his back on Anur and followed the *chathula* down the worn path leading into the valley. A lone soldier wearing Alexandrian blue rose up from the soil, his eyes glowing. Before Bredych could unsheathe his sword, Avishai swiped out with her claws and ripped several gashes in the man's stomach. He tumbled back to the ground, but for how long, Bredych did not know. "We should move quickly."

The two of them ran towards the water, Avishai reaching it first, and once there, a light green mist enveloped Bredych. *You are protected but hurry.*

Cold water flooded into Bredych's boots as he stepped into the river. Even with the warmer temperatures, it was still Luthian, the beginning of winter, and the water coming down from the mountains spoke of the season. His teeth chattered as he stood beside the *chathula*. "Can I speak to them all through you?" he asked.

"We will t*rr*y. Whenever*rr* you a*rr*e *rr*eady."

Bredych closed his eyes. Something about the motion felt right, and he breathed deeply of the cold air.

My name is Eli Bredych, former Grand Master of the Order of Amaska, though I was born with another name... Malaki Abner. His voice echoed in his head but as it did, fighting in the Pass stopped. Even the risen turned in his direction as if every being heard him. Nodding to himself, he continued.

As Amaskans, we are taught to serve Justice, to serve Anur. Our very texts tell us that we are Justice, we judge in the face of crimes committed against Boahim, and we seek justice for all those harmed by sin. But the Senate has fallen to corruption, to dishonesty and fear. This is why we fight. For our own Justice.

But it is not fair to ask you to fight, to potentially die, unless you know what you are fighting for. You have heard that the Senate is our Thirteen. This is true. The gods we followed have twisted their power, their magic, for their own good.

But so has the Order.

Under my leadership, the Order of Amaska committed crimes in the name of Justice that were not always just.

Amaskans who were otherwise good people were sent to commit crimes because I too had fallen to corruption. I grew greedy with my power.

Somewhere across the Pass, Bredych imagined Miriam standing with others in the Order as they listened to him confess, and he prayed they would all forgive him.

I manipulated people for my own benefit, much like the Thirteen. I ordered my own sister killed because she would not cave to my demands. I have done horrible things, committed awful sins. A moment ago, I stood near Anur, God of Justice and War, and realized that in fighting, we give him what he wishes.

'Justice is found only through the truth seekers. Truth is not a comfort, but a liberation; a resistance to falsities and corruption, for only those two have reason to fear.' So it is written in the Book of Ja'ahr. *But it is also written that 'Those who would seek vengeance, seek destruction.'*

I came here believing in a prophecy, that in order for goodness and justice to win, I had to be strong enough to fight, to die, but I realize now that all that is required is the truth.

The truth is, the Amaskans formed in order for truth to prevail in the face of corruption, but we have become that corruption. Not just us, but our rulers as well. If we are to live free, we must live in truth.

Bredych swallowed hard before he withdrew a thick, folded parchment from beneath his leather chestplate and held it in the air. *On this is the name of every man, woman, and child I have killed or ordered killed. There is also a list of every known death ordered by or attributed to the Boahim Senate as well as the Little Dozen Kingdoms' rulers.*

"Hurry, please," whispered Avishai, and when Bredych glanced down, he could see the whites of her eyes as sweat trickled down her fur.

I give this information knowingly, not so that violence and vengeance rule us, but so that we might heal. Together. In light.

No more Amaskans. No more Tribor. No more gods. No more Senate. Just Boahim.

"I'm done, Avishai."

As he finished her name, some lone soldier cried out a single word: Boahim. Several more took up the cry until the Little Dozen Kingdoms' individual armies united in their chant. The dead soldiers raised by the Thirteen crumbled into dust as an army of the living surged forward.

A pitiful mew sounded at his feet and when Bredych glanced at the river shore beside him, Avishai had collapsed into the cold water. Anur stood over her, sword raised as his face twisted with a singular fury.

There was no time to draw his own sword and block, no time to cry out for help. Bredych leapt forward, placing himself between Avishai and Anur.

A pillar of light ripped through him as Anur's sword drove into his side, the same place Agaia had wounded him, though this time, he did not feel it. There was no sound of metal tearing into his flesh or the searing pain that followed. If anything, the light that enveloped him was warm. Loving.

Beneath him, Avishai still lay in the water, and he frowned. His actions had not saved the *chathula* after all.

Young Bredych would have wished for Anur's death and for his own to be avenged, probably with some verse or another about Justice wrapped around it, but he was not a young man anymore, with much to prove to an Order that had outlived its usefulness.

Bredych was old. His time was done, and his life, at the end, well lived.

THE MASS of soldiers made keeping track of Bredych a near impossible task, and Margaret lost him almost immediately.

Instead, she found herself pulled from her horse as a dead Sadain tried to claim it. The *Amaskan* battlesteed grabbed hold of the dead soldier with its teeth and ripped off the man's forearm. With a loud whinny, the horse bolted back towards the horse pen. Someone wearing Estona's purple stepped in front of a blade that threatened to take off Margaret's arm, and before she could do more than blink, the soldier had fallen, only for someone else to take his place.

"This way!" A woman in the burgundy of Merriwynne pulled Margaret away from one scuffle and into another where she fought off several of the risen before making her way to the edge of the conflict. From there, she found someone's abandoned horse and mounted it in hopes she could get a better view.

The area closest to the bridge held the most fighting. She had assumed the rulers had remained at the command tent, still arguing over what to do next, but a shout nearby came from Shad's marshal. Several fights away, Havin hacked away at someone who would fall, only to rise back up, and Margaret searched the hills for the Thirteen.

She spotted them by the shimmering blue wall in front of them, though she could not see the gods behind it. She urged her horse in that direction when everyone in the field froze. The magic washed over her a moment later, the tingling less painful than before. When Bredych's voice echoed in her mind, she gasped. How was he doing this?

My name is Eli Bredych...

At some point, she began to cry, though she only noticed when Bredych stopped talking. Her cheeks were damp and her eyes burned. All around her, soldiers cried out the name Boahim. The roar shook her bones, and she gripped the reins in her hands until her fingers ached.

His confession had united the Little Dozen Kingdoms in a way her plans had not. When the mass of risen soldiers dissolved into dust, the armies cheered and a nearby soldier clapped her calf.

"We won!" he yelled before clapping another soldier on the back.

Up on the cliff, the Thirteen remained behind their blue wall. Nothing was won yet.

The wall fell, and Margaret urged her horse forward. She did not know how, but the Thirteen were no longer protected. Hoofbeats sounded behind her and when she glanced over her shoulder, Leolin was several horse lengths behind her.

He yelled something, but she could not hear him over the shouts and cheers of the combined armies. When she continued towards the cliff, he shouted again and pointed. A white haired man stood near the river, his entire body glowing.

Anur.

It had to be, which meant that Bredych was at the river. Who else amongst the Thirteen would seek out the former Grand Master? Soldiers parted as her horse galloped towards them.

She was a few heartbeats away when she saw Avishai collapse. Anur raised his sword, and Bredych moved like water. One moment he stood beside the *chathula,* and the next he was between the creature and Anur's blade.

Margaret cried out, and a pillar of white light blinded her. When she was able to see again, Anur stood over Bredych's body, a grin on his face. Her horse stopped at the water's edge, and she slid from the saddle.

It would have been easy to cry then, to wallow in the loss that threatened to swallow her, as it almost had when her father had died. Instead, her sister's voice whispered in her ear from the *Book of Ja'ahr.*

Empty the vessel. Like water, I flow to the sea. Nothing between it and me.

Grief left her, as did the bubbling rage. Anur stood over

Bredych's unmoving shape, and Margaret stepped across the space, her sword in her hand. His knees shook as he took one step towards her. When he pointed a finger at her, it too trembled. Anur turned the finger towards himself and stared at it.

"It's gone," he said.

She shifted her stance as she watched him fall to his knees. Whatever he had done to Bredych had left him weak. She pulled back her sword to thrust it into him when he held up his hands.

"Please, mercy."

"No, Justice."

He had a single moment to look up before she slid the blade between his ribs. Anur's eyes widened in shock as he coughed, blood painting his lips bright red. His gaze slid to the carved circle on her jaw.

"You...you aren't one of...mine." He struggled to say the words as he coughed.

Margaret smiled at him as his gaze found hers. "None of us ever were," she said as she shoved her sword into his torso again, her hands coated in his blood.

When she tried to remove her sword a second time, it caught on something, so she released the hilt and watched as the God of Justice tumbled into the river. The other gods were vulnerable, but as the calmness left her and she saw Bredych's body, thoughts of the Thirteen left her. She rushed over to the second father of her heart.

Her teeth chattered, though whether it was the water's chill or her actions that brought it about, she could not say. She turned Bredych over and cried out at the gaping wound that had ripped a hole through the *Amaskan*.

His eyes were still open—their blue-gray staring at the clear skies above. She could almost see the twinkle in them if she stared hard enough, but when she pressed her fingers to his neck, nothing beat inside of him. Ragged cries sounded but it took Leolin shaking her for her to realize the sounds came from her.

"He's gone, Maggie."

She shook her head. "He can't be. We need him. *I* need him."

Leolin tried to pull her into his arms, but she pushed him away. "No, there is more killing to do. I will cry later."

She stood up and when Leolin paled, she glanced down at her armor. The symbol of Alexander, two oblong, conjoining circles painted in blue, was soaked in Anur's blood, staining the leather and marring the symbol. "I'm unharmed. It's Anur's blood," she said.

"I saw."

Something moved in the river bank, and Margaret turned to see Avishai struggling to stand. Her hind legs were trapped beneath Bredych's body. "Help me move him," Margaret said.

They rolled Bredych off the *chathula*, and while Avishai was able to stand, she wobbled as she walked. Leolin dragged Bredych's body to the shore with Avishai following along.

"I hu*rr*t. I am ti*rr*ed." When Avishai reached Bredych's body, she curled up beside him and tucked her tail beneath her. "I will wait he*rr*e fo*rr* the fighting to stop."

Margaret hesitated a moment before she rested her hand on the *chathula*'s head. "He can have no better guardian."

Leolin handed her the reins of the horse she had found, and she pointed at Anur's corpse. "I couldn't remove my sword."

He strode over to the god and gave the blade a good tug. Once removed, he wiped it on Anur's white cloak before returning to her side and handing it to her.

When he touched her shoulder, she swallowed hard and tried not to think of Bredych. Of her father. Her sister. Everything and everyone she had lost. Anger burned in her chest as she looked over Leolin's shoulder at the cliff where the remaining Thirteen stood.

"Just...be careful. I can't lose you, Maggie."

"You won't lose me. Besides, I'm owed. For everything I have lost, the Thirteen owe me." She stuck her foot into the stirrup and heaved herself into the saddle. When she glanced down at Leolin, his face remained neutral. "Let us end this."

23

Seeing Sharmus not only alive but helping the Little Dozen Kingdoms against his own was an insult Adlain tucked away as he struggled to help his brothers and sisters. While Farimun maintained the protective wall, Adlain set forth raising dead soldiers from the earth. The idea had worked at first as the living threw themselves at those risen again, but when the soldiers united in their cries of Boahim, Adlain's magic fizzled.

For all that Luthia pretended to help, she did not bear the signs of exhaustion that the rest of them did. When Anur had ordered Farimun to remove the magical wall, all Luthia had done was give him a look and the God of Journeys had followed Anur's orders. The consequences of that action meant another god was dead, and Adlain ground his teeth together.

Delorcini huddled with Luthia, her eyes wide with fear—true fear—and Adlain approved. Perhaps if those two had understood the danger the Poncett family posed from the beginning, none of them would be mortal. Adlain turned to his brother, Farimun, and pointed to Margaret as she rode towards them. "I don't care about the little ants cheering for their own death, but we must end the Poncett line if we're to survive this."

"All we need do is wait then."

Adlain shook his head. "A good marshal knows when to attack and when to retreat and regroup," he said, and he glanced at Delorcini and Luthia. "Perhaps if you and I were to withdraw and regain some of our strength, we could determine the when and where of the next battle."

When Farimun stepped toward the two goddesses, Adlain barred the way.

"Leave them."

"But they—"

Adlain's black eyes sparked with fury as he stared at Farimun. "I said leave them. They weren't of any use anyway."

The God of Journeys hesitated a moment before giving a brief nod and touching Adlain's forearm. One moment they stood on the cliffs and the next, they were a day's journey from the Pass, in the middle of an open field.

"Where are we? Why did you bring us here?" asked Adlain.

"The magic...of walking...is hard." Farimun's skin was almost gray in the sunlight, and he panted, his arms wrapped around his great middle. When he caught his breath, he said, "This was as far as I could take us."

"Even you, the God of Journeys? I thought no journey was forbidden to you."

Farimun shrugged. "I was wrong."

Adlain waggled a finger and a cup of wine appeared before him, which he offered to Farimun. The god took the cup and drank from it, though he frowned.

"Why do you look like a storm cloud, my brother?" asked Adlain.

"If you're going to bother using magic, you might as well waste it on something useful."

"Such as?"

"A water skin instead of a mere cup. I don't know if you've noticed, but we're no longer near the river. I hope your plan to regroup is a quick one, or it will be a long day of walking ahead."

Adlain ran a hand through his black locks. Nothing was going as planned, and the fact irked him.

"Now who resembles a storm cloud, hmm?"

"I am the all-father of creation. I should be able to blink and their miserable little lives end, but instead, I am stuck in this field while my heart beats too hard in my chest. Margaret Poncett will pay for this."

Farimun frowned. "And her child too?"

Adlain flinched. Of course the queen was with child. Well, he would have to make sure they both died. It was long past time for that family line to wither on the vine.

THE PATH between the river and the cliff was short, especially on horseback, and Margaret and Leolin mounted it in time to see Farimun and Adlain disappear in a green mist. Delorcini and Luthia huddled together nearby where they clung to each other, eyes closed. Margaret dismounted and withdrew her sword as she approached.

"Careful," said Leolin.

Margaret nodded but continued forward until she stood beside the two women. Her weight shifted as she drew back her sword, and Delorcini opened her eyes. The Meridi Pass disappeared as Margaret met the goddess's gaze. In a world of greens and browns, Margaret was four again, standing beside her mother and sister in a field. Sounds of laughter and the smell of wildflowers reached her, and when she glanced up at her mother's face, it was her own.

Older and wiser, but the shape was hers, including the scar on her jaw. Her breath caught in her throat, and she blinked, only to return to the Meridi Pass. Delorcini reached for Margaret, who tapped the goddess's hand with her sword.

"I only meant to check on the child," said Delorcini.

Leolin approached, his own sword drawn. "Keep your hands to yourself."

"You know who I am." The words were directed at Margaret, who nodded. "Then you know I would no more harm you and the child you carry than I would harm any living creature in this world."

Margaret ground her teeth. "Tell that to Master Bredych who lies near the river below. Tell that to all those who died today fighting against an army you raised, an army of soldiers who died the last time Alexandrian blood was spilled at this pass. You could be the goddess of peace, and I would not believe a word from your lips."

Luthia pressed a hand against Delorcini's outstretched arm until it lowered. When the Goddess of Silence opened her mouth to speak, her deep voice reverberated in Margaret's bones. "We were given no choice. Participate or be banished."

"Then be banished," Leolin said.

Delorcini hissed. "Luthia speaks and you dare mock her? You insolent child."

Margaret poked Delorcini's chest with the tip of her sword. "Do you know why we're here on this cliff?"

"To k-kill us."

Leolin nodded. "So tell us why we shouldn't."

"If we were any threat to you, Farimun and Adlain would have taken us with them. They left us here to die. With magic fading, we have nothing more we can offer you," said Delorcini.

Margaret tilted her head as she stared at Luthia. Eyes and hair like night, her gaunt frame gave her the appearance of someone weak or sick, but every painting and carving she had ever seen of the goddess portrayed her in the same manner. But this was the being before the gods, the silence that stretched across the stars and brought Adlain into form. Margaret shifted her sword so it was in front of Luthia. "Delorcini may have nothing of any use, but you do. If the creation tales have any truth to them, you are the reason anything exists. So we ask again, why should we allow you to live?"

A sigh escaped Luthia and when she spoke, her body sagged like the very act cost her greatly. "I am old, child. Older than the stars and the sun. I was old before Adlain was sung into form, but even I'm dying. Everything has its time and place, and ours has passed."

When Margaret stepped forward, Luthia held up her palm. A small globe floated above it and as it spun, the continent that once formed Boahim floated in a giant body of water. The globe glowed white, much like the orbs that had once been scattered across the Little Dozen Kingdoms. "When the world was new, it was filled with magic, with power, and with life. The people of this world worshiped the gods, and we gave our gifts aplenty."

The globe spun faster as she spoke, and the glow changed. "As time continued, the people of this planet changed, and the magic began to fade. In some areas, it disappeared altogether. Many gods died until few remained."

"The Thirteen," said Margaret.

Leolin frowned. "But there are other gods. Avishai spoke of hers. Alisher, I believe."

"There were many gods across this world, more than the Thirteen worshipped by those of Boahim, but people found other ways to live that did not include us. And so our magic faded, *all* magic faded, until we found ourselves mortal." Luthia swallowed hard and rubbed her throat. "By becoming the Senate and involving ourselves directly in the very nature of this world, our power changed us."

"It corrupted you."

Luthia nodded at Margaret. "Indeed. The rot began with the breaking of Boahim, and while I saw it, I could do nothing to stop it. It festered in each of us. The more magic we used, the worse it became."

"That still doesn't answer the question of why we should allow you to live. If anything, it means we should kill you as soon as we can, to prevent the corruption from spreading," said Leolin.

"Please—" cried Delorcini, and Luthia touched a finger to her lips to quiet her.

"Adlain and Farimun will return. They have fled in hopes their magic will strengthen, but it will not," said Luthia as she waved her hand, and the globe fizzled into nothing. "You will need protection when they arrive."

Margaret frowned. "If their magic is so little, why would I need protection?"

"Adlain forced each of us to exhaust ourselves repeatedly. While the magic is fading, he is more rested. But if we live, Delorcini and I can weave the wall to protect you while you fight."

"But it will kill us—"

Luthia silenced Delorcini with a look. "Yes, it probably will."

Delorcini's lip trembled as she stared at Luthia. Before Margaret could stop her, she touched Margaret's stomach with her finger and warmth spread throughout her body. "I, Delorcini, bless your daughter's life. May her life be full of family and...oh!"

"What is it?" asked Margaret.

"Perhaps if I survive, I will tell you."

Margaret slapped the goddess's hand away. She was not surprised by Delorcini's cryptic message, or the promise of an answer should she live. For all that she was the Goddess of Family and Love, her reputation as a selfish being preceded her. "You know nothing of my child. If I allow you to live, it will be because you may have some use to me yet."

Footfalls sounded behind them, and Delorcini gasped. When Margaret glanced over her shoulder, Sharmus was helping Miriam up the pathway. The *Amaskan*'s eyes were rimmed red, and she avoided meeting Margaret's gaze.

"You escaped," said Luthia as she stared at Sharmus.

"I did. Thank you."

Sharmus walked up to Margaret, though his hooves on the ground made no sound. It was something she would have to remember when fighting the others.

"I have a favor to ask, Your Majesty."

She gestured for him to continue. By the way he hunched over and his eyebrows slumped, she suspected she already knew what he would ask for...mercy.

"Rather than kill us, allow us to help you. Three building the protective weave is better than two. If we survive and the battle's done, we will return to our island to die." He held his hands out to her, and she stepped back. Rather than touch her, he turned his hands back and forth slowly. "Do you see the lines in my flesh? There was a time when they weren't there, Your Majesty. We are aging. It's never happened before. Since we can be killed, I can assume only that we are dying as well. Like mortals."

"How can we be sure you remain on your island? How do we know you won't use magic to continue to influence the shape of this world?" she asked.

Luthia cleared her throat. "Magic. One last spell to keep us there...until we die."

"The Senate relies on supplies from the Little Dozen Kingdoms to survive...or they appeared to do so," said Leolin, and he shrugged. "Do you even eat?"

"And what happens if you die first, Luthia, and the spell breaks? Nothing about this plan ensures the Little Dozen Kingdoms' safety," said Miriam.

Sharmus untied his green cloak and set it on the ground. His tunic hung from him as if it were the wrong size, and when he raised it, Margaret could count his ribs. "At first, we did not have to eat, though we enjoyed the process and the taste... Now we eat, but it does not nourish us. Queen Margaret, we are *dying*. There is nothing that can stop it now."

"Why do you think we fight so hard to live?" asked Delorcini, her cheeks flushed. "Every day is numbered as easily as yours. Moreso as we are beings of magic. Magic is not just something we use, it is something we *are*."

"If you die, will all magic die?" Margaret asked Luthia.

The goddess shrugged. "I do not know."

Margaret gave a slight nod. "We will bind you together and take you to my tents until a formal decision is made, as it's not one I can make alone." When Luthia frowned, Margaret added, "All of the Little Dozen Kingdoms must make this choice."

"We understand," said Sharmus.

Halfway down the path was a small group of Amaskans, and Leolin sent for rope to bind the remaining Thirteen. While they waited, Margaret leaned close to Luthia and asked, "You mentioned fighting Adlain All-Father. What will keep us from overwhelming him? He is mortal now, and we far outnumber him."

"He will fight only you, Your Majesty."

"Why?"

Luthia stared at her, her gaze slightly unfocused as if she

were far away. "You are descended from King Dama Yachad of Boahim, who saw our rot when it was merely a seed. Adlain encouraged the people to burn him alive as a heretic, but the histories were not forgotten."

Margaret did not know Miriam had overheard until the woman said, "Yachad's beliefs that corruption would keep something like the Boahim Senate from being successful led to the formation of the Order of *Amaska*."

"Not quite. It was his suggestion that the Senate form to enforce the Thirteen laws, but it was the people who decided it would be the Thirteen gods who served them in the Senate," said Luthia.

"That...that's not in our histories." Miriam frowned.

"There is much missing from your histories. I could help with this if given the opportunity."

Margaret asked, "But why does being his descendent matter to Adlain?"

"Adlain believes if your line ends, so does the line of power. He believes we will become immortal beings again."

"Is he correct?" Margaret tightened her grip on her hilt. If her death meant the gods' return, she would end these three now.

Luthia shook her head, her gaze on Margaret's face.

"How do I know you aren't lying to me in order to keep me from running you through?"

"I cannot lie."

Margaret laughed. Leolin carried rope in his hands as he approached, and when he saw her laughing, he asked, "Did I miss something funny?"

"Luthia claims she can't lie."

"I cannot."

Leolin raised an eyebrow. "Why?"

Having first searched her for weapons, several Amaskans bound Delorcini's hands in front of her. They moved to bind

Sharmus, and Miriam shook her head. Sharmus held his hands out in front of him. "While we have grown to know each other, it is better if we are treated as one."

Luthia held her hands in front of her as well. "Deceit lies in silence, in everything unsaid. If I were silent, you would have no way to trust me, but I am speaking. Prior to this year, the last time I spoke was many, many centuries ago. If I am compelled to speak, it is only the truth that I can utter. It is how the world came into being—I spoke truth and purity."

"I thought you sang," said Leolin.

She smiled, her gaunt cheeks stretched by her wide lips. "I did that as well."

A group of Amaskans surrounded the three gods, who had their hands tied, as they began walking down the pathway. It would be a long walk across the Pass to Margaret's tent, and as she watched the three hobble down the hill, she frowned.

"Don't pity them. They brought this upon themselves," said Leolin as he held the reins to her horse.

Margaret paused for a moment and leaned her head against his shoulder. "Every ruler does," she whispered.

"That's not a valid comparison."

Every death she had ordered as queen weighed upon her shoulders as she stood near Leolin. Where they all listed on the parchment Bredych carried? A piece of her hoped so, for every death she had committed was carried with her into every battle. For all that he was a lieutenant in her army, he dispatched his duties with an ease she could not understand.

He cupped her face in his hands and raised her chin so he could see her eyes. "I know that being queen wasn't the role you envisioned for yourself and that you don't relish making difficult decisions, but that's what separates you from the Thirteen, Maggie. You don't want it for yourself."

"I don't," she whispered.

The muscles of his face relaxed and his eyes widened. "When this is done, leave."

"What do you mean?"

"Leave. Who says you must be queen? We can marry and go off somewhere together. We can be two normal people alive in the world."

A laugh escaped her. "We could sail across this Great Sea Avishai keeps talking about and see the land that lies beyond it."

"Exactly!"

"I would no longer have to make these decisions. I could just disappear." Her laughter ceased as she considered it. "Let somebody else bury the bodies and mourn B-Bredych."

The sobs ripped through her then as he held her. Her sister. Her father. Bredych. Even dear old Darras. Senator Montero or Asti, the God of Peace, who had tried to help her in the forest. Grand Marshal Doublis and his son, Philip. The Amaskans she had killed shortly after her sister's death. Dead bodies stacked deep enough to drown her. "Curse the Thirteen," she said as the tears slowed.

Leolin squeezed her hand. "Marry me."

"You would truly have me run away with you?"

He nodded. "Anywhere you wish, Maggie."

She hesitated and found herself looking down towards the river. A group of people carried Bredych's body away. She would need to plan for his burning and those of her soldiers slain today, and she sighed. "You said I was different from the Thirteen because I didn't want to rule, because I didn't want this power and responsibility, but that's why I can't leave. I'm a good queen because I care about what happens to my people and leaving them to ruin is not something I can do."

"I knew when I said it that you wouldn't do it," he said as he gave her hand another squeeze. "But you can still marry me, you know."

Margaret shook her head, and when his eyes widened, she placed a hand over his heart. "Do not mistake my words for something else, Leolin. I love you, but I can't have a consort."

He paled. "Why not?"

"No one expected me to rule. Everyone expected me to marry someone of power, someone like Gamun, and he would rule Alexander. If I marry you, people would look to you instead of me. I would become what they expected of me."

"You have proven time and again you are capable, Maggie."

"Not enough to stop tongues from wagging. It doesn't mean we can't be together, love, just not in the way you are asking." She nodded down the hill where the Amaskans were escorting their prisoners. "We should join them. What was it your Doughal said? The work is never finished?"

Leolin gave her a leg up as she mounted her borrowed horse. Sorrow swam in his eyes as well as joy, a battle she understood too well, and she urged the horse down the path. There were decisions to be made.

A heaviness settled across Margaret's shoulders and weighed down her chest. If Adlain killed her, at least the work would be done...for her.

24

The day would certainly stick in Margaret's mind for many years as it was the day many died, particularly Bredych, but also the day the Little Dozen Kingdoms agreed on something together without argument. The sun was setting by the time Margaret arrived at her tent with Luthia, Delorcini, and Sharmus, and all three sagged to their knees when they stopped moving.

Many rulers wanted to give them a chance to prove themselves before deciding on whether or not to exile them, but a few like Havin planned to use them against Adlain and Farimun before killing them. *That* decision would be made later. For now, the gods were placed in a heavily guarded tent to rest. Several monarchs wished to use Avishai, little healed through she was, and Margaret was thankful when those few where outvoted. The challenge from Adlain would likely come on the morrow. It was better to rest now while everyone had the opportunity.

Back in her tent, Margaret sat on the cot that served as her bed. Her steward had offered to send a stuffed mattress with her entourage, but she had refused. What her army slept on would be what she slept on, though at five months pregnant, she had some regret as her lower back ached. A second cot for Leolin had been brought into her tent and pushed beside hers, and he lay on it asleep.

Even exhausted, sleep eluded her, and she rose as slowly as possible to avoid waking Leolin. Her nighttime pacing had worn a tread in the dirt floor of her tent, and she stared at it. Bredych would never hold her hand and pace beside her again as she worried about her decisions. He would never chastise her for not seeing his attack coming as they sparred. He would never smile in that knowing way he had while he waited for her to process something he felt she should know.

Too much grief weighed down her feet for pacing, so Margaret stood on the cold, dirt floor. A small rock poked her heel through her slippers, but she ignored it. The pain meant she was alive.

She blinked, or at least she had intended only to blink, but when she opened her eyes, Senator Montero stood before her. It was impossible as he had died in Alesta Castle during the first quakes, but nonetheless, he was here. She reached out to touch him, and her hand passed through his form.

"Asti?" she whispered. It was odd calling him by his real name. Margaret had spent her entire life knowing him as a kind old senator for Alexander, but he was more than that. Or he had been.

When she glanced over her shoulder, there were no cots behind her, no Leolin to wake, no worn tread in the ground. Just a darkness stretching forever. "Where am I?"

"I don't have long, Queen Margaret. I shouldn't be here at all, and neither should you, so listen."

"How do I know you are yourself? You could be a trick sent to me by Adlain."

The God of Peace smiled as he furrowed his brows and seized her hand. The memory of her in the forest outside Alesta and his visit flashed through her mind. "Few know I came to you then, to bless you, as I come now. Please listen."

His body had disappeared into dust when he had died but here he stood. Margaret gestured for him to proceed.

"I wish I could tell you more than this, but it's forbidden, even to me, but all this loss? I promise there's a purpose. It hasn't been for nothing. There's goodness in this world because of your actions. You must continue to fight." He glanced over his shoulder for a second time, his eyes wide with fear.

"Are you safe?" she asked.

"Not in this place. None of us are."

She looked around her, but other than Asti's shape, there was nothing but darkness. "Where are we?"

"It's not for me to say."

When he stopped talking, she frowned. "Is there more you have to tell?"

Asti smiled and released her hand so he could touch her stomach. "Margaret Poncett, your child is blessed, but more than that, she is a gift to you."

"She?" Margaret's heart sped up. When Delorcini had named her a daughter, Margaret had thought it a trick, but Asti had never lied to her. A tear trickled down her cheek.

"Every heartbreak and death has shaped you, Queen Margaret. Without sadness, there is no happiness, yes? Even in loss, no one is ever truly gone. Do not despair. There is work to be done."

Asti's form faded, leaving Margaret in darkness. Panic threatened to overcome her when she saw a figure sliding through the pitch. He moved like water across river stones until he was close enough to identify.

Bredych.

He whispered something but it escaped her. "Master, I can't hear you," she said. When he repeated it, his mouth moved without sound, and she shook her head.

"When an avalanche threatens to take down the mountain, rise above it."

"I don't understand." His figure faded too quickly, and Margaret rushed forward. "Come back! Please!"

Darkness, thick as tree trunks, enveloped her until she struggled to breathe. In it, she saw another figure whose body blended in with the black, all except her bald head. Then that figure disappeared as well, swallowed up by the night.

Margaret reached out to grab hold of it, to fight it off, but what her hand touched was soft. She clawed at it and kicked, tossing it away from her. Moonlight struck her vision as she stilled.

"Maggie, stop, you're safe," said Leolin as he grabbed her by the shoulders.

Her legs were still tangled in the blanket, though she had thrown the rest off. "Where am I?" she asked.

"You're in your tent at the Meridi Pass, remember?"

She glanced down at the dirt floor with its familiar worn path and then at Leolin. "Asti was here."

He touched her face with his hand, his eyes narrowed.

"I'm not feverish, Leolin. Asti was here, I tell you."

"Perhaps you were dreaming, Maggie. Asti's dead, remember?"

Margaret pulled the blanket off and rose from her cot. "Listen to me, Leolin. I was not dreaming. This pregnancy... I've had trouble sleeping so I was pacing," she said as she pointed to the dirt tread. "The tent grew dark, as if there were no moonlight streaming in, and Asti appeared. He told me not to give up and to fight, but he also said our daughter is blessed. Then Bredych appeared and said something from the *Book of Ja'ahr* before the darkness swallowed me."

Leolin frowned as he stood and took her hands in his. "Maggie, I can't say whether it was a dream or something else, but think for a moment. You're exhausted, you've lost people close to you, and more may die tomorrow. You haven't been eating well either. War is hard on everyone, and it wouldn't surprise me if you were being troubled by bad dreams."

"It was real."

"If it was, we're all in trouble. Think about it, if Asti returned from the dead to see you, what's to keep Anur or any other god from returning?"

She shook her head. "He came to speak to me, but he was still dead. I'm not one of the Holy Few, but I think it was his spirit, Leolin. If Anur or even Itovah wished to plague me, they could do little more than talk in that state. I don't think Asti could affect the world. Not really."

When he pulled her back to their cots, she allowed it, though she waited until Leolin's light snores filled the tent before she left. A light snow was falling, and she pulled on her boots and a heavy cloak before walking to the area where the Order had made camp. Amaskans surrounded the tent holding the gods, and when she stopped outside of it, one stepped forward to ask her business.

"I am Queen Margaret of Alexander, and I need to speak with Sharmus."

The *Amaskan* eyed the heavy cloak around her shoulders before landing on Margaret's jaw. "Are you carrying any weapons?" she asked, and when Margaret nodded, the *Amaskan* held out her hands.

Margaret handed over her short sword as well as her dagger and several throwing knives. She had intended to keep one but thought better of it. The *Amaskan* parted the tent flap to allow her entrance. Inside, several cots had been provided, along with a few chairs, the latter of which the gods had set around a small brazier where they huddled.

While they all appeared fatigued, none looked sleepy as they all turned to her, their eyes alert. Sharmus stood and offered his chair to Margaret. When she shook her head, he said, "You need this seat more than I do, Your Majesty. Please sit."

"Welcome to our prison. What may we do for you?" said Delorcini, and Luthia scowled at her.

"For someone who's supposed to represent love, you represent bitterness more, I think," said Margaret.

Sharmus frowned. "Fear does not rest well with any of us, I'm afraid. Perhaps when we know our fate, it will be easier to be amenable."

"I had a visitor to my tent, and I'm not sure what to believe."

At this, Delorcini tensed as she glanced around the tent.

"Was it Adlain?" asked Sharmus.

Margaret shook her head. "Asti, though I know that's difficult to believe as he's dead, but he came to my tent to bless my child and to tell me to keep fighting. His form was not solid, but it was him as I know his smile well. He also brought me another visitor, though that message was a personal one I won't share."

"Can you be sure it was him?" Sharmus crouched beside Margaret as he studied her. "Could it have been a dream? Or even a vision from Adlain meant to distract you? You don't look like you've slept much."

"That is why I came here. I do not know."

Luthia asked, "Did he come to visit you in your tent or was it somewhere else?"

The sensation of the darkness tickled Margaret's mind as she looked at Luthia. "I thought it was my tent but it was dark. The only light was Asti's face and...something vexed him. He was afraid, I think."

"He walks in the silence." Luthia's black eyes stared

through Margaret as she swayed. "I walked there for so long before I found my voice. I am saddened that he is bound there."

"What is this place you speak of? I thought you were the Goddess of Silence, so does he walk within you?"

"I am the Goddess of Silence because I am *of* the silence. Silence is what was and what will ever be. It is the end and the beginning and the middle."

Margaret frowned. "I don't understand."

Luthia's gaze refocused as she glanced at Margaret. "It's not for you to understand, Your Majesty. If I can, I will help Asti...and Bredych."

Margaret had not named the second visitor. For Luthia to know.... It was not a dream. Whatever this silence was, it was connected to Luthia. It had to be. Margaret inclined her head to Luthia and stood to leave.

"Your Majesty, a moment please," said Sharmus as she neared the tent flap. When she halted, he smiled at her. "I know you don't trust us, but we do not wish you harm, I swear it. Whatever message Asti intended for you, whatever blessing he gave, the stress of all of this can be difficult on someone with child. After all of this, when Adlain and Farimun have been slain, I would like to remain in Alesta until the birth of your child."

"Why?"

"I am the God of Healing. If something were to go wrong, I would be there to help if I can."

Margaret studied Sharmus's face as she searched for some sign of malice, but there was none. If anything, his features were softer than she had seen many moons ago on the cliff. They were older too. "You may not live long enough to see the birth of my daughter. There are many months ahead before she's born."

His mouth twitched. "Indeed. If I am still here, I will do

what I can to protect her. What was it you said, 'The Thirteen owe me'?"

She reached for a weapon that was not there. "How could you know that?"

"We may be dying but we are still gods," he said and gave a sad half-smile. "But you are correct. You are owed. I will make good on this, I swear."

The prickling of magic crossed her skin as he spoke, a sensation that faded as did his words. The god sagged against the tent's brace, and Delorcini and Luthia rushed forward to help him back to his chair.

"Go rest, Your Majesty. We will see to Sharmus," said Luthia, and Margaret exited the tent.

Her weapons were returned to her, but they felt useless against so much that she did not understand. Emotions spiraled inside of her, threatening to overwhelm her, and Bredych's words echoed back to her from the silence of night.

When an avalanche threatens to take down the mountain, rise above it.

She could not cut off her emotions, not in the way the Order did. The *Book of Ja'ahr* spoke often of being like stone, and she had tried, but the meditations did not work for her. Marked though she was, she was no *Amaskan*. She was something different.

But stones sank. What had he meant by "rise above it"?

Margaret was no closer to deciphering the *Amaskan*'s message when she arrived back at her tent. As she lay down beside Leolin, her mind worried at it like a puzzle and rather than sleep, she walked through what she could remember of the *Amaskan* text.

As the sun peeked over the horizon, she sat upright as it clicked into place.

She knew how to win against Adlain.

25

Our prisoners were correct," said Margaret as she sat on a fallen tree trunk, a bowl of soup in her hand. She sipped it as all around her army broke their fast. This morning, titles meant very little as they were each fighters, each hoping to earn their freedom from the Thirteen. "Adlain wants to challenge me, but I think that is how we win."

Leolin ladled up some soup in his own bowl and then sat on the fallen tree trunk beside her. "How so?"

"We will use our prisoners, mystics, and whoever else can wield a spell to ensure there's a fight between Adlain and me. While I fight him, everyone else can handle Farimun."

A snort escaped Leolin. "It's not that I don't think you capable, Maggie, but Adlain's a god. The All-Father. I-I don't know that you can fight him alone."

"But I can. All I have to do is rise above the avalanche."

"Bredych's message?"

"I spent most of the night puzzling it out, but I was

thinking too metaphorically. I kept searching for some hidden meaning about how to be a better person or be more *Amaskan*." She brushed a hand over the circle on her jaw. "But I don't need to be *Amaskan*. I need to be a fighter. Nothing more. What he was telling me was to move. How does one avoid an avalanche? By not being in the way of it."

Leolin tilted his head. "How does that help you fight Adlain though? You can't avoid the fight altogether."

"The gods are dying, and their magic waning. I'm younger than him, so if I keep moving, I can exhaust him. He won't be able to fight me if he's worn out."

"You try and outlast him."

Margaret nodded. "The goal will be to keep Farimun away from the battle with me. If they are working together, that makes the fight an avalanche."

His gaze moved across the army in front of him and beyond, to the other armies of the Little Dozen Kingdoms. "Seems like we went to a lot of trouble to bring everyone together for a fight between two people."

"That's my worry—you and others assuming this will be easy. The entire Little Dozen Kingdoms against Farimun, but this is Farimun. His magic is different. Every step he takes is a journey, and he can move between places in a heart-beat. The only way to defeat him is to be everywhere at once."

"Which requires an army. Or several."

"Exactly."

The camp fire near them flared a sudden crimson, and several soldiers stumbled away from it. Margaret set her soup on the ground, hand on her sword's hilt as she waited. In the days leading up to this, she had grown used to the skin prick-ling sensation that came with magical usage, so when the needles pricked at her, she brushed it aside as she unsheathed her sword.

Leolin followed her lead. "Magic?" he asked, and she nodded.

"He's here."

"Where?"

Margaret searched the faces around her and shook her head. "I don't know. Only that he must be here for my skin to crawl like this." She placed a hand over her eyes to shield them from the sun and peered up at the cliff. No one stood up there that she could see. Admittedly, she stood across the Pass, but Adlain was difficult to miss. "I thought he would want to be seen. Who issues a challenge from the shadows but a coward?"

Someone behind her hissed, and she spun around to find a small group of soldiers with their own swords drawn. Standing in the middle was Adlain.

The soldiers who comprised her army were hearty folk, but beside Adlain, they almost resembled children. His muscular frame stood out, as did his jet black hair that curled around his ears and nape. When he smiled, the jovial look left some soldiers unsure of whether he was friend or foe, but Adlain ignored them as he stared at Margaret.

He held no visible weapons that she could see, nor did she see Farimun, which meant Adlain had used his own magic to appear before her. More power remained with the god than she had thought. Luthia's warning held true. Margaret gave a brief incline of her head, and her soldiers stepped back to leave a clear path between her and Adlain.

If the god noticed, he gave no indication, and instead, gave a deep bow to Margaret. When he spoke, every person in the Pass must have heard him by the way everyone froze, or perhaps magic caused people to stop, spoons halfway to their mouths. When she glanced out of the corner of her eye at Leolin, he stood perfectly still with his sword thrust forward. The whites of his eyes were visible as they turned her direction.

Short of his eyes, he could not move.

"Let us save more deaths, little queen," said Adlain as he stepped towards her.

She did not step back or change her stance. Something in her gut told her that he would not attack her here. Not yet. Besides, if he moved close enough, she might be able to end the fight before it had begun.

"When the sun reaches midday—"

Margaret waved her hand. "I will defend the Little Dozen Kingdoms' peoples against your corruption, yes."

Adlain's eyes narrowed. "When I defeat you, Alexander will be mine. Your family will forfeit all rights to its lands, its wealth, and its people. Agreed?"

"And when I kill you, the Little Dozen Kingdoms will no longer be held prisoner by tyrants."

Alexandrian soldiers took up the cry of Boahim, which spread across the field. They might be frozen in place, but they could still speak. Off to her left, Havin yelled something else, but it was lost in the chanting of two thousand.

Adlain's grin increased until it marred his features, twisting them around in a macabre manner. His form dissolved into dust, which lay on the ground for a heartbeat until the wind blew. The dust mixed into the lightly falling snow until it was indiscernible. Only then were people's bodies released from whatever held them.

For all that she had spoken with strength and kept her sword firmly in her grasp, inside Margaret quaked with fear. Adlain held far more power than she had imagined if he had been able keep so many still.

When she turned towards Leolin, his face held the same fear. They sheathed their blades as soldiers returned to their morning soup. Margaret returned to her fallen tree, though her stomach rebelled at the thought of food. In a few candlemarks, she would be fighting for her people's souls.

Her soldiers stepped aside to allow King Bajit entrance to

their camp. "You have no idea what you're doing, Queen Margaret, and I request the right to fight Adlain in your stead. I have magical gifts where you do not. I should be the one to face the All-Father."

Not that she had expected him to bow, being her equal, but a nod or even a greeting would have sufficed. She resisted the urge to stand, choosing instead to remain in a relaxed and seated position as she waved away concerned soldiers as if Havin were little more than a nuisance.

"Cousin, welcome to our camp. Would you like to join us in breaking our fast?" she asked.

"No, thank you. I...apologize for the interruption, but as midday approaches, such decisions must be made with haste."

His face flushed as he apologized, though Margaret doubted it was from embarrassment. Beside her, Leolin bristled, and she rested a hand on his. "Unfortunately, Adlain requires a battle with me, a descendent of King Dama Yachad of Boahim." If she could have foisted the fight off on the King of Shad, she would have, though she kept such thoughts to herself. "But since you have knowledge of magic that I do not, any advice you wish to impart would be appreciated."

"Descendent of King Yachad? You?"

"There were rumors of this in our histories, but Luthia herself confirmed it."

Havin ground his teeth. "Luthia spoke? To you?"

Again Margaret nodded.

When he glared at her, she noticed that he stared at her jaw and resisted the urge to raise her hand and cover it. Rather than comment, Havin spun on his heel and strode back towards his camp.

"It would have been nice if he had given us some indication of how strong Adlain might be and what sorts of magic he might still be able to use. I wonder if Havin's magic is fading as well..."

Leolin nodded. "Shai noticed that even the magics used for healing are less powerful than before. Wounds they used to be able to fix, they now can't. Sharmus used a good deal of power healing Bredych. He will probably die sooner because of it."

"And yet Bredych died anyway."

She stood to stretch her legs, and Leolin's gaze fell to her midsection. "Do what you can to rest before this battle, and not just for you. Please," he said.

There was no way she could rest. Several candlemarks until she fought Adlain meant several candlemarks she could be studying magic and planning how best to protect herself. But she nodded to Leolin anyway.

Let him believe her well rested if it helped.

As Leolin worked with her army to better prepare for the upcoming battle, Margaret called Shai to her tent. He, too, had been ordered to rest and preserve whatever magic he still possessed, but from the bags beneath his eyes, he listened to orders as well as Margaret did.

He seemed unsurprised by her summons as he sat in the proffered chair. As she gathered her thoughts, he said, "You won't know until you try, Your Majesty."

"I do not understand."

Shai pinched two fingers together and stared at them. A small ball of light appeared which he quickly allowed to dissipate. "Magic. You won't know if you can do it until you try. That *is* why you brought me here, yes?"

Margaret nodded. "In our fight, Adlain will use magic, but I don't understand how to protect myself against it. Every time magic is used near me, my skin is stuck by needles. I can sense it, but how do I know if I can *use* it?"

The mystic nodded. "Hold up two fingers together as I did," he said, and when she followed his instructions, he continued. "Think about a tiny ball of light. Don't worry about where, just the what. Clear your mind of everything else and think only of light."

Shoving aside her thoughts of the Thirteen was as easy as climbing a mountain with one leg. Even the act of trying not to think of Adlain made Margaret think of him, so she focused on the light instead. She pictured the ball Shai had created in her mind and mentally repeated the word light while she stared at her two fingers. When minutes passed and nothing happened, she stopped. "I believe I have my answer."

Shai smiled as he shook his head. "If magic were that easy, everyone would use it. It took me a season of trying before I managed the tiniest of lights."

Margaret's stomach dropped as he spoke. "I don't have a season to try and make a light."

The mystic nodded. "This is why I came when you summoned me, Your Majesty. You're looking for a simple solution to a complex problem, and that won't work. You aren't going to be able to use magic against Adlain."

She remained silent for several heartbeats as Bredych's words ran circles in her brain. Shai reached out to pat her hand, and she smiled at him. "I suspected you would tell me this. I'm not distraught, only disappointed. I've lived this long without magic in my life, and I will continue to live without it. I don't suppose there is any way to lessen the pain of magic's presence?"

"Without understanding more about why you feel it, I couldn't say. There are herbs that would put you to sleep, and then you wouldn't feel magic's touch, but I believe you wish to be awake for the upcoming battle."

"That would be helpful, yes. If I had been able to create the light, would that mean I could use magic against Adlain?"

"No, Your Majesty. While one's will and desire drive their magic, it takes years of study and practice to do what I do in the healing arts. Even longer to wield magics like King Bajit is rumored to use. I don't think anyone can do what the Thirteen are capable of." The mystic's shoulders slumped as he spoke, and his eyes stared at something far away.

When Margaret tried to meet his gaze, he glanced away. Shai did not believe she would win.

"Is there anything else I can do for you, Your Majesty?" he asked.

She shook her head. "I appreciate your help, Mystic Shai. May we have the luck we need today."

He gave a brief bow before leaving her tent.

Alone, she held up two fingers and stared at them, her mind focused on light. For a time, nothing happened. After half a candlemark had passed and her mind wandered, she gave up.

A gust of wind sent the winter's chill through her tent, and Margaret rubbed her tingling fingers together to warm them. She stood and turned towards her cot, a small ball of light hovered over it. Her eyes widened as she approached. The size of her thumbnail, it floated in front of her, and when she moved her hands above and below it, nothing held it in place.

When she touched it with her finger, the light disappeared.

Whatever ability she possessed, it was too late to help with the upcoming fight against Adlain. Still, her will had created light in the universe where there was none before.

As she left her tent, she smiled.

THE CLEARING CHOSEN by Margaret was halfway between the bridge and the cliff overlooking the Pass. Originally, she had wanted to meet Adlain on the cliff itself, but it was too small to hold those needed to protect her from Farimun. The chosen space was out of the way the camps and provided a level terrain.

Luthia, Delorcini, and Sharmus would form three anchor points, while another would be held by Shai and some of those he had brought with him. The remaining mystics would form another point, while Avishai would form the last while standing in a large basin of water. It was not the same as standing in a lake or a river, but according to Avishai, it was better than nothing at all.

The six points formed a star, a symbol Luthia said the original Amaskans used to represent truth before the symbol morphed into the circle used now. Considering they were fighting against Adlain, they needed every advantage they could get.

Those soldiers who could sense magic's use would form a second circle around the first, in order to better detect if Farimun was attempting to force his way into the fight with Adlain. Leolin had cocked his eyebrows when Margaret had asked them to think of protecting everyone, but she had offered no explanation. Now was not the time to have that conversation. The Amaskans would form a third circle, followed by the rest of the Little Dozen Kingdoms' armies. The two outer circles would engage Farimun and with hope keep him away from the main battle.

Margaret stood in the clearing's center as the sun moved across the sky. Clouds mostly blocked the sun from view, and while it was no longer snowing, the smell of water and cold indicated that it soon would be. She sighed. Snow was not what she needed during a fight. But then, perhaps snow could help Avishai's magic. Her brain turned over each thought out of boredom and a healthy amount of fear as she waited.

Miriam walked over to Margaret and gave a brief nod. "Your Majesty, I have a request before this battle begins."

"What can I do for you, Grand Master?"

Tears gathered in the woman's eyes as she stared at Margaret. "I've not had much time to think on his passing, though I know he died protecting the *chathula*. B-Bre...He died a hero's death, and justice will be served when you have slayed Adlain. But this fight, you have to know Adlain means to kill us all."

Margaret nodded. "I did not get to tell you how sorry I am that he is gone. He was family to me as well, and I—I wish he were still here."

"He and I loved for many years, longer than you have lived, Queen Margaret. When he left the Order, I knew he would never return. My favor is that you make sure Adlain dies."

"Of course."

When she answered, Miriam wiped a tear from her cheek and turned away. As she walked back to her place with the Amaskans, Margaret's heart ached for the woman. Bredych had been a mentor to her, a father-figure, but to Miriam, he had been everything.

Margaret would kill Adlain and quickly.

The moment the sun reached its midpoint, Adlain and Farimun arrived in a light mist. The latter whispered something to the former before stepping aside. A sword hung on the thick leather on Adlain's waist, the brown belt a contrast to the white clothes he wore.

"To ensure this fight is fair, we ask that Farimun step outside of the circle," said Margaret.

Farimun whispered something else to Adlain, who shook his head. Farimun's legs trembled as he ambled to the inner circle. He glanced over his shoulder at Adlain before the Amaskans broke the circle long enough for him to pass.

Almost immediately, the six anchors closed their eyes, their mouths moving soundlessly.

"A protective weave. Interesting," said Adlain.

"It's for your protection as well as my own."

Adlain laughed as he untied his thick cloak and let it drop to the snow below.

The god wore no armor, only his tunic, vest, pants, and boots. The lack of protection sent a shiver down Margaret's spine. Either he was foolhardy or she was going to lose, leaving her people to his torture. She unsheathed her sword and held it in front of her.

Rise above it.

If he were smart, he would avoid using magic and attack her with his sword. His body was that of a fighter, and his abilities with a sword would far surpass hers, but with youth on her side, she could outrun him. She hoped.

A pale, white dome covered them as the gods and mystics worked their magic. The ground trembled briefly as the weave locked into place. The moment the ground settled, Adlain rushed her, sword in hand. His muscular frame moved faster than Margaret had expected and while she danced out of the way, she did so narrowly.

He spun on his heel and faced her again, waiting only a moment before advancing a second time. While she could have blocked, she slid out of the way instead. The next lunge, he changed course midway through, his sword aimed at her left side rather than the right. She brought her blade up at the last minute, and he pushed, their swords grinding against one another.

As her sword came closer to her face, she wrapped her other hand around the hilt and shoved. Adlain retreated, and she used the opportunity to sidestep away from his reach. Despite the cold temperature, perspiration gathered across her forehead. Behind her, shouts sounded as fighting broke out, but she had to trust that the circles protecting her would keep the combat away. Adlain glanced over her shoulder, and she used the opportunity to throw a knife at him.

A small trickle of blood stained the shoulder of his white tunic where the small blade connected, but he flung it aside as if it were little more than a bee sting. Margaret feinted towards the same side as his wound and when he stepped forward, she sidestepped again, dancing away from him altogether.

He stepped back, sword in front of him, and waited.

She retreated a step and still he waited. He was waiting her out. He was using *her* strategy.

Dammit.

THE MAGICAL WEAVE rose from the ground with the briefest of quakes, and two heartbeats later, Farimun clasped his hands together and pulled them apart to expose a short sword glowing hot with magic. He turned the sword towards the nearest *Amaskan* and thrust the blade through the woman's side. She fell without a sound and another stepped forward to take her place. This *Amaskan* parried as several soldiers rushed toward the god.

Someone swung a sword toward Farimun's back and he disappeared, only to reappear several horse lengths away. Leolin studied the pattern as the god worked. He would strike, and then step back before reappearing in another place to strike again. The god appeared to move in a circle of his own as he carved his way toward the six anchors, though the sword dimmed with each death.

If Farimun continued his pattern, he would reach Avishai first, and Leolin ran towards the *chathula*. The basin's water had mostly evaporated, leaving her standing in an empty basin. While Avishai could work without water, Leolin did not want to know how fast it would drain her, and he ordered a nearby soldier to fetch a bucket of water..

He stood with his back to the *chathula*, and a nearby *Amaskan* gave him a slight nod as they both waited.

The longer they stood, the more people died around them, but with the god disappearing as he was, there was little Leolin could do to avoid their deaths. As more Amaskans caught onto the pattern, a few tried to fight the god before he reached Avishai.

Someone cried out to his left. A sweaty man with a large gash in his side narrowly escaped the god and when the man turned, it was King Havin Bajit. He retreated, almost stepping on Leolin's feet in his haste. "He'll be here next," said Havin.

"We'll be ready." Leolin gave the king a brief nod and gripped his sword's hilt tighter.

Several soldiers fell to the ground in a splash of red, and the god disappeared. When he did not reappear, folks glanced around in a slight panic.

"Where'd he go?" an *Amaskan* asked.

Leolin shrugged in response. Several heartbeats passed without Farimun, and several soldiers lowered their blades. "Stay alert. He'll be back," Leolin called out.

A nearby soldier rang the loud bell in his hand, a signal that he felt magic cross his skin. Several others joined him. Leolin could not feel it himself, but the sound of bells moved through the army in a direct line towards Margaret.

Had the god figured out a way to get past the magical weave?

When Farimun appeared, his heft shoved several soldiers aside as he strode towards Avishai. Despite the delay, the god had held to his pattern. His sword's glow was gone, leaving a sharp, metal weapon behind. While it lacked its magic, it cut well enough as Farimun swung it in front of him.

The *Amaskan* beside Leolin fell, his head completely separated from his body. As the god turned toward Avishai, Leolin thrust his blade at the god's unprotected side arm where it stuck in his thick bicep.

The god dropped his sword and laughed, his chins quivering as he punched Leolin with his free hand. The blow made the world spin as Leolin blinked hard. He heard the swish of fabric as Farimun stepped closer to Leolin and winced, expecting another blow. Instead, Havin stepped forward, his hands glowing a deep red as he laid them on the god's back.

Farimun screamed, a sound like a thousand swords tumbling down a well. Havin's eyes glowed and sweat poured down the king's face. The god's skin bubbled and blistered as it cooked. When Farimun stepped toward Havin, the ground trembled again, and the king stumbled as the earth bucked around him. Leolin's vision cleared in time to see the god disappear.

"Where did Farimun run to?" Prince Amar asked as he ran to his father's side. The prince offered his father a hand, which he took. The king trembled as he stood, his skin pale as the snow on the ground. "Are you well, Father?"

Havin nodded, though doubt hovered in his eyes. A rumble of thunder sounded and heavy flakes of snow fell around them. "That...that should have killed him," said the king as he stared at his hands.

"Magic is fading for everyone," said Leolin, and the king nodded.

Blistery and red, Farimun was easy to spot when he reappeared near Delorcini. Leolin ran for her with the prince and king at his side. Tears streamed down the goddess's face as she caught sight of Farimun. He slammed his meaty fist through several soldiers as he reached toward her.

With a burst of speed, Prince Amar rushed forward with his sword held high.

It was a fool's move. When Leolin called out, echoed by

Havin, the young man paused but it was too late. Farimun reached forward, wrapping his hands around the prince's throat.

The god squeezed, and Amar gasped, his fingers clawing at Farimun's hands.

Havin roared and charged forward, his sword sliding into the god's chest. Farimun's hands remained around the prince's throat, and Leolin raised his sword to hack at the god's arms.

The color faded from Farimun's face as he fell, though his hands remained firmly around Amar's throat. The prince fell to his knees, tears streaming down his face, and his father knelt beside him as he too clawed at the god's hands. When they remained, Havin shouted, "Somebody help him!"

Leolin knelt beside Farimun, whose eyes were open and searching. Somehow the god still lived. He plunged his sword directly into the god's heart, where he twisted it until Farimun gave one last shudder. The hands around the prince's throat fell away, and the prince collapsed on the snow. Havin shook his son by the shoulders, but the prince did not move.

Farimun was dead, but so was Prince Amar.

As the fighting outside the circle intensified, Farimun's yells reached Margaret, and her stomach knotted in response. Were these cries because he was losing or because he was winning? Was Leolin still alive, or had he fallen in battle? A million thoughts fragmented themselves across her mind as Adlain watched her.

If she lifted her heel, he shifted in response. No move was made without his noticing. Rather than focus on her moves as a swordsperson, Margaret relaxed her arm, tilting her sword down until the tip touched the ground.

Adlain frowned. "Giving up already?"

"Not particularly. Boredom would be more accurate."

His face flushed red as he raised his empty hand. In his fist was a ball of white energy which crackled. The air around her prickled, and her nose itched with the smell of a storm.

Margaret remained relaxed, though inside she wished to flee. Unless he exhausted himself, there was little chance she could win, so she taunted him. Thunder rumbled overhead, and heavy snowflakes began to fall. While she could still see Adlain, her vision of the protective weave was obscured by the snowfall.

Delorcini was the closest to Margaret, as she stood a few feet to Margaret's right. Out of the corner of her eye, Farimun's robust form lunged through the Amaskans to stop before Delorcini. His skin resembled that of a roasted boar as he shouted something unintelligible in the air. Tears fell down the goddess's face as her gaze met Margaret's.

If the goddess fell, so would the protective circle.

Something hit her, like falling out of a tree, and Margaret could not breathe. She struggled to take gasps, but no air reached her lungs until something popped in her ribs. The air rushed in too fast, and she leaned over as coughs shook her frame. If his ball of energy hit that hard, she had best avoid it. When she raised her head, Adlain laughed as he watched the struggle just outside the inner circle.

Farimun had grabbed hold of someone, a feral grin on his face. The god squeezed the man's neck until someone swung a sword at Farimun's arms.

Margaret peered across the falling snow when she spotted the double-oval symbol of Alexander on the man's cloak. It was Leolin! He was still alive!

A ball of energy landed near Margaret's feet, and she jumped aside. She would have to trust in the fighters outside the weave to handle Farimun. Adlain called forth another ball and tossed it at her.

Margaret leapt out of the way, though her body moved slower than she expected, and Adlain almost hit her. He held another ball of energy ready. This one sputtered, and when he threw it at Margaret, it flew wide, bouncing harmlessly off the protective weave.

The god's magic fizzled as a cry sounded to their right, and Adlain turned to see Farimun's head rolling to a stop at the circle's edge, reds and pinks leaving a trail in the snow.

Adlain's arm fell to his side as his sides heaved. Had he been using Farimun for magical energy? The god stared at his hand, but no energy came forth. With a growl, he gripped his sword and charged Margaret.

While she watched his sword, something sharp landed in her shoulder near the collar bone. When she glanced down, a small throwing knife stuck out of her. When he had grabbed it, mattered little now. The wound stung, and she used her free hand to pull the knife out.

She parried his sword attack and as Adlain stepped backward, his face almost gray, she continued to push forward. The god's feet slipped out from under him, and he fell, his sword sinking into the snow. He threw up his hands in defeat, but Margaret refused to stop.

Her sword slid through his fingers and toward his throat. Adlain's eyes glowed in one, last attempt to ward off her attack, but the spell died on his lips as her sword plunged into his throat. Blood sputtered from his mouth as he stared at her.

Margaret removed her sword long enough to swing at his neck. She did not know if beheading was necessary, or if it had been done to Farimun by coincidence, but the action had killed Itovah and Agaia. Rather than take the chance, she chopped at Adlain's neck until she severed his head from his body.

He landed in the snow with a thud, and moments later, the protective weave fell. Delorcini wavered before collapsing into the snow. Margaret spun around to check on the other anchors.

Shai had collapsed as had the rest of his mystics. Sharmus and Luthia remained standing, though both were visibly shaking. Avishai the Fierce lay in her basin of water, unmoving.

Margaret ran towards the basin, her feet skidding and slipping across the new snow, and when she reached it, she tugged at the *chathula*. "Help me!" she cried and several Amaskans grabbed the Avishai's body to lift it from the water. Her sides did not move, nor could Margaret feel any heartbeat.

Someone grabbed her shoulder, and she cried out as the hand touched the wound left by the knife. She turned away from Avishai to find Shai at her side.

"You're wounded, Your Majesty," he said.

She shook her head, Avishai's head in her arms. "Help her."

The mystic touched the *chathula* and sighed. "I don't have enough magic left to save her."

Margaret craned her neck to find Sharmus. "If you want to stay alive, fix her!" she yelled at the God of Healing.

His steps were slow, his knees shaking as he walked. Luthia supported his weight as he leaned on her. Several dozen agonizing heartbeats passed before he knelt at her side. Sharmus laid Avishai's head in his lap and dug his fingers into her fur as he closed his eyes and concentrated.

Snow coated the shoulders of his green overcoat, turning it white as Margaret waited. At some point, Leolin reached her and slipped his hand in hers. The wound on her shoulder burned, but she pushed it aside as she waited and thought of healing.

Grunts and protests reached them as someone pushed their way past the gathering crowd. Margaret glanced up to see Havin in front of them, the side of his tunic bright red with blood. She hoped it was his.

"Why are you wasting what little magic is left on this...this animal? My son—you have to help my son!" the King shouted.

Sharmus opened one eye and glared at Havin. "Your son is dead, King Bajit. He is beyond my help."

"But you are a god! Your gifts are of healing, so...so heal him!"

When Sharmus closed his eye, his concentration on Avishai, Havin unsheathed his sword and lay it against Avishai's neck. Margaret pulled out a throwing knife from her boot and with the flick of her wrist, tossed it at the man's leg where it stuck in his thigh.

Havin's sword tumbled from his hands as he grabbed at the wound. "How dare you!" he yelled before falling hard into the snow. Shai leaned over and raised the king's outer jacket. A jagged wound ran down the length of his torso.

"He must have been injured in the fight with Farimun," said Leolin.

Sharmus gave a deep sigh as he opened his eyes. "I have done all I can for Avishai. It's up to her now," he said.

Avishai's chest rose and fell with each breath, and when Margaret rested her fingers against the *chathula*'s fur, her heart beat. "Thank you, Sharmus."

The god tried to stand and fell back on his rear. Several mystics rushed forward to help him, and Margaret said, "Make sure Sharmus and the others are returned to their tent, and please take Avishai with them."

Her teeth chattered as the wet snow worked its way beneath her armor. Havin glared at her as she stood, his face a wall of fury and grief. "You are the bane of sons. May you never know the joys of one," he said as she passed.

Everywhere around them, people gathered the dead for yet another burning in the Pass. The wounded would be treated as best they could but without the use of magic. Even if enough existed to help, no one had the energy to use it. Those who could walk, headed back to their camps as marshals recalled their armies. A soldier offered Margaret his horse, and Leolin helped her into the saddle. Her shoulder throbbed in rhythm with her heartbeat.

Havin would bear close watching. Freedom from the Thirteen meant there was no one to ensure he remained an ally, but perhaps that could change. Tomorrow, the Little Dozen Kingdoms would meet to discuss the future, but today, Margaret planned to fall into her cot and sleep.

Leolin held the horse's reins as he led the horse across the Pass. The horse's gait across the flat plain was like swimming through water, and Margaret was asleep in the saddle before they ever reached her tent.

26

The tent that once held twelve people with ease struggled with the additions of the remaining Thirteen. Everyone crowded together in a tight circle around the brazier. What had begun as a heavy snow had transitioned into a storm, leaving the rulers' armies to shelter in place rather than prepare for the trek back to their kingdoms.

Not to be outdone by Margaret battling Adlain, Queen Helena Lorellyn of Liallan had joined her army in the fight against Farimun and suffered a fatal wound. Sitting in her place was her son and heir, Damon, a young lad of fourteen. Also missing was Havin, whose wound had festered in the night. Sharmus doubted the King would survive and with no direct living heir, questions floated about the tent on who would succeed the King of Shad.

Margaret's shoulder wound had been bandaged and only hurt when she moved it, and she counted herself lucky that her injuries were not worse. The baby gave a solid kick as she sat with the others, a reminder that the decisions she would make today would affect more than her.

Leolin, Miriam, and Shai were not allowed in the tent as it was a matter for rulers and heirs only, and Margaret sighed. She could have used Leolin's humor about now as King Marco of Halelind gave a lengthy speech on why he felt the remaining gods best exiled.

It was not that she disagreed with him; in fact, Margaret was sure that all rulers felt as he did, but every ruler would be given an equal opportunity to speak on the topic before a vote was taken.

Marco's voice had a low and relaxing tone, and she struggled to stay awake. The baby kept her up at night, and during the day, all Margaret wished to do was nap. Rather than be rude, she tapped her foot against the chair's leg to stay awake. As the man finished speaking, he scowled at Margaret. "I apologize, Queen Margaret, for taking up your time. Your impatience is noted."

"She's with child, Marco. Movement helps with the leg cramps," said Queen Catia Racci of Estona as she smiled gently at Margaret.

The scowl remained firmly in place, though Marco indicated he yielded with a shrug of his shoulders. King Ermen Clavine of Naribor cleared his throat as he stood to address the group. "While I believe the three remaining gods contributed to the protection of Queen Margaret while she fought and killed Adlain, I worry about allowing them to live. Who's to say that they won't regain their power and create other gods, stronger gods that could then punish us for what took place here at the Meridi Pass?" he said.

Many nodded their heads in agreement. Margaret opened her mouth to interject, but Sharmus stood and all eyes shifted to him.

"I promise you all that we are harmless. I could not so

much as heal a papercut now. Ask the mystics, but magic is almost gone from the Little Dozen Kingdoms. Even if magic were to return, we are old. When I arrived here, my hair still held some of its color, but now I am gray as Adlain was. My wrinkles have wrinkles, and every joint in my body aches with the decay and promise of death." Sharmus sat slowly, his knees trembling.

Ermen nodded though he did not look convinced. Others spoke of their concerns but the general belief was that the gods could do no more harm. Margaret was the last to speak, and she stood in the small space between her chair and the brazier.

"When I first asked you all here to the Meridi Pass, I did so because I believed that destroying the Thirteen and freeing our kingdoms from their corruption was our only choice. Many of you were incredulous that the Senate was the Thirteen until Sharmus arrived. He convinced you all to side with me in this decision. What god would do that if he intended to harm us? Why would he encourage us to destroy him unless he believed it to be the right decision?"

"It could be a deceit," said Ermen.

"A deceit where we could kill him before ever deciding his fate?" asked Margaret as she pointed at Delorcini. "This goddess almost died protecting me. Farimun stood close enough to stab her. She could have fled, but instead, she remained a part of the protective weave."

"And Luthia?" asked Catia.

Margaret pursed her lips together for a moment as she thought. "Honestly, even if we struck down Luthia in this form, I don't believe she would die. She is the silence that was before and will always be. Itovah may have been the Goddess of Death, but I believe Luthia to be what comes after. I do not believe her to be a threat to us in this life."

Several rulers paled as she spoke but asked no more questions.

As Margaret returned to her seat, Queen Helena Lorellyn's son, Damon, stood. "M-My mother has gone on to whatever you spoke of, Queen Margaret, and has passed because of a decision I was not a part of. While I acknowledge that she agreed to defeat the Thirteen and why, I do not feel I can be a part of this vote as I would not have agreed to the murder of our gods so easily."

Margaret flinched, and Catia reached out to pat her hand. "He's young," she whispered in Margaret's ear. "Give him time to walk the world a bit."

"With Damon Lorellyn abstaining, we will take a vote," said Margaret as she held one hand out in front of her. "If you are in favor of exiling the three remaining gods to their island until their deaths, please place your hand out, palm-side up. If you believe we should execute them, place your hand out, palm-side down."

One by the one, the Little Dozen Kingdoms' rulers placed their hands in front of them, their palms up, the exceptions being Damon and the absent King of Shad. Vote taken, Delorcini burst into tears as she clung to Luthia.

King Adir Monsine of Sadia glanced at Sharmus as he spoke. "While I agree to exile them, I'll not be responsible for ensuring they are safely escorted to their island, nor will I provide supplies for them any longer. If they wish to live out their remaining days, let them figure out how to survive on their own like the rest of us."

As the other rulers voiced their agreement, Margaret said, "Since I was the one who suggested exile in the first place, my kingdom will ensure they are given safe passage via ship to their island."

"Where you'll let us starve to death?" said Delorcini.

Margaret shook her head. "Assuming you live long enough to require supplies, Alexander will provide them."

"Thank you, Queen Margaret." Sharmus bowed before her, and several rulers gasped.

While he was their prisoner, he was still a god—a god who had bowed to a queen. Margaret called for a soldier to escort the remaining Thirteen to their tent. "With that decision out of the way, let us talk of our future…"

SERVANTS HAD BROUGHT in a midday meal and taken the remains away a few moments before, while another servant had cleared the tent's smoke hole from snow. After a brief break to stretch legs and take care of necessities, the rulers gathered again in the command tent. Outside, the snow had stopped, but the air hung heavy with moisture.

"With the Senate gone, we are free to make our own choices with regards to how we manage our kingdoms, but I have a suggestion to make to help us keep the freedom and peace we have fought for," said Margaret.

Adir frowned. "I sincerely hope you are not about to suggest we form another Senate."

"Of course not. The Senate created secrecy and corruption. The very group intended to help prevent another war, not only failed at that, but they caused one. Even together, our armies sustained large casualties by the very gods sworn to protect us."

"Then what are you proposing, Queen Margaret?" asked Adir.

If the man would allow her to finish her thought, perhaps she could tell him. Other than Damon, who was still a child, Margaret was the youngest ruler present. The assumption that her ideas lacked any wisdom rankled her, and she resisted the urge to grind her teeth. Instead, she smiled and said, "Part of the reason that conflict has occurred between our kingdoms is a lack of communication. A message here or trade agreement there is not enough for us all to benefit from our neighbors. Coming together here at the Pass, as we have twice done, has allowed us to work together in a way not seen since Boahim."

Again Adir interrupted her as he stood. "And now she wishes for us to give up our thrones to form Boahim, with her as the ruler."

"I said no such thing."

"Queen Margaret, I heard you when you told Havin that you were a descendant of King Dama Yachad. It's no secret that your father stretched the boundaries of Alexander every opportunity he had, and now you wish to do the same to encompass us all." As chatter broke out across the rulers, Adir regained his seat, a smirk on his face.

Rather than address all the rulers, Margaret stood and walked over to Adir. She crouched in front of him and met his gaze. "King Adir, I was too young to know what my father did or did not do or his reasons for any of his actions, but he is dead. *I* rule Alexander now, and I have no interest in ruling all of the Little Dozen Kingdoms. What can I do to make peace with you?"

"You can stop acting like the leader of this meeting."

All chatter was hushed at his words, and Margaret nodded. "My apologies, cousin. I have an idea I think could help us all, several in fact, but it is not my intention to be seen as the leader. The point is that no one of us is 'the leader.' We should all share ideas in this rare time that we are together and make plans as we see fit."

Ermen clapped his hand on Adir's shoulder. "My friend, I think what the young queen is suggesting is that perhaps meeting together like this should be a regular occurrence. We wouldn't need to bring our armies, best if we didn't, but we could meet every so often. What do you think of this?"

"I would need more details, but the idea is not abhorrent."

As Margaret returned to her seat, she ground her teeth until Catia leaned over to whisper again into her ear. "It would have to be a man suggesting it to gain Adir's attention."

"If I may continue...?" asked Margaret, and when Adir nodded, she said, "This is why I thought up this plan before our meeting here. The petty arguing that has happened several times when we have been together could have been avoided if we had stayed in better contact with each other, if we grew to know one another. If you knew what I have done and had to do in order to...gain the information we needed to overthrow the Thirteen, you would not dismiss me so easily as an ignorant child playing queen. Of course, you may not wish to hear my plan or agree to it, which is your right. I have no wish to rule over anyone but those in my kingdom."

"What is your plan, Queen Margaret?" asked Ermen.

"Every five years, we agree to meet here at the Pass."

"Hopefully not in the middle of winter," muttered Adir.

Margaret shook her head. "We could figure out a better time for all considering the travel required. I propose that by meeting like this, we could use the time to discuss and sign new treaties and trade agreements. Doing so in person would help communication, and encourage better brokering of said agreements."

"Sounds boring," said young Damon, and several rulers chuckled.

"In Estona, my vassals gather annually in the City of Ibani during spring for the Atlin Festival," said Catia. "As the snow melts and the ice breaks in the river, there are wagers on what day the ice will break, with a prize to the winner. There are other games, and crafters set up booths. Those who can, travel into the city for the day of celebration. While less entertaining plans are made, we make time to enjoy ourselves as well. This five-year meeting could be something similar."

"While I believe this to be a good idea, the Meridi Pass is

covered in the blood and bodies of our dead. Hardly a place to have such a gathering," said Ermen.

"Alexander would gladly host—" Margaret stopped as Adir glared at her. Something was bothering the old king, and she wished she knew what it was so she could fix it.

Catia said, "Perhaps it could be rotated? Hosted by a different kingdom each time so no one kingdom bears the brunt of hosting such a gathering."

Marco, who had been eerily silent through the conversation, grinned. "I have a suggestion. Since the Pass is a decent halfway point for most of us, but the location itself is not ideal, I offer up the city of Lowell. It's near enough to the Pass and easily reachable. It's also sizeable enough to host such a gathering." When Adir raised a brow at the old king's willingness to play host, Marco continued to grin. "I'll be honest, having eleven kingdoms tromping across my borders every five years gives me a bit of a fright, but it'll keep us all honest. Besides, all the money spent in Lowell—I can't see anything detrimental in that!"

"Now wait, how come you get all the benefit of such a gathering?" asked Adir.

Several others joined in to protest Marco's hosting of the meeting, and when Margaret stood to stretch her legs, Catia joined her. "Don't worry, the men will argue themselves out soon enough. They will agree to Halelind hosting so they don't have to do the hard work of planning such a gathering."

Queen Delia Benavent of Ethenium stood and walked over to stand beside Margaret. She pointed at her midsection and asked, "How far along are you?"

"Five months as near as the healers can guess."

"I remember those earlier months when one could still move around. I'm glad you didn't wait much longer to challenge the Thirteen. Soon enough you won't want to sit on a horse for one candlemark, let alone a full day's travel," said Delia.

The two queens continued to offer advice to Margaret until Adir cleared his throat to recapture their attention. "If you three are done, perhaps we could continue planning the future of our kingdoms?" he said.

"We were waiting for the men to stop bickering, so we could return to the discussion," said Catia.

Adir snorted, and as everyone returned to their seats, Margaret hid a grin behind her hands. Originally, listening to everyone in the tent had felt similar to getting children to agree to the same meal, but amidst the jeers and critiques, there was the hint of balance that reminded her of when her father would sit with his advisors in the afternoons. Their idle bickering was made of long friendship rather than ill will. For all that Adir acted as if he were not interested in her ideas, the way he leaned forward to engage in the debate said otherwise. Perhaps there was hope for them learning to work together.

"I realize that everyone runs their kingdom uniquely, and we are each used to being the deciding voice amongst our people, but I hope we can develop a sense of community and goodwill with each other. My father spent his entire life at odds with the Bajit family. Personally, I would like to avoid that." As Margaret stopped speaking, the tent flap was pulled aside to admit Havin.

He used a cane as he shuffled in, his skin pale as he struggled. "I believe I heard my name."

A servant helped him to the empty chair waiting for him as Adir reprised the conversations. Havin avoided looking at Margaret, though he listened intently as plans were outlined on what would be needed to host the gathering, when they would meet, the guidelines for what types of trades and treaties would be kept for their in-person meetings and which could be discussed in the time between the gathering. A scribe was sent for to take notes on the details which were drawn up into formal documents.

"Perhaps we could call this gathering *pasetivi*," said Margaret, and when Catia tilted her head, she added, "In the old tongue of Boahim, it means a gathering or a caucus. A gathering fits as those who can travel will do so in order to take part in the festivities, and caucus works as we rulers will also gather in order to better our kingdoms through treaties and trade agreements."

"Fitting that the Little Dozen Kingdoms would agree to join together at something named in the original tongue of our land." Havin's words were slow as if the very effort of speech was too much. "Perhaps we should vote."

Twelve hands were raised quickly, palms up. Only Havin hesitated before agreeing. Soon after, they signed an accord that the first *pasetivi* would be in held in the month of Echain, at the beginning of summer, in the year 262 in Lowell, Halelind. Additional details would be solidified as Marco planned.

Margaret sent a servant to fetch Miriam, and when the Grand Master of the Order walked into the tent, Adir sprang to his feet. "Why are you here? This is a meeting for nobility only."

"I have no idea, Your Majesty. I was sent for and told to come to this tent." Miriam did not bow but merely inclined her head in the monarchs' direction.

"I'm the one who sent for the Grand Master," said Margaret. While she had shared her ideas of a general gathering with both Leolin and Bredych, her next plan was something that had remained a secret. Not that there was any reason to do so, but a part of her worried that had she shared them, Bredych or Leolin might have chastised her for it.

Margaret stood and turned to face Miriam. "The Kingdom of Sadai has been home to the Order for the entirety of its existence. During this time, Amaskans outside your kingdom have been forced to hide in order to stay safe, all while seeking justice."

"Most of that is because of your kingdom," said Adir, and Margaret nodded.

"Amaskans were given a reputation as killers and assassins. The former grand master, Bredych, confessed to us all. The documents he left behind detail a grisly past where some grand masters ordered the deaths of people purely out of service to vengeance rather than justice."

She reached out a hand to receive a stack of parchment from Miriam. "I could read these crimes aloud, as they not only list crimes committed by Amaskans, but monarchs as well, but it would serve little purpose. Our gathering here marks a new beginning."

Margaret walked over to the fire pit and held the documents out over the flame.

Catia stood and reached for them too late as Margaret dropped them in the fire. "That was useful information you destroyed."

"Useful only if we intend to live at each other's throats. I don't know about you, but I would rather live in a world where peace fought for and earned so preciously means *peace*. I don't wish to look over my shoulder waiting for my neighbor to betray me."

"Such thoughts are naive at best," said Havin. He coughed and a bit of blood appeared on his lips.

"You are not well, cousin. Perhaps you should return to your tent so the healers can look after you."

Havin waved a hand at her. "Tell us this idea of yours."

"With the Senate gone, I propose a new way for the Order. What if the Order were given access to every kingdom in order to create places of learning? Places were anyone could go to learn more about their kingdom, the laws of their homeland,

and their rights as citizens? What if a new type of *Amaskan* were born of citizens who helped keep the peace and seek justice for everyone?"

"How does that differ from our peace keepers and jailers?" asked Ermen.

"Rather than seeking out criminals so they can be jailed or executed, Amaskans could work with our peace keepers. If someone had a problem with a land dispute with his neighbor, he could start by going to the Order. They could teach him about his rights and the best way to approach the dispute, which may be to talk with his neighbor. Perhaps they could sit in on the talk as a form of mediator. If the dispute can't be solved through discussion and compromised, then they can involve the peace keepers or petition the courts."

Ermen nodded. "So this would focus on educating the public and involving the monarchs less in petty troubles that could be solved more easily."

"In a sense." Margaret disliked his framing of people's trouble as petty, but the point was close enough that she accepted it. "If we teach our people more about the laws that govern them and the why, and we teach them how to work together to solve common issues, there is less of a need for justice seekers."

Miriam pursed her lips together. "Queen Margaret, while the idea has merit, the Order has never been about solving small land disputes. Our search for Justice came from people's need to see murderers, rapists, and other horrors laid in the dirt. People who would harm others must be dealt with, no matter who they happen to be friends with."

"I understand that. Master Bredych spoke at length about the importance of the Order's work, and I know from my sister's journals about the role Justice serves in an *Amaskan*'s life."

Damon pointed at her jaw, his eyes wide. "She's only saying that because she's one of them."

Margaret raised a hand to her jaw, her fingers brushing the circle that marred her skin. While healed, the skin over the mark was slightly raised and red in color. She gave a sad smile to the young lad before she continued. "I don't wear this mark by choice as it was given to me by a *Tribor* assassin named Till. He was sent to kill me and before he tried, he carved this into my face with a hot knife."

The boy paled but his jaw jutted forward. "Amaskans killed my father!"

"I know. They took my sister from me when we were little and tried to kill my father and me many times."

"Then how can you help them?" asked Damon.

"Sometimes we must make peace with the past in order to have peace in the future. Sometimes that means forgiving those we hate." Margaret glanced at Havin as she spoke. He returned her look but said nothing in response.

"I think this is a conversation to be decided at this *pasetivi*. It would give each ruler time to consider your words," said Catia.

"Agreed," said Adir as he nodded. "I would also say that no one kingdom should feel they have to agree to house Amaskans in their home either."

"I used to think Amaskans were no different from the *Tribor*—contract killers who lacked morals—but in now knowing several Amaskans, I learned that they are people, same as you and me. They seek only to help solve problems, sometimes problems that are beyond a king's notice. I'm not suggesting that anyone give up their crown to the Amaskans or that they be given the ability to rule over us. We do not need another Senate. I'm suggesting they find honor and justice in a new way. There have been too many secrets separating us. Too much bloodshed. The time for that is done," said Margaret.

"Let us vote. All of those in favor of discussing this again at the *pasetivi*?" asked Adir.

Margaret's hand was the only palm facing down. Change would be slow, if ever.

Miriam asked, "What makes you believe the Order wishes a change like this?"

"The *Book of Ja'ahr* states 'I am Justice: *Amaskan* judge in the face of your crimes.' Amaskans have always served others as judges. But rather than executioners, I would see them become educators. Justice is better served by helping others and giving them a chance to do right," said Margaret as her eyes teared up.

"As you did with Bredych."

Margaret nodded. "But I've been outvoted, so we will discuss it again in five years' time. Though I would welcome a conversation with the Order."

The comment raised some eyebrows, but what Margaret did in her own kingdom was her decision. Miriam nodded before she left the tent. A moment later, another cough ripped through Havin. Blood splattered on the ground as the man struggled to stay upright.

"Fetch a healer, quick!" Catia called out and outside the tent, a servant trudged through the snow.

Havin reached into a belt at his waist and threw something in Margaret's direction. The small blade missed her side by a handswidth and struck the dirt.

"Did he hit you?" asked Adir, and Margaret shook her head.

When Havin reached for his pocket again, his body seized, and he slid from his chair. He took another, deeper breath, which he exhaled before a sudden pop sounded and he breathed no more.

27

The snow storm lasted another day before it blew itself out, but by then, the Meridi Pass was coated in a thick layer of white. With the loss of their king, Havin's camp was the first to pack up, his nephew and field marshal, Celil, in charge. The lad was next in line and while young, a nicer person than his predecessor. The Little Dozen Kingdoms would watch and wait to see how events changed inside of Shad. Most of the other monarchs broke camp as quickly as possible as winter hurtled into them, but Margaret delayed packing up as she sat with Miriam in her tent that morning.

"I have no intention of waiting until the *pasetivi* in order to make plans for Alexander," Margaret said as she sipped from a cup of warm tea. "In the end, Bredych believed the Amaskans could be something more, that they could do more for the world than kill. He died in hopes of bringing honor to the Order, and I would see that belief made real."

Miriam sat beside Margaret, her hands in her lap. Her cup

of tea sat untouched as she listened and after a moment's thought, she shook her head. "You say he wished this, but the man I knew would want the Order maintained. I'm sure perhaps that he felt some jobs assigned to Amaskans bordered on vengeance, but the Order's ways have been since the fall of Boahim. We are the ones people come to for help when there are no other options. Why should that change now?"

"Because this is the way things are done, this is the way they should always be?"

"Honestly? Yes."

Margaret frowned. "This rigidity of thought is how we ended up following corrupt gods down a path full of misery. Change should always be considered."

"Change for the sake of change doesn't make it the correct path."

"I...I know that you knew Bredych for many years, but I saw a change in him in the time he spent in Alexander. His own admissions here, admissions he made so that everyone could hear them, demonstrated his unease with his past. They demonstrated a belief that the Order must change if it is to survive," said Margaret, and she took another sip of tea. The warmth seeped through her, but it did little to help the chill in the room.

Miriam glanced at the wooden cup on the small table between them. "Bredych's guilt is his own, Your Majesty. The Order won't become answerable to the Little Dozen Kingdoms because of the regrets of an old man." Despite the *Amaskan*'s words, Miriam's voice quavered.

"Bredych and I spoke at length about the Order, but he also spoke of you and of his love for you. He believed you to be the best choice for his replacement, but not just because of his feelings where you were concerned. Did you love him?" The moment Margaret asked the question, she realized the mistake in it as Miriam hissed.

"You dare ask me that? B-Bredych..." Tears gathered in the *Amaskan*'s eyes as she glared at Margaret. "You will never understand...perhaps I should ask, did you, Your Majesty? You claim he was like a second father to you and yet you ask me this."

Margaret's cheeks grew warm, but she relaxed her shoulders as she breathed. "I did not intend for this conversation to turn adversarial. Please forgive me. I asked because loving someone sometimes means doing what we don't wish to do because it's what's best for them, or in this case, their memory. We can't ask Bredych his wishes now and can only make our choices based on what was."

"And I say he would not want this."

"I believe he would."

"Then we are at an impasse, Your Majesty."

"I can't make decisions for King Adir, but Alexander is mine to make decisions for. It's for the betterment of my people that I do this, Grand Master. I will build an academy for those who wish to help others. It will be open to any and all to learn and seek justice. Everything I spoke of in the meeting with the monarchs will come to fruition in Alesta, and I hope other monarchs will follow. I had hoped to build the Abner School of *Amaska* with your help, but if necessary, I will build it without."

Miriam stood, her lips a grim line across her face. "If you do this, you will make an enemy out of the Order."

"Why? We both want justice for everyone. How are our goals in opposition?"

"I expect Bredych's body to be brought to the Order's tents by midday as we'll be leaving on the morrow," said Miriam as she stood beside the tent's exit.

"No. Bredych will be burned and honored in Alesta so that a portion of his ashes might mingle with that of his sister's."

When Miriam turned, her hand rested near a pouch at her waist, and Margaret raised her hands in the air.

"The remainder of his ashes will be sent on to the Order."

"He was *Amaskan*!" shouted Miriam.

"He was more."

Miriam's eyes sparked, but she made no move to attack Margaret. Instead, she strode from the tent, leaving the tent flap open. Margaret set her tea cup down as the bitter cold settled about her shoulders. She was not wrong about what Bredych would have wanted as they had spent many candle-marks discussing their goals for the future. Had Bredych lived, he would have opened the school himself. Margaret had nothing on paper stating such, but she did not need it as his wishes lived on her heart.

By the time she reached the tent's flap, Miriam was nowhere to be seen, and Margaret sighed. This was supposed to have been a goal that united rather than separated them. Margaret beckoned a nearby solider. "Alert Field Marshall Fenton to pack up the camp. We leave the Pass in the morn-ing," she said.

After all, there was no other reason to stay.

28

The sun shined almost perversely the day of Bredych's burning. While the chill of winter left everyone bundled up, the temperature rose higher than normal. One day prior, one of Her Holiness's acolytes prepared to carry out the burning ritual, though without the Thirteen, it mattered little to Margaret who conducted the more religious portions.

Bredych's body rested on a stone and wooden cairn near the front of the castle. Black silk wrapped his corpse from head to toe. He was not a member of the royal family to be wrapped in deep blue, but as an *Amaskan*, black fit him better.

Margaret dressed herself in a simple red gown, the same she had worn to her father's burning, though it draped differently. The seamstress had stayed awake half the night releasing stitches so it would fit her expanded middle. At first, she had chosen her sister's silks but changed her mind a candlemark before. She was not *Amaskan*. She was the Queen of Alexander and her people needed that reminder on this day. A slight grin crossed her lips as she glanced at her stomach. Adelei's silks would not have fit her anyway.

They were past the thirteen day mark after Bredych's death, but with the hard travel back from the Pass, it could not be helped. Her Holiness's acolyte had turned almost purple with the changes Margaret had ordered, but when Sharmus, Delorcini, and Luthia had spoken to her, she had prostrated herself before them and agreed to any changes made.

Leolin would stand beside Margaret during the burning, though it chafed him to do so. Despite the return of his memories and the help given by the Order, a piece of him could never forgive Bredych for the damage he had caused.

A knock sounded before her lady-in-waiting announced a visitor. Margaret stepped into her sitting room to find Her Holiness waiting for her. The woman no longer wore the robes of her order and her long, blond hair fell down past her shoulders rather than being pinned beneath a cowl.

When Margaret reached for the dagger tucked in a dress pocket, the woman raised both hands in front of her. "Peace, Your Majesty. I-I am not here to harm you."

"Then why have you returned?"

"Word reached me of the battle at the Meridi Pass. I remember what you claimed and originally returned...well, out of curiosity, I suppose. When you arrived home with Master Bredych's body...I'm sorry for his death."

Margaret frowned. "Why would you feel sorrow at the loss of an *Amaskan*?"

"In the end, the Amaskans and the Holy Few are not so different. We both believed in the Thirteen and their laws. While we took a more holy path, it mattered very little. Our gods were corrupted by power and sin." Her Holiness glanced at her hands. "Malaki Abner was an intelligent man, flawed but fascinating. I would have liked to have talked more with him."

The admission surprised Margaret, though she kept the emotion from her face. Instead, she removed her hand from her pocket, leaving the dagger inside. "What will the Holy Few do now the Thirteen are dead or dying?" she asked.

"I don't know. You will have to ask them."

"I don't understand, Your Holiness."

The priestess smiled. "I am no longer a member of their order, and please, call me Celesa."

Had the woman left or had they removed her? Margaret opened her mouth to ask, then closed it. Despite Celesa's assurances that she meant her no harm, the woman had tried multiple times to read her thoughts. Perhaps it was better not to know the why. Instead, Margaret said, "The burning will begin soon, and I am needed. You are welcome to remain in Alesta for it, but I would ask that you move on from this city afterward."

Celesa did not protest but nodded in response. "I understand. You should know that I plan on traveling with Luthia and the others to their island. I think there is much to learn from these old gods."

"Are they aware of this plan?"

"They are."

Margaret mentally reminded herself to ask Sharmus if this were a correct accounting. If they wished to bother themselves with the woman, that was their decision. A servant stepped inside and bowed. "Sunset approaches. They are ready for you, Your Majesty."

Celesa bowed before leaving, something Margaret had never seen the woman do. All around Margaret, the world was changing. Tears gathered in her eyes as she thought about all of those who were not here to see it.

Especially Bredych.

⚔

W HEN   M ARGARET   APPROACHED   the   dais   where
Bredych's body waited for burning, she carried her sister's
Amaskan silks in her hands. Leolin already stood beside the
cairn, his clothing dyed almost crimson. The tunic was longer
than those he typically wore but more fitting for the ceremony. He might not mourn the loss of Bredych as she did,
but he would be there to support her throughout the
ceremony.

Burning the body for thirteen candlemarks was a tribute
to the Thirteen, and Margaret had almost changed it, but the
Little Dozen Kingdoms' people held fast to their rituals. Word
of the Thirteen's corruption swept across the land, but for
some, it was little more than rumor. Too much change too
quickly could cause unrest, and in the end she had acquiesced
to the Holy Few's recommendations.

In front of the dais stood Celesa's acolyte, her face covered
by a red veil as she used a silver dagger to cut away a small piece
of the burial shroud, or the *meshoi*. She handed it to Margaret,
who placed it on her tongue. Miriam should have been the one
to carry out this task, and Margaret had extended an invitation
to the woman to attend, but the *Amaskan* had declined. The
Grand Master had ordered all Amaskans from not just Alesta
but Alexander itself, an action that caused Margaret much
sorrow.

"This temple hovers between this world and the next.
Only the flames can carry the vessel to the afterlife," said the
acolyte.

Some of the city had turned out for Bredych's burning,
though not as many as Margaret had expected. As she looked
out across the crowd, Mademe Pouffaur stood a few rows back
with Jessa and a few other workers from the public houses.
The more Margaret studied the crowd of mourners, the more
she spotted their clothing's wear and the way most avoided her
gaze. Folks who Bredych used to send messages sprinkled

through the crowd, and Margaret wondered how many, if any, were *Amaskan*.

"The temple is sacred. The temple creates life."

Margaret repeated the phrase along with the audience. Memories of previous burnings darkened her mind, including her mother's, which was little more than a hazy memory from childhood. She rubbed her back and hoped her ankles would not swell with all the standing. Leolin took her hand in his and gave her a small smile.

The acolyte retrieved an unlit torch and held it high in the air. "The temple is a gift—a gift of life everlasting."

As everyone echoed the words, another priestess stepped forward with a flint stone and the silver dagger. She struck the two together thirteen times. Sparks landed on the torch, and the acolyte blew on the tiny flame until it birthed fire. "Life should be loved and in the end, honored," said the acolyte.

Margaret spit the *meshoi* into the acolyte's waiting hand and took the offered glasses of brown liquid. Margaret swallowed it without hesitation, though her nostrils flared at the medicinal taste, which was almost as sharp in flavor as the *meshoi* had been.

In the time it had taken Margaret to swallow, the torch's fire leapt across Bredych's body. With magic fading, the flames did not erupt into the colorful display they had in the past, though whatever herbs were used helped them remain lit. Before anyone could stop her, Margaret tossed Adelei's silks into the flames where they caught. Better they should burn with their master.

The acolyte frowned but continued the ritual as she handed Margaret a blackened bowl of herbs. "Malaki Abner has been anointed and blessed by the Holy Few. May his spirit travel easily to...whatever lies beyond the silence."

The Holy Few had baulked at this change in ceremony. Normally they would lay Farimun's blessings upon the dead as the soul traveled to Itovah, but Bredych would have wanted neither. Murmurs from the audience reached Margaret, but she remained still, eyes on Bredych's burning body as was appropriate.

The acolyte stepped down from the dais to join the nearby priestesses from the Holy Few. They would remain there with Margaret until the burning was finished to ensure the flames lived through the thirteen candlemarks required.

"Some of you know who Malaki Abner was," said Margaret as she stared over the heads of those in attendance. "While he was born Malaki, he was born again as Eli Bredych, former Grand Master of the Order of *Amaska*."

While some of the crowd shuffled, most remained silent. Amaskans had moved throughout Alesta and Alexander for months now as Bredych used his network to bring peace and change to the Little Dozen Kingdoms. Few who knew him would speak ill of the man at his burning. To the audience Margaret said, "While he spent many years in pursuit of justice, he remained in Alesta to help us find the truth. Today, we honor his sacrifice as he gave it to save another."

Margaret's mind drifted for a moment to Avishai, who was not amongst those gathered to witness the burning. The *chathula* did not feel comfortable walking amongst those grieving as death was observed differently amongst her tribe. Instead, she hunted in the forest in Bredych's honor. Her kills would be left on the leaves of the forest floor for other forest dwellers' benefit.

Also absent were the remaining Thirteen, who were settled into the Holy Few's rooms until after the birth of Margaret's child. It was one thing to tell people that their gods were corrupt and dying, but another to have them walking amongst them. The Holy Few had been shocked silent at the three gods' arrival as it was.

As the sun sank below the horizon, the flames licked their

way across the shroud covering Bredych. Attendees approached the dais one by one to pay their respects. None who approached disrespected Bredych by tossing sand at the fire or breaking the silence. Margaret lost count at how many faces bore the circle of *Amaska*, and it gave her hope to see them there despite Miriam's order.

When all who wished to stand before the flames had done so, Margaret began to step toward the cairn. Leolin tugged her back and stepped forward. Margaret's breath caught in her throat, but he gave only a partial bow to Bredych before returning to his place behind Margaret. He, too, had paid tribute to the Grand Master.

She breathed a sigh of relief as the long night began.

It had been at her father's burning that she had first met Bredych. He had saved her life from an assassin and lied his way into her castle so he could discover the truth of what had happened to Adelei. It was their shared love of her that brought them together, and now he would join Adelei wherever souls lived after death.

With the Thirteen's fall, Margaret had questioned whether there was an afterlife at all, but Asti and Bredych both had sought her out in dreams. Luthia spoke at length about there being more, so Margaret tucked that knowledge into her heart as she thought on the dead.

Whatever came after, she hoped her family—including Bredych—were together again.

THE MOON HAD RISEN and set in the thirteen candlemarks of burning. Margaret's feet were numb and not just from the cold. Her back ached while her right calf threatened to cramp, and she counted the heartbeats until she could move.

"While this being has passed beyond, the living remain.

May we find peace in the knowledge that the dead have found everlasting life. The very chill of today's winter air is but their breath reminding us that they live again in our memories," said the acolyte as she returned to the dais.

Rather than spreading Bredych's ashes in the royal garden, the Holy Few scooped the bulk of the ashes into a black urn engraved with sigils known only to them. The remainder stayed on the dais, and people murmured in response.

"Bredych's ashes will be returned to his people at the Order where they will honor the man he was. We honor him here and now for the man he became, a second father, a mentor, and a friend," said Margaret, and she stepped back from the cairn.

Shai stepped forward from the crowd, his arms raised in the air. They trembled from the effort as he worked the smallest of magics. A gust of wind with a sprinkling of rain carried Bredych's ashes into the air. "May his memory live with all of Alexander," he said as he returned to his place in the crowd.

The acolyte frowned as she stared at Margaret. They had not discussed involving the mystics, but Margaret knew the man they honored would appreciate the honor more than the approval of the Holy Few.

When the acolyte made to follow Margaret as she stepped off the dais, Margaret shook her head. "I have no need of your assistance."

"It's important that you—"

Margaret stopped, forcing the acolyte to stop as well. "If the dead cling to me, so be it. They won't harm me as I'm sure they have better things to do. You are dismissed."

The acolyte remained outside, a frown on her face, as Leolin followed Margaret's slow steps through the castle in silence. He did not speak until they were in the privacy of her bedchamber and her lady-in-waiting and servants had been dismissed. "Come," he said as he opened his arms. She fell into them with a sob.

So many dead.

Margaret cried for them all as he held her, and when she ran out of tears, he helped her undress. A small laugh escaped her as she stepped into the bathing tub filled with hot water kept warm by the coals beneath it. "I have cried so much. Do I even need a cleansing bath at this point?" she asked, but a glimpse in her mirror showed puffy eyes and black hair littered with ash.

When he did not join her in the half-hearted joke, Margaret reached out her hand for his. Leolin sat at the tub's edge, his face unreadable. "Share your thoughts with me," she said.

"I was thinking of my mother."

She nodded. "I was too, and my father. Adelei. My mother, though my memories of her are fuzzy. Perhaps the cleansing baths are for removing more than ash from a person."

Leolin shook his head. "Water won't remove their deaths or our sorrow. I didn't like Bredych, but I can feel your grief for him. I remember when my mother killed my father. Some days it's only a memory, but others, I'm a child again, and he's in front of me, dead."

While the blizzard had blown through the Pass, Leolin had shared with her those lost memories regained. "From the moment her parents died, my mother did what she had to do in order to survive, but so did Bredych. It's easy to blame him for trying to kill her or for any number of other grievances, but when you needed him, he was there. If he hadn't been, Agaia might have..."

"She didn't succeed. She's dead."

He nodded, but his eyes were moist with unshed tears.

"Bredych saved your life multiple times. He saved Avishai. I can't hold onto this hate for a man who died saving others."

Margaret reached up to pick a piece of ash out of Leolin's dark curls. "You need a bath," she said as she picked up the white bulb soap. "It might make you feel better to wash the death from you. There is plenty of room for us both."

At that, he grinned and shed his tunic first before removing his undershirt. Red clothes piled on the stone floor. If she stared at them long enough, they became a puddle of blood. Margaret splashed water over her face while Leolin climbed into the steaming water.

They both took several candlemarks to help each other forget the death that surrounded them.

29

Summer began with a heat wave that swept through Alexander and sent its people seeking the comfort of the shade. The castle's stone walls kept the place cooler than the rest of the city and many citizens sought its interior during the afternoon heat. Some remained as long as they could as Margaret paced, heavy with child. Magic continued to fade from the Little Dozen Kingdoms, but Sharmus had assured Margaret that he would be there, magic intact, should some difficulty arise.

Her back and hips ached as she paced in her private study. While the heat rose, Margaret ran her fingers across the quill's feather. A stack of documents sat on her desk for her to sign, but she could not sit still long enough to look at them, let alone sign them. Another labor pang passed through her, painful but not painful enough to warrant telling anyone yet. The midwife had explained the signs of early labor, along with the warning that it could stretch out for many candlemarks or even days. Considering her restlessness had driven Leolin from the room, Margaret hoped it would be the former.

While pacing helped some with the back pain, it did little to alleviate the pressure in her hips from the baby, and she returned to the chair at her desk. It had been her father's and as she stared at the inlaid carving of several hunting hounds playing, tears gathered in her eyes. He would have been ecstatic at a grandchild. The study had not been his for over a year, yet hints of pine cones and eucalyptus tickled her nose at random times. Nothing in the room spoke of her mother other than the tapestry of her that hung on the wall.

The Holy Few had wished Margaret to stay secluded in her suite the last month of pregnancy, and while Margaret had agreed to rest as much as possible, she had refused their archaic request. Her mother had remained in isolation and not even Margaret's father had been allowed to see her until both Margaret and Adelei were born out of some superstition about influencing the baby's will to be born.

The parchments she was meant to read were updates on the construction of the Abner School of *Amaska*, but rather than read them, Margaret stood again and trudged over to the study's lone window. Double the width of an arrowslit, she could see enough of the building to render the documents useless. Its walls were finished, and Leolin had walked through it the day before to check that Margaret's plans were being followed. They were on time for its completion next spring, and she could not wait to be able to see it for herself.

Another pang, this one surprisingly stronger, caught her off guard, and she gasped. Her lady-in-waiting must have been listening at the door as the young woman gave a brief knock before she opened the wooden door, her eyes wide with excitement. Lady Claretta de Gant had been a mere slip of a girl when she had arrived, but helping Roland with the wounded during the war had given her some resolve. She no longer looked at her 'cousin' like Margaret would have her flayed alive. When Margaret sighed, the young women asked, "Nothing yet?"

"Minor pangs, but no, nothing to report to Roland."

Claretta pursed her lips together for a moment. "My aunt says pickled vegetables and wine will bring on labor in even the most stubborn of infants."

The thought of eating made her stomach turn, and Margaret shook her head.

"Are you counting the pangs?"

"Counting them?"

"My aunt also says twenty pangs, and the baby should arrive."

The midwife had told her to pay attention to the distance between the pangs but nothing about counting them. Besides, Roland had told her that every woman's experience was different, especially for a first child. Margaret said, "Send for Leolin."

"But—"

"Seeing Leolin won't change how quickly this child will come, Claretta. Send for him."

When the door to her study closed, she clenched her jaw as another pang hit her. As it passed, she shifted her weight from side to side in hopes that it would take the pressure off her hips. Leolin rushed into the study, his face flushed from running.

"Any-thing...yet?" he asked as he panted.

Margaret shook her head. "A few pangs but that is to be expected."

A deep pressure pushed at her and when she stood thinking she needed the chamber pot, a burst of water fell from beneath her skirt. The bathing waters were here. "You ran all the way up the stairs, but now I need you to run down them and fetch Sharmus," said Margaret as she waddled towards the door.

Leolin paled, his eyes wide. "And Roland?"

"I'll send Claretta for him though the midwife won't approve." Margaret gave a brief chuckle before she placed a hand on Leolin's arm. "Women have been having children since the beginning of ages. This is just another day, and I'll be fine."

He leaned down and kissed her before he opened the door. Once he was gone, Margaret stepped through the other door that led to her bedchamber. The midwife took one look at her wet skirt and set down her embroidery.

"Claretta, send for Roland," said Margaret, and her lady-in-waiting rushed for the door.

"Why you feel you need for a man to help with a woman's work makes little sense to me, if you don't mind my saying, Your Majesty. How long between the labor pangs?" asked the midwife as she stood from a nearby chair. As she walked, her large hips swayed.

Margaret had hoped pregnancy would grant her the hips she envied on the women around her, but even now, her frame remained slim. Perhaps that would change with a few more children as the midwife had six of her own.

"Your Majesty?"

Margaret shook her head. "I apologize for my lack of attention. I have not been able to focus much the last few days. I-I think it has been a few pangs in the last candlemark."

Several servants entered her bedchamber carrying cloth, a deep blue velvet blanket, and a basin of water. The midwife directed them to bring the birthing stool to the room's center, and she took Margaret's arm to guide her to it. "Remove everything except for her chemise," the midwife said to a servant, who helped Margaret remove her clothes before sitting her on the stool.

As another pang hit her, she hissed at its strength. "So soon?" she asked the midwife.

The woman lifted Margaret's chemise to look beneath. Without a word, the midwife stood and busied herself at a side table. "This tonic was my grandmother's recipe and will help with the labor," she said as she mixed liquids from various vials. When the woman returned to Margaret's side, she handed her a glass with a warm liquid in it.

"What's in this tonic?"

The midwife made a clicking sound with her tongue. "Some raspberry leaf, red clover, chamomile, and yarrow, mixed with a few other things. Drink."

Margaret sniffed the cup, which gave off an herby smell, and when she swallowed a mouthful, it burned all the way down into her stomach. She gasped and coughed, and the midwife pushed her to finish it.

Someone knocked on the door and when Leolin poked his head inside, Margaret handed the cup back to the midwife and gestured to him. He rushed over, followed more slowly by Sharmus, Delorcini, Luthia, and Roland. She had not called for the other two gods, but seeing them somehow brought her comfort. When the midwife saw the entourage, she ignored everyone except for Delorcini and prostrated herself on the stone floor before the goddess.

Delorcini touched the midwife on the shoulders and when the midwife looked up, the goddess took her hands to help her to her feet. "I appreciate your readiness to help your queen and all the preparations you've made. If you are willing, I would assist you in the birth of the queen's child."

"Assist me?"

The goddess nodded. "Between us both, this baby girl will be born soon enough."

The midwife blinked at the baby's gender and glanced at Margaret, who merely shrugged. In the months leading up to today, she had grown used to the three gods referring to the baby as a girl. If it was, she held the perfect name for her in her mind, and if it were a boy instead, no one would mind if she took some time to decide upon a proper name.

Another pang, this one much stronger than the previous, and Margaret grabbed Leolin's hand and squeezed it. "I...I think perhaps you and Roland should wait in the sitting room."

Leolin furrowed his brows and nodded, but Roland shook his head. "As your physician, I should remain here to help." When Delorcini glared at him, he paled. "But with the Goddess of Family here, perhaps I should wait with Leolin."

As the two men left the room, Sharmus chose a seat in the corner behind Margaret and Luthia joined him. "If I'm needed, know that I'm here," Sharmus called from behind her. Margaret had not realized how comforting his presence was until he spoke, and her body relaxed...at least until a pang made her hiss.

The midwife grabbed a bottle of primrose oil and settled in a chair in front of Margaret. "This will help with the birthing," she said as she reached beneath Margaret's chemise.

The oil smelled of spring and wildflowers, though she would have preferred it on her skin rather than where the midwife applied it. A servant brought another chair for Delorcini, who placed it beside the midwife.

With the common knowledge of childbirth between them, the midwife and Delorcini chatted at length about techniques while Margaret listened. She was sitting in the chair when the tonic hit her, and the room grew fuzzy. When she smiled, her lips felt like they were sideways, and she asked, "Is my smile lopsided?"

When Delorcini frowned, the midwife said, "The tonic I gave her has some spirit to it. Helps with the pain. Her Majesty should stay relaxed through the birthing, or as relaxed as any of us get."

"You said this could take some time. Is there not a more comfortable chair I can sit in?" Margaret rubbed at her lower back. Not even the tonic could take away the painful pressure in the lower half of her torso.

"It will proceed faster than you think, Margaret," said Delorcini.

As if her baby heard the goddess, the baby gave a swift kick, followed by another labor pang. Despite it, a slight giggle escaped her.

"How much was in that tonic of yours?" asked Delorcini, but the midwife merely shrugged.

The two women's yammering blurred into the background as Margaret waited. Another candlemark passed until the labor pangs transitioned from semi-regular to regular.

With the next pang, the goddess raised Margaret's chemise and rested it across her hips. Whatever Delorcini saw made her smile. The midwife nodded as she wiped Margaret's forehead with a cool cloth and beckoned to a servant. Margaret squeezed the stool's sides as another pang hit her. A servant spread several layers of heavy wool on the floor beneath Margaret and set the basin of water next to the stool.

The midwife moved behind as Delorcini moved her chair to be directly in front of Margaret. "Are you feeling the need to push?" she asked, and Margaret shook her head.

"There's pressure, like I need to use the chamber pot, but it's tolerable."

Delorcini smiled. "You are blessed then with an easier birth than most. On this next pang, I want you to take a deep breath and hold it. Then when I tell you to push, you'll tighten the muscles here and push," she said as she touched Margaret's abdomen.

It was not long before another pang ripped through

Margaret, and she cried out. This was what she had been led to expect pain wise, and she pushed when the goddess encouraged it.

Her mother, Catherine, had struggled for half the day with the pushing, and Margaret bit her lip hard enough that she tasted blood. A servant darted forward to dab at her lip, and Margaret resisted the urge to swat her away.

After the first few pushes, the midwife wrapped her arms around Margaret from behind. At the next push, the woman used her hands to push down on Margaret's belly. Being held in the woman's soft frame helped and while she cried out with each push, Margaret felt safe and protected.

"I wish...my mother was...here," she said as the contraction ended, her breath coming in short pants.

"On the next pang, I want you to push hard," said Delorcini as she glanced up at the midwife.

Her face was unreadable, and Margaret opened her mouth to ask what was wrong when another pang passed through her. Margaret tried to catch her breath, but there was no time as her body commanded her as readily as if Delorcini had spoken.

"I see the head."

The afternoon sun shone into the window behind Margaret, causing sweat to pour off her body, and she tugged at her chemise. "Get this off."

"It would be better to keep it on, Your Majesty," said the midwife from behind her. A servant dabbed again at her forehead, the girl's eyes glancing to the man in the room.

"I would kill the sun if I could," said Margaret and as she tried to laugh, another pang hit.

"Push!"

Margaret did not need the order as she took a deep breath and pushed again, her jaw clenched shut.

"One more, Margaret," said Delorcini.

A wave of fatigue rolled through her as she panted and when she thought she could not push again, the next pang left her no choice. Delorcini guided the baby out and onto the wool below. Margaret barely noticed the activity below her until her daughter's cries filled the air.

The goddess rinsed the baby clean in the water basin before wrapping her in the blue velvet cloth. The cord connecting her to her child had been tied off, and when Margaret felt the urge to push again, she frowned. Delorcini nodded. "If you need to push, it is safe."

Once the afterbirth was delivered, several servants helped clean Margaret before taking her to her bed where the goddess handed her her daughter. Sharmus walked over as Margaret held her close to her skin.

"She's a beautiful baby, Your Majesty. How are you feeling?" he asked.

When she smiled, her expression felt almost as loopy as before, but it did not matter. She held her daughter in her hands. Hers and Leolin's. "Leolin!" cried Margaret as she glanced at the door.

Someone opened it to allow Roland and him to enter. Avishai followed them, her snout high in the air. While Roland chatted briefly with the midwife and Delorcini, Leolin rushed to her side. He stopped just short of the bed as he stared at his child.

"Would you like to meet your daughter?" asked Margaret.

Leolin nodded and held out his arms to receive the child. "Do you have a name for her?"

"Her name is Catherine Adelei Poncett." When Margaret said the name, something inside of her hummed. This was her child and her child was perfect.

While Leolin held her, a goofy smile on his face, Delorcini walked over and placed a finger on the baby's forehead. "Your Bredych was wrong about the prophecy," said Delorcini as she removed her finger. For a moment, the spot where she touched glowed.

"What do you mean?"

"Bredych's death may have been the spark, but it was not his confession nor his death that brought back honor to the Amaskans. It was you, Queen Margaret, who has returned honor to the Amaskans. You have given us all a second chance, and for that, I bless you and leave you a gift."

At first, Margaret thought she meant the birthing process or perhaps being with child to begin with, but as Margaret held her daughter again and looked into her daughter's eyes, Adelei's dark brown eyes stared back at her. She gasped. "Adelei?"

Leolin frowned. "I...I know you're one of the Thirteen but—"

When the goddess touched his forehead, the tall *Amaskan*'s face popped into his head. He could see who Adelei had been and when he looked to his daughter, the same familiarity lay in her dancing eyes.

"But how?" asked Leolin.

Sharmus smiled. "The amount of magics left to us was small, but not so small we couldn't help with some of the pain we caused. Her death was premature, at our hands, but in restoring the honor of *Amaska* through the changes Margaret seeks to make, in her love of Bredych, and her forgiveness of him, Adelei's soul was not yet lost to Luthia. So we made a sacrifice."

While Margaret held her daughter to her chest, Delorcini said, "Adelei's soul has a second chance. An opportunity to live the life she possibly would have lived had she not been taken by the Order."

"What do you mean by sacrifice?"

"It is unlikely that we three will survive the winter. Many days were lost but we gave them willingly to your daughter," said Luthia. She still sat in the corner, her eyes dark as she watched the child.

"When I chose her name, I had no idea you would grant me such a gift. I merely wished to honor my sister and the sacrifice she made. I—" Margaret's throat tightened as tears ran down her face. While her sister would never walk beside her again, her spirit would in the form of her daughter.

Margaret touched her forehead against Catherine's. "Welcome to the world, my child. May it always bring you joy...and justice."

EPILOGUE

258 Diomusin 12th - City of Alesta

I write this letter to my daughter as a continued accounting of the love that brought about her life. Not long after her birth, the heat wave broke with a summer storm, one that threatened to undo much of the repair work happening across Alesta, not to mention the new school. Luckily, no serious damage was done, and Leolin tells me the city has rallied together to fix any small damage.

Sharmus, Luthia, and Delorcini, along with Celesa, rode out of the city a week after Catherine's birth. They made their way towards the Port of Lyon to the southwest before setting sail for their island. I hope the sea carries them with the swiftness of *Amaskan* horses so that they finally might rest. In the few days they remained in Alesta, the wrinkles in their face deepened, and their steps slowed. They risked much to help us, and I will owe them a debt as long as I live.

I thought perhaps that Avishai would remain in Alexander, but she still seeks many answers to her past and word of her father. The *chathula* decided to join those traveling to the Senate Isle, at least to the Port of Lyon. Beyond that, only the *chathula* knows where her journey will take her.

Leolin holds Catherine at every opportunity. I think he loves her more than he loves me, and as I write this, he begs me to mark out this sentence, as he swears he loves me as much as our daughter. When I caught him looking over my shoulder again, I told him to love on his daughter, which he did with glee.

Catherine will always have our love to guide her, of that she can be sure.

The other day as we were walking through the garden, there was a smile upon his face that I thought long gone. He was at peace with himself and the world around him; perhaps that is how he loves our daughter so, but I suspect that when he looks at her, he does not see what I do.

Adelei, I see *you*.

Being new to the world, Catherine does not do much more than sleep and eat, but when I hold her, there is a feeling in the very center of my being. I can't explain it, only that I know it is Adelei who looks up at me from those eyes. The gods have given me such a gift that I wonder if I can ever repay it.

Once we returned from the Meridi Pass, I thought perhaps that Leolin would protest my decision to rule alone, but some-where in all of this, he has made peace with that as well. That same day in the garden, he mentioned that his mother, Ida, would often help my father in the decisions that he made for his kingdom. She did not need marriage to love him or to help him, and Leolin did not either, though I did bestow upon him the title of *sepier*.

While I hope to see the Order of *Amaska* change, I wish to see the role of *sepier* change as well. With better and more communication amongst the Little Dozen Kingdoms, I hope never to need a spy. An advisor and confidant, yes, but never again a spy.

The world does not need assassins. It needs lovers and educators and leaders.

Much to the horror of the Holy Few, I met with Mademe Pouffaur to discuss the public houses. Their people did much to help in the rebuilding of Alesta, more than the nobles of the city, and I wished to honor that as well. Perhaps if the public houses were regulated like other trades, everyone could benefit from their existence. Leolin believes it a foolish pursuit, but I will continue to meet with the Mademe in the hope honor can be brought to her people as well.

When we are not holding our daughter, Leolin and I are run over with decisions to be made for the future, and I'm sure King Marco of Halelind feels a similar pressure as he plans for the first *pasetivi*. Sometimes I wonder whether the peace we have fought for will hold. I have to believe it will, and that all of those who died did not die for naught.

The weight of this sits on my shoulders as I nurse Catherine late at night. Those I would share my concerns with are now beyond me, except for Leolin. His strength and laughter carry me through those moments and reminds me of why we fought in the first place. It is more than justice that people need now.

It is hope. Where there is hope, all things are possible.

Penned by the Hand of

Queen Margaret Poncett of Alexander

ACKNOWLEDGMENTS

Where to begin... The past five years have been...challenging. Complex. Unique. I've lived through COVID *(pre-vaccine)* decimating my life through long-COVID and pummeling my body with all sorts of newfound hell. Then I watched it do the same to my wife. I watched her lose her job because yet again, a company chose profits over people. They let her down when she needed them most. Then we needed a new roof we now couldn't afford. Kitty Riley had a heart attack, died, was resuscitated, and surged back to his 18-year-old kitten self. Kitty Malley blew out his knee and with his surgery unsuccessful, he now limps around the house. Kitty DiNozzo almost died of neurogenic bladder. My relationship with my narcissistic mother imploded. I came out as nonbinary trans. My wife came out as transgender during a timeline that wishes she were dead rather than living as her authentic self. I could go on and on.

As I said...challenging. Complex. Unique.

To My Readers: There aren't enough thank you's in the world for you, especially all of you who stuck with me through the above chaos. When I started writing this book in February of 2020, I had no idea what was to come. None of us did, yet so many of you had faith in my ability to finish this tale, faith I sometimes didn't have in myself. So for that, thank you. ALL the thank you's.

To Mimi, My Editor: Thank you as always for your keen eye and ability to find issues that I miss. Good editors are underpaid and underappreciated, much like teachers. My books wouldn't be what they are without you.

To Tammy and Emily: I found a new writer home in our daily Zoom calls where my struggles were understood and my progress cheered on like nowhere else. Without our body doubling group, the past five years wouldn't have been nearly as survivable. Honestly, I don't have enough words for the support and encouragement you both have given me.

To the Rest of the Body Doubling Crew and the Wit 'n' Word Group: Thank you for your enthusiasm, sense of humor, and support as well. Writing can be a lonely endeavor and you all keep reminding me why I do it.

To My Wife, Molli: Growing older with you these past 28 years has been a wild ride. It's been the kind of adventure I could never write and give it proper justice. The future is unknown, especially with long COVID and such complex disabilities, but with you beside me, I know we'll be okay. I can tell stories like this one because you give me the strength, love, and support to do so. There aren't enough thank you's for you either.

ABOUT THE AUTHOR

Multi-international award-winning speculative fiction author Raven Oak (they/them) is best known for their epic fantasy *Boahim Trilogy* (*Amaskan's Blood, Amaskan's War, & Amaskan's Honor*) and their space opera, *Class-M Exile*. Also, they have almost two dozen short stories published in various anthologies. They're even published on the moon! Raven spent most of their K-12 education doodling and writing 500 page monstrosities that are **forever** locked away in a filing cabinet.

Besides being a writer, they're a disabled, nonbinary artist who enjoys getting their game on with tabletop games, indulging in cartography and etymology, and staring at the ocean. They live in the Seattle area with their wife, and their three kitties who enjoy lounging across the keyboard when writing deadlines approach. Their hair color changes as often as their bio does, and you can find them at www.ravenoak.net.

You can also find Raven Oak on the following social media platforms:

- instagram.com/author_raven_oak
- facebook.com/authorroak
- bsky.app/profile/ravenoak.bsky.social
- threads.net/@author_raven_oak
- tiktok.com/@author_raven_oak
- youtube.com/kaonevar
- bookbub.com/authors/raven-oak

Please enjoy this excerpt from the upcoming book *Ear to Ear: The Collected Stories of an Amaskan.*

Upcoming 2026 from Grey Sun Press.

EXCERPT FROM EAR TO EAR

Black hair, blue eyes, tall frame for a girl. Throat slit ear-to-ear. The newest victim could've been a younger version of me, a *much, much* younger version if I ignored the number of silver hairs on my forty-five-year-old head. As King Leon's *sepier*, gathering information was what I did best as an all-around spy and problem solver, but a string of deaths—all women—had pulled me back toward Justice and the town of Loughrie.

As I stood outside the Merc's Guild, my throat throbbed in response to the report in my hands. I could feel the knife against my throat all over again. Had these women known their attacker? Had they struggled, as I had, or had their lives been over in a single gasp? The report sent to the king stated the Merc's Guild had handled the burning of all four victims, though they hadn't bothered reporting the murderers to the crown. Curious that they'd covered up their burning, leaving someone else to report it. The decision left me wishing I was back in Alexander rather than staring down my past.

It couldn't be coincidence that this girl looked like me.

The change in Loughrie was obvious in the line of mercs outside. Not one of 'em a woman, and none of 'em young. I nodded to 'em before glancing over their heads at the newly posted jobs. Caravan guards. One call for an archer at the border. None of it complicated, and none of it local.

I passed through the open door into the Guild itself where a whip of a girl scurried over. "Welcome to the Mercenary Guild. Fair work for fair pay. Are you lost?"

The round man nearly attached to her elbow could've been her father by the look he gave her, and she disappeared behind a curtain before I'd done more than open my mouth. "My apologies," he said, and I sidestepped his attempt to grasp my forearm.

I'd been here before—twenty years ago, not that the man recognized me now—and little had changed. Master Alfred and his three brothers grew fatter on crowns and notches earned by negotiating poor deals for those willing to live by the sword.

"The Guild currently does not have any jobs available."

Master Alfred's frown deepened when I smiled. "The line of mercs outside at that new postin' says otherwise."

"Well, yes. There are those jobs, but it would not be appropriate for a...woman," he said.

"And why not?"

His gaze followed along the adornment that curled around my leather armor before finally resting on my polished sword. "A woman of your...age might be better suited to work in a castle or large manor rather than on the dangerous road."

My cheeks grew warm, but I bit my tongue, choosing instead to fetch the scrap of parchment I carried bearin' the Guild's crest. He recognized my mercenary name as his green eyes popped against his face's sudden flush, then his eyes noted the *sepier* star pinned near my collar bone. "Lady Ida, it's been a long time since you've visited the Guild. Far too long! I meant you no slight, only...."

"Only?"

"Last job you had, you abandoned. Word was you left for a comfortable palace job, and well, the Guild has a reputation to uphold."

While tossing his ample rear across the room was my preference, I forced myself to smile. "Course ya do. But I'm not here about—"

He leaned close and whispered, "Besides, have you heard of the Merc Meister? It's not safe for women fighters—not in Loughrie anyway. My apologies, but I have nothing for you. Maybe you can check in one of the larger cities or Alesta itself."

It wasn't good enough. I wasn't leaving 'til I had a clear path to tread. "Tell me more about these murderers," I said.

His stiffened posture shifted as his hands thrust forward. Perhaps I'd gotten soft as a *sepier* or perhaps it was my old age. Either way, he'd shoved me out the door before I'd finished speaking. When the door closed in my face, I turned to find a line full of men shuffling their feet as they suppressed laughter. If I couldn't get answers from him, I'd get 'em elsewhere. "The nerve of him," I muttered, only half-way an act. Fools had no idea the dangers of being a *sepier*. All they saw was an old woman who'd gained a boon from the king. "As if I were some common merc. Damn fool."

I shoved my way through the crowd to stop before the board where I pretended to study it. Ten minutes in, someone slipped some parchment into the palm I held against my back. I didn't open it 'til I wandered away. Another ten minutes saw me tucked into the west corner table at a tavern called *The Drunken Footsman* while I waited on whoever had taken my bait.

Shortly after sundown, a young man with shoulders nearly as broad as the table claimed the seat across from me. He inclined his bushy red beard in the direction of my almost empty cup, and I shook my head. His gaze flitted around the tavern while the din carried on around us. "Lady Ida hasn't visited Loughrie in over a decade. One might wonder what brings her out of her cushy retirement now," he murmured.

"Maybe she needs a little coin, is all."

Laughter erupted from the bar, and he glanced over his shoulder at a man attempting to juggle mugs while hopping from one leg to another. "Or maybe it's the Merc Meister," he said, and I shrugged. "What have you heard?"

"Four victims, all women. All died the same way."

When I didn't elaborate, he said, "Actually, there've been five victims so far. Guild only knows of four because the other one wasn't a merc." At my raised brow he added, "Commoner. Maybe she saw something."

It was plausible. If all of 'em had been mercs, that'd explain why the Guild covered their burning. And why it was set on keeping word quiet. "Why only women?" I asked.

"No one's sure...though I have some ideas." He pointed to my throat. "The way you fled the Guild for a King is a famous tale around here. So's that scar of yours. Though no one knows how you got it. I heard some Amaskan in Sadai gave it to you."

Bile tickled the back of my throat as my muscles tensed. Who was he to know so much?

Blue eyes, twin to my own starred down at me. His dagger was against my throat as he laughed. "Leave? No one leaves the Order of Amaska. Not even you, sister dear. No one leaves...not alive anyway." The pinprick, then a sting as sharp as my sword slit my neck from ear to ear.

"Lady Ida?"

I opened my eyes to find the merc's hand shaking me. "Sorry," I muttered and downed the last swallow of ale. My gaze sought his jaw line, but no tattoo marked it. "Where'd ya hear this?"

"Around. People talk if you pay. If you did get that scar

from them, I don't blame you for being afraid. Amaskans are born to kill. They may think they're doing holy work by killing sinners, but my Da always said 'Bad depends on your point of view.' Nothing but rotten assassins, they are."

I nodded, but settled my hands in my lap to hide their trembling. "Why bring up my scar?"

"I think it's connected. This murderer's trying to find you. Think about it—all women with dark hair, mostly fighters, and all with their throat slit. Until I saw you outside the Guild today, I hadn't made the connection."

I swore under my breath. How many others were making the same connection? To him, I asked, "How do I know ya aren't the killer yourself?"

"You don't. Folks figure it's a merc though. The killer seems to know where we gather, how we move, and the weapons we use." He traced circles across the tabletop with his finger as he spoke. "Details like someone's been studying mercs for a while now. But if I was the killer, I'd have just killed you rather than meet with you."

A little laugh escaped me, and he smiled—a grin made more earnest by the way his bushy, red beard danced. Something about it felt familiar, though I couldn't place it. "Have we met before?" I asked.

"I'd have remembered the honor of meeting the great Lady Ida. It's not something I'd forget."

I flushed, though whether it'd been a compliment or insult, I couldn't tell. The tavern door opened to allow entrance to a disheveled man in a black cloak. A few called out greetings as he folded his tall frame into a chair at the bar's end. His hood shadowed all but a scruffy beard and lips that trembled.

"That's Marc Silversmith," the merc said, and I glanced at the bar a second time.

Last time I'd seen Marc, he'd been one of the wealthiest

caravan guards this side of the mountains. He carried the right bumps and lumps to be well armed, but the way he'd moved through the door was like a man with one foot in this world and one foot into the next.

"Now *he's* the man you want to chat with."

"And why's that?" I asked.

"The first victim was his sister."

By the time I'd fetched another cup of ale, my informant had fled, leaving me alone with a stomach full of squirming vipers and the need of a few more cups to settle 'em. Rather than wallow in my fear, I elbowed the juggler out of his seat beside Marc Silversmith. It hadn't been all that hard considering the mixed scent of sour ale and sweat coming off my old friend. I breathed through my mouth and said, "It's been a long time, Marc."

At first, he didn't move—he kept his gaze on the bit of ale that ran down the side of his cup—but the moment I swiveled toward him, Marc fumbled for the bulge at his hip. My hand reached his dirk first, which I pressed deeper into its scabbard.

"Easy," I whispered into his ear. "It's Ida. Remember me?"

His brows furrowed as he blinked, and like someone clearing away sleep, his gaze focused on my face. "Lady Ida?" His hand went limp against mine. "You can le-go. Surprised me is all."

I released his dirk and waited another heartbeat before sliding into my seat. "I'm sorry about your sister, Dorine," I said.

"Yeah, ain't everyone."

"Can I ask ya about...what happened?" When he reached for his cup, I slid it out of reach. "You've had enough, friend. Answer a few questions for me, and I'll let ya get back to it."

"Always were a royal pain," he said with a sad little smile. "Don't know what good it'll do, but ask away."

"Where was she before the attack?"

Marc swung his arm wide. "Here. Where she always is...was. Working the bar."

"Were ya here?" Those soft, brown ovals hardened at the question, and I asked, "Did she leave with anyone? Say anythin' off or unusual?"

"No. Wish she had."

"Was she friends with any mercs in town?"

"All of them. Since you left, all she ever wanted was to be was a merc like you. Even after..."

I winced, and when I pushed the cup back at Marc, he drank like a man trapped in the swirling sands of Sadai. I set a few coins on the bar before leaving him to it. What little conversation there was lulled as I passed.

Loughrie wasn't the merc's town I remembered. Not anymore.

The pounding on my door lasted a few good minutes after I'd opened my eyes and another two minutes past my shout to go away.

"Please, there's been another death," the innkeeper shouted.

Red-beard had me spooked, and I'd been all set to leave Loughrie in the past where it belonged, but another dead woman? I dragged myself out of the sad excuse for a bed with a sigh.

"Be down in a moment," I said before pulling on a linen shirt and breeches. I stuffed my feet into my boots, buckled myself into my leather armor, and was down the tavern stairs at a pace that left my old joints complaining. A man wearing the King's Army uniform chatted with the inn keep, the latter of which shoved a cup of ale and small plate of food in my direction. "I hear we have another body?" I asked and bit off a chunk of cheese.

"Lieutenant Colby," the man in blue said as he nodded at me. "Word is I'm supposed to report...to you?"

So this was the Lieutenant who'd sent word to the King. "Thanks for the reports on the victims. They were quite helpful." As helpful as too much ale the night before.

"I was expecting someone—"

I slid the coin from my pouch and held it up to stop him talking. If he'd finished that sentence, I might've had to kill him. Etched into the coin was a silver star marking me as *sepier*. When he opened his mouth, I shook my head to silence him.

"Um, yes, if you'll follow me," he said.

At least this fool knew who and what I was. I trailed along as he led me out of the inn and towards a lean-to held together by little more than luck and a prayer. Inside, a soldier with a lantern stood guard over a body. When the lantern light reflected off his face, I closed my eyes. Marc's disheveled black cloak was gathered around him like a shroud, but his throat wasn't slit. The place reeked of sour wine, and a quick glance around left me wondering when he'd last been home as a layer of dust coated everything. "When was he found?" I asked.

"Landlord was around this morning to collect rent. Found him passed out. Thought him drunk until he turned him over. You think it's related to the others?" the lieutenant asked.

I ignored him as I searched Marc's pockets. His registration with the Guild was wadded up in his pant's pocket along with a lock of hair. Probably his sister's. I set both aside and checked the pouch at his waist. A few coins but nothing else. I nudged his head with my boot. "Bring the lantern here," I said as I leaned closer. Something discolored his jaw near the ear, and I grabbed the throwing knife from the top of my boot.

"What are you doing?" the lieutenant hissed, and I brushed aside his outstretched hand.

"There's somethin' on his jaw." I held his beard hair taut and gently pulled the knife-edge across the hairs, cutting 'em a bit to get a better look at his skin. My insides shook as the hair fell away.

It wasn't the Amaskan tattoo I'd been dreading, but it *was* an intentional mark all the same. Someone had scratched three slanted lines into his skin.

"Looks like he scratched himse—"

My glare silenced the lieutenant. "The marks are evenly spaced and even in length. No one scratches themselves that cleanly. It's recent, too."

"Then what's it mean?"

I shook my head. No need to tell him. There wasn't anything he could do to stop what was coming or what was already here. Only an Amaskan would use that symbol. Marc had been spotted talking to me, and they'd silenced him— marked him an oath-breaker. He wasn't one, but it was a symbol I'd recognize. One meant to silence me.

The red-bearded merc had been right. The Amaskans *were* here, and from the looks of it, they were looking for me. My hands trembled as I returned my knife to its sheath.

"Burn the body immediately. Tell anyone who asks that Marc drank himself to death."

The lieutenant saluted me as I left the lean-to, my steps a lot less sure than they'd been before. It'd been twenty-five years since my brother'd left me for dead. Why would Bredych choose now to hunt for a woman believed to be dead?

I rubbed my jaw. The puffy scar marred it, but if I pressed against it, the tattoo was still there under the scar tissue. Like a curse.

A light drizzle left the morning chilly and gray as I set out for the Merc's Guild. Somewhere in this town was a red-bearded man who'd asked all the right questions. Maybe he knew more than he was letting on. Either way, I needed to find him before anyone else died.

Or before he did.

Several hours and a parched throat later, the red-bearded merc was nowhere to be found, though I'd had several folks tell me he'd last been seen at the tavern in the company of some lady merc. As afternoon rolled in with a storm, I settled into the tavern's back corner with a glass of wine and a hearty meal, though I only picked at it. Once done torturing myself with the idea of food, I tossed up my cloak's hood and retreated to the shadows.

When he walked into the tavern, the merc who I'd since dubbed Red-Beard, glanced around at the dozen occupants before settling at the bar. Every time the door opened, his fingers squeezed his mug, but he otherwise kept his gaze straight ahead. A candlemark passed before he gave up waiting for me, assuming that was his goal, and left. I followed a few heartbeats behind and winced when I opened the door to the downpour.

The rain would disguise the sound of my footfalls, but it'd be harder to track him in all the shadows, which he hugged like a mistress. I used an empty wagon to reach the tavern's roof and ignored the groan in my right hip as the old injury reminded me how young I wasn't. Jumpy as Red-Beard was, I needed every advantage, and lucky for me, the buildings in Loughrie lay close together.

He was good, but not *that* good. Which meant he couldn't be Amaskan. Or if he was, he'd have to be new. Like the rest of Loughrie, he'd underestimated me, and I grinned as I followed along from the rooftops. While he meandered in the rain for a few minutes, he eventually circled around to the road leading out of town. I used the shutters on a house to climb down, careful of where I placed my feet when I landed. A light flickered in a barn up ahead as the door opened, and he stepped inside.

I spent the next few minutes dodging puddles as I prayed to the Thirteen that the storm would hide my approach. The barn was a smart choice--no real windows and two doors, three if ya counted the hay door in the rafters. My hip ached as I peered up at the hay door. It was reachable with some inventive maneuvering though I'd pay for in the morning.

Thunder rolled overhead, and I used the opportunity to walk around the barn's side. The wood siding was too slick to scale in the rain, but luck was with me. In the rear, a ladder leaned against the barn. Perfect.

A moment later, I'd climbed in through the open hay door and sat dripping in the rafters. Below me, three voices, including Red-Beard, murmured, and I crept forward 'til I'd reached the railing. Two of the men sprawled across hay stacks while Red-Beard approached. "She wasn't there," he said.

"Do you think she's on to you?"

The man who asked this slid forward off the hay, giving me a good look at his clothing. Black from head-to-toe, the fabric was fitted at the joints and waist, yet stretchable elsewhere. Cloth shoes covered his feet and when his hood fell back, his bald head shined in the lantern light.

Amaskan.

I didn't need the tattoo to confirm it, though I caught sight of the circle on his clean jaw when he turned his head my way. I held my breath, but the darkness hid me.

The face was older, the lines and wrinkles deeper, but it was the scar across his nose that confirmed it. The man pacing before Red-Beard was none other than Ilan, my brother's second-in-command. He'd been like a brother to me growing up in the Order of Amaska, and bile burned the back of my throat.

Watching him, the urge to flee was overwhelming. It'd be what he'd expect too. Always playing it safe—that was how he probably remembered me.

Red-Beard flinched as Ilan leaned close and whispered something in his ear. Red-Beard nodded, then left the barn. Fleeing was exactly my plan, but Ilan chose that moment to look up into the rafters. Behind me, the open hay-door swung in the wind and tapped against the siding.

"Got to close that door. Storm's getting worse," he said to the other guy, who shrugged in response.

I crept back as slowly as I dared and didn't turn around 'til my feet touched the ground outside. Long after I'd dried off in the warmth of the tavern, my body shivered and my skin crawled. I could've sworn his eyes still watched me. I took a long swallow of ale and waited for Red-Beard's return.

Desperation usually drove people to stupidity, but also to the familiar, and Red-Beard was no exception. Not long after I'd nursed my third glass of wine, he stumbled into the tavern, his cheeks flushed and his beard a dripping mess. When he spotted me, he grinned and made straight for my corner. "I've been looking for you," he said, and I nodded to the empty chair in front of me.

"We seem to have spent most the day looking for each other then."

He frowned at this. "Seems odd we couldn't find one another in a town this small, but we've found each other now. I have a proposal for you."

"Indeed? A job?"

"I...I know you've been looking into the murders, but I could see it in your eyes last time we talked."

"And what did ya see?"

"Fear. When I mentioned the Amaskans, you froze. Maybe you need a good job to forget the past. My employer's looking for those who're good at talking to people. He's looking to set up his business here in Loughrie, but the towns-folk might not be keen on the competition."

"What's he do? Your employer?" I asked.

Red-Beard pointed at my glass. "In Sadai he runs a very successful vineyard, but he's looking to expand here as the weather's more hospitable to growing grapes."

I took a sip of wine to cover my laughter. The Amaskans used both horses and wine to fund the Order. Whether he knew it or not, he'd tipped his hand with that story.

"If I decide to take your employer up on this offer, what'd I be doin'? Guardin' the wine?"

"Some, though mostly just making sure the good people of Loughrie let him make his wine in peace. Maybe some negotiating with the locals."

The tavern door opened and Red-Beard's friend, a tall man whose name I hadn't deciphered, walked in. His hood covered his bald head, but it didn't matter. From the way he slid through the space to his awareness of everyone in the room, his very movement screamed Amaskan. He tucked himself into a table alone, but his eyes flickered once in our direction.

"I'm interested, though I need to let the Guild know I've found work." While Red-Beard pretended to think it over, I studied his face. Only a few inches long, the red, wet locks of his beard curled around his face, almost hiding the tattoo on his jaw below his ear. Dry, the beard had covered the tattoo completely, but now, the barest hint of a circle was there if I stared hard enough. When he nodded agreement, I said, "I can meet your employer in the mornin'. Does he already have a spot in mind, or would ya like to meet here? Usual table?"

"You know the old barn at the edge of town? Has a big tree out front?"

"Used to be a sheep farm, right?"

Red-Beard nodded. "Now it's a vineyard. Or it will be come this time next year. Locals aren't too pleased with him for buying the land, so that's where you come in. We can meet there around noon."

"Noon sounds fine. Say, never did catch your name. I figure if we're goin' to be workin' together, I might want to call ya somethin' other than 'Red-Beard.'"

He laughed and held out his arm, which I grasped by the forearm and shook. "The name's Morei," he said.

"Nice to meet ya, Morei. I'll be seein' ya tomorrow then." Or sooner if all goes well.

I stood up first and left the tavern knowing full well that both Amaskans watched me. Once outside, the downpour continued, and I sighed as I rounded the corner to the alley. I grabbed a few rocks, which I tucked into my pouch, then grabbed a handful of mud. I smeared the thick stuff across my face 'til it was mostly covered. Hopefully between the darkness and mud, I'd blend into the shadows. I climbed into an empty wagon, unsheathed my sword, and removed my cloak, tossing the latter over me like a tarpaulin.

It didn't take five minutes for someone to exit the tavern, and Morei stopped a few feet in front of my hiding spot. He glanced about, and seeing nothing in the dim light, swore. I took one of the stones from my pouch and tossed it down the alleyway, a good twenty feet away.

Morei peered into the alley as thunder rattled the buildings around us. I tossed a second stone, which bounced off a stone wall before landing in a puddle, and he stepped into the alley. I held my breath as he passed by the wagon but almost laughed aloud when a rat scurried in front of him and he flinched.

Stepping from the wagon would've made all sorts of sounds but the Thirteen must've been on my side as a bolt of lightning hit a nearby tree and set the air a-buzz. The reverberating thunder covered most of the noise. Morei spun on his heel and turned into my blade as I drove it into his gut.

"It *is* you," he muttered as he stumbled back, hand clutching his innards.

"Ya couldn't let the past stay buried anymore than my brother could. I'm sorry, Red-Beard, but ya left me no choice. I wanted to run—probably should've—but I can't let 'em die for me. I'm sworn to protect these people, which I can't do if I'm dead."

Morei dropped to his knees and held out his hand. Clutched in his fingers was a silver ring. "B-belonged to Marc's sis-sister," he said. I took it from him, and he smiled. "Sorry, Lady Ida."

Damn him. I hadn't wanted to kill him. Why couldn't he have left it alone? Why join the Amaskans?

He exposed his throat. "Make it q-quick."

Before my blade moved, another blade sliced through his flesh from behind, nearly taking his head clean off. "Don't be sorry. Be Amaskan," the man muttered as he continued his forward momentum until I stood face-to-face with the third, unnamed Amaskan from the barn. He grinned and as lightning struck, he was on me, moving faster than I thought possible in the muddy mess. I brought my sword up in time to parry, but my feet slid backward in the mud. I fell to one knee, and his next blow knocked my sword from my muddy hands.

A miracle had saved me back then, but there wasn't one to save me now. His feral gaze left me shivering in the mud, and I thanked the Thirteen he wasn't my brother. If he had been, I'd already be dead.

"Ilan wanted the honor of killing the mighty Ida, King Leon's *sepier* and whore, but he'll have to forgive me this," he said.

I let him step into my space as he blathered, and I slid my fingers into my boot cuff. As thunder rattled overhead, I shoved my knife into his heart. He grunted with surprise, then fell to the ground.

The rain pelted me, washing off the mud and blood as I stood, chest heaving in the cold. My hip throbbed, the scar at my neck pricked a million pins, and my stomach churned. As much as I wanted a strong ale and good, long nap, both would have to wait. Unlike his new recruits, Ilan wasn't stupid. Too long without checking in, and he'd know something was up, so I left the bodies in the alley and set off for the barn at the town's edge.

And prayed to the gods that I wasn't about to get myself killed.

The hay door still flapped in the wind, though a little less now that the rain was easing up. Ilan. He'd been my best friend and the first man I'd ever loved. He was family. Or had been 'til he'd held me down while my brother slit my throat.

Could I kill him as casually as I'd killed the two Amaskans in the alley?

From the rafters, I could kill him with one throw of my knives. It'd be done. And the past could stay in the past— where it belonged. Leon never need know about who I had been or how I'd gotten my scar.

But was that the Amaskan in me talking? The killer in me? Or was I more than that now?

I shook my head, and a few pieces of hair that had escaped my thick braid in the fight stuck to my neck. The front door slid open without much effort, and Ilan grinned when I stepped inside. He held no visible weapons, but I wasn't foolish enough to think him unarmed. No Amaskan ever was.

"It's been a long time, Shendra...or should I say Ida?"

"Shendra died when her brother slit her throat," I said. His authentic smile caught me off guard, and I asked, "Does he know?"

"Who?"

"Bredych."

"Aren't you curious how I found you?" he asked as he pulled out a piece of parchment bearing King Leon's seal. "It was a beautiful thing. A King choosing his lover for his _sepier_. A woman who'd saved so many at the Little War of Three only to rise through the ranks to Captain of the Royal Guard. It's unusual for a woman to make it that far, so when the rumors reached me, I was curious, as I'm sure you understand. And my plan worked! Kill a few women, and you come running. You never were good at staying dead."

_He_ was curious. _He_ killed the women. Not my brother, Bredych.

I rushed him, sword before me. It was a risky move—one knife and he could end me—but he'd be expecting me to play it safe. To be the same Shendra he'd known before.

And he'd be wrong.

He was still talking when my sword plunged into him. Ilan's eyes widened as his mouth moved soundlessly for a moment. "Ya always had to gloat, didn't ya?" I said as he dropped off my blade and fell into the hay.

Unlike Red-Beard, there was no apology. No remorse to make his death easier to bear. Just the same smirk he'd worn when he'd held me down and betrayed me twenty-five years ago.

"Itova be merciful," I whispered as I closed his eyes. "But not *that* merciful."

Five murdered women had forced me to face my past. What would these three dead Amaskans do to me?

My hip, which had stopped aching somewhere in the fight, reminded me that for the moment, I was alive. I left the barn and walked into the night.

And into my future, whatever that would be.

Raven Oak's Conspiracy is for readers of intriguing speculative fiction. Join now to get sneak peeks at upcoming stories and art from author & artist Raven Oak as well as free books, book signing news, and more!

Join the newsletter version at:

http://conspiracy.ravenoak.net

Or join the Facebook Group at:

https://www.facebook.com/groups/ravenconspiracy/

ALSO BY RAVEN OAK

THE BOAHIM TRILOGY

Amaskan's Blood

Amaskan's War

Amaskan's Honor

STAND ALONE TITLES

Class-M Exile

*The Eldest Silence**

*Ear to Ear: The Collected Stories of an Amaskan**

Dragon Springs & Other Things

Space Ships & Other Trips

The Bell Ringer & Other Holiday Tales

Voices Carry: A Story of Teaching, Transitions, & Truths

ANTHOLOGIES

"Eye of the Beholder" with Jennifer Brozek in *Interdimensions* (Atthis Arts)

"Not Today" in *99 Fleeting Fantasies* (Pulse Publishing)

"Drip" in *99 Tiny Terrors* (Pulse Publishing)

"Weightless" in *Soul Jar: Thirty-One Fantastical Tales by Disabled Authors* (Forest Avenue Press)

"Scout's Honor" in *The Last Cities of Earth* (WordFire Press)

"Wrinkled" in *Clarity: Queer Sci-Fi's Flash Fiction Anthology* (Other Worlds Ink)

"Amaskan" in *Swords, Sorcery, & Self-Rescuing Damsels* (Clockwork Dragon)

"The Ringers" in *Joy to the Worlds: Mysterious Speculative Fiction for the Holidays* (Grey Sun Press)

"Ol' St. Nick" in *Joy to the Worlds: Mysterious Speculative Fiction for the Holidays* (Grey Sun Press)

"Mirror Me" in *Magic Unveiled* (Creative Alchemy Inc.)

"Q-Be" in *Untethered: A Magic iPhone Anthology* (Cantina Publishing)

** forthcoming from Grey Sun Press*

BUY DIRECT!

While all of Raven Oak's books are available at bookstores worldwide, buying books directly from Raven helps ensure that more of your money goes to the creator and less of it into the pockets of billionaires and corporations. Also, buying direct means autographed copies and sometimes free artwork.

You can buy most* of Raven's art, eBooks, and physical books at:

SHOP.RAVENOAK.NET

* NOTE: Some anthologies are not available directly if the publisher does not allow for direct sales. If there is something you are looking for and can't find it, please email orders@ravenoak.net for assistance.